"You were a vi⋯⋯⋯⋯⋯⋯⋯⋯ con-versationally.

Well! That had come out of nowhere. She forced a laugh. "How many virgins do you know who'd pick up a strange man in a bar?"

"Only you." He pushed away from the desk, tucking the towel more firmly around his hips as he stalked her. Close enough for her to see jade flecks in the paleness of his eyes. The eyes of a hunter with the target firmly in his sights.

"Touch me again and I'll break every finger in your hand, buster," she warned, feeling for the doorknob behind her as he stepped into her personal space.

"Ah, jungle girl. If wishes were horses . . ." His thumb moved to caress her bottom lip. "Hell with it . . ." He bit off the words as his mouth crushed down on hers. This was no soft tender exploration. The fever-ish heat was instantaneous as his tongue played against her lips, teasing them open. She responded without conscious thought. Her hands lifted to bury themselves in his long, thick hair. To pull him closer. . . .

By Cherry Adair
Published by The Random House Publishing Group

RED HOT SANTA
HOT ICE
ON THIN ICE
OUT OF SIGHT
KISS AND TELL
HIDE AND SEEK
IN TOO DEEP

HIDE AND SEEK

Cherry Adair

IVY BOOKS • NEW YORK

An Ivy Book
Published by The Random House Publishing Group

Copyright © 2001 by Cherry Adair

Published in the United States by Ivy Books, an imprint of The Random House Publishing Group, a division of Random House, Inc., New York, and simultaneously in Canada by Random House of Canada Limited, Toronto.

Ivy Books and colophon are trademarks of Random House, Inc.

www.ballantinebooks.com

ISBN 0-449-00684-0

Manufactured in the United States of America

First Edition: October 2001

For my dad, Ralph Campbell
(The best father in the whole P.T.O.)
Who taught me all things are possible—
Including reading the Rosetta Stone

Chapter One

"Well, well, if it isn't Miss Eastman. I'd recognize those tits anywhere."

Delanie froze, the bright tropical sun suddenly cold on her bare skin. Even with her eyes shut she recognized that deep velvety drawl.

Kyle Wright.

The only man who'd ever seen her naked.

Here? Impossible.

No, more like, *improbable.*

What were the chances of Kyle bearing witness to the only two outrageous, out-of-character acts of her entire twenty-seven years? Delanie had to admit, her one step on the wild side all those years ago had been incredible, but she'd never expected to see him again.

Besides, it was highly unlikely he'd turn up here, on this inaccessible mountaintop, deep in the jungles of South America, thousands of miles from San Francisco, and light-years from the last time she'd seen him.

After all this time she was *still* mortified by her uncharacteristic lack of restraint with the man. She was a woman who needed to be in control of her emotions at all times. With Kyle Wright she hadn't been capable of remembering her own name, let alone maintaining her equilibrium.

"Ah," he said, and God help her, no matter how unlikely it was, there was no doubt whatsoever that the man walking purposefully toward her *was* Kyle. "The perfect woman. Beautiful, practically naked, and mute."

Fiery red burned through the thin membrane of Delanie's

eyelids. She sensed the head-to-toe skim and scorch of his gaze as she frantically tried to think of something sophisticated and witty to lob back. The bottom half of a string bikini, a thick gold necklace, a nice tan, and nerves of steel had sufficed until a few moments ago. Now her small bare breasts felt as prominent and conspicuous as mountains.

Come on, she thought frantically. *Think, damn it. Think.*

Okay. So what if it is *Kyle. I'm sensible. Pragmatic. Competent. I can handle this.*

Their fling four years ago had been like a comet ride. Quick. Hot. Intense.

And history before they'd learned much more than each other's erogenous zones.

Chances were, she was overreacting—

No she wasn't. After all this time, he'd recognized her by her *boobs.*

But their blazing seventy-two-hour sex marathon hadn't exactly included delving deep into each other's lives. She'd fibbed, no, downright lied, to him that weekend in San Francisco, pretending to be considerably more sophisticated and experienced than she really was. That would work to her advantage now.

Same pretense.

Higher stakes.

The fine hair on Delanie's nape prickled as Kyle's deliberate footsteps scraped on the brick surrounding the swimming pool. His shadow slid over her. His knee brushed the top of her head.

The thought of his large hands trailing up the swell of her bare breasts brought back memories best forgotten. Nevertheless her nipples immediately perked up in response to the mental stimulation. Sweat pooled at the small of her back with the determination to remain motionless beneath Kyle's up-close and personal scrutiny.

Time's up. Think faster, damn it!

Delanie pretended she was her sister Lauren. Confident in her beauty, comfortable with her naked body, secure in the knowledge that whoever the man may be, he'd wait for *her* next move.

She finally found her voice. "Don't even think about it, pal."

"Talk about wishful thinking." Kyle's laugh was arrogant and mocking. "My hands are in my pockets, honey. But if you're advertising your wares and offering freebees we'd best go inside."

"If you know anything about our host, you know Ramón doesn't share." Delanie felt each individual throb of her heart beneath the gold necklace at her throat.

"If Montero isn't prepared to share, he shouldn't allow you to sunbathe out here stark naked, now should he?"

Had anyone ever died of humiliation? Delanie wondered, hot with embarrassment. Could this be the same man who'd crooned love words to her?

This wasn't the time or the place to dredge up long-buried memories. She'd better get her act together and remember that embarrassment and hurt were the least of her problems. She was in a place where one screwup could get her killed.

Slowly she opened her eyes and sat up, deliberately keeping her expression bland as she swung her legs over the side of the chaise before standing.

Positive ID.

Kyle Wright in the flesh.

He was all hard muscle and razor-sharp intellect. Big, solid, and achingly familiar.

Delanie's first impulse was to fling herself into his arms. She squashed the ridiculous notion in a heartbeat, grateful that she wasn't known for impulsive acts. Casually she strolled around behind him, making no move to cover herself, despite the overwhelming desire to do so. Until she knew what part Dr. Kyle Wright played in Ramón Montero's plans, she had to keep her head and play the role she'd cast for herself.

Barefoot, she was eye-level with Kyle's broad shoulders, which were clad in a black silk T-shirt, and with the extraordinary sight of his dark hair hanging in a braid down his back, almost reaching his fancy tooled-leather belt. It was impossible to ignore the shoulder holster and gun he wore as unceremoniously as another man might wear a watch.

For several moments she mimicked his scrutiny. "Funny. You don't *look* like a doctor."

He gave her an up-and-down scan as she completed her circuit, his eyes cool, unreadable. "And *you* don't look like a—what was it you said you were? I forget."

That's because "kindergarten teacher" hadn't sounded nearly as sophisticated and cool at the time as "dancer."

She'd implied exotic dancer, when all she'd been was the third swan from the left in the corps de ballet.

Part-time.

On weekends.

During the summer.

In the local amateur ballet company.

The fib had been easy to sustain for three days. Especially since they hadn't done a whole hell of a lot of talking.

"Oh, yeah, that's right," he drawled, "a *dancer.*"

Rude, arrogant bastard. She wanted to slap him, but reminded herself that unlike her mother and sister, she could control her temper. There was no point going off half-cocked until she knew what he was doing here and how his agenda might interfere with her own.

Except for his sensual mouth, his face could have been carved from unemotional granite. Kyle was six-foot-four of pure heartache, with dark hair, and darker slashing eyebrows over penetrating pale green eyes. He hadn't changed that much since last she'd seen him, although the lines beside his mouth were deeper and she didn't remember his mouth having the harsh sardonic curve it wore now. All he needed was a gold hoop earring and a cutlass between his teeth.

He looked older, harder, more dangerous than the day he'd taken her virginity. It would've been easy to forget this man with the razor-sharp tongue and ice-hard eyes.

Within hours of their first meeting they'd been hot and sweaty in her hotel room. Would she have left the bar with *this* Kyle?

Not in a trillion years.

That Kyle had made her feel safe. And beautiful. And cherished.

This Kyle made her want armor plating.

She'd have settled for a bra.

She compromised and, as usual, used her tongue as a shield. "Well, well." She widened her eyes wide in feigned surprise. "If it isn't the wrong Dr. Wright." Proud her voice was steady, Delanie lowered her sunglasses to the end of her nose to look up at his face. "I recognize you *so* much better from the back."

"As I recall, we had more contact face to face," he said silkily.

"Funny." Delanie picked up her glass of soda from the table and drained the ice-diluted contents. "That's not *my* most lasting memory." *That* was the view from the bed as Kyle's silhouette was limned against the open hotel room door, just before he shut it behind him.

Without warning his hand curled around her waist to draw her closer. Her sunglasses fell to the brick at her feet with a small clatter.

"Perhaps you need a refresher course." His fingers skimmed down, the G-string no barrier, as he caressed the firm flesh of her behind, drawing her even closer.

Her gaze locked with his and she lifted her glass, giving the contents a dangerous tilt. "Perhaps *you* need to be cooled down." Lauren would've known how to handle him with one hand tied behind her back and her eyes closed. But she wasn't her sister.

Figuring even a bimbo had standards, she inserted her hand between her mouth and his. "Back off."

His breath scorched her fingers. Her breasts flattened against his chest, smearing the fine silk of his T-shirt with coconut-scented oil. Dropping her hand, she stared up at him, keeping every nuance of emotion off her face. His fingers tightened on the cheek of her butt. The second he dropped his arm she put a few feet of patio between them. His studied equanimity didn't fool her for a moment. She was pretty sure the cool, calm, and oh, so collected *Dr.* Kyle Wright was furious.

Logic dictated he couldn't be angry with her. They hadn't seen each other in years.

Whatever the reason for his anger, the look he was giving her chilled her to the marrow. She felt the imprint of his fingerprints pulse on her skin.

Oh, Lord. She couldn't pull this off with him here, she just c—

Damn it! She *had* to. Her sister's life—for that matter, her own life—depended on everyone believing she was a not-too-bright chorus girl.

"See those men?" She glanced casually to the opposite end of the enormous patio. Normally Ramón's militia gave her the willies, but she welcomed their presence now. The uniformed soldiers, as conscientious as ever, had their camouflaged backs turned to the pool area. Cradled in those minimum-wage arms were maximum-wage Uzis. "All I have to do is—"

"Whistle?"

Her bare toes nudged the sunglasses she'd dropped. She bent to pick them up, forcing each breath to mirror the last. Slow. Easy. Unaffected. She straightened, settling the frames back on her nose. During the last few months, every second of every day had stretched her nerves to the breaking point. Montero's private mountain retreat in San Cristóbal was absolutely the last place she knew to search for Lauren. Four weeks with him in the States, and almost a week up here, and she still hadn't found even a hint of her sister.

Ramón Montero terrified her. For that matter, he'd scared her long before Delanie had ever met him. She'd had a bad, bad feeling about Lauren's infatuation with Montero the first time her sister had called her. The more Lauren had raved about the wealthy Las Vegas casino owner she was dating, the more worried Delanie had become.

Lauren had sloughed off all her questions. And the few times Delanie had managed to pin her down for answers Lauren had laughingly told her Montero was gay. All the millionaire wanted was a pretty girl on his arm for show. In exchange he lavished her beautiful sister with expensive clothes and jewelry. It all sounded sordid and unlikely. Not to mention dangerous.

But Lauren, like their mother, thrived on excitement. They could skydive their way through life with impunity. Delanie was always their safety net.

Scared on behalf of her sister, Delanie had gone on line and researched Ramón Montero. The man was a suspected terrorist. He was a drug dealer. And if he was indeed gay, he covered it well. There was no mention of it in any of the hundreds of newspaper articles about him Delanie had forced herself, with mounting alarm, to read. There were countless mentions, however, of death, destruction, and mayhem that seemed to follow him like a thick black cloud.

The man was scary as hell.

Delanie couldn't figure out for the life of her how the authorities could know so much about Montero and not slap him into a cell for the rest of his unnatural life.

She'd called Lauren and begged her to come home to Sacramento.

Naturally her sister had laughed. Delanie was such a prude. Always had been, always would be. One of these days she should try getting a life, and having some *fun* for a change. Sheesh. What a drag her older sister was, what a stick-in-the-mud!

Then that last frantic call two months ago.

Lauren finally admitting she *might* be in way over her head. Delanie *might* be right about Montero. If big sis could just come and bail her out of this latest screwup, this would be absolutely the last time, she promised, sounding hysterical.

It was a couple of weeks before spring break, money was tight, and besides, Delanie was up for a part in that year's production of *Swan Lake* and didn't want to miss any rehearsals. She'd booked a flight to Las Vegas for ten days later.

Too late.

By the time she'd arrived Lauren had disappeared.

Guilt-ridden—it was the first time ever that she hadn't rushed to her sister's side—Delanie had applied for a job at Montero's casino that very day.

Getting a job at the Cobra hadn't been easy. She'd had to lie through her teeth about work experience, and make it look convincing. The personnel manager at the hotel/casino wouldn't have hired a kindergarten teacher for any of the jobs Delanie knew she'd need to attract Montero's attention.

Dancer was number one. She had the long legs required to be one of the Cobra's showgirls, and she was a pretty good dancer, not great, but good enough to pull it off if she had to. Luckily she hadn't had to.

There was that clothes thing again. Unlike Lauren, Delanie preferred keeping hers on. She'd been relieved when she'd been offered the job as cocktail waitress in the high-stakes area instead.

It had taken several weeks to bring herself to his attention. Then the last five weeks in Ramón's company. None of which had changed her mind about the suave man who'd so infatuated her sister. The son of a bitch had something to do with Lauren's disappearance, she knew it.

So here she was, in the middle of a jungle, high on a mountaintop, behaving as recklessly as Lauren ever had.

She was already living on her ragged nerves. She didn't need the unexpected and unnecessary ingredient of her one and only ex-lover added to the already toxic soup bubbling around her.

Lord. Fear was exhausting.

From the roof of the hacienda, the tiny eye of the surveillance camera tracked a slow circuit of the patio. Montero would hear about this meeting; he didn't need to see it, too.

"Don't touch me again," Delanie warned, her gaze steady on his face. "Ramón won't like it. And more to the point, *I* don't like it."

"Is that any way to talk to an old friend?" Kyle asked.

"We were *acquaintances*."

"Ships that passed in the night?"

"The *Titanic* and the *Andrea Doria*," Delanie agreed sweetly.

Kyle laughed, his eyes sweeping her body. "Honey, there wasn't an iceberg in sight."

No kidding. They'd gone supernova. Which was beside the point. "How did you know I was here?"

"What makes you think I'm here because of you, jungle girl?"

She wasn't vain, but why else would Kyle Wright be here at precisely the same time she was? "Just because I was naive enough to sleep with you the first time we met doesn't mean I'd be stupid enough to do it again."

"*Sleep* wasn't the operative word."

"No. *Stupid* was." She pushed a strand of shoulder-length, Nice 'n Easy number 98, Natural Extra Light Blonde, hair behind her ear. "What *are* you doing here, Kyle?"

"Ramón invited me. And I might ask you the same damn question."

Delanie ignored both the question and the sudden spurt of obvious anger in that demand.

The temperature in the shade must be a hundred degrees; Kyle hadn't even broken a sweat. She, on the other hand, perspired from every naked pore.

Never let them see you sweat. "Where is Ramón?"

"Still in San Cristóbal, waiting for a few more business associates." For a second his gaze dropped. "Christ, I can't believe you're parading around outside half-naked like this. That dental floss you're almost wearing would get you arrested even in Palm Beach."

She felt the heat of his stare on her breasts, but raised *yeah-so-what?* eyebrows.

"Those guards are already having a hard time keeping their eyes where they belong. Yeah, honey. You *should* blush. Why don't you cover yourself and put the poor bastards out of their misery?"

It was none of his damn business, but the soldiers were so terrified of Montero they'd never noticed anything lower than her nose. Thank God.

"Don't be a prude. They're here to protect me." She looked at him under her lashes, a small smile barely curving her mouth. Her little students would never recognize their Miss Lanie's feral smile. Delanie knew how it appeared, she'd practiced the vapid-avaricious-dumb-blonde act in the mirror several times a day to remind herself of just why she was here. And just what was at stake if she failed.

"How many notches have you carved on your lipstick case since I last . . . saw you?"

His not so subtle slur threw her for a moment, but she rallied quickly. "Goodness," she said, wide-eyed. "I've completely lost count." One notch had been more than enough for this girl. She wasn't stupid, she was acting. And from his reaction doing a fairly good job of it, too.

"I just look for men who'll give me what I want, when I want it." The huskiness in her voice was from strain. Not suppressed tears. She hadn't cried in years and didn't intend to start now. "And Ramón treats me *very* well."

"What the hell do you see in him?" Heat emanated from his body and she could smell the faint, familiar tang of his aftershave and the muskiness of clean sweat as he crowded her from three feet away.

Delanie looked him dead in the eye. Defiantly. "He has something I want."

My sister first.

Revenge as dessert.

The barely polite mask dropped from his face, leaving more than a hint at his awesome fury. "Wealth and power."

"Oh, much more than that." She wanted to cheer. Kyle didn't know Montero was gay. She wasn't sure how, but she'd find a way to use that to her advantage.

She touched the quarter-inch-wide herringbone necklace around her throat with her fingertips. She couldn't find the clasp to take it off, and the thing always irritated the hell out of her. It was more uncomfortable outside in the heat.

Green eyes made another leisurely survey of her body. She dropped her hand. It took every ounce of fortitude to stand still for his scrutiny. He reached past her to snag a towel off the inside skeleton of the umbrella, then draped it around her neck, holding the edges between her breasts. His hands felt cool and steady against the hard flutter of her heart.

Delanie resisted the overwhelming urge to beg his help in locating her sister. But for all she knew, he was part of Montero's plan. No. She dared not. Besides, when had she ever asked for, or received, help resolving her family's problems? Never.

She took a step back from temptation. "What's the matter, Doc? Don't trust yourself?" She shrugged and the towel landed at her feet. She bent to stuff a bottle of oil and a paperback romance novel into a black canvas tote and slung the straps over her bare shoulder.

The bag banged against her hip. It was never out of her sight for a second. It contained everything she thought she and Lauren might need when they left.

Delanie slipped on her high-heeled, gold sandals. Eyelevel with Kyle's chin, she managed a credible "hostess" smile. "Let's go inside, cool off in the air-conditioning, and have something cold to drink."

She had to touch him. To show them both that his nearness no longer had any affect on her. She tucked her hand through his arm.

His forearm felt as unyielding as his attitude. The feel of his cool, hard skin, liberally matted with crisp, dark hair, made her suck in a sharp involuntary breath.

Oh damn.

"Jesus," he said under his breath at the same time.

They stared at each other in alarm for a split second before Delanie released his arm, and said quickly, "Ramón likes guests to dress for dinner. We have a few minutes before I have to change."

"At least you dress for dinner," he muttered as they passed beneath a pergola covered in a thick canopy of lush vines. Magenta flowers spilled in a delicate, sweet-smelling carpet onto the brick patio. Set into the thick adobe walls, French doors led to the living room. A soldier, eyes averted, rushed ahead of her to swing them open.

"I admire your self-control, *amigo,*" Kyle said, as the man, eyes locked on his boots, backed away.

Scorching white light changed into the blessed dim coolness of the house. Chill air immediately raised goose bumps on Delanie's skin. "Beer? Soda? Iced coffee?"

"Coffee's fine."

She removed her sunglasses and shivered as she crossed to an intercom, where she gave orders to an unseen servant. Then she nonchalantly picked up the flimsy beach cover-up she'd left draped across the back of a chair. Drawing it over her head, she remembered belatedly it was about as effective as wearing an ounce of Saran Wrap.

Kyle strolled over to the far wall to inspect a metal sculpture on a marble pedestal. "Fascinating. Who's the artist, do you know?"

He ran his hand down a smooth curve of copper. "Looks remarkably like the Leggett in the Louvre. What do you think? Is it real, or is it Memorex?"

Delanie stared at his back and shook her head. Here she was, practically naked, pretending she wasn't humiliated and scared out of her wits, and *he* wanted to know her opinion on a chunk of metal that looked like something one of her six-year-old students had done? Men.

He glanced around at the expensive dhurrie rugs covering the glazed terra-cotta tile floor of the vast room. Half a dozen butterscotch-colored leather sofas were arranged between lush plants. The combination drew the rain forest inside. Ceiling fans moved the languid air; an enormous three-tiered fountain in the center of the room splashed water onto lacy ferns and tiny yellow orchids. On the whitewashed walls, in full view of several surveillance cameras, hung part of Montero's extensive, priceless, and no doubt stolen, art collection.

The cameras were everywhere. The only way a thief could get on or off this peak of Izquierdo was by helicopter, parachute, or transporter beam. There wasn't a doubt in Delanie's mind that even the small airfield behind the sprawling hacienda was constantly monitored. Obviously Ramón Montero didn't even trust the friends he invited to his private retreat. But then a guy like Ramón didn't *have* friends. Only acquaintances who hadn't bumped him off yet.

She gave Kyle an assessing glance as she swept her hair out of the neckline of her cover-up. A house servant came in and set a large tray on the elegant rattan sideboard across the room. When the man left the room Delanie poured two iced coffees, then floated dollops of sweet, heavy, whipped cream on top. After liberally sprinkling both cold drinks with grated, bitter dark chocolate, she handed Kyle a tall frosted glass and took her own with her to the sofa by the window overlooking the pool.

Except for the hot and cold running servants, she and Kyle were alone in the house until Montero returned. She wasn't sure that being alone with Kyle was the lesser of two evils.

Licking cream off her upper lip, she settled in the corner against the scrolled, curved arm, and crossed her long, bare legs. "Do you have a clue just how powerful Ramón is? If not, let me give you a friendly warning, Kyle. He doesn't suffer fools lightly."

A single dark, mocking eyebrow rose. "You've known him how long?"

"A couple of months." A lifetime. One month, one week, four days and nineteen hours.

"Yeah? Ramón and I go back to our first year in med school at Stanford. Nice try, but no cigar."

"Holy Hannah! Ramón has a *medical* degree?"

"No."

Delanie frowned. "But you just said—"

"I said we went to med school together. He didn't finish."

"Did that have anything to do with the fact that he was at least ten years older than his classmates?"

"He wasn't," Kyle told her shortly. "I was eight years younger than the average."

"Doogie Howser, huh?"

"Something like that," he said dismissively. "I'll make arrangements for you to leave tomorrow morning."

"I beg your pardon?" That had certainly come out of left field.

"Sorry." Kyle said, not sounding in the least bit apologetic. "Was that sentence too complicated for you? How about this. You." He pointed. "Leave." He made a running motion with his fingers. "Tomorrow." The finger took a dive.

"You should've been a comedian. If you're so offended by my presence, *you* leave."

"You don't know what the hell you're in the middle of, Delanie." Kyle kept his voice low and cool, and the fire in his pale eyes banked. "You don't know him like I do."

"He's *my* lover," she reminded him coldly, wishing she had an antacid for her revolting stomach. "I assure you, I know him as well as I need to."

"Somehow I don't think so." His brow cocked as he scrutinized her. Kyle Wright had an uncanny way of watching her that made her feel as though he could read her mind. It wasn't going to be easy hiding anything from him.

"Once you dissect a cadaver together after an all-night keg party, you get to know the other guy pretty damn well. And believe me, Montero and I did our share of kegs and corpses together. Wanna compare notes?"

She shook her head. He crossed the room toward her, his stride long and loose. His clothing was expensive, well-tailored, fitting his rangy body well. He *could* be a doctor, or an investment banker, or a businessman. But one look at his ice-floe eyes, and a person would know he wasn't anything so tame.

Just *what* he was, she wasn't sure.

She frowned when he sat in the middle of the same sofa and sprawled against the glove-soft leather, stretching out his legs, crossing them at the ankle. Speculation, and something else, flickered in his expression. It was the something else that made her heart lurch.

Determined not to let him rattle her, she studied his face.

"What could you have that a man like Ramón Montero would want?" she mused aloud. "It can't be your . . ." she eyed his black T-shirt, black jeans, black boots . . . black scowl. "Flair for fashion," she managed dryly. "And surely you've both outgrown keggers. Are doctors making house calls these days?"

She hadn't missed the obscene chunk of gold and diamonds he wore on the pinkie finger of his right hand. A twin to the ring Ramón wore. She loathed jewelry on men.

Half turning, he rested an arm on the back of the sofa. It was a very relaxed pose, yet Delanie could almost feel the crackle and pop of energy emanating from him. "I'm not a medical doctor anymore."

"Shitty bedside manner?" she suggested sweetly.

"PhD. Switched to biotechnology and virology research." He tasted his drink and assessed her over the glass. "And you took a different career path, too, right? From showgirl to playmate? Were you aware of what Montero was before you . . . hooked up with him?"

Oh, you mean a drug-dealing terrorist and a sadist? Delanie forced a laugh. "Do you think I'd come to the middle of nowhere with him if I didn't?" She leaned back, flinching when she encountered his hand on the cushion behind her head. "And the reason I changed career paths ought to be obvious. Money. Glamour. Nice clothes. It only took a few weeks working at the Cobra before he singled me out."

Agonizingly embarrassing weeks. Weeks of worrying and questioning her sanity. Weeks of mingling with and befriending people she would've run from in real life. She'd lived in her sister's apartment, worn her sister's clothes, and God help her, practically absorbed her sister's personality. And existed on antacids.

She'd done, and said, whatever it took to gain the attention of the big boss.

Nonchalantly she reached for her glass and took another sip of iced coffee. "And obviously I knew he owned the casino."

His eyes flickered for a nanosecond to the corner camera and back. "Owned the ca— Yeah, right," Kyle said drolly, proving he, too, knew of Montero's criminal activities.

Delanie felt ridiculously disappointed and more afraid than ever. Of course he knew. He was here, wasn't he? She got up and strolled to the sideboard across the room. If she didn't get out of here soon, she was going to do something really stupid. Like have a nervous breakdown.

She held up the frosted glass carafe. "More coffee?"

Kyle stood, draining his glass before following her. "Perhaps in the next couple of days you'll give me a guided tour of the compound." He gave her an ironic look. "If you can find time to squeeze me into your busy schedule, that is."

She felt stalked, and hitched a hip on the sideboard as he handed her his empty glass. "Sorry. You'll have to ask someone else. I've only been here a week myself and Ramón keeps me pretty busy."

An iridescent beetle the size of her fist scurried across the floor toward her. If crushed, the smell alone would be overpowering enough to evacuate a large room. Its sting could kill in minutes. Her sandals clattered to the tile as she swiftly lifted herself onto the sideboard and swung her bare feet out of harm's way.

She read Kyle's intention a second before he managed to step into the V of her thighs. "Oh, I don't think so!" Delanie jumped down and grabbed her sandals.

"Your mother should have taught you not to grab." She managed to sound amused as she stepped around him. "Just because something's for sale doesn't mean *you* can afford it."

"True. There are some things not worth keeping around at any price."

"Don't—" she warned as Kyle lifted a booted foot to step on the lethal beetle. Ignoring her warning, he crushed it beneath his heel, then turned and strode from the room.

The second the stench rose, Delanie slapped a hand over her nose and mouth, then watched Kyle's retreating back through tear-drenched vision.

"Damn you, Kyle. Damn you."

Chapter Two

Still furious ten minutes after their encounter, Kyle removed his shoulder holster and weapon and placed them on the foot of the enormous bed in his suite. He'd left his stinking shoes outside for one of the invisible servants to dispose of.

What in God's name was Delanie, with her soft, pouty, lying mouth and those deceptively innocent baby browns—which did a piss poor job of hiding secrets—doing here? Her presence complicated everything. And her presence at both the inception and completion of this assignment was suspect.

Coincidence, or something far more calculated? With Montero one never knew. This entire mess was tenuously built on lies, fabrication, and bullshit. One truth and the entire operation would come down like a frigging house of cards. All he had to do was maintain for five more days.

Five days compared to the last fifteen hundred? No sweat.

Kyle yanked off his clothes and walked naked into the opulent cream-and-gold marble bathroom and cranked on the shower.

Hearing about Montero's new girlfriend-in-residence at lunch this afternoon had thrown him a curveball. Kyle had spent the previous six weeks in Atlanta arranging the last delicate chess pieces, the *final* pieces, and setting the stage for the grand finale. Up until then he'd known all the players in Montero's game, and Delanie Eastman's name had never been mentioned. And God only knew, even if it *had,* he wouldn't have connected the woman he'd met briefly all those years ago with someone Montero would have any interest in now.

Someone's ass was grass for not being more thorough and keeping him properly briefed. Lives depended on his knowing Montero's every blink and fart.

Kyle savagely loosened his braid, his yardstick, as it were, of how long he'd been undercover and on this particular job. Four years, three months, and four days.

He stepped beneath the cool, hard jets and let the pulsing water pummel his neck and shoulders, causing his hair to glue itself uncomfortably all the way down his back.

He reached for the shampoo.

He'd inform Ramón at dinner that he didn't want her here, especially at this crucial time. That if she stayed, he'd walk. He knew his unstable, unpredictable host well enough to know that he'd better take this carefully. No sudden moves.

Just because his scrotes pinched, knowing the kind of danger Delanie was bringing down on her own head, didn't mean he had the luxury to go off half-cocked. He hadn't gritted his teeth, gone at a frigging snail's pace, and controlled his every urge to take Montero down *now* for all these years, just to blow it at end game.

Damn it to hell. How was he supposed to keep her safe for the duration when she was way the hell 'n' gone on the other side of the hacienda and under Montero's watchful eyes?

He'd have to hurry the hell up slowly. She didn't deserve what would surely happen if she was still around at the end of the week.

He had five days to get her off the mountain.

Sooner—he wiped shampoo out of his eyes and reached for the soap—would be better than later.

It shouldn't take much to get rid of her. Like cotton candy, she'd melt after one bite.

Kyle gave the empty dining room a cursory glance when he arrived a few minutes early for dinner. Reflected in a wall-size gold-veined mirror behind it, a large, quite magnificent Ming vase, filled with tropical foliage and golden-green orchids, was showcased on a centuries-old Spanish sideboard. Kyle strolled over and poured a glass of wine from the silver serving tray there.

Across the room hung an enormous oil: a Spanish Mediterranean villa, purported to be the original home of the Montero family and dating back to the sixteenth century. Montero flaunted his Spanish ancestry and expected his acquaintances to attach as great a prestige to his pure Castilian blood as he did. In reality, Montero's late father had stolen the painting from a Spanish monastery thirty years before. The history of the Montero family fortune could be traced no further than Ramón's introduction to terrorism twenty-two years ago. There wasn't a drop of Castilian blood to be found anywhere down the line. Ramón Montero had been inconveniently born in Monterey, Mexico, and had dragged himself up by his sandal straps.

Everything about Montero's hidden hacienda was a testament to how good taste could be bought. A decorator on retainer, an art restorer on his payroll, and a scout who brought his boss the best that money could buy. Or in many cases, steal.

And one leggy, brown-eyed blonde.

Few people were left who knew of Ramón Montero's humble beginnings, and fewer yet who would dare voice disbelief. Terrorism and the cocaine trade had made him one of, if not the, richest men in the world.

A generous philanthropist, Montero's "legitimate" art collection alone was appraised into the millions. His acquired artwork was worth at least that much, if not more. As part of his diversification into legitimate business, Montero owned coffee and orange *fincas* and one of the largest horse-breeding farms in Kentucky. He was also heavily invested in real estate all over the world.

Not to mention, he was head of one of the world's most powerful drug cartels, involved in international-scale money laundering, and the leader of one of the most vicious and profitable international terrorist organizations ever known.

Over the last ten years various law enforcement agencies had tried, and failed, to put a stop to his activities. Montero was too fast and too clever. But what he now wanted to unleash on the world had brought together some of the most powerful international agencies in a collaborative effort to end Montero's reign of destruction. The logistics, intricate and on a need-to-know basis, spanned the globe. Once and for all, they were going to take down Ramón Montero and all his associates.

In five days Ramón Montero would be stopped. And stopped dead.

Kyle was merely the sharp tip of the wedge that would finally put an end to Montero's terrorist acts for good.

And Delanie was smack dab in the middle of it.

"Casing the joint?"

"Only for what I can get into my pockets," Kyle said dryly as he turned. "Yowza!"

Unlike this afternoon, tonight Delanie wore full battle garb. The fire engine–red dress, consisting of a scrap of latex, clung to her breasts and thighs as if painted there by a miserly hand. She was an insanity-inducing combination of Michelle Pfeiffer and Jessica Rabbit.

And if he didn't miss his guess, she was blushing as he let his eyes take a leisurely tour. Nevertheless she spun around, arms extended, so he could get the stereo version of what passed for her dress. She dropped her arms when she came back to face him again. "You like?"

"What's not to like?"

The changes in her appearance in the years since he'd last seen her were subtle. Hair a little blonder, clothes a little tighter.

Her eyes appeared even darker surrounded by smoky color, her already-long lashes thicker and more seductive. Slick red lipstick painted her succulent mouth with moisture. Streaky, honey-blond hair had been pulled up and away from her face in loose, just-got-out-of-bed curls. She looked good enough to eat, and knew it. As overblown and overt as she appeared, Kyle still experienced the familiar immediate arousal he'd relived at the pool earlier.

He had the strongest urge to toss her over his shoulder caveman style and run like hell. Far and fast.

"Welcome to my home at last, *amigo,*" Montero said from the doorway, where his arrival had been silent. He paused for effect. "I see you and my Delanie are renewing old acquaintances." He stepped farther into the room to make his grand entrance, followed by several servants.

He indicated his guests take their places at the table.

Kyle on his right. Delanie on his left.

"I thought you were bringing the others back with you." Kyle was eager for all the ducks to be in a row.

"I returned with both Kensington and Sugano," Montero said smoothly as Bruno flicked open a snowy linen napkin and laid it on Montero's lap before stepping back behind his master's thronelike chair. "They will join us shortly, but we will not hold back our meal to wait for them." He snapped his fingers without glancing at the hovering servant.

"You find your quarters satisfactory?" Montero asked.

"For the duration," Kyle answered coolly. "The sound system was unwelcome and excessive, however." The bugs were a given. He'd found the five in his rooms he was supposed to, and the three he wasn't. He'd removed the obvious and left the others.

Communication worked both ways.

"An oversight. Merely installed for the last visitor, *mi amigo.* I will, of course, have the staff remove any offending equipment from your suite immediately."

"I saved them the trouble." Kyle took a sip of his wine. "When can I see the lab?"

"Everything is exactly as you requested. The top of the line equipment. The best of the best. The Rolls Royce of—"

"That's a given, and wasn't the question." Kyle narrowed his eyes. "When do I get to see my lab?"

"What lab?" Delanie asked.

"We can go there tonight if it pleases you," Montero said, as if she hadn't spoken. "Or we can wait for full daylight and go first thing in the morning."

"Tonight. Tomorrow I'm returning to San Cristóbal to pick up the rest of my equipment from customs."

"Ludicrous," Montero snarled, gulping his wine. "That imbecile. I told him the urgency of your medical samples, and yet he insisted everything go through customs in the usual way. Bah! His departure will be no loss."

"There's nothing they can open," Kyle assured him. "One more day won't make that much difference. I just want to be sure my lab is ready to receive the viruses and vaccines as soon as I return with them."

With a frown Delanie glanced from one man to the other. "What vaccines?"

"Everything is in readiness for you," Montero promised Kyle. "Down to the last biohazard suit and lab coat."

"Good." A servant placed a gold-trimmed bowl before each of them. "Another thing." Kyle picked up his spoon and dipped it into his soup. "Just to be on the safe side, I'd suggest you have a chopper ready at the airfield, and you also inform your guards that I have immediate access to you twenty-four/seven."

Montero's swarthy skin blanched. "Everything is contained."

"Yes," Kyle said quietly, enjoying the mushroom soup. "And I intend to keep it that way. But it's wise to have contingency plans."

Kyle took sadistic pleasure in scaring the shit out of Montero and his business partners. Between tonight and Saturday he planned to torque the sorry son of a bitch's nerves to the breaking point.

The surge of adrenaline pumping through him felt terrific.

After more than four years it was finally coming together.

They were close. So close.

The soup tasted like nectar.

The ratio of two waiters to one dinner guest was overkill, but then, that was Montero's style. He had a flair for the dramatic. Behind his chair, guarding his back, Montero's personal bodyguard stood with arms folded across his massive chest, mahogany head gleaming in the candlelight. Bruno could bench-press four hundred pounds without breaking a sweat. Kyle had never heard the man utter a word.

Beyond the wide double doors, open to the slate hallway beyond, two bodyguards stood ready to apprehend anyone foolish enough to try anything with *El Jefe*.

The security cameras were obvious and everywhere.

Delanie's reserve tonight was perfectly controlled. She gave not one iota more conversation than was necessary to be polite, not one scrap more attention to him than was absolutely called for.

Dangling red earrings brushed bare, tanned shoulders as she turned her head to listen to Montero whispering sweet bullshit in her ear. Montero, a young George Hamilton look-alike, thrived on having sexy, leggy blondes hanging on his every word. Delanie was eye candy. But any attractive blond would have suited his purpose. Montero's 'dates' had remarkably short runs. They were eliminated before they could reveal any of his bad habits. Montero took care of his enemies execution-style. His discarded girlfriends disappeared, never to be heard from again.

Kyle raised his magically refilling wine glass and drained the excellent Chateau Lafite Rothschild '52. He knew more about the sick bastard than he wanted to. Hell, he probably knew more about Ramón Eduardo Montero than the man's own mother.

But did Delanie know what a sick bastard she'd latched onto? Obviously she knew the man was homosexual. But did she know *how* brutal, *how* depraved Ramón Montero could be? And if she did, what in the hell was she doing pretending to be the egregious bastard's girlfriend?

Her reasons, thought Kyle, forking up some kind of highly spiced fish, were immaterial. No matter *why* Delanie Eastman was here, no matter *what* she thought she knew about their host, she had to go. Before she left in a body bag.

She was nervous as hell, though she covered damn well. He'd noted it at the pool this afternoon. Good. If she was afraid of Montero then she was smarter than she appeared. Then again, if she were so damn smart, what the hell was she doing on top of Izquierdo?

He found himself at the starting post with more questions than answers. A situation he didn't like and wouldn't tolerate.

A warm breeze brought in the scent of the citronella candles winking around the patio beyond the French doors. His keen hearing picked up the bug zapper, which was just out of sight, as insects got incinerated for their audacity to come close to the light.

"Sorry I'm late." Peter Kensington strolled in, interrupting Kyle's musings. A servant immediately filled his wine glass, while another brought his dinner.

Kensington had an Ashley Wilkes feyness about him. Wiry, with thinning blond hair, he used his slight build and general air of anemic weakness to good effect. A slippery bastard, he was second in command of a small, but powerful, terrorist group based in Ireland and had recently been involved in the bombing of three U.S. planes out of Heathrow and Orly. He didn't enjoy playing second banana and was here because Montero had encouraged him to be.

Kensington acknowledged Kyle with a slight, and subtle, shift away from him in his seat. He graced Montero with a fawning, ingratiating smile, ignoring Delanie completely.

"You found your quarters agreeable?" Montero asked, his mouth full as he gestured with his fork—a mannerism he retained from his humble beginnings. It was an indication of just how relaxed he was in his protected little kingdom. Anywhere else, Montero played his fabricated past and his wealthy, high-class playboy image to the hilt. He never forgot *anything*. Not even something as inconsequential as table manners. Montero's inattention to detail here on Izquierdo suited Kyle just fine.

Cheeks flushed, Kensington managed a reply, struggling to swallow without choking, as he tried valiantly not to let his nervousness show. Kyle could have told him that the only kind of enemy a man should have was a *dead* enemy. People with a lot to lose couldn't afford to make foolish mistakes. He let the dissolute conversation between Montero and Kensington ebb and flow around him as he relaxed in the high-backed, velvet chair.

"So, Kyle." Montero turned soulless black eyes to him, cutting Peter Kensington off in midsentence. "You and my Delanie are old friends."

"Not quite the word I would have used, but yeah. We knew each other years ago." Kyle smiled at his host, a man-to-man look that had Delanie's grip on her glass white-knuckled. Montero chuckled. Kensington concentrated on his dinner.

"As I offered at lunch, you have my blessing to resume your friendship while you are both here."

Kyle saw Delanie's color drain beneath her makeup and her chin jerk up a notch. He'd found grim satisfaction in watching her nervousness escalate. She *should* be nervous. Damn nervous.

"Generous." He kept his voice dry and his gaze on Delanie. "But totally unnecessary, my friend. The lady and I have no fresh avenues to explore." He held her gaze. "Do we, babe?"

The gold necklace vibrated at the base of her throat as her pulse leapt in response to his volley. If looks could kill, he'd be rotting in his grave. He smiled gently at her, impressed when she managed to switch her venomous glare to vapid disinterest.

"I'm sorry." Her eyes told a different story as she gave him a singularly sweet smile. "I really don't *remember* one way or the other, ya know?"

She turned to Montero, laying a slender hand on his arm, red nails long and startling against the darkness of his sleeve. Kyle distinctly remembered her having short, clear nails this afternoon at the pool. *All she needs to complete the picture,* he thought, biting back a grudging smile at her chutzpah, *is a wad of snapping gum.* He was surprised she hadn't thought of that prop.

"Of course I'd do anything for you, baby, you know that. It's just . . ." She managed to look beautifully flustered while shooting Kyle a smart-ass glance. "Well, how can I say this without hurting his feelings? What I *do* remember was just so . . ." Red beaded earrings tinkled against her shoulders as she shrugged. "So, well, boring, ya know?"

Kensington swallowed the wrong way, choked. Kyle slapped him on the back and stifled a laugh. He remembered one "boring" night when Delanie's legs had damn near vise-gripped him in half as she'd climaxed. So hard that heel-shaped bruises had decorated his back for days. Her eyes said she remembered it, too, but she didn't look away. Instead she composed herself and gave him a vacant, unconcerned stare.

Kyle noted the personality change when she was with Montero. He didn't like it, but she was good. Damn good. *Little girl,* he thought with regret, resignation, and faint admiration, *you have no idea just who you're playing with.*

Kyle held her gaze.

She blinked. Her gaze skittered around the room.

That's better, sweetheart, look away. If Montero doesn't scare the hell out of you, then I will. He wanted her scared and running. No matter who had to do the dirty deed.

All his attention appeared to be on his food, but he observed the other two men covertly. This was an ingrained part of his life, like muscle and bone. He was a man with many skills. Because he'd been so much younger than his contemporaries, and always too young to participate in school activities for most of his life, he'd learned to sit back and watch. It was what also made him good at what he did.

While his peers played football and romanced the cheerleaders in high school, Kyle obtained his medical degree. He'd streaked ahead of his much older classmates at med school to become an epidemiologist.

He'd wanted to help fight the occurrence of disease in large populations. To detect the source and cause of epidemics and to find cures. The *last* damn thing he'd ever thought he'd be doing at this point in his sterling career was manufacturing and weaponizing the smallpox virus for Montero.

Montero had approached him just over four years ago. Kyle had been his first pick. And he knew why. He was top of his field. The best. The youngest. The brightest. And Montero wanted the best money could buy.

Kyle had done small jobs for the government and a small, elite antiterrorist group called T-FLAC since he'd left high school. He also had brothers in the business. He'd gone directly to his oldest brother Michael for direction, then contacted his superiors at T-FLAC.

T-FLAC had mobilized immediately. Within twelve hours, Kyle had agreed to spearhead Montero's plan to manufacture the smallpox virus, and every legitimate law enforcement agency around the world was in.

England joined forces, then France, then South Africa, then Israel. Small European countries followed in quick succession, offering money, manpower, or tactical options. They all came to the table determined to vanquish Montero once and for all. No small tentacles were to be left to flourish after his annihilation.

No one was prepared to risk a smallpox epidemic let loose on the world. There were perhaps seven million doses of the vaccine available worldwide. Not nearly enough to combat what Montero had planned. Every step of this maneuver had been choreographed backward and forward every step of the way.

Kyle was excited, invigorated, and scared shitless. A million things could go wrong.

There was too much riding on this assignment, too many people depending on him, to allow for any distraction.

Circumstances had always mandated he be a loner. He'd never felt it more powerfully than he did here and now. In five days this place would be crawling with good guys. But until then he was it.

Conversation was stilted as each course was consumed, and the next set before them. Montero had coerced the chef from a top-rate hotel in Spain into service, and the food was superb.

Kyle enjoyed every bite.

"None for me, thanks," Delanie told the waiter as he approached with dessert. She bunched her napkin on the table. "I'll leave you gentlemen to your dessert. I'm going to change now." Sinuously she uncurled her body from her chair. "If that's okay with you?" She stood behind Montero and ran her fingers lightly over his immaculate black hair.

He reached up and took her hand, bringing it to his lips. The diamond in his pinkie ring glinted tiny rainbows on her cheek.

"Go, *mi dulce*." Montero smiled indulgently, releasing her hand to pluck a cigar from the humidor a servant placed beside him. "But don't be too late." Snipping the end off the fine Cuban, he caressed it between finger and thumb. "I will not wait up for you." He motioned a servant to offer the Montecristos to his guests. Kyle almost expected Delanie to take one on her way out.

"I'll jog fast," she assured Ramón. She left the dining room without a backward glance.

Delanie's taut ass in that tight red dress made Kyle grateful he was sitting down. He dragged his gaze away.

Kensington ignored her to concentrate on his cigar selection.

Montero watched Kyle, not his departing girlfriend. He smiled. "Not intelligent, but enthusiastic."

"When's she leaving?" Kyle asked coldly, waving away servant and humidor. He walked a fine line with this. If he pushed too hard, Montero would off her without compunction. Kyle wanted her gone. Not dead.

Montero blinked into the flame a servant held to his cigar. "Delanie? Why would she leave?"

"You know I don't do business with women around," Kyle said. "And particularly not *that* one. I don't trust her."

"She is my gift to you." Ramón Montero's obsidian eyes lost their glitter. "If you don't like or trust her, do whatever you want with her."

Kyle laughed dryly. "Meaning she's my problem now." Picking up the brandy snifter, he warmed it in his palm.

"She's too self-absorbed to have any useful knowledge of our business. I'll pay her off, and take her into San Cristóbal when I go back. Get her out of our hair."

"I prefer she remain here, old friend."

Shit. "Do you?" Kyle glanced at Montero. "Why?"

His host frowned. "I just do."

Crap, shit, and damn, Kyle thought as he leaned back in his chair with studied casualness. This was not good. Not good at all. *Her sweet ass better be outta here before Montero acts out whatever's in his whacked-out mind.*

"If you insist, *amigo.* A not altogether unpleasant task, I suppose. For a short while. Don't forget though, my attention span with the weaker sex is almost as short as yours."

Montero preened. Kyle wondered which of them would win the Oscar after their performance this week and toasted Montero with the glass.

It might be hard on his body parts, but at least this way he could keep a close watch on her until he flew her out tomorrow.

A cloud of pale cigar smoke drifted about Montero's head, as he, too, picked up his snifter and swirled the amber liquid meditatively. "The reason I so enjoy your company is precisely because of your, shall we say—" he savored the bouquet of the Bas-Armagnac, not taking his eyes off Kyle's face "—creativity, in the face of adversity." He paused to roll the brandy on his palate before setting the glass down and smiling across the table.

"Which is, after all, the reason *precisamente* for wanting you to join me on this new venture. Not so?"

Yeah. Creativity in the face of adversity was another one of his talents, Kyle thought hours later, standing alone on the dark patio. He leaned his shoulder against one of the fluted Doric columns supporting the latticed roof over the pool.

Everyone had gone to bed. Behind him, the hacienda was dark. Outside lighting would attract insects and animals. Although a barely discernible chain-link fence ringed the circumference of the clearing to keep out both two- and four-footed game, insects and small animals were always a problem.

There'd been a moon when he'd come outside. Now, no stars pierced the thick cloud cover in the black canopy of the sky. The air felt hot and oppressive.

The four men had gone to see his brand-new, top-of-the-line lab after dinner. It'd been a small trek through the jungle, and within eyesight of the drug lab.

The chickens, for use in hosting the virus, were happily pecking at their feed in a newly constructed coop. The building was air-conditioned, freshly painted, and damn it, *perfect*.

Kyle had taken his time inspecting every Bunsen burner, every petri dish, every last little detail before admitting his satisfaction.

Hell, what was not to like? The best of the best as decreed by himself. The *good* he could do with a lab like that and Montero's kind of funding—

Too bad in five days it would be rubble.

He glanced impatiently at the face of his watch.

Delanie had gone *jogging* for God's sake.

In his peripheral vision, Kyle detected a slight movement a less observant person would have missed. A blacker-than-black shadow moved slowly, silhouetted by the trees encroaching on the perimeter of the clearing.

His night vision was excellent—something that had saved his ass a time or two. The shadow was just a soldier. He had long since marked the guards patrolling the perimeter of the compound and knew their schedules and individual habits inside out. He also knew the range and timing of the various cameras positioned around this section of the patio. There was one directed at him now, where he stood painted by shadows.

No one could approach him without his being aware of it, and checking his watch every five seconds, like the irate father of a past curfew teenager, wasn't going to make the time go any faster.

Aside from Ramón Montero's efficient soldiers, the compound bristled with the latest in security systems. Cameras, an electrified fence, a radar grid, and three thousand acres of unexplored jungle should be a big deterrent. If not, the two strategically placed SAMs would. The surface-to-air missiles utilized lasers and an infrared homing device, enabling them to differentiate between friendly and hostile aircraft. They were top-of-the-line U.S. issue. So new, so revolutionary, only a handful of people knew of their existence.

Several fly-over reconnaissances in the last few weeks had shown him where everything and everybody was. Infrared had pinpointed the size and location of the compound's buildings and the accompanying number of personnel.

There was only one way in and out—by chopper. Which for the moment was just the way Kyle wanted it. Except for the immediate problem of his little thorn in the side.

Little fool. She was ass-deep in alligators.

Tomorrow when he got back from a quick trip to the port of San Cristóbal he would have achieved two things.

One pickup.

One delivery.

Although Montero hadn't seemed concerned by Delanie's long absence after dinner, Kyle *was*. She'd been gone for hours. He couldn't put her on the damn plane Stateside if he couldn't find her. Where in hell would she have trotted off to in the pitch dangerous darkness of the midnight jungle?

A soft breeze drifted across the patio, combing ripples in the dark water of the swimming pool and rustling the foliage of distant trees.

He heard her first. Her breathing came harsh and erratic, over the hard, rapid slap of running shoes on brick as she raced across the patio out of darkness, arms and legs pumping.

His raking gaze saw everything. Scraggly ponytail bouncing on top of her head, sweat sheeting her skin, the darkness of her eyes and the length of her long legs in skintight black leggings.

Fear came off her in palpable waves.

Kyle had his SIG P210 in his hand before he'd taken step one as he scanned the darkness behind her. She was alone. As she came closer he could smell her perfume, mingled with a good dose of healthy sweat. He had an immediate hard-on.

Flicking the safety on his gun, he tucked it out of sight. Before she could pass, he wrapped his large hand around her upper arm, jerking her to a standstill in midflight. Her scream would have woken the inhabitants of the San Cristóbal cemetery, a hundred sixty miles away, if he hadn't palmed her mouth with his other hand.

She struggled for a second, then froze in his hold. Tendrils of hair stuck to her damp cheeks. Her eyes flashed sparks in his general direction. She couldn't see him nearly as clearly as he saw her.

He had a feeling that was going to be a defining problem for them.

In his family, hell in his *profession,* women were to be loved and cherished. Protected. Respected.

Yet here he was. About to violate every damn code ingrained in him.

So, what the hell was he going to have to do? Which would scare her more? The cynical bad guy, or the ex-lover who'd never forgotten the taste and texture of her lush mouth?

The sweet softness of her succulent lips moved like a caress against his palm. Her eyes strained to see who held her.

Resigned, Kyle murmured softly. "Ssh, it's m—"

Delanie bit down on his hand.

Hard.

Chapter Three

Delanie tasted blood. "Bstrdth!" She'd known who it was the moment Kyle had put his hands on her.

With a muttered expletive Kyle jerked his hand from between her teeth. "Bitch," he said mildly.

"Bastard!" she shot back, this time more clearly. Served him right. He'd scared the bejesus out of her, coming out of the dark like that.

Blood pounded in her ears. The timbre of his voice brought back memories of things better forgotten; the gentleness of those hands on her sensitized flesh, his scent as it had lingered on her skin when he'd made love to her. Way back in the mists of time.

She hadn't forgotten.

She'd never forget.

And she *never* repeated a mistake.

Life was crammed with just too damn much to repeat lessons she'd already learned. She *had* to keep her focus.

Especially now.

She swallowed, drawing back mentally. "Let go."

The pressure of his fingers lightened. Infinitesimally. He slid his hand down her upper arm to lightly circle her wrist. There was the subtle threat of both pain and pleasure in his grasp and she jerked her arm away, glaring up at his ghostly presence. She licked her lips. He might be invisible, but no ghost tasted salty and musky.

"What . . . are you doing . . . out . . . here?" she panted, hoping her heartbeat would stop threatening to choke her.

33

"Waiting to see if you'd come back alive, or if we'd have to retrieve your decimated bones from the jungle tomorrow."

His low, perfectly pitched whisper showed he wasn't a happy camper. Which was just fine and dandy with her.

"Gee. I didn't know you cared." Bending forward, she braced her hands on her knees and dropped her head, dragging great gulps of sultry night air into her burning lungs.

"I'm taking you into San Cristóbal tomorrow."

"Nope." She felt the heat of his eyes on the top of her head, but made no move to unfold herself. The tendons behind her knees screamed for mercy. She bounced them into submission, her fingertips brushing her toes.

"It wasn't an offer," he stated flatly. She heard him shift his feet on the brick, and a shower of sweet-smelling flowers drifted from the lattice above him at his movement.

"In case you didn't recognize it—" she straightened and peered in his general direction, barely able to make out his denser shadow from the darkness "—that *was* a refusal." She felt rather than heard his snarl.

"What the hell are you up to?" He paused a beat. "Whatever Montero is paying you, I'll pay a hell of a lot more for you to disappear."

"Give it up. I'm not for sale, and I'm not leaving. This has nothing to do with money. And nothing whatsoever to do with you."

"What's he holding over you?"

"Not a thing," she snapped. "Ramón Montero has something I want. When I have it, I'll be happy to trot off into the sunset. Until then, leave me the hell alone."

"Tell me what it is," he drawled, suddenly, suspiciously affable. "*I'll* give it to you."

She didn't trust him any farther than she could spit. "You're not in a position to do so."

"Then you'll have to do without it." Now his tone was uncompromising.

Damn him for making her feel even more vulnerable and scared. Very carefully she slid her hand under her shirt and down the back of her leggings where the narrow Tampax box had been digging uncomfortably into her damp skin. She pulled it out. "Don't make me use this."

There was a moment of silence and then he gave a bark of laughter. "What are you going to do? Shove a tampon up my ass?"

Her cheeks flamed with fury. She didn't bother to ask how the hell *he* could see what she was holding, when she couldn't even see it herself. She mangled the flap of the sweat-dampened box with fingers made clumsy by impatience. White cylinders dropped like pickup sticks around her feet. Her fingers touched the metal barrel of the gun. She pulled it out, dropping the box and the rest of its contents on the ground. She pointed the business end of the little .38 Colt directly where she hoped Kyle's chest was. Right at his black, octagonal heart.

"Get out of my way and stay the hell out of my sight. I don't care what business you have with Ramón, just stay away from me."

"Hmm. Little thing like that can make a big hole."

"Don't tempt me." Six shots would clean up his attitude quite nicely. "I'm not in the least bit afraid to shoot you. In fact, I'm sure I'll enjoy it."

"Ever shot anyone before?"

"No. But there's always the thrill of the first time," she lobbed back sweetly, her hand sweaty on the grip. Acid churned in her stomach.

His sigh caressed her forehead. "Then I guess since you've shown me yours . . ." Delanie heard the rustle of his clothing. "I'll show you mine." She felt the cold caress of hard steel against her temple. "And mine's bigger than yours. Sorry, honey, you'll have to put away your toy and play the game my way."

Her heart beat so fast it made her light-headed and blurred her vision. Mouth dry, palms wet, the sweat on her body turned to ice. She might not be able to see him, but she could feel the antagonism radiating from his body. She could only draw shallow staccato breaths at the sensation of that deadly, round black hole against her pulse.

God, *could* he kill her? The answer throbbed on the next heartbeat. Yes. This Kyle Wright was quite capable of pulling the trigger. She'd seen it in his eyes this afternoon. The answer was in his voice now. He didn't want her here.

Lauren will be lost forever if I'm dead. How would Mom and the others cope?

Instinct whispered he wouldn't do it now. Not in the dark where soldiers would return fire before asking questions. She hoped.

Coolly, she reached up and shoved the barrel away from her temple with her open palm, then crouched down to scoop up the tampons. "You really bring out the worst in me, Wright." She jammed the Tampax, packed around the little silver gun, into the squished-up box.

She wished he'd disappear. She wished he'd— The question she should be asking herself was, could *she* shoot *him* if he interfered with her search for Lauren?

"There." Delanie stood defiantly, not answering her own question. She pushed the box down the back of her leggings. "Happy now?"

"You have no idea," Kyle said dryly. She heard him put his own weapon away.

"Well, entertaining as this has been, I'm too tired to play cowboys and Indians. I'm going to bed," she managed carelessly, even as her body still pulsed with residual adrenaline. Her stomach burned, and she dug an antacid out of her shirt pocket, chewing it quickly. The breeze, while warm, felt chilly through her damp shirt. She shivered, turning blindly toward the house, her hand pressed to her midriff.

She should have known better than to try walking away. Gripping her elbow, Kyle firmly and inexorably herded her away from the house and across the pitch-blackness of the patio.

She pulled against his implacable hold. When his fingers tightened, she demanded, "Do you mind telling me where you think you're dragging me off to?"

He must have eyes like a cat. She couldn't even see her hand in front of her face. She glared up at the cloud-covered sky— The moon had shone very nicely for her earlier. She put up a token resistance, but allowed him to steer her to a lounge chair.

"Right here. For now."

She dropped onto the chaise, smelling the chlorine of the nearby pool and a subtle masculine aroma that was tantalizingly familiar as Kyle sat beside her.

Close, too damn close. Delanie could just see the gleam of his eyes in the darkness and feel the press of his knee against her thigh.

"Why do you think Montero offered to let us renew our acquaintance?"

"I don't have the foggiest idea." Delanie sounded as surly as she felt, and that was pretty darn surly. "Since it isn't going to happen, I don't really care one way or the other. But if I *had* thought about it, I'd guess it'd be a test to see how loyal to him we both are."

"Good guess, but not in this case."

"And I suppose you're just dying to enlighten me." A warm breeze caressed her cheeks; it smelled of green things and danger. Exhaustion dragged at her. Abject terror and sleeping with one eye open for nights on end did that to a girl. She leaned back against the soft cushions, yearning to close her eyes. Obviously she dared not. Her biggest danger at the moment was sitting right here with her.

He shifted, his voice coming to her out of the dark, curling around her like smoke. "He wants to make damn sure I'm happy."

"There, see. Someone cares."

"Because," Kyle's voice was hard, and she could feel him watching her in the dark, "if I'm not happy, I walk. If I walk, I take my contribution with me."

Unless it had something to do with Lauren, she didn't care who did what to whom.

There was a lengthy pause. "You heard what we were discussing at dinner. You know what he's—"

Her eyes shot open. "Don't you get it? I don't give a rat's patoot *what's* going on between you and Ramón." After the

first few minutes she hadn't bothered to listen to a word the
men had said at dinner. She'd been too busy trying to decide,
on her mental grid, which area she was going to search later.
"I have my *own* damn problems, Kyle. Just tell me what you
have to tell me so I can drag myself off to bed."

"One way off this mountain is with Montero's say-so. The
alternative is a damn sight less pleasant than a short, volun-
tary helicopter ride."

Considering she hated to fly that wasn't saying much.
Besides she'd already figured that out for herself. There was
a long, pregnant pause. An animal growled in the distance,
the sound carrying clearly on the still night air. Nothing
she'd heard tonight at dinner had really surprised her. She'd
been aware Montero was a drug lord, or whatever they were
called these days, and that he laundered money through the
casino. She hadn't cared. He'd pay for that, just as he'd pay
for whatever he had done with Lauren.

She shrugged. "What's *your* contribution to all this mayhem and murder?"

"Among other things," Kyle said with quiet menace, "I'm
the one Ramón trusts enough to off the president."

"Of America?" Delanie asked, horrified.

"The president of San Cristóbal. For God's sake. Weren't
you listening at dinner?" Silence throbbed, then his voice
came out of the darkness and he said flatly, "I'm the designated assassin."

She'd been thinking about the ramifications of Kyle's presence here and about her sister. She'd asked questions that
both men had naturally ignored. Not that Delanie expected
them to fill her in.

Their casual mention of labs and biohazard suits was
alarming to say the least. She didn't remember hearing anything about an assassination.

Her necklace threatened to cut off her air at his words.
"You're an *assassin?*" She stared at him, sick. "So much for
your *hypocrite* oath. You told me you were a doctor. Was that
a lie, too? Were you . . . when we met . . . were you doing
this?"

"Amongst other things. Now," he said, almost gently, "would you like to reconsider my offer of a ride into San Cristóbal tomorrow?"

"No. Your Mission Impossible has nothing to do with me." She was rapidly losing her bravado and had to swallow the metallic taste in her mouth.

Oh God, oh God. Please. I want to get the hell out of Dodge. Where *are* you, little sister?

"You're mine to do with as I please," he told her coldly. "I can hurt you. Never doubt that for a minute."

Unfolding her cramping legs, she stood. "You couldn't hurt me, Kyle, no matter what you did."

"Why? Do you think I'd draw the line at breaking someone smaller and softer than I am? Consider my profession." He rose. "I know as many pain centers as I do pleasure points. Willing to give it another crack?"

His shirt brushed against her chest, but Delanie stood her ground. "Let's just say you've given it your best shot and let it go at that, shall we?" She spun on her heel, headed for the house. What she needed was a cool shower, lots of soap, and breathing space. Half a bottle of antacid. And a new plan.

What she got was a dizzying spin into Kyle's arms. "Damn you," he snarled against her mouth.

"Don't you dare—"

He dared.

Trapped against his chest, she tried to shove his bulk away. His hold was unbreakable. No preliminaries, no feeling his way, no Mother-may-I? Just a lip lock as he held her face between his hands and kissed her deeply; a starving man graced with a banquet.

His taste and texture were hauntingly familiar, sending sharp, poignant longing to her breasts and groin. And a red alert to her brain. She kept her arms at her sides, but couldn't prevent swaying against him in the pitch darkness. The sounds of the jungle beyond the fence intensified the aura of steamy mystery, leaving only the sensation of touch, taste, and the intoxicating scent of him to fill her senses.

Oh, God. She knew better. She really did.

She'd known from the first moment she'd met Kyle Wright that he'd hurt her in ways she'd never been hurt before. Known within minutes what drove the women of her family like lemmings to the sea. Known the wild sense of addiction. Need.

Known then, as she did now, that she had no defenses against him. There was no way on earth she could protect herself from a man this compelling. This powerful. This tempting.

And she'd been right.

Which is why she'd planned to leave him sleeping in their sex-rumpled bed in the middle of the night four years ago. Only to find he'd beaten her to the punch and left her first.

It was a good thing she was immunized, Delanie thought vaguely as Kyle's large hands tunneled through her sweat-dampened hair to cup her head. He stroked her cheek with his thumbs as his tongue plunged and stroked. A soft moan broke free when he sucked her tongue, and she opened her mouth wider to receive him.

She ignored the now muted warning sirens as another shock of desire darted through her. Her legs went wobbly and she stood on tiptoe to slide her arms around his neck. The kiss was long and deep. The rhythm drugging.

Lips wet and swollen, she felt both stunned and disoriented when he finally held her away from the furnace heat of his body. It was as sudden as being taken off life-support without notice.

"What . . . ?"

"Go in the house and pack." His voice sounded raw. "We leave first thing in the morning."

"Don't I wish," Delanie muttered under her breath, too softly for him to hear. Blindly, she walked in the direction of the largest dark shadow, hoping it would turn out to be the house. Her lips tingled as blood rushed through compressed nerve endings and her nipples went from engorged to soft beneath her shirt.

Somehow she found her way to her room, not bothering to

turn on the light. Her breath wheezed in and out, as labored as if she'd only now finished her run.

She shouldn't have let him kiss her. What on earth had she been thinking? She stripped off the long-sleeved shirt and tossed it in the general direction of the chair, then toed off her running shoes.

Okay, so Kyle Wright was just as potent now as he'd been four years ago. He was a good kisser. So what? There wasn't a law saying a murderer couldn't have a good technique. She wasn't that naive. Not only was Kyle the wrong man, but this was definitely the wrong time and the wrong place for anything even resembling attraction. She resented the hell out of her body's betrayal. If ever there was a man to be afraid of, Kyle Wright was it.

She finished stripping off her clothes and made straight for the shower, feeling better after she'd washed off the scent of a man she'd believed she'd forgotten. She walked back into the bedroom rubbing her hair dry with a towel. She'd find her sister, then they'd *both* leave. Until then, she'd do whatever necessary to avoid Kyle. If she had to hide out tomorrow until he left Izquierdo, so be it. She was *not* leaving without Lauren.

A half second later she realized her problems were far more immediate. Ramón and Bruno had entered her room while she'd been in the bathroom and stood waiting for her.

Ramón's flat perusal skimmed neutrally over her naked body as she unhurriedly snagged her robe off the back of the bathroom door. The silk clung uncomfortably to her damp skin. "Goodness, you gave me a fright." She casually tied the sash at her waist. "What are you doing here? Is something wrong?"

Let me count the ways, she thought dryly, trying to figure out Montero's agenda from his expression. Although she and Ramón always had connecting rooms, he'd never so much as put a foot in her bedroom until tonight. She glanced from one man to the other.

"Did you forget, little dove, this is my house?"

"No, of course not." Delanie unwound the towel from around her head and finger combed her wet hair before crossing to the dressing table for her silver-backed brush. It was gone. Punishment for some infraction?

Her eyes skimmed from the neat dressing table to the empty closet, doors still open. Apparently the longest day of her life was about to get even longer.

She watched his reflection in the mirror as he sat down on the foot of her bed, Bruno a sentinel at his side. The bodyguard held a flame to the cigar Montero withdrew. For several seconds there was silence.

Mesmerized by the glowing tip of the cigar, she couldn't help the tremor that swept across her skin. She had no idea what he wanted tonight. But she just bet, whatever it was, she was going to hate it.

"Did you enjoy your run tonight, my dove?" Ramón asked.

"Oh, yeah." Her heart did a double thump as she turned around to face him. "It was great. In fact, I managed to run twice as far as I did last night." She had to be sure he was convinced she loved to jog. It was the only time to search for Lauren without having everybody's eyes on her.

Smoke drifted lazily about his head. "And nothing bothered you?"

She frowned, not liking the way this conversation was shaping up. "Uh-uh." She deliberately misunderstood. "I doused myself with insect repellent and wore long sleeves." She glanced at Bruno's impassive face, then back to Montero. "It's sweet of you to worry abou—"

"Did he touch you?" Ramón asked conversationally, watching her without a blink. He held out his open hand. Bruno handed him a small silver nail file. Inexorably her gaze moved from the shiny file to the scarlet tip of the cigar and back again. Light glinted off the utilitarian nail file as he worried it between his fingers.

"Who?" She was letting her imagination get carried away, she admonished herself.

"Come here, *mi paloma*," he said so softly, she had to

strain to hear him. She hesitated too long. At his nod, Bruno moved forward to grab her wrist, exerting just enough force to show he was willing to break her arm if necessary. As soon as she stood before his boss, Bruno released her, returning to his post.

Montero rose, handed the cigar to his bodyguard and took her face between his icy fingers. He squeezed her cheeks. He did it so gently, so gradually, it took seconds for her to realize just how painful it was.

His liquid black eyes gazed coldly into hers. "Don't ever lie to me, *puta*." His mocking drawl sharpened. "He touched you. He more than touched you, and you want each other, *verdad?*"

God, his digging fingers hurt. She controlled the desire to flinch, keeping her expression blank. Damned if she did. Damned if she didn't. "I have no idea what you're talking about—"

The pressure increased, cutting off the words. She dug her nails into her palm, kept her eyes steady and refused to wince.

"You were about to tell me of your desire for my friend." His head tilted to the side, waiting. Watching.

His other hand came up, as he very gently ran the cold, smooth edge of the fingernail file under her right eye. "Did Kyle admire these pretty eyes, my dove?"

The threat was chillingly effective. "He was out on the patio when I came back from my run," she admitted cautiously. "We talked for a while. Then I came in to shower."

He released her, settled back on the edge of her bed, and waved away Bruno's attempt to hand back his cigar. She swallowed bile; her heart's uneven rhythm throbbed in the fingerprints he'd scored into her cheeks. The delicate skin beneath her right eye felt chilled.

She'd never been intentionally, *physically* injured by anyone in her life. She closed her eyes briefly and conjured up the sound of children in the playground. The sound of giggles and happy laughter— Her heart rate skipped several beats before starting to race painfully.

"Did he put his hands on you?" He resumed cleaning his nails.

She'd forgotten the damned cameras.

"He kissed me." Her heart still beat much too fast. He'd *given* her to Kyle, for God's sake. What did he expect?

"Did he appear to enjoy the experience?" Ramón glanced up, his expression intent, as if her answer held the hope for world peace.

"He seemed to." She fervently hoped that had been the right answer. She ran her finger around the inside of the tightly woven links of her necklace to hold it away from her damp skin.

"Ah." Perfect teeth shone in a brilliant smile. He sounded pleased. "Good. I've known him for many years, he is a brilliant man in his field. The best. A man many fear because of his expertise." Reading between the lines she figured *he* was afraid of Kyle. She didn't want to know just what Kyle's field of expertise was. But she wondered, if Montero *was* afraid of Dr. Death, how the knowledge could help her.

"Kyle and I are like this." He held up twined fingers, his Cobra pinkie ring glinting in the lamplight. "It was my good fortune to persuade him to join me in this venture. He has shown his trust by coming here to my home. Alone."

This was apparently a big deal. Delanie could tell by the almost hero-worship on Ramón's face as he finished softly. "I wanted to return his trust with a gift. A matter of honor, one that a mere woman could not understand."

Delanie waited for the punch line.

He handed the nail file to Bruno, and accepted back the cigar, and drew in smoke, before he said silkily, "Your things have been moved to Kyle's room. Make him a happy man."

Sheer force of will helped her hold his gaze as she swallowed the helpless frustration she felt. Keep calm, sound vaguely stupid, *and don't tick him off.*

Intellectually she *knew* there was no reasoning with a psychotic. She held her temper as she'd learned to do, but she couldn't let this go.

"That wasn't the arrangement we made, though, was it, love bug?"

"The arrangement has changed. I want to give Kyle a gift he can use." He gave her a singularly sweet smile. "And you know I always keep my promises."

"So do I." The voice might be pure bimbo, but she made it a promise. "I thought you wanted people to see you had something they couldn't have, sweetie. You insisted I flaunt myself so everyone knew what they were missing. I agreed to play *your* whore, you never said anything about sharing me with your friends." She pouted, wanting to puke.

There was a long silence as he scrutinized her face. She must have done a credible job looking vapid.

"I think my friend Kyle appreciates your assets very much." Obviously prepared to go the extra mile for a friend, he said generously, "Make sure he is kept satisfied, and your benefits will remain the same."

Great. She got to keep the bimbo clothes and jewelry he'd lavished on her. All she had to do was give her body to the devil.

She wouldn't do it.

"You don't understand, sweetie, I don't *want* to have sex with your friend." Delanie struggled to stay in character. The way Montero was watching her right now made her question her sanity in standing up to him.

"My job was to *pretend*. Nobody suspects we aren't sleeping together, do they? You never even suggested the arrangement would change." She was desperate now. She absolutely had to convince him not to give her to Kyle.

"We had a deal." She realized too late that she'd not just shown irritation, she'd done it in her natural voice.

"I don't like your tone, *puta*," he said sharply, black eyes opaque as he tugged at his eyebrow; a habit she'd quickly learned meant he was extremely annoyed.

To him she *was* a whore. She changed her defensive stance, and voice, to meek submission. "I'm sorry, baby, of course I'll do whatever you want." And pigs will fly. "I'm just worried, how will it look if you give *your* girlfriend to one of your associates? I mean, jeez, it's cool if the big boss is the only one with a lady friend, but if you give . . ." she almost begged. "If you give me to Kyle, the others might think it's unfair and want women, too."

He wasn't buying it. "Kyle is my brother, my *compañero,* my right hand. To insult him is to insult me." He rose. "Very well, *mi paloma,* I would, of course, never force you against your will."

Like hell, Delanie thought, swallowing hard.

"Bruno will take you to San Cristóbal tonight. I'll have your things sent to you in a few days."

From the merciless look in his black eyes, Delanie knew, without a shadow of a doubt, he'd have her killed before she ever reached the small airstrip behind the house. Would Montero have Kyle dispose of her? What ironic poetic justice *that* would be.

Like a shadow, Bruno followed him to the connecting door.

"I will not tolerate disobedience," Montero continued coldly, his absurdly handsome face flushed. "Do you understand me? I will not tolerate it."

Damn it. Even if he didn't kill her first, there was no way she would ever make it back up here alone through hundreds of miles of jungle.

So, the bottom line? She'd do whatever it took to find Lauren.

"Gee, honey, I didn't know you felt so strongly." The words felt forced through her frozen lips as she struggled to sound humbly contrite. "Of course I'll do whatever you want, sweetie."

"A wise choice." Ramón's benevolent smile showed her capitulation had been a given. "Kyle is waiting for you. Bruno, show Miss Eastman to Dr. Wright's quarters."

The bodyguard reached her in three steps and wrapped an enormous hand around her upper arm.

"I haven't got any clothes on," she pointed out, ignoring the beefy shackle holding her in place. She was *not* going to be delivered to Kyle like some sacrificial offering naked under a flimsy robe.

"What you are wearing will suffice." Montero, obviously bored with the conversation, pulled open the connecting door to his room. "If Kyle permits you to dress, he has access to your clothing." He motioned Bruno to take her and vanished into his own room, leaving behind the acrid smell of smoke and brimstone.

The tampon box lay on the floor by the chair, where she'd dropped it earlier. She glanced up at Bruno's implacable expression. She wasn't going to leave it there.

"I need this." She nudged the box with her bare toe.

He released her for the half second it took to stoop down, shove the box into the pocket of her robe, and grab her canvas bag from the chair. "Okay. I'm ready," she lied through clenched teeth.

Keeping a firm grip on her upper arm, Bruno herded her through the dim house to the wing on the other side of the family quarters. Oblivious to the maze of her chaotically churning thoughts, Bruno was unstoppable. Whatever she was going to do about this situation was going to have to be done behind closed doors.

Kyle's closed *bedroom* door.

Think. Think.

"Thanks, Data." The quiet sarcasm sailed over his bald head as they stood at the dead end of the corridor outside what was obviously Kyle's suite. Suddenly Bruno's silent bulk seemed reassuring.

"Don't suppose you'd like to hang around?" She regarded him hopefully. He gave her an impassive look, and she sighed. "I kinda thought you'd say that."

Her thumping heartbeat threatened to choke her. She straightened her shoulders under the flimsy silk robe and faced the double doors with her heart pounding and her chin up.

Chapter Four

Bruno reached over Delanie's head and gave the solid wood a sharp rap with a ham-sized fist. She shot him a dark look. She'd have gotten round to knocking. Eventually.

Staring straight ahead, jaw tense, she pulled the robe's lapels up around her throat seconds before the door swung open.

Kyle didn't appear the least bit surprised to see her. Silently he motioned her into the room.

He was fresh from the shower, and the white towel slung around his narrow hips made his skin appear darker by contrast. His hair, wet and slicked back, hung loose down his back and clung to his biceps in dark licks, like question marks. Diamond drops of water glistened in the crisp, dark hair on his chest and arms.

God help her, he looked absolutely delectable.

She glanced back at the door. Every escalating heartbeat throbbed behind her eyes. "Bruno—"

"—is gone." Kyle hitched his hip on the burl writing desk to the right of the door. Behind him, the colors of the small sitting room blended into the shadows. Only the light from the other room illuminated his harsh features and limned the muscles on his arms and chest like a golden caress. An ocean-size bed loomed through the arch leading into the bedroom.

"Was this your brilliant idea?" Delanie asked coolly, pretending she was wearing one of her favorite ankle-length floral skirts and voluminous sweaters instead of the skimpy silk robe. It helped. A little.

He gave her an amused look. "Let me put it this way, jun-

48

gle girl. I asked Ramón for the favor." Bracing his arms behind him on the desk, he crossed his ankles. "He doesn't need to know it's because I'm not letting you out of my sight until tomorrow."

Caught between a rock and a hard-ass.

At the moment she'd have felt safer covered with honey and running naked through the rain forest.

"I'm touched by your concern. But I'm a big girl. Ramón and I understand one another. I'll just trot back and tell him that you've changed your mind."

Without volition she skimmed the damp towel Kyle wore like a sarong, and the shadows beneath it. Her body vibrated with tension, and her ears buzzed. Face flaming, she whipped her gaze back to his face.

He gave her a quizzical look, and asked in a dangerously soft voice, "Just who the hell are you, Delanie Eastman?"

A sexy, vital man like Kyle wouldn't have looked at the real her twice. Her personality was far from submissive. Her body was okay. She exercised and ate right. But her real hair color was brown. Not dark brown, not blonde brown. Just plain old brown. Her eyes were ordinary old brown, too.

And she'd never worn clothes like this in her life. The only time Kyle had ever seen her was when she was wearing her sister's clothes and pretending to be something she was not. Which she intended to continue doing until she was safely back home with Lauren.

Kyle's eyes narrowed. "At the pool this afternoon you were the vamp. At dinner tonight, the seductress. And now here you are. No makeup on this beautiful skin, no teased and tortured hairdo." He lifted her hand and stroked a thumb down the back of her fingers, making her shiver.

"No long red nails." Still holding her hand, he glanced up with a frown. "You bite your nails. You crunch antacids like you own stock in a pharmaceuticals company . . . and just looking at me makes you blush. What gives?"

"That's not a blush. It's a flush of annoyance." She tried to tug her hand away. He held fast. "And it must be obvious why I'm not wearing makeup. I just took a shower, and was planning to go to bed, before Ramón instructed me to come to you." She curled her fingers defensively in his hand.

"Honey, I have three brothers and a sister. Don't try and kid a kidder. You're crazy if you think I believe this act of yours for a second."

"I have no idea what you're talking about. But if you insist on chatting I'd like at least one of us to be dressed. Where are my clothes?"

"Bedroom."

Delanie stalked into the other room and threw open the mirrored doors. "How cozy," she muttered under her breath. His and hers, side by side. Not wasting time searching for underwear, she yanked a pair of jeans off a hanger, and snagged one of his T-shirts, because it was huge, off a shelf.

Staying behind the open closet door she pulled the denim up over her bare behind and the soft white shirt over her bare breasts. A cursory glance in the mirrored door showed her decently covered, the T-shirt hanging to her knees. She immediately felt better equipped to handle Dr. Kyle Wright and strolled back into the other room.

He was just where she'd left him. Unfortunately.

"Better?"

"Soon."

"You were a virgin in San Francisco," Kyle said conversationally.

Well! That had come out of nowhere. She forced a laugh. "How many virgins do you know who'd pick up a strange man in a bar?"

"Only you." He pushed away from the desk, tucking the towel more firmly around his hips as he stalked her. Close enough for her to see jade flecks in the paleness of his eyes. Eyes of a hunter with the target firmly in his sights.

"Touch me again and I'll break every finger in your hand, buster," she warned, feeling for the doorknob behind her as he stepped into her personal space. The door was still slightly ajar behind her. She wasn't foolish enough to run, even if there'd been a place to run to. But the temptation was there. Big time.

Delanie realized she was pinning her hopes on the Kyle she'd known for three days, four years ago. A man she'd believed to be decent, caring, honorable. Unfortunately, that memory was disintegrating before her eyes like wet tissue paper.

He smelled of soap and man. She tried to compensate by inhaling and holding her breath, which only made it worse. Closing her eyes for a second, she struggled to think calming thoughts, trying to center herself. There wasn't enough time in the universe to compensate for what she'd gone through in the past couple of months. Days. Hours. Minutes. Wetting her lips she looked at him again.

Kyle sighed, rubbed his hand across his jaw, and said tiredly and very softly, "Fine. Keep your secrets. For now."

His gaze roamed her face. A murderous expression flickered across his face for a split second. Gently he turned her head one way and then the other, studying the marks their host had left on her cheeks.

"Montero did this to you?" he asked, deadly calm. She could only nod as his thumb gently traced the fingerprints left on her skin. His breath fanned her face and she could feel the heat of his body seep through the thin fabric of the T-shirt. Her eyes closed as he cupped her face, running a callused thumb backward and forward over her bruises.

"Ah, jungle girl. If wishes were horses—" His thumb moved to caress her bottom lip.

Delanie had difficulty swallowing, her tummy felt like a clenched fist.

"Hell with i—" He bit off the words as his mouth crushed down on hers with a hunger that seemed to explode out of nowhere. This was no soft, tender exploration. The feverish heat was instantaneous as his tongue played against her lips, teasing them open. As much as she would have liked to pretend that brute strength had compelled her acquiescence, she knew it would be a lie. She responded without conscious thought. Her hands lifted to bury themselves in his long, thick hair. To pull him closer.

She rose on tiptoes to better reach his mouth. The door

snapped shut as his full weight pressed her against it. One hand curled around her hip, the other moved inextricably up her rib cage. Delanie groaned low in her throat as his strong fingers closed over her breast, knowing he could detect the wild cadence of her heart. His hand felt hot and hard as his thumb made a sweep across her beaded nipple. She pressed against him from breast to knee.

It wasn't enough.

The taste of him flooded her senses with tactile memories. Of a hotel room, tangled sheets, room service trays forgotten, and three days out of time. She wanted those nights back with an intensity that shook her.

"Kyle . . ." Delanie moaned, and his mouth left hers only to come down hot, wet, and open against the pulse throbbing at the base of her throat, just above the necklace. Her breathing grew more ragged, she bared her neck in supplication as he tasted her skin with his tongue.

Her eyes fluttered open as he held her hip, rubbing her in a slow sensuous glide against his erection. The damp towel around his hips had fallen unnoticed to the floor. Kyle pressed her between his hot arousal and the cold hard door at her back. His eyes, as green as the impenetrable jungle at night, searched the depths of her soul.

His head blocked out the light as he kissed her again, his voracious tongue dueling with hers, mating and then sliding away. Delanie moved restlessly between his hands. He spread her legs with his knee. She was desperate to feel the erotic scrape of rough hair against the tender skin on her inner thighs. She grabbed fists-full of his long hair, the tangled skeins cold and wet, his scalp hot. Blood pounded furiously in her lips. His tongue forced her to accept the rhythmic seduction. His hips teased a duplicate rhythm that drove her wild with need.

She made a small sound of protest. Of surrender. His lips and body pressed harder. Heat rose on her skin in waves. She wanted to bite him, drive *him* as wild as he drove her.

It had always been this way with them. Their lovemaking had had this intense, almost violent edge to it, as if neither could ever get close enough, as if they lived on the brink of a terrifying precipice and would tumble in an agonizing free-fall unless the other were there to stop their descent.

Oh God, it was so tempting to allow herself to be enticed, seduced, and distracted by him. Just for the moment. Just until she could forget for a few blessed seconds why she was here at all. He cupped her behind, pulling her in closer. Her muscles softened, flowing into his heat. Her fingers twisted into his incredible hair.

But she was no longer naive, and she wasn't ignorant about sex this time. This was dangerous ground. Hurtling off this particular cliff would do more than break her heart. This time, it might kill her. Kyle's carnal lovemaking had almost made her forget.

Lauren.

A dousing of ice water couldn't have cleared her mind any faster. Kyle Wright had a bad habit of making her irrational. Their magical days in San Francisco had been the only time she'd allowed herself the blessed freedom to be selfish. In the midst of a climax, she hadn't been able to think about her mom, or Lauren, or anyone else in the family. Only herself.

She couldn't afford the distraction now.

With a violent wrench she pulled her head away, using both hands to push at the rock-solid width of his chest. Delanie covered her face with both hands. "Damn it, I won't—"

He gently removed her hands from her face. "Wrong place, wrong time, wrong continent." The heat drained out of his eyes, leaving them once again cool and unreadable.

"Right! I'll stay because I don't have a choice, but if you so much as look at me the wrong way again, I'll—"

He smiled. A smile that didn't reach his eyes. "Shoot me with your pea shooter, Annie Oakley?"

"Do a *Bobbitt* on you while you're sleeping," she shot back, stalking through the arch into the bedroom to yank the serape-type bedspread off the bed. On her way back, she snagged a pillow. He was still standing at the door when she dumped the bundle onto the sofa.

"Take the bed." He sounded as exhausted as she felt.

"This is fine. Don't let me keep you—" She scanned him derisively from top to toe. "—up."

She plopped down on the sofa, pulling the spread over her before giving the pillow a punch. She closed her eyes. By imagining the life she would have, once she had Lauren safely home with her, Delanie managed to keep her breathing slow and deep.

Another teaching job. Sweet, innocent little faces . . . She'd buy a small house . . . trees and grass . . . civilized rows of flowers.

Knowing Kyle stood there watching her made her skin itch. She controlled the nervous urge to scratch.

Breathe, she instructed herself.

In.

Out.

In.

Lauren.

Out.

Lauren . . .

Lauren—

—Kyle.

God save him from stubborn females. Kyle waited until Delanie's faked slumber became real.

She looked small and defenseless curled there, one cheek cradled in her hand. Her skin appeared translucently pale, and smudges lay beneath the fan of her lashes. He shook his head and moved closer. Even in the muted light her hair shone, thick and silky to the touch. For years he'd remembered its texture in his dreams.

Using just his fingertip, he moved the strand covering her nose, his index finger lingering on the softness of her cheek. He trailed his finger over her chin, down the silky warm skin of her neck, then lingered on the fragile pulse beating in the hollow of her throat. He knew how easy it would be to exert just the right amount of pressure to break her. Some in his line of work would consider her immediate termination mandatory. Montero and his new threat were far more important than a single, easily-disposed-of woman.

He removed his hand from her face and dressed. Opening the door quietly he padded down the hallway and through the dark house.

Instructed to give this guest immediate access to their boss, the guards stepped back as Kyle traversed the long hallways of the house.

Slipping through another set of double doors, Kyle snapped on the bedside light and waited. He wanted his business partner's full attention. He got it as, blinking in the light, Montero reared up in bed, his face puffy with sleep.

"Kyle? *Qué pasa?*" Beside him his companion, a lump under the covers, groaned and rolled over.

"Do you want your present back?" Kyle kept his tone affable as he strolled toward the four-poster bed, his hands in his pockets.

"What . . . ? Oh, the girl? No, no." Montero raked back his hair, obviously trying to figure out what the hell Kyle was doing in his rooms. "She was your gift, my friend."

"Yes. That was the impression you gave me." Kyle withdrew his hand from his pocket and poured the microsurveillance bugs in his fist onto Montero's naked chest. He'd removed the rest the moment Delanie's clothing had been delivered to his suite this evening after dinner.

"I won't have an audience while I'm having sex," he said coldly. "If I find any more of these, I'll take my toys and go home. Either you trust me or you don't."

"Trust you?" Montero glanced about nervously. "But of course! I . . . I trust you with my life." Kyle saw the telltale movement of Montero's leg under the covers as he tried, subtly, to nudge his companion awake.

Kyle turned to go. When he was almost at the door, he paused to give Montero a hard stare over his shoulder. "And Ramón, old friend, old pal. I insist my playmates be unmarked, *comprende?* I won't tolerate anyone, other than myself, disciplining my property. Don't touch her while I have her. If you do," he said gently, "I'll have to kill you."

The open French doors leading out to the pool flooded the dining room with squares of buttery early morning light. Delanie, gorgeously overdone in a bright pink sundress and carrying a wide-brimmed straw hat, became an exquisite work of art framed by sunlight.

She owned the room in that moment, oblivious to the presence of strangers, enemies, or thick undercurrents. The rest of Montero's nasty little group had arrived early this morning. She didn't so much as acknowledge them as she strolled to an empty seat at the table.

Delanie's all-male audience, however, focused on honey hair sexily tussled, succulent fuchsia lips, and sultry bedroom eyes. All conversation came to an abrupt halt.

Which was another damn good reason to get her the hell out of here, Kyle thought. The conversation had just been getting interesting. Montero took great pride in his charitable pursuits and had casually announced his appointment to the board of directors of a well-known international children's foundation. With the man's interesting methods of recruiting, Kyle knew those same kids could end up as part of his network of dealers and suppliers, not to mention customers.

Their host scrutinized Delanie speculatively as she sashayed into the room. Despite her war paint, she gave the appearance of a woman who'd spent half the night indulging in sexual gymnastics. Only Kyle knew how she'd tossed and turned in restless slumber until he'd scooped her off the sofa and tucked her into bed beside him. Rather than a night of wild sex, she'd slept deeply, cradled in his arms. When he'd left her this morning, she'd been curled in his bed in a sweet-smelling little dream ball.

Thank God in a couple of hours she wouldn't be here to distract him. The fragrance of soap and strawberry-scented shampoo followed in her wake as she strolled behind his chair to an empty seat. What was going on in that clever little brain of hers? The glance she gave the assembled guests was only vaguely curious. Whatever her agenda, obviously she considered it far more important than anything going on here. Or what he could easily have done to her last night. With their host's blessings. The woman knew how to play chess.

Kyle accepted another cup of coffee from the servant behind him, settling back to enjoy the show. Her run might be short, but she was a pleasure to watch in action.

"Good morning, *mi paloma*," Ramón greeted her, all affable charm, friendly smiles, and bonhomie. "I trust you slept well?"

"Just peachy, thanks," she said coolly, and started to pull out the chair beside him.

"No, no." Montero waved her away with an avuncular, too-white smile. Like a cartoon character, he was too handsome. Kyle almost expected to see the flash superimposed on his teeth. "Kyle has kept a space for you, there by his side."

Jaw tight, she spun on one high heel and took the chair to Kyle's right, handing her large hat to a hovering servant who didn't know what the hell to do with it. It passed down the line of servers until it disappeared out the door. Delanie ran her index finger under her necklace in an unconscious gesture he'd noticed several times yesterday. He wondered why she wore it if the thing bothered her so much.

"And who is this delightful young woman, Ramón?" The question broke the silence punctuated by cutlery and crockery chinking.

Montero glanced up. "Takeshi Sugano, Delanie Eastman."

Sugano scrutinized her for a moment before his sumo wrestler shoulders dipped in a small formal bow. Despite his roly-poly appearance Sugano was no benign despot. Kyle had firsthand experience of how well the Yakuza operated. They gave the Italian Mafia a run for their money in creativity alone. Five-foot-two in his heel lifts, his appreciation for tall blond American women was legendary. And he liked what he saw.

Next, Montero introduced Karl Danzigger. The man flushed, running his freckled, chalk-pale fingers through his red hair. "Miss Ea-Ea-Eastman." His stammer sounded strangely musical with his Dutch accent. In his early fifties, Danzigger lived a reclusive lifestyle, seldom removing himself from his high-security estate in Holland.

Through Montero, Kyle had met him on his home turf in Delft two years ago. Like Sugano, Danzigger's reign of terror across half of Europe was renowned, despite his seclusion.

Kensington hadn't shown for breakfast. Kyle had been unpleasantly surprised last night to learn that he'd arrived with Montero's mother in tow the day before. Apparently the woman had decided on the spur of the moment to take a vacation with her son. Another female complication he hadn't anticipated.

He still wanted to recon the compound to get the lay of the land. The infrared was good, but nothing beat up-close-and-personal verification. There were final arrangements to be made, and a myriad of other small vital bits of business to wrap up before Saturday.

But first things first.

Kyle dropped his napkin beside his empty plate. "I'm taking Delanie with me into San Cristóbal this morning," he informed Ramón when the other man glanced up. "I'll take care of the other matter at the same time."

Ramón frowned. "Is that wise, *amigo?*"

Kyle cocked an eyebrow.

Montero smiled, waving away his own concern. "You know what is best, of course."

Kyle rose, placing both hands on Delanie's tense, bare shoulders. She felt fragile. It wouldn't take much to break her bones. He wondered how much it would take to break her spirit. He let his thumbs brush against her neck and felt her shiver. Stubborn and foolishly brave as she was, he couldn't afford to take pity on her.

He kept eye contact with Montero. "Perhaps your mother requires a ride back to the city, too?" he added pointedly. "I'd be happy to escort her to a comfortable hotel in San Cristóbal."

"Thank you for offering, Dr. Wright." A sultry voice,

tinged with annoyance, made all heads swivel to the open door way. Isabella Montero was stunning in the way that only a woman of means could afford. It was hard to believe she was Ramón's mother. The plastic surgeons in Switzerland were true artists.

"As I have only just arrived, it would be foolish to have the pilot take me back." She gave him an assessing look. "Would it not?"

Elegantly smoothed-back hair accentuated a widow's peak above striking dark eyes. The loose knot of black hair coiled at her nape set off a pale olive complexion, wine-red lips, and expertly kohled eyes. She had the toned body of a thirty-year-old and accented the positive in the understated linen dress with a large, rather barbaric, gold pendant hanging on a long heavy chain to rest between her voluptuous breasts.

Regally she strolled to the seat beside her son. Taking the chair a servant held out for her, she accepted the air kiss Montero directed at her cheek. "You may resume your seat." She glanced pointedly at Kyle. He ignored the command, and her gaze flicked to Delanie. "And to whom do you belong?"

Beneath his fingertips, Delanie's slender shoulders tensed.

"I don't *belong* to anyone," she said sweetly, ignoring the warning pressure of his fingers. "Ramón and Kyle kinda share me, ya know?" The "bimbo" voice grated, as it was supposed to.

"You might have potential, my dear, but I can assure you it is not being realized." Isabella's eyes reminded Kyle of two hard, dark cherries as she took in Delanie's bright dress and pink-plastic flamingo earrings with obvious distaste. "I'm surprised at Dr. Wright's lack of . . . discernment."

Before Delanie could volley that one back, Kyle got a grip on her arm and hauled her troublemaking little ass out of her seat. He gave her a shut-your-mouth-and-don't-stir-up-shit look. Delanie's eyes went dark. His fingers tightened in a warning to keep those luscious fuchsia lips pressed together.

She acquiesced with a squeak of annoyance before she slid her hand into the curve of his elbow and gave him a sensual smile. "These boys of mine are always in such a hurry, ya know?"

Oh Lord, Kyle thought, unwillingly amused. "Don't overdo it, Sarah Bernhardt," he cautioned under his breath.

He glanced at Isabella. "I'll take her off for a little refresher course in interpersonal skills." He refused to release her, even when Delanie squirmed. He wasn't hurting her, despite his fingers covering the days-old marks on her arm.

Mamá Montero gave him a sultry smile. For all her beauty there was something rather unsavory and predatory about her bee-stung mouth. Kyle managed a counterfeit smile. He still had an old-fashioned notion of what a mother should look like. Isabella Montero didn't even come close.

"Say good-bye, Delanie."

A meaningful glance passed between mother and son. Isabella leaned in to whisper to Montero. He rose, cutting off Delanie's next salvo.

"I'm afraid your excursion into town must wait until later, if you will, my friend," Ramón said. "I'm taking all of you on a little outing to a special place."

"Something more important than my errand into town?" Kyle asked tersely. Now what the hell was Montero up to? The damn clock ticked with annoying volume in his head. No way in hell was he keeping Delanie up here for another twenty-four hours.

Montero pulled at his eyebrow. "It was scheduled for tomorrow, was it not?"

"I'd prefer to get it over with and bring my supplies back here so I can get started," Kyle said flatly. "Every day wasted is another day without the money in the bank. Your choice."

"I'm sure a few hours won't make any difference at all, Doctor." Isabella Montero smiled. "Don't be impatient. Whatever it is, will wait."

Montero couldn't tie his shoelaces without Mommy's sayso? The Oedipus complex was another facet of Montero's personality unexposed.

Curiouser and curiouser.

When he went into San Cristóbal he'd have his people dig

deeper into Isabella's background. There was something about the woman . . . something Kyle couldn't quite put his finger on.

His gaze went from mother to son and back again. He quirked a brow.

Montero shrugged and glanced away to address the others. "I suggest everyone change into sturdy shoes and comfortable clothing. We'll meet on the patio in, say, fifteen minutes?"

Sugano and Danzigger rose agreeably. No stress there. They, and Kensington, were full partners in this. All they planned to do this week was kick back, relax, and rake in the dough.

Were they in for a surprise!

Delanie's earrings jiggled as she threw Kyle a mock smile. "I'll just stay right by the pool and do my nails instead, okay, sweetie?" Big brown eyes sparkled with triumph.

Little witch.

"No, *mi paloma.* You will come, too," Montero insisted charmingly, giving his mother his arm. Like a ridiculous wedding procession, they walked into the wide hallway. Montero paused, glancing back at her. "You will enjoy the nature lesson, little dove. There are some interesting sights to see."

Delanie rolled her eyes in a "yeah, right" gesture when he turned his back. Obviously the last thing she wanted to do was go with them on this oddly timed nature walk.

Why? What did she want to do back here at the hacienda on her own? It was a mistake for her to telegraph her emotions the way she did.

Being that transparent could prove deadly.

Chapter Five

Even at ten in the morning, the sun filtering through the trees was dim and oppressive. A variety of exotic undergrowth thrived in the dark, rich soil. Vegetation struggled for control of available space, vying for the occasional ray of sun filtering through the dense foliage canopy overhead. The tropical jungleness was not nearly as attractive in real life as it was in the movies. Steamed, eaten alive, and drowning in perspiration, Delanie wondered how it was possible a body could sweat so much and not shrivel into a prune.

She'd changed into thin, bright yellow cotton pants, a matching long-sleeved top, and sturdy lace-up boots, her hair stuffed into a baseball cap, ponytail pulled through in back. She'd never given a rat's patoot about fashion until she'd assumed the bimbo persona, which would, no doubt, earn her a spot on Mr. Blackwell's list of the fashion impaired.

As soon as this was over, she'd return to her normal couture; the baggier and more comfortable her clothing the better. She'd borrowed the outfit from Lauren's vast closet in Las Vegas. The boots were her own.

On a positive note, the dreadful outing provided an opportunity to look around in broad daylight. She could practically hear a giant clock ticking in her head with each footstep she took.

Lauren *had* to be somewhere here on Izquierdo. There was nowhere else to look.

Almost stumbling over a twisted vine, she could practically feel Kyle's eyes on her butt. Trotting along behind Ramón and the others, she kept a respectable distance between those in front and *him* behind. Why he was lagging, she hadn't a clue. She'd refused to speak to him since she'd slammed and locked his bedroom door in his face so she could change for this mandatory outing.

Kyle had behaved like a Neanderthal at breakfast. Putting possessive hands on her while sending flirtatious glances at Isabella. The woman was old enough to be Kyle's mother.

Delanie did a hop-skip to keep her balance on the uneven terrain. Too bad Mommy Dearest didn't act her age. Isabella, of course, was back at the compound, no doubt sipping a cool drink under a fan, while they got chewed alive by nasty little bugs as they hiked to China.

Visually exploring, Delanie pretended a fascination with the vibrant orange and fluorescent pink orchids hanging in masses from the trees. She ducked as a scarlet macaw swooped just over her head to land in a nearby tree.

Kyle moved up beside her. He wore jeans, black of course, with a T-shirt and heavy boots. And the ubiquitous shoulder holster. Thankfully, he'd waited until she was done in "their" bedroom to change his own clothes, managing to avoid more conflict. He hadn't broken a sweat, naturally, and she wished he'd worn something other than the thin, black silk T. It stretched across his chest and abs, and accentuated his biceps.

"What are you so pissed off about now?"

"Me?" She opened her eyes wide. "Now why should I be pissed off?" She kept her voice low, although there were enough jungle noises to drown out the Boston Pops. "Goodness, could it be because I *live* to watch macho men attempt a little male bonding while they show off their survival skills?" She paused. "Or gee, could it be because somehow I woke up in your bed this morning?" She was on a roll. "Or how about the prehistoric way you behaved at breakfast, or the—"

"Don't blame me if you insist on taking risks."

"What are you talking about?" She shoved a hank of damp hair back into her cap and kept on walking, her black canvas beach bag swinging against her hip.

"I'll give you a piece of advice, jungle girl. The fates have conspired to allow your continued presence here. At least for another day. Don't aggravate Isabella. Tick off either of the Monteros and you'll be gone so fast your head will spin. *If* your're still alive, of course."

"I'll take that under advisement."

His eyes narrowed as he watched her speculatively. "Have any idea why Montero touched your neck back there?"

"Back where?"

His braid slithered over his shoulder as he jerked his head back in the direction of the compound. "When we passed through the gates near the generator building."

"I don't remember. Why?"

"He was deactivating that necklace of yours," he said conversationally. "The one that irritates you so much."

She stopped dead to stare up at him. "D-deactivating?"

"Ever own a dog?"

"Damn it, Kyle—"

"There's a small sensor hidden in it. The second you move beyond that chain-link fence . . . Zap!"

Her fingers shot to the flat, half-inch-wide gold band around her throat. "Zap?" she asked faintly, holding it away from her clammy skin. She'd been girding her loins to leave the protection of the compound tomorrow if she didn't locate Lauren tonight.

Zap?

"Probably a radio-controlled fence buried out here somewhere this side of the chain-link fence. They use them to confine dogs. An electronic deterrent. This appears considerably more sophisticated, of course. But then our friend has acquired somewhat refined taste. Twenty-four–carat gold—"

Delanie gripped the restrictive band in a tight fist and gave him a pleading look. "Get it *off* me."

"No can do, jungle girl. I'm sure Ramón will want it back when you leave, though."

She shot him a fulminating look before storming off. He made no more comments, which she appreciated enormously. The necklace that had merely annoyed her for the last few days, now gave her the willies. The few ounces of gold, pretty and delicate, felt like a garrote at her throat.

Could she remove it right now? she asked herself. No. Delanie put the necklace out of her mind. There wasn't a thing she could do about it for the present.

She concentrated on her nemesis instead. The way he switched from lover to villain, and then back again, made her damn wary. He did it in the blink of an eye, with no warning, and there was no avoiding him.

Tree trunks spread their leafed branches hundreds of feet in the air, while underfoot, wrist-thick roots looped and snaked beneath the detritus to trip the unwary. Moss fuzzed the tree bark, a verdant home to the insect population that made the air hum and buzz in a muted undertone overshadowed only now and then by an occasional birdcall or a monkey's shrill howl.

Her shirt clung unpleasantly to her back in the stifling hothouse atmosphere. Every surface either oozed or dripped water. Thick and hard to breathe, the humid air felt like a living presence as she and the others followed single file in the wake of half a dozen locals using razor-sharp machetes to hack a path through the jungle.

The thick carpet of dead leaves underfoot felt spongy and dank, the undergrowth littered with man-size ferns and knots of leafy vines. Delanie watched for snakes.

Concentrating on where she put each foot, she worried her lower lip with her teeth. She'd skillfully managed to push reality out of the way in the past week.

My God, how will *I get Lauren out of here? And how am I going to get this blasted necklace off?*

She glanced over her shoulder. Kyle clearly wanted her gone. What if she asked him to help her find Lauren? She could offer him money. It was obviously important to him.

She mulled over the idea of putting the house she'd worked so hard to get up for sale. Combined with her 401K, minus the IRS's take, she could come up with about a hundred thousand dollars. Would Kyle help her find Lauren and get them both safely out of here for that amount?

The first, optimistic thought was that he'd say "certainly." Lead her to her sister, fly them out, and wave them good-bye.

The second, far more realistic thought was that Kyle knew exactly where Lauren was and had something to do with Montero taking her in the first place. In which case, alerting him to who she was and what she wanted would be really stupid.

Nope. She was all on her lonesome.

Practical was her middle name.

Lauren was somewhere nearby. Delanie was sure of it. But in the meantime, God only knew what the rest of the family was up to. She hadn't talked to anyone in over a week. And in her family that was a lot of time for the shit to hit the fan.

She'd always taken extinguishing the constant fires and dramas stirred up by them in her stride. Lauren. Mom. Grandpa and Aunt Pearl and assorted cousins, aunts, and uncles who came to her. Their ups and downs were all a safe and familiar routine in her life. Disruptive, but familiar.

Sandy better not be in jail when she got back, Delanie thought grimly as she trudged along. Her youngest cousin and Lauren were two peas in a pod. Too beautiful and too vivacious for their own good. They attracted the wrong kind of men to them like ants to a picnic. But where her sister was truly sweet and good inside, Sandra had always been hell on wheels and hard to control. She'd have to talk to Sandra again when she got home. *When* she got home.

Delanie sighed. She missed her family.

She missed the smell of chalk and uncontrollable giggles in her classroom.

She missed her life, damn it.

Lauren, where the hell *are* you?

"My grandmother used to tell us the clock would strike, and our faces would stay that way forever. Why're you frowning?"

Her eyebrows shot up. "You have a grandmother?"

"She died a few months ago. But I do have a father, three brothers, a gorgeous sister and a cool brother-in-law if you want references."

She frowned. "I thought all you soldier of fortune types were loners."

Kyle held a man-size leaf aside for her. His lips twitched as she passed beneath his arm. "Known many soldiers of fortune, have you?"

"Not a lot, no." Delanie gave him a curious glance. "Why do you work for a man like Ramón, Kyle? Surely there are legitimate private investors who would give you anything you wanted to work for them?"

"Montero's supposed to be the richest guy in the world," Kyle said, pale eyes shuttered, expression unreadable. "Why the interest? Trying to reform me?"

The others were some distance away. Delanie stopped on the rough path to put a hand on his arm.

"Not reform. But we both know what he is— Doesn't working for him scare you at all?"

Kyle's expression softened a little and he brushed a strand of sweat-dampened hair off her cheek, keeping his fingertips on her face for a moment.

"Yeah, he scares the hell out of me, jungle girl. But the money's good, and the hours suit me just fine. And once in a while my pal gives me a present I can really enjoy." He grinned. Cocky. Sure of himself. Confident of his place in the hierarchy of Montero's empire. "Don't knock the bad guys, honey. They have all the fun."

She frowned "How old are you?"

"Thirty-two."

"Are you the oldest?"

"Second youngest."

Delanie scuffed a toe in the slick ground beneath her boot. "Figures, your sister's the oldest. She must worry herself sick over you."

It was Kyle's turn to frown. "Why would you presume that? Actually Marnie's the baby of the family, and we all did our share of worrying about *her.*"

She started walking again, reluctantly. Kyle stayed right behind her on the narrow path.

"You an only child?" he asked.

"No. I have a younger sister, Lauren." And a flaky mom, and my grandfather and aunt living with me, and numerous other family members who depend on me to worry on their behalf when they go off half-cocked into the wild blue yonder. "I come from a pretty big family, though. Lots of aunts and uncles and cousins."

"And they let you come all the way to South America alone?"

"Yes." Facing front, she rolled her eyes, amused. "What were they thinking?"

"Yeah," Kyle said grimly. "What the hell were they thinking?"

"Probably that while the cat's away the mice can play," Delanie said absently as they closed the gap between themselves and Montero and his merry little band up ahead. "When we—when I get back home, they'll all be waiting for me out on my front lawn."

"Family's great."

Surprised, Delanie glanced over her shoulder to look at him. "You're close?"

"You bet. When we're lucky enough to get together."

Delanie faced front again and resumed walking, an uncomfortable ache in her chest. "Us, too." The only reason her family stayed together was because she held them that way. Tightly binding them together with love so fierce, so big, they couldn't all go to hell in a handbasket and scatter to the four winds.

She scowled as a vine caught in her hair, and paused to untangle herself. She hoped Auntie Pearl was taking her medicine like she was supposed to, and that Grandpa wasn't driving her nuts in Delanie's absence . . .

Ahead, Ramón and the others slowed, surrounded by his guards who all wore camouflage and carried Uzis. Handy if a wild boar decided they were the smorgasbord of the day. She heard the shrill, tortured cry of a bird, the rustle of leaves as a small animal rushed through the forest unseen, and the splash of water.

"We came all the way out here to go swimming?" Delanie asked Kyle incredulously. "With a nice, clean, Olympic-size pool behind the safety of a chain-link fence back at the house?"

"There's no accounting for tastes, jungle girl. Remember that," he warned, his voice hard, as he gave her a meaningful look.

The guards stood back, holding the feathery emerald ferns aside as Montero and his guests emerged into a small, bucolic clearing in the middle of the jungle, à la Tarzan.

A small pond shimmered in the half light, idyllic and tranquil. Huge sprays of magenta orchids flourished on the mossy banks and dozens of brilliant coral-colored butterflies sipped their reflections on the mirrored surface. A trickling stream fed a narrow silver ribbon over slick green rocks, then tumbled into water so transparent Delanie could see the small stones and debris on the sandy bottom.

In fact she wouldn't mind a quick dip in that cool water right now. The thick air wrapped around her, humid and heavily fragrant. It was a beautiful spot.

Ramón snapped his fingers and one of his guards approached carrying a large plastic bag. He set it on the loamy earth and Montero opened it, nodding in satisfaction.

"You will all enjoy this. It is one of my more amusing entertainments when I'm home."

Danzigger, red hair sweat-slicked to his pale skull, appeared more concerned with the sweat drenching his clothing than whatever their host was up to. Kensington stood well back, out of the line of fire, apparently attempting to blend his scarecrow-thin body into the foliage. Like an albino, his thin, blond hair disappeared, almost invisible in the damp heat. He'd started the outing in neatly pressed khaki pants and shirt; now both were sweat—and vegetation—stained. He didn't look any happier than Delanie felt.

Delanie glanced at Sugano. Now there was a man intrigued. His small features were lost in the fleshy sag of his shiny face as he watched Montero avidly. He moved as if his shoes pinched and his underwear had given him a wedgie.

Welcome to the club, pal, she thought. So far *everybody* was giving her the creeps.

Montero's fingers snapped again. This time in her direction. The implication, and the gesture, annoyed the hell out of her. She almost told him what he could do with those fingers, then remembered herself and gave him a vapid smile.

Going to his side, she hooked her hand through his arm, the bulky purse between them. At her feet the large plastic bag had been opened. She wrinkled her nose. Whatever was in it stunk to high heavens.

Ramón smiled radiantly. "Would you like to throw first, little dove?"

"Throw . . . ?" She peered into the bag. It looked revoltingly like . . . ground hamburger. She shot Ramón a blank look.

He wrapped a strong hand about her wrist, then plunged her hand into the moist, glutinous mess.

Oh *yuck!*

Raw, bloody meat squished between her fingers. She tried to pull back, but he held her fast, his fingers tight about the fragile bones of her wrist. Reflexively her eyes flew to where Kyle stood apart from everyone else, his shoulder propped against a tree. He watched impassively, his arms folded over his chest.

"Close your hand, *mi paloma,*" Ramón purred. She squeezed her eyes shut; at the same time he yanked her fist out of the plastic bag. Coagulated fat and bits of meat clung to her skin. She shuddered, opened her eyes and stared unblinkingly at the romantic little pond until the orchids and butterflies blurred.

"Throw it into the water."

Grossed out, she did an underhand throw. Speckled bits of raw flesh arced through the air before pitting the reflective surface. She watched them slowly drift beneath the clear tranquil water.

The change happened swiftly. One second the transparent water was mirror calm, the next, from beneath the rocky overhang and from amid the grasses, came a furious churning. The water turned to bubbling pink froth within seconds. Vaguely aware that her hand was still hanging in the air, she dropped it to her side, swallowing hard as she took several steps backward.

Piranha.

Sugano, Kensington, and Karl Danzigger seemed fascinated by the macabre spectacle. The soldiers stood at attention on the perimeter of the small clearing, feet braced, Uzis at the ready.

Ramón smiled his wholesome, boyish grin. "Always wash your hands well after handling raw meat, my dove," he cautioned, taking her elbow in a firm grip.

She was damn sick of being manhandled. "Let go of me," she said, trying to shake free. He gave her a puzzled stare, as though he couldn't understand why she was protesting when he was giving her such a nice treat.

She dug her boot heels into the loamy earth. His grip tightened. "Ramón, for God's sake—"

"Excuse me, gentlemen," he said unctuously, and Sugano and Danzigger parted for them, watching her curiously as Montero inextricably guided her forward until her boot tips were on the rocky outcropping over the water. It seemed as though the whole jungle held its breath. A toucan shrieked in sympathy from a nearby branch. She could hear Montero's easy breath as his hand moved from upper arm to her wrist in an implacable grip.

The son of a bitch intended to force her hand into that surging water.

She didn't move, didn't breathe, wasn't capable of a coherent thought for long, long seconds. Blood pounded in her ears.

The man was crazy. *Crazy.*

The oscillation of the water settled, no longer even faintly pink as, lunch over, the silver bodies looped gracefully in search of dessert. A hard shudder raced down Delanie's spine as Montero forced her down, closer to the water, dragging at her wrist in a death grip.

Gritting her teeth, she got a firm toehold on the moss-slimed rocks, resisting the downward pull by locking her knees. She'd throw Montero in before she put a pinkie into that liquid diet.

She presumed the guards, the rest of Montero's merry men, and Kyle were still there. It never occurred to her to yell for help; she was too busy resisting and worrying how far the lunatic would go.

Off-balance in his grip, she teetered on the edge of the rocks. One boot-shod foot slipped. Her heart slammed up into her throat as she managed to steady herself, and the muscles in her neck pulled taut with the strain of resisting. Montero smiled at her struggle to find purchase.

Sadistic bastard.

She turned her head. Just enough to see what he was going to do next. For a split second she read determination in those glossy black eyes. She spread her feet, centered her weight and kept eye contact, every muscle quivering in anticipation.

"If I go in, I'll take you with me." It was a grim whisper, as she tightly gripped the front of his shirt with her free hand. He was observing something, or someone, over her head, and she braced herself.

Something flickered darkly in his eyes and then with a laugh he abruptly released her, patting her cheek as if she were a fractious child. "A joke, my dove. Just a small joke."

He yanked her hand from the front of his shirt, then turned back to his associates, smile in place, leaving her stunned and shaken on the edge of the water.

Son of a . . . Spinning on her boot heel she got as far away from Montero and the pond as she could.

When she was a safe distance away, she looked up. And caught Kyle's eye. He was still leaning casually against the tree trunk, but she just knew he was the one responsible for Ramón letting her go. For a moment they stayed that way, looking at one another.

"Not one's normal pets, but entertaining nevertheless." Unruffled, Ramón gestured for a soldier to offer the plastic bag to his associates. "Help yourselves, gentlemen." His open smile stayed in place even as he tugged at his eyebrow.

Delanie searched for a wet wipe in the black hole of her purse. The second she found the pack she pulled one free and attempted to rub the greasy mess off her hand. Her skin felt clammy, and she couldn't help the shudder that wracked her body. If he did this to her, with absolutely no provocation, what had he done to Lauren?

Oh God—

"Need to sit down?" a quiet voice asked beside her. Kyle. Faster than a speeding bullet. He took hold of her upper arm in a large steady hand.

She swallowed hard. "It was only ground meat. The same kind I use to make meat loaf." *Which I'll never eat again as long as I live. So help me God.*

"Didn't bother you, huh?"

She shrugged, keeping her bloody, yucky hand away from her clothes.

He kept a straight face, but his eyes had those damn crinkles beside them as he scanned her features for God only knows what. "Scared of snakes?"

Yes. "No."

"How about spiders?"

Them, too. She glared at him. "No."

"How about rats? Toads? Deadly poisonous wild Bora-Bora butterflies?"

"There's no such thing," she said, feeling a foolish smile tug at her mouth.

"That's better," he said softly, "You were starting to go an interesting shade of ash-gray." He gave a quick glance over at the other men tossing hamburger patties into the water, then released her arm to join them.

She had a funny feeling he'd been holding her up.

The moment they returned to the house the men convened a meeting. As much as she'd have liked to hide out in the bedroom, Delanie wasted no time changing into the most circumspect swimsuit she'd brought with her. The lime-green maillot covered her decently and she went out to the pool.

Heading straight for the denser shade of the vine-covered pergola, where a large table had been set for lunch, she dropped her canvas bag beside a chair.

The way Montero smiled while doing something heinous was unnerving. She had a feeling that if it hadn't been for Kyle's presence at the pond, Montero would have forced her hand into the water as some perverse form of entertainment to amuse his associates.

She leaned back against the padded cushions and propped her bare feet on another chair, staring across the Olympic-size swimming pool. Lined by natural rock, it disconcertingly mirrored the pond in the jungle. Only much, much bigger. Her skin crawled as though ants swarmed over her. Montero's casual cruelty made her blood run cold and froze her to the marrow. Just like last night when he'd gripped her face and held the nail file under her eye, this morning he'd delivered his sick "discipline" with an angelic smile.

God. She'd actually believed she could steal Lauren from under his nose and emerge unscathed. She shuddered in the heat, feeling nauseated.

Was Lauren alive?

If Montero hadn't thought twice about terrorizing her, God only knows what he could've done to—

Don't go there. *Don't.*

Lauren was alive. Her heart told her so. And damn them all, she was going to find her sister and get her home.

Wherever she was.

Somehow.

Desperate for a distraction, she watched as servants brought out a cold lunch and several frosted pitchers.

With hands that still shook, she set the small radio she'd found in Kyle's room down on the table. After pouring herself a glass of fruit juice, she stuck the little earpiece in her ear and turned on the radio, fiddling with the tiny dial. Finding nothing more than annoying static, Delanie flicked the off button, yanked out the earpiece, and stuffed everything into the cavernous bag beside her.

She shivered despite the hundred-degree heat and bit into the sweet, juicy pulp of a pale-pink melon, willing her mind to go blank.

A giant blue-and-gold macaw glided down to land on the table a few feet away. It picked up an orange slice and proceeded to nibble at the juicy center. That pretty much summed up how she felt about Kyle. He was nibbling at her center, knowing just where the soft tender parts of her were hidden.

On the other side of the house she could hear the faint, but unmistakable sounds of soldiers drilling, as they did twice every day, and from an open window, the sibilant tones of men's voices.

Blocking out the sheet of bright white light the pool had become, and the sight of the parrot, now beak-deep in a plum, she closed her eyes behind her sunglasses.

"*Qué pasa,* Delanie?"

Delanie glanced up, and almost groaned out loud.

Chapter Six

Isabella Montero wasn't exactly the distraction she'd been looking for when she'd come out to the pool. Delanie sighed; she'd been too wired to nap anyway. The macaw gave an annoyed squawk before flying off. She wished she could do the same.

"Fine thanks," she answered belatedly, feeling awkward with Ramón's mother for reasons she couldn't fathom. Dressed elegantly in a saffron linen sheath, hose and high heels, gold jewelry and hair immaculate, the older woman made her *feel* like a bimbo.

Delanie started to remove her legs from the chair she was using as a footrest. Isabella stopped her with a wave of her hand.

Ramón's mother wore a heavy, spicy fragrance and a hard gleam in her onyx eyes as she pulled out a chair and sat down.

"You look very—refreshed after your little walk." The pause was filled as Isabella's gaze scanned her from the crooked ponytail on top of her head to her red toenails.

Delanie withdrew her legs from the chair and set her feet firmly side by side on the brick beneath her own chair. "It was . . . interesting, all right. You should have joined us." *Since I have a sneaky suspicion it was your stupid idea in the first place.*

"I was expecting an important package." Isabella shifted, folding her long-fingered hands gracefully on her lap. Sunlight glinted off the chunk of gold around her neck. "Ramón

tells me he gave you to his good friend, Dr. Wright. He is
well pleased with both of you, yes?"

Delanie shrugged.

"The good doctor, he is excellent in bed?" Isabella asked
with a lascivious smile.

Delanie almost choked on the notion of Isabella in bed
with Kyle. "Yeah, actually, he is a good lover." *Was* a good
lover.

"Inventive?" Isabella leaned back against the cushions of
her chair and gave her a considering once-over. "Passionate?
Creative?"

"That's an extremely personal question." Holy Hannah in
heaven, what was this about?

Isabella pouted. "You Americans have an aversion to discussing something natural and enjoyable. We are both
women. It should not be awkward to discuss such a subject
with one another."

Gross. "We're strangers," Delanie pointed out. "Where I
come from, people only discuss their sex lives with very
close friends. And I tend to, well, you know? Have more *men*
friends than girlfriends."

"Then we must become *very* close friends." Isabella's red
lips parted in a smile. "We are the only two women here.
What could be more natural than growing closer and sharing
confidences?"

Oh, ugh! Delanie thought with misgiving. Suddenly it
dawned on her what the other woman had just revealed.

"There aren't any other women in the compound?" she
asked casually, picking up her glass and taking a sip of tart
juice while her tummy churned. God. If Ramón had "given"
her to Kyle, who had he given Lauren to? And when? And
where *was* she, damn it!

"Only men attend my son when he returns to his mountain, my dear. Their women remain home." Isabella reached
out to pat Delanie's knee. Unlike her eyes, her hands were
ice cold.

"I am just his *madre*. So you see," she shrugged and

spread her hands, rings flashing, "I am in desperate need of a friend in this all-male bastion." Isabella gave a tinkling laugh as she rose, coming to stand beside Delanie. "You and I will become *very* good friends I think, *mi bonita*."

Taking Delanie's chin firmly in her cupped hand, Isabella tilted her face up. She stood disturbingly close, her fragrance making Delanie's eyes itch. Black eyes moved over Delanie in an assessing way that brought hot color to her cheeks.

With a gentle squeeze, which reminded Delanie disconcertingly of Ramón doing exactly the same thing to her last night, she let go to pat Delanie's cheek with just the tips of her fingers.

Delanie shivered, despite the heat that rose in a shimmering mirage off the brick patio. She watched Isabella saunter back into the house. Like everyone else on Montero's mountain, *Mom* gave Delanie the heebie-jeebies.

Filled with a restless energy as though she was going to jump out of her skin at any moment, she shifted her sweaty back against the dark blue canvas cushion.

She couldn't even *start* to look for Lauren again until dusk, when she went out for her evening run. There were only a few more buildings unchecked within the compound.

Delanie touched the activated necklace. She had to get the damn thing off somehow. Possibly she could pretend she was willing to go with Kyle tomorrow. The necklace would have to be removed . . . Then what? Make a break for it? With umpteen soldiers after her? Into the jungle?

She'd always been resourceful. Despite the lack of choices, she'd find a way. She had to. In the meantime her insides roiled against the inactivity and frustration.

She didn't want to analyze the bone-deep fear seeping ever deeper into her marrow. *That* would incapacitate her. When she and Lauren got home she'd indulge in a nice nervous breakdown; now she needed to hold herself together and believe she and Lauren would get out of here safely.

Both of them.

But it was hours before dusk, and hotter than the hobs of hell.

At the far end of the swimming pool, fluorescent pink orchids and trailing vines with tiny bright green leaves grew profusely in the crevices of a "natural" rock wall. A twenty-foot waterfall showered a crystalline rainbow into the water below. A pillar-supported lattice roof, covered with the same plant, shaded the deep end of the pool.

Cold. Wet. Exercise. Easy decision.

Jumping up, she raced across the scalding hot bricks, pausing just long enough to toss her sunglasses on the rocky ledge by the waterfall. She dove into the clear, lukewarm water.

She swam five hard laps before doing a lazy crawl to the shaded end. There she let her feet drift so she could rest and catch her breath. A glance at the table she'd vacated showed the men had come outside and were seated for lunch. Isabella had joined them. Kyle was nowhere in sight.

Delanie figured she could happily stay here in the water until they were done and gone. She closed her eyes and floated lazily on her back until a splash alerted her to another presence. Flicking water out of her eyes, she kicked off, only to find she was caught between the falls and Kyle as he broke the surface of the water in front of her.

"Doesn't chlorine turn blond hair green?" he teased, eyeing the scraggly lopsided ponytail on top of her head.

"Doesn't water turn you back into a frog?" Delanie shot back, moving arms and legs to stay afloat.

Kyle grinned, his teeth white and straight in his tanned face. "I'm a prince?"

"Only by Machiavellian standards." She tilted herself upright. " 'A prince must use cunning and ruthless methods to stay in power,' " she quoted. "Does that about cover it?"

"I wouldn't have let him do it, you know."

"So say you." Barely a foot separated them. She noticed a compelling glimmer of amusement in his eyes and felt an answering heat surge up out of nowhere. He was a dangerously potent male animal and knew exactly how he affected her. One of the many things about this man that made her uneasy.

Why did he *do* this to her? Chin up, she back-paddled, giving herself a bit of distance. At least physically. "I noticed how quickly you jumped right in to stop him from trying to feed me to his pets."

He gave her a steady look. "He didn't do it, did he?"

The directions she was getting from her brain didn't seem to matter to her body. She trembled with the need to touch him. To feel the solid presence of his large body against her. Predatory and altogether too dangerously sexy for her to cope with.

In an attempt to appear causal, she floated farther back. "And that's because—why?" She found herself unreasonably annoyed. "Because you did *what?* Stood there leaning against the damn tree with your mouth shut while he tried to force my hand into that piranha soup?" Somehow without her being aware of it, he'd maneuvered her to the far side of the falls, blocking them from view of anyone on the patio. "What *I* think is that you have your own agenda and rescuing damsels in distress isn't part of it."

He narrowed his eyes, and said tightly, "I've saved your ass twice in two days."

"I was fine and dandy before you got here, and trust me, I'll be fine and dandy once you're gone."

"I'm not going anywhere," he said tersely, hardly moving but somehow getting closer. "I told you before, you're in way over your head, jungle girl. Now you know what I meant. Montero was proving a valid point. He can do whatever the hell he likes, and nobody will stop him. If I'd interceded this morning, we'd *both* have been tasty morsels."

"That's what I like so much about you, Dr. Jekyll. You're nothing if not predictable. A real hero. I'll be sure to put your name down for a medal when I get home."

"When's that going to be?"

"When I'm good and ready. If you're in such an all-fired hurry to get away from me, why don't *you* slither off?"

"I have business here."

"So do I." She rolled her eyes. "Must be a guy thing, presuming *your* business is more important than *mine*."

"Want to compare notes?" He gazed at her with those disturbing eyes, schooled in the art of concealing his feelings.

Delanie threw him a wary glance and shook her head. White flag. He was much better at this game than she was.

Checkmate.

"How was your meeting?" she asked, to change the subject.

"Educational and annoying." He paused. "Do you really want to discuss my business meeting?"

"Not really." She paddled in place, bone weary. Too much tension, too much uncertainty, and too much Kyle Wright.

Things were happening too fast for assimilation. She longed for a momentary break in the hostilities to regroup and refocus. This morning was the first time she'd felt her own mortality. She shivered. If she died, Lauren was lost. It was as simple as that.

Kyle's broad shoulders were shiny wet, his slicked back hair like black ink as it floated in the water around him. He should have looked feminine with such ridiculously long hair. Instead he looked like some ancient pagan water god, wild and untamed, his pale eyes eerie in his darkly tanned face as he watched her.

Her legs were starting to get tired treading water, when she realized she could stand, too. The water came almost to her chin. She backed up just enough to have her shoulders clear the water.

Kyle's eyes crinkled and he gave her a quirky smile that did strange things to the pit of her stomach.

"I think I'll go in. I'm getting pruney." Despite her words and strong desire to put distance between them, she stayed where she was. She wasn't sure why she stayed. It was ridiculous to stand so close to him and try to ignore the way the water beaded on the crisp dark hair of his chest and the sensation of her heart as it picked up speed. He was dangerously compelling when he smiled at her like that.

A teasing, sexy smile she remembered only too well.

He drifted closer, brushed a dripping strand of hair off her cheek, and murmured, "Chicken."

Delanie lifted her eyes to his face. Her heart missed a beat. "Don't even *think* about it," she said weakly, annoyed for allowing herself to be in such close proximity to a man she found hard to resist.

His legs brushed against hers under water. Her muscles tightened for flight as his hand moved down the small of her back.

"I had something a little more active than *thinking* in mind, jungle girl." The low, lethal murmur rumbled like a warning.

A heat wave broke across her skin. "I—"

"Look at me," Kyle demanded, holding her fast.

"I don't want to look at you, you barbarian, I'm going . . ." She swallowed the words as they died in her throat. "Will you please let go?"

He pulled her in closer, and gently but firmly took her chin between his fingers and thumb. His cool, wet mouth touched hers. His chest brushed against her breasts. In response her nipples puckered, sending a red-hot spiral of desire shooting downward. Weightlessly her legs drifted against his. A zing of electricity shot up, deep inside her as he wedged one hard, muscular thigh firmly against her pelvic bone.

"Don't make me have to hurt you," she said. He wasn't playing fair, damn it!

"Scared of a little kiss?" The taunt mocked her.

"Not scared. Not interested."

"Liar."

"You don't do anything in half-measures," she said tightly, wanting to resist the lure of his mouth and unable to look anywhere else. Damn him.

She placed a defensive hand on his chest to shove him away, and felt the steady thud of his heart. Her fingers curled and kneaded the taut flesh. He felt strong and safe, and she closed her eyes and indulged in the luxury of not being terrified out of her wits for a few moments.

She wished he'd say something annoying, which would

snap her out of this trance. *No, I don't,* Delanie admitted wistfully, as her search traveled from his eyes to his mouth, and then to the pulse at the base of his strong throat. There was no law saying she had to trust him to let him kiss her.

Her arms slid about his neck, her breath suddenly shallow and rapid. She could smell the faint trace of his woodsy aftershave, and the lingering scent of coffee on his breath, as he held her, his feet steady on the bottom of the pool, her only anchor in the buoyancy of the water. She had to hold onto him to remain upright.

Two layers of wet swimsuit felt like no barrier at all. The hair on his chest grazed her nipples and she felt the solid ridge of him at the juncture of her thighs. Slowly her lashes drifted up, and she met his eyes.

With his smoldering scrutiny, she was surprised the water wasn't boiling around them. Strands of his long hair wrapped around her like a caress. Nerve endings pulsed; the throbbing, building excitement made her eyes glaze. He was lethal to her peace of mind. Dangerous. Not to be trusted.

She lost the thread of her thoughts as her entire being focused on the exquisitely pleasurable sensation his touch was arousing. Fool. She was dangerously tempted by a weakness she hadn't felt in years. And although she'd never been partial to danger, right now she found the idea of being this close to it exhilarating.

"Did we ever make love slowly?"

"I-I don't remember."

Kyle smiled. "Yeah, you do. And the answer is no. We never did. We were so hungry, we devoured each other in ravenous bites because we couldn't get enough. I want it different this time," he said with bone-melting heat. "I want to make love to you slowly . . . in a cool room . . . on a big bed. For hours. Then I want to start all over again, until neither of us can move— Want to come, jungle girl?" he asked in a hoarse whisper.

"No."

"Liar."

She gave him a steady look. Broad daylight, she reminded herself. People over there . . . Lauren— "Let's say we did, and *not*."

His eyes glinted with amusement. "Jungle girl," he said half to himself, "why is it you're always either seriously overestimating your willpower, or underestimating my powers of persuasion?"

Kyle reached out to cup her face and felt her shiver. She glared up at him, her eyes slits of annoyance. But it was just an act now. He felt the electricity pulsing off her skin in palpable waves.

"I never underestimate myself." She met his gaze evenly. "Or my enemies."

Her nails dug into his forearms, but he didn't let go and after a few moments of obvious internal struggle, she relaxed against him.

He recognized the tactic for what it was.

She was plotting.

He could practically hear her mind working.

Unfortunately his body was reacting to far more tactile stimulation. Her skin, cool and slippery, smelled faintly of coconut oil and felt as smooth as satin under his fingers. Her lush mouth, soft as rose petals, her eyes, reflective in the water, scanned his features. He wondered what truths she saw there as he stroked the corner of her mouth with his thumb. Her lips opened on a sigh and her eyelids fluttered closed.

He held her silently, studying her upturned face, his primal need to protect her overwhelming. Unfortunately, for both of them, she was not his prime directive. There was so much more he wanted to know about this stubborn, intractable woman. Who was she? What drove her to sacrifice herself to a man like Montero? What was she hiding?

Immaterial, Kyle reminded himself. Whatever the hell she wanted from Montero, she'd just damn well have to do without. Her time was up. Especially after the piranha episode this morning. It didn't matter *what* the hell she wanted here, it wasn't as important as keeping her skin intact. Tomorrow he'd be in San Cristóbal. She'd be there with him. When he returned to the elaborate laboratory, he'd be alone and she'd be on her way Stateside.

It was a given that she wouldn't take her departure lying down. Delanie was stubborn and too goddamned tenacious for her own good. If he had to he'd drag her kicking and screaming to the chopper. In fact he wouldn't object to her being unconscious at the time, if that's what it took. But like the proverbial penny, she was bound to find a way back. Anyone else would find several thousand miles of jungle a deterrent.

Not Delanie Eastman.

She had the will and, knowing her, she'd find a way.

He considered for a moment the best method to handle her departure in the most expedient and permanent way possible without blowing all he'd worked for.

The longing he'd had for years, the longing to hold her body close, to feel her mouth respond under his, was a dangerous preoccupation he couldn't afford right now.

He had the opportunity to taste her one last time before he banished her, but he had to ensure while doing so that she would be compelled to go. Even her fear of Montero was subjugated by her desire to stay. What in the hell could be so damn important?

He'd get the skinny on the way into San Cristóbal when she couldn't run or evade the questions.

It wasn't the fact that Montero didn't scare the hell out of her—it was the fact that whatever kept her here was far more important than her own physical safety. He had to present something guaranteed to frighten the crap out of her.

He'd have to threaten her emotions, the ones she kept in such tight control.

He knew exactly which type of kisses would affect her in which way. She was so close to the end of her emotional rope it shouldn't be hard to give her the necessary nudge.

He teased with gentle but demanding nibbles as he coaxed

her lips apart using his teeth, then used his tongue as a masterful lure. She pressed closer, responding blindly, arms tight around his neck, her mouth open and greedy. She tasted unbelievably sweet.

He put a rough hand on her breast and squeezed without finesse, her nipple a bud beneath his palm. The diamonds in his Cobra ring glinted in the sunlight, reminding him of just why he was doing this to her. He tightened his fingers and felt her corresponding flinch.

"God, baby." He toyed with her nipple, watching her eyes, watching her mouth, reading the myriad emotions sweeping across her features. Dazed pleasure.

She teetered—

He had to remember not to fall into the same dark pit he was preparing for her.

He dropped his voice to a thick suggestive drawl. "I'd forgotten how responsive you are. You make me so goddamned horny, all I can think about is screwing you again."

She dragged in a hiss of air. When she tried to pull away, he jerked her back against his erection knowing his words, coupled with the feral glitter in his eyes, were doing exactly what he'd wanted.

Scaring the hell out of her.

And making him feel like slime.

His hand submerged beneath the water to unerringly cup her through the thin fabric of her swimsuit. He slid two fingers under the leg opening as he ground his mouth against hers. She jerked as he slipped his fingers inside her.

He almost exploded. She was hot. Wet. Ready. Pulsing with need. She gasped as his fingers plunged more deeply, her body starting to spasm. Christ. *He* wasn't supposed to be affected by this.

"God, you're hot. Let's go in the house. I can't wait to get some of what you've learned since the last time."

She opened her mouth to let him have it. His arm was already across her back, effectively pulling her closer. Her oath died in a strangled gasp as he once again fastened his mouth on hers in one quick move. He felt her internal muscles tighten around his fingers. God Almighty. He had to let her go before he lost it.

He couldn't. He'd started down this path. He'd burn in hell for this, but he had to make sure she got the message. With no room for interpretation.

To be effective, Kyle knew his attack had to be intimate and very, very personal. And with extreme prejudice.

Struggling in earnest now, Delanie made a furious muffled noise against his lips. He didn't have to fake the hard-on. Just the smell of her skin triggered some primitive response inside him.

Jesus. Shame curled ugly in his gut.

"Show me what you've learned, baby," he taunted, "show me—" He murmured against the impenetrable seam of her lips. He used a little pressure, her mouth opened, and she moaned in frustration, the kick she tried to administer thwarted by the water.

She bit his lower lip and struggled harder. She pushed at his shoulders, her hands skidding off his wet skin. He pulled her up, hauling her tighter against him. Grinding his mouth down on hers. Pressing his flattened palm hard against her under the water between their bodies. Hot, tight female muscle started to spasm.

She shuddered.

And helplessly kissed him back.

The hands that had been trying to push him away clung, eyes squeezed shut, her internal muscles tightened with the force of a powerful orgasm. Christ.

She whimpered.

He answered with a rasping curse.

And let her go.

He couldn't take any more.

She'd swum a good five feet away before her eyes lost their glazed look and she said venomously, "You are such a . . . such a . . . pig." Her voice wobbly, her color high, she glared at him, as she trod water.

He gave her a nasty smile. "Wanna get porked?"

"Get near me again, and I'll throw up on you." She

scrubbed at her mouth with the back of her hand. "You really are a sick excuse for a human being, aren't you? No morals, no principles, no . . . whatever!"

"Ethics? Integrity? Moral fiber?" All things he'd woken in a cold sweat thinking about in the lonely hours before dawn for the last four years.

Delanie glared at him. "All of the above." The smoldering fire in those eyes was for real now. "Let me make something perfectly clear, Dr. Romeo." Breathing hard, she yanked up stretchy fabric, covering the tanned globe of her breast, and leveled him with a dark look. "Keep the hell out of my way. Don't touch me. Don't talk to me. In fact, don't even *look* at me."

She swam away with long angry strokes, a flume of white water frothing behind her. He ran a careful tongue inside his lower lip, tasting blood and regret, then followed her at a more sedate pace.

He caught up to her without effort, but she stopped so suddenly his arm almost clubbed her on the head.

"What the hell—?" He put out a reluctant hand to steady her, then dropped it uselessly into the water when the color leached from her face. *Be careful what you wish for—*

"There's—" Her lips moved without sound. She cleared her throat, eyes fixed, and said roughly, "S-something in the water."

Kyle followed her line of sight to a rapidly moving V-shaped ripple in the water. His heart lodged in his throat.

The large head of a snake broke the surface of the water, as deadly and direct as a heat-seeking missile.

Forty feet away. And closing.

"Jesus." he grabbed Delanie's arm. *"Move!"*

Chapter Seven

They shot back the way they'd come, through water suddenly as thick and viscous as honey. At least thirty feet separated them from the safety of the rim of the pool. Delanie's arms and legs sliced automatically through the water beside him. But she was slow. Too damn slow.

The anaconda, all fifteen-plus feet of it, swam with amazing agility and speed. Its dark green-and-black body sinuously glided through the water, as its powerful muscles propelled it across the pool. Closer and closer. Close enough for Kyle to see its elliptical eyes. Venomous or not, he knew all it would take was one bite for it to grab and never let go. The result would be slow death within its coils.

Despite her protests, he flipped Delanie onto her back midstroke, and using an almost superhuman spurt of energy, managed to haul her across the pool and shove her out of the water onto the blistering hot cement apron. He was a split second behind her.

He saw the icy rush of fear in her eyes as he helped her to her feet and turned back to gauge just how close a shave they'd had. Mesmerized they watched the snake S lazily through the water. Standing above it, the damn thing seemed a mile long, its strong, muscled body terrifyingly graceful as it made its way under the waterfall and out of sight.

"You're certainly having an exciting day, aren't you?" Kyle said wryly, wringing the water out of his hair, then securing it with the thong from the inside pocket of his trunks.

"Aren't I just?" Delanie rubbed her hands up and down

her arms, shivering despite the heat. She chewed her lower lip. "I'm going to s-sue my travel agent when I get home."

Adrenaline leaked slowly out of him, leaving Kyle chilled to the marrow and more terrified than he'd ever been in his life. And that was saying a hell of a lot.

Tomorrow wasn't damn well soon enough to get Delanie the hell off this mountain, and away from these people. All his years of patience would be worth nothing if he spent every moment worried she was going to be dead on her next breath.

Patience had kept him alive, and *necessary,* thus far. More lives than their two were at stake. He couldn't forget that.

No matter how terrified Delanie was.

No matter how scared he was *for* her.

Delanie's brow knit. "How'd a snake that big get in the pool?" She continued to stare at the water. "There's a boy who's supposed to keep the pool clean and watch out for snakes."

Kyle wanted to run a hand up and down her back in a gesture of comfort, but restrained himself. Coupled with his crude seduction attempt, this might work to his advantage. Problem was, her shell-shocked eyes damn near twisted his gut.

"I guess he was taking a siesta," she answered herself, then glanced up at him with narrowed eyes. "Unless *you* had something to do with it?"

He gave her a faint, mocking smile and heard her teeth snap together. Good. She'd already managed to put starch in her knees.

"I'm sorry I warned you your *brother* was in the water. With any luck you might have come out on the unpleasant end of some sibling rivalry."

Not giving him a chance to retort she said savagely, "And I'm even sorrier I didn't shoot you when I had the opportunity last night. You really are a despicable piece of—"

"I get the gist," he paused. "Are you done?"

"N—"

He grabbed her hand, dragging her after him to the table

where the others were finishing lunch and staring at the two of them in puzzlement.

"For goodness sakes, slow down." Delanie hurried to keep her balance, her feet burning on the hot brick.

"Move it." He didn't slow his pace. Right now having her pissed *and* terrified seemed like a good thing.

Montero rose, Bruno, his "Mister Clean" shadow, right behind him. Both men impassively observed Kyle, a belligerent Delanie in tow, approach the table.

"Tell me you had nothing to do with that snake being in the pool," Kyle demanded in a deceptively affable voice, keeping his razor-sharp gaze on Ramón Montero's ridiculously handsome face. Delanie yanked her hand free and flopped down in an empty chair to glare at them.

"Claro que no, mi amigo," Montero protested, hand over his heart.

"Of course not" my ass, Kyle thought, annoyed. He didn't appreciate Montero's dangerous games. He'd seen the son of a bitch lie through his teeth with the same altar boy–sincere smile he wore now.

"I've had about enough of this crap. I'd've been considerably more amused," Kyle said to him, "if *I* hadn't been the one it was aiming for."

"I will take care of this immediately, my friend. You can be assured." Montero snapped his fingers. A soldier raced across the steaming patio in full battle fatigues, sweat standing out on his face as he came to swift attention.

Montero fired rapid instructions and the man strode off, his sweat-darkened uniform clinging to his back as he rounded the side of the house and disappeared.

Delanie said something snotty under her breath, but Kyle kept his focus on Montero. No one else at the table uttered a word. In a state of relaxed alertness Kyle watched as the soldier returned poolside, dragging a kid dressed in servant's whites. The pool-boy's eyes rolled with fright as Montero strolled toward them.

The kid tried to run.

His guard wasn't having any of it. As he bucked, trying to

break free, the guard tightened his fingers on the boy's skinny arm, propelling him inexorably to *El Jefe*. Sweat beaded the teenager's face, and his hands balled into impotent fists at his sides. His mouth twisted in terror the closer Montero came.

Out of the corner of his eye, Kyle noticed the avid fascination on Isabella's cameo face as she set her fork down and turned her chair slightly for better viewing.

Montero, followed by the soldier and struggling kid, moved closer to the edge of the water. For a few moments, there was much pointing and gesturing.

Shit.

Montero's voice was calm, low.

The kid gestured wildly toward the pool, the fence, the back of the house.

He pleaded. Fast. Frantic. Terrified.

Kyle *knew*. He just damn well *knew* what the sick little prick was going to do next. He shot to his feet—

Too late.

The black shape of the Magnum, obscene in the brilliant sunshine, came up in Montero's hand. The kid saw it, too, his eyes wide, white, wild.

Delanie's shoulders went rigid as her fingers white-knuckled the arm of her chair.

"Hey, Delanie! Pour me a drink." Kyle's words dropped into the highly charged atmosphere like confetti at a funeral. "Delanie!"

Her head whipped around and she glared at him over her shoulder. "Are you crazy? Pour your own damn—" She flinched at the deafening hollow crack behind her. For the split second they kept eye contact, he saw the spark of realization in her eyes. He'd protected her from seeing the actual hit.

Then she spun around, both hands gripping the arms of her chair again.

Well, no one could say he hadn't tried, Kyle thought as he leaned against the trellis post, his pose deceptively casual.

He was going to enjoy breaking Montero. Personally.

It took every ounce of self-discipline Kyle could dredge up to keep from grabbing Montero by the throat and playing anaconda until the sick bastard quit breathing.

Montero stood over the body, the Magnum loose in his hand, the pool-boy sprawled like a disjointed puppet at his feet in a pool of blood, dead before he'd hit the ground.

A .357 between the eyes will do that.

Kyle waited to see if Delanie would puke.

Isabella leaned over, saying something that caused the younger woman's spine to straighten. Delanie shook her head. Isabella brought her hand to Delanie's cheek, her expression almost maternal. More words were exchanged. Delanie's chair scraped against brick as she pushed away from the table.

Her face was taut and leached of color under her tan as she carefully pried her fingers loose from the arm of the chair and rose. Despite it all, she was steady as a rock. Without a word, she walked past him and into the house.

Kyle didn't realize he'd been holding his breath until she was gone, Isabella close on her heels.

The soldier struggled to get two hundred pounds of snake out of the pool. Sugano strolled over to stand beside Montero and was quietly chatting to him as two more uniforms arrived. The three soldiers battled to heave the twenty-foot, animated length onto the apron of the pool with the help of a long pole.

Kensington, his face flushed, started to join them, then changed his mind and subsided into his seat. "Christ."

He glanced up at Kyle, then shot a quick look at Montero, before looking back. "He's going to feed the kid to that thing?"

Kensington, Kyle knew, wasn't concerned with the morality of Montero using the dead pool-boy as snake food, if the zealous intensity in his eyes as he watched the proceedings was any indication. Kensington must have forgotten that Kyle had observed him offing someone in a far more brutal manner than a point-blank shot and a creative disposal of the body. The victim had been Kensington's wife. The infraction—a fabricated affair. Fabricated by Kensington himself for the girlfriend du jour.

Danzigger walked out onto the patio, a straw hat on his head, wearing his swimsuit, a Hawaiian shirt, and an expression of obvious disappointment that he'd missed the beginning of the drama.

"Don't worry, Danzigger. It'll take weeks for the anaconda to consume the body," Kyle assured him with a touch of irony. "There'll be plenty of time for you to watch each gory phase." *Not.*

He forced himself to wait an interminable twenty minutes before leaving the patio and making his way to his rooms to change. It irritated the hell out of him to find Isabella inside, waiting for him like a praying mantis rubbing its hands before dinner.

The room was dim, the slats of the shutters closed to block the early afternoon sun. She hadn't bothered with any of the lights. An oversight he rectified at once by turning on a table lamp.

"Where is she?"

He clicked on the second lamp and gave her a cool glance. He hadn't missed the wine bottle and glasses on the table. He hoped to God he was wrong about what he thought Mamá Montero wanted. She had a damn odd expression on her beautiful face as she uncrossed her legs and rose from the sofa.

She picked up the two filled glasses from the coffee table. "She is in the bedroom, *querido.*"

He waved away the glass she tried to hand him. Kyle headed straight for the archway and the dark bedroom beyond. Isabella stopped him with a hand on his bare arm. Her eyes glowed black.

"You do not have the same proclivities as Ramón, do you, my dear?"

"Why?"

She shrugged, the curved chunk of gold between her breasts glinting. "I am not considered an unattractive woman," she purred, stepping closer to engulf him in a cloud of expensive, and freshly applied, perfume. When he didn't say anything, she smiled coyly and shot him a considering look. "You are supposed to assure me that indeed I am."

"Look in a mirror, Isabella."

Her nails dug into his arm as he tried to move. "My breasts are larger, my body just as firm as that of Miss Eastman." She gave him a sultry glance under her lashes. "And I have considerably more experience." She pressed herself disconcertingly closer. He felt her surgically enhanced breasts against his arm with a shudder of revulsion.

"Perhaps that's exactly what prevents me from taking what's offered," he murmured silkily. With dispassionate carelessness, he plucked her carmine-tipped nails off his arm. "What were you thinking? That I would take you here, in your son's home? With Delanie in the next room?"

She smiled, running a practiced tongue over her lips in a meaningful gesture.

"Where *she* could walk in at any moment?" he asked with marked disinterest. "I prefer more of a challenge than you present, Isabella. I doubt you could offer me anything I haven't experienced before. However creative you are. And I've never needed an audience to perform. Sorry, I won't play."

"You won't play with Delanie either, will you?" she said waspishly. Something more than annoyance flashed in her cold, dark eyes. It vanished almost immediately behind a mask as she followed him into the bedroom.

The room was as dark as midnight. What the hell was going on here? "That's none of your business, Isabella. Remember that," he finished softly, turning on the overhead light a second before Delanie flung herself off the bed and into his arms. He braced her weight as she burrowed her face against his shoulder.

Quite a switch from half an hour ago in the pool, he thought dryly, as his arms wrapped around her automatically. He could smell Isabella behind him.

Delanie's flushed face rose from where it had been buried against his chest, her eyes dark and slumberous. He could feel the sharp points of her nipples against his bare chest as she rubbed against him. His fingers tensed against her scalp as he felt her hot, hungry breath across the bare skin of his throat. She pressed her hips against him.

Jesus. Were *both* women turned on by violence?

Delanie suddenly struggled in his grasp, and he unglued her from his chest, holding her by the shoulders to keep her steady on her feet.

She was incorrigible. He was hard pressed not to laugh at the ludicrous situation. Not half an hour ago he'd been deliberately, aggressively, and crudely to the point and she'd torn a strip off his hide. *Now* she was all over him like a rash. Hell. She managed to surprise him at every turn.

He gave her an assessing look. "What are you up to?"

"Come 'ere, I'll tell y—" She stood on tiptoe to whisper in his ear, but didn't say anything. After a moment, she shifted her head and stared up at him blankly. She shook her head as if to clear it, bleary-eyed as though she'd just woken from a deep sleep.

His gaze sharpened and his hands tightened on her upper arms. This was no act. He turned his head to glance at Isabella, surprised to see her right behind him instead of over by the door. "How long has she been like this?"

The older woman shrugged. "Perhaps it is the heat-stroke?"

"If you didn't know what was wrong with her, why the hell did you give her wine?" He could smell it on Delanie's breath as she nuzzled his chest again.

"We were thirsty! Goodness, *lo siento,* Kyle. I thought I could help her. The wine was in the room." Isabella smoothed Delanie's bangs off her face. "I thought she was distressed about the *serpiente.*"

Christ, this was all he needed. Delanie had finally snapped. He'd take long enough to pack her stuff, then get her on the chopper Montero kept at the small airfield behind the house. It wasn't going to be a moment too soon.

Delanie looked at Isabella with dazed eyes before petulantly waving the other woman's hand from her face, then rested her cheek against his chest again and closed her eyes.

He swung her up into his arms as her knees buckled. Hell. A small cut could become infected here in the jungle, any number of microscopic insects were poisonous. She could have been bitten—

Had the bastard drugged her? Jesus. Montero had more drugs than Carter's Little Pills. It could be any one of dozens of the bastard's products.

"Kyle . . . feel . . . strange."

"Strange how?" he demanded. Her skin felt fiery hot, her eyes glazed as he laid her on the bed. Her arms shot up around his neck to pull him back.

"How, Delanie?" He picked up her wrist. Her pulse was thready and fast. Too fast.

"Like—" She licked her lips. "Like I'm going to jump right out of my skin . . ." She grabbed his hand and pressed it hard against her breast, flattened by slick nylon. "Like— hmmm, a cat and my fur's been rubbed the wrong way. Kyle?"

He lifted her lid and scrutinized her frantic brown eyes.

Glassy. Pupils dilated. Crap'nshit.

"Kyle. What's happ—" She faded, staring up at him blankly before she tightened the hand she held over his on her right breast and pressed it down hard. He felt the sharp erect peak in the center of his palm.

He looked up at Isabella. "Out."

"Oh, but—"

"Now," he snarled unequivocally, turning back to his more immediate problem, spread diagonally across the wide bed.

"I hate this." Delanie sounded panicky. "Kyle, help me."

He heard a movement behind him. Creepy Isabella stood a few feet away, watching them avidly. "I said get the hell out of here. Move it!" Kyle kept his eyes on her, while Delanie clung like a limpet to his arm, trying to drag him onto the bed. The moment he heard the outer door slam, Kyle focused on his prime concern.

Those sons of bitches had given her one of their filthy drugs, he thought murderously. What the hell was it? And how long would this last?

"Who gave it to you?" he demanded, trying to get out of her frantically grasping hands. She was like a wild woman now, and had the attention span of a water newt. Her brain couldn't focus, and he gave up.

"Hell, sweetheart. Your timing stinks, you know that?" he said with grim amusement as she managed to ram his hand between her thighs against her damp heat, clamping her legs together to hold him there. He could smell her arousal as she ground her pelvis against his wrist in a desperate bid for release.

Her body bowed, her eyes rolled back, and her soft mouth was a rictus of pain/pleasure. He had never seen a woman climax that fast. Which was probably not a good thing, he thought grimly. He had a sinking feeling it wasn't going to last her.

"Delanie?"

She was out for the count. Just like that, she sprawled across the mattress on her back, her eyes closed, her breathing ragged.

Carefully he extricated his hand from between her legs. She moaned. He swore.

He placed one knee on the bed beside her hip and gently pried open an eyelid. Oh yeah. She was drugged to the gills all right.

Annihilating these bastards would be more than business. It was going to be a pleasure.

But first things first.

Levering himself off the edge of the bed he ran his hand over his jaw, gritted tight with fury. At himself. He'd screwed around too long. Now, God only knew what crap she'd ingested or what the ramifications of *this* scenario could mean.

First, he confirmed Isabella had left. He locked the double doors to his suite and dragged the writing table across it for added protection.

Swearing under his breath, he strode to the closet to start packing her stuff. The servants had stashed her Louis Vuitton on the top shelf. Holding a handful of rubberized, elasticized, and transparent garments he paused. Hell, she'd be better off leaving everything behind, he decided, and tossed the clothes onto the floor of the large closet, about to close the louvered doors when a hand grabbed him from behind.

By the balls.

He froze.

Ah, hell. "Delanie, don't."

Her fingers tightened on his scrotum. "I was wild about you, Kyle, did I ever tell you that?" Unfiltered by her normal stubborn, intractable thought processes, the words tumbled out uncensored. Her moist breath feathered his back.

"No," his voice was hoarse, "you never did."

Through the far too-thin fabric of his swim trunks he felt Delanie's fingers cup and stroke until he practically bit a hole in his tongue.

"Oh yes." The drug made her voice thick, syrupy, and amazingly poignant. "Remember the night we met?" Her lips nuzzled his shoulder. "I'd never felt like that. Hot. Cold. Shivery." She pressed her hips against him, and he could feel her skin touching all the way down his back. "From that first moment—" Obviously buck naked, she trailed her hands up over his erection to reach the waistband of his trunks and lost track of what she'd been saying.

He felt the lush brush of her breasts against his back, the nipples hard pebbles. God, she was going to be doubly pissed when this was over, *if* she remembered this little conversation. From what he was rapidly learning about her she didn't like admitting any vulnerability. Particularly where he was concerned.

"I waz so nervous—kind of icky in my stomach, you know?—when I walked into the bar. 'N I *felt* all you guys looking, looking, looking. 'N I thought 'Who cares I'm a virgin? Nobody! That's who. Except for stupid Anthony-baby!' Then I saw you, and my heart went . . . zoooooom! Jus' like that! Zooooom! An' I want to." Her hands were busy as she spoke, her voice far away and dreamy. "With you. I loved your calm eyes. Trusted—"

With a reluctant oath, Kyle put a restraining hand over both of hers. "God, I'd love to hear about it any other time, but this is bad, bad timing, honey. Trust me." He turned to gently guide her back to the bed. "Take a nap while I—"

In one quick move she had his swimsuit yanked down to his knees. Which brought her mouth, quick as a lick, against his rampant erection, where she proceeded to try to devour him with lips and tongue and a clumsily endearing technique that almost brought tears to his eyes, it was so frigging effective.

She paused, giving Kyle a reprise and a second to catch his breath. He found his fingers tangled in her damp hair.

"I went there to sh-shleep with Anthony-baby, did I mention that little f-actoid?"

Her breath fanned his crotch and Kyle stared at the top of her head in bewildered amusement. "No, as a matter of fact you—Jesus, don't bite!—didn't."

"Yep. I was the virgin fiancé. Really, really pissed off good ol' Anthony-baby."

Virgin fiancé? "Sounds like a fascinating story." He tried to pry her hand off his body parts, which were starting to turn an interesting shade of purple, and draw her to her feet. "Why don't we get dressed while you tell me the rest of the story. Okay?"

"Shr." She looked up at him for a second, her heart in her glazed eyes. "*Prove it!* Not prudey and cold annny more." She shook her head adamantly, obviously reliving a past conversation with someone.

Someone Kyle was beginning to dislike intensely. He'd rip the bastard's heart out.

His hands clenched in her hair.

"I *said* to him." Delanie absently stroked her tongue down his hipbone. "I *said* 'Silly! I *am* a kindergarten teacher! Of course I look like one! If you want to see someone parading around half nek-naked, you'll have to go see Lauren.' I did *not* want him—Lauren. Anthony-baby would've fallen in love wit her for sure. *Everybody* loves *Lauren.*"

A *kindergarten* teacher?

"Sweetheart, that carpet can't possibly feel good on your knees. Let me help you up, and we can—

Her giggle teased the damp tip of his penis. If this wasn't the most bizarre encounter Kyle had ever had, God only knew what was.

"Said, if you change your mind, buy crotchless panties and get your ass on a p-plane to Frisco. Does thith tickle?"

"Not even close." Kyle told her, his voice grim. She'd bought the panties, crotch intact. They'd been red satin with little black bows at her hips. The tiny red satin bra she'd worn that night had matched. The sight of her in her underwear was a memory he'd never forget.

"We're slow now. Right?"

"Slow now?" *Lord,* Kyle thought, his body thrumming, *I can't keep up with her stream of consciousness thoughts.* Ah. At the pool. He'd asked her if they'd ever made love slowly.

"So I got on the plane. I hate flyin', did I mention that? I am *so* scared of flying. Waaaay scared," she added lugubriously.

"Shhhh!" She used his penis as one would a finger up to her lips. Kyle choked back a laugh. "Don't tell, 'k?"

"Sweetheart, I won't tell a soul— Whoa! that's not a rubber hose, gently there." He stroked the bright silky mass of her hair, his tenderness in no way mirroring what Delanie was up to.

He felt as if he were in a porno flick as she fueled his own powerfully dark needs.

"All right, that's it, upsidaisy." He managed to drag her to her feet without hurting either of them, his erection abundant and painful. He tried to read the fleeting expression on her face. God. There was nothing simple, nor easily accomplished with this woman. She was a mass of contradictions even when she was almost mindless with desire. Her damp body felt absurdly light. Her sultry brown eyes showed both need and vulnerability; she felt fragile between his hands.

So she'd gone to the hotel to have sex with the fiancé who thought she was a prudish kindergarten teacher. The son of a bitch had given this woman an ultimatum. A crude, cruel, insensitive ultimatum, by a crude, cruel, and insensitive lout. Show up at the hotel in appropriate underwear or else.

Well, you jerk. She showed up. But somehow or other *I'm* the one who got lucky.

"Let's reserve a date to discuss this when you know what you're doing, okay?"

" 'kay," she agreed, worrying her lower lip for a moment as he got a firm grip on his trunks and started to pull them up. Agile as a gymnast she inserted one foot into the crotch of his restrictive swimsuit and stepped them to the floor before flinging herself against him, rubbing and grinding her body in a motion guaranteed to make him as wild as she was.

"No fair." He couldn't help his body's immediate reaction, but he firmly held her away from him, feeling the perspiration of control bead his skin. The imagination that had kept him going, kept him alive many a time, paled at the reality of seeing Delanie Eastman naked, and *willing,* again.

God, she was gorgeous. Sleek, toned, tanned all over, small high breasts flushed with the drugged fever racing through her veins. He couldn't remember when he'd ever been this hard.

Or hot.

Or honorable.

"I am not going to make love to you now," he told her regretfully. "Soon, but not *now,* and not *here.*" He gave her slender shoulders a shake. She licked her lower lip in a provocative manner meant to drive him to the brink. He closed his eyes briefly, praying for the strength not to jump her bones and say hell with the whys, whos, and wheres.

"Good," she said grimly, "I don't *want* you to make love to me." She looked him straight in the eye, edging him toward the bed. "I want you to fuck my brains out. *Now.*"

Kyle groaned.

She pushed.

They fell on the bed together in a tangled heap of arms and legs. Their lower bodies miraculously, perfectly, aligned.

He must have been a very bad boy at one time, he thought fleetingly, to be punished like this. Delanie was frantic, her skin felt hot, moist, electrified. She licked his nipple, then sucked it. He almost came out of his skin.

She whimpered, looking up at him with beseeching, dilated eyes. He *had* to help her.

Yeah, right, he mocked, *how altruistic of me!*

It would be unconscionable of him to make love to her when she had no control over what was happening, he warned himself.

"Help me," she moaned, gripping his hand so hard he winced. He was beyond feeling pain, but obviously so was Delanie in her frenzied plea for release.

She didn't seem to care which body part fitted where. Just that he did the deed quickly. "Now," she begged. "Do it now."

She was quick. God, she was quick. Flinging one leg over his hips to hold him in place, she plunged herself to completion. All he had time for was to marvel at the furnace of slick heat surrounding him and it was over. She slumped against his chest, her slender body racked with shudders, her skin damp with sweat, sawing breath antagonizing his already raw nerve endings. He was hard as a rock inside her, tortured by a million contracting muscles, a hot wet mouth, and siren hands.

She pulled his mouth to the voluptuous moistness of hers for a mind-blowing mating of teeth and tongue and then dragged her upper body off his chest. Sweat ran down her temples into her hair as she kneaded his chest with her hands and squeezed her knees around his hips.

"Don't stop," she sobbed, "for God's sake, don't stop."

He flipped her onto her back without breaking contact. Half-lidded eyes glittered feverishly as, using both hands in a rough sweep of his back, she dug her nails into his butt urging him deeper inside her. With a driving thrust that had her fingernails drawing blood, he did exactly as the lady asked.

He knew he was going to pay for this. And pay big.

Then he just didn't give a damn anymore.

Chapter Eight

"How're you holding up?" Kyle's voice reverberated through her headset over the *whop-whop-whop* din of the blades above them.

"Just dandy." Horny, embarrassed, angry, scared. All of the above about covered it. So much so, in fact, that her normal sky terror hadn't even figured into the equation. Not so far anyway. Thank God for small mercies.

"No thanks to you," she added.

"What do *I* have to do with it?"

"Are you saying you *didn't* Mickey my drink?"

"Yeah, sure. Right after I hauled two hundred plus pounds of snake into the swimming pool and took the risk of it choosing *me* for an afternoon snack."

Delanie had no idea what *he* was so mad about. He'd gotten what he'd wanted. In spades. She refused to turn her head. Instead, she concentrated on their slow descent to the pencil-thin dirt airstrip as she crunched a couple of antacids and clung to the seat with a white-knuckled grip.

She didn't know whether to believe him or not. Only minutes before the drug had taken its disastrous effect, he'd been threatening her. In the swimming pool. With a woman-eating snake. What was she supposed to think?

She wasn't paranoid for God's sake.

They *were* all out to get her.

Delanie rubbed the nagging ache between her eyes, feeling lost, scared, and totally out of her depth as the helicopter rose again to make a lazy circle over the field below. Her memory, after he'd dragged her from the swimming pool, was hazy at best. She remembered Montero shooting the boy. She remembered creepy Isabella in her room. She remembered drinking a glass of wine ... She remembered feeling her senses expanding beyond normal bounds. And she remembered enough of what happened with Kyle between then and now to be mortified.

If she ever remembered *all* of it she would probably have to move to the farthest reaches of the Antarctic. Or have a frontal lobotomy.

She looked down. This was the same airstrip she and Montero had departed from only a few days ago. God, she'd had no idea what she was letting herself in for then.

Montero's people ruthlessly sprayed the area around the small landing strip to keep out fast-growing vegetation. The resulting scar was the small, discreet clearing, effectively hidden by the dense rain forest.

Behind them now rose the high peaks of Izquierdo, and Ramón Montero's compound with its cloak and dagger atmosphere and its shadowy memories of the past several hours. Delanie was unsure if she had indeed left the danger behind, or if, instead, she'd accompanied the worst of it to San Cristóbal.

Unfortunately it was particularly hard to concentrate, feeling as she did. Horny, nauseous, and terrified. She tried to focus on something else. Choices were sadly limited at the moment.

Her nipples still throbbed beneath the circumspect white T-shirt. Obviously one of his shirts he'd shoved over her head before their hasty departure. She gave up trying to think about other stuff. She was consumed with thoughts of what the drug had done, and was *still* doing to her.

"What did you tell them we were doing in there for hours? I presume it *was* hours?"

"In the bedroom, two hours and twenty minutes. Considering you were wailing like a banshee it would have been damn impossible to convince them we were in there playing

Parcheesi." He paused. "On the way to the chopper, forty minutes, in the maintenance shed? Only thirty." Kyle's voice was dry. Delanie gritted her teeth.

He brought the chopper down lightly in the middle of the airfield. The rotors kicked up clods of dirt and vegetation.

"What a prince." Feeling grimmer, she waved away Kyle's helping hand and removed the headset and seatbelt herself. She'd rather die than have him know she needed sex again. "I meant about why we had to race from bedroom to helicopter and hotfoot it to town."

"I told them I preferred to screw without everyone hearing me in surround sound."

"And here I thought you weren't a gentleman, silly me."

"I have a job to do here. Trust me, no one gave a shit what I did with you one way or the other."

"Oh, someone cared all right," she said bitterly, still filled with annoying yearnings and throbbings. "Enough to give me their very best anyway." She didn't want to think about the repercussions of just *what* it was they'd given to her. Not now when she had other, more important things to concentrate on. Like keeping one step ahead of Kyle Wright. She shot him a look filled with suspicion. "What kind of job?"

"A shipment to pick up at customs and a little favor to perform for Montero. It should all be taken care of by lunchtime tomorrow."

"Thanks so much for dragging me along." She was being sarcastic, but what would she have done if Kyle had left her there feeling like this? She shuddered at the thought.

"Hey, you told me you loved me, how could I leave you behind?" he asked lazily.

Her heart stopped midbeat. Sadistic swine. She was pretty sure she hadn't said any such thing. She'd never even *thought* the words, let alone said them out loud. "People on drugs believe they can fly, too," she managed calmly. "If I did say anything like that, it didn't mean anything. I would have told Ross Perot I loved him to get what I needed at the time."

"Just wanted me for my body?" he lamented. "How lowering."

"I didn't need *you* personally, nor did I require a whole body," she pointed out pithily. "How long do you think this will last?"

"No idea." He paused. She could feel him watching her. "Still have the hots?"

Yes. But it wasn't nearly as intense as it had been a couple of hours ago. Not that she'd tell him, either way. "Do you think whatever it was is addictive?"

Kyle laughed darkly. "It is to me."

She scowled. "*You* weren't the one who took it."

"I'm the one with bloody claw marks on my back and bruises on my ass from your heels digging in. I think I took it like a champ."

"I'm delighted you were so entertained."

Two men raced across the small airfield, ducking under the spinning rotors to open the doors. Delanie got enough of the conversation to understand that the disreputable vehicle parked a hundred yards away was for their use. Slinging the strap of her canvas bag over her shoulder, she accepted a hand down from the soldier on her side of the chopper and strode to the military jeep parked under the trees. Walking fast made her legs rub together, which made the problem worse.

The vehicle was unlocked, the keys in the ignition. Delanie slouched in the passenger seat and stared at the green canvas ceiling. Kyle wasn't going to be able to get rid of her this easily.

Okay, so they'd managed to give her some kind of sex drug. She'd live.

She was perfectly aware she was in way over her head. She'd make that work for her.

And yes, damn it, she *knew* Kyle Wright was the *last* person she should ever have had sex with. That didn't mean she'd ever do it with him again.

Kyle slid into the car, and adjusted the torn plastic-covered seat to accommodate his long legs. He glanced over at her before starting the jeep.

She slouched down lower. The harder she tried to ignore

the rapacious need for having Kyle hard, naked, and inside her, the more difficult it became. She crossed her arms tightly over her chest as her nipples pulsed. She crossed her legs, then uncrossed them. God, how long could this stuff last?

It already felt like an eternity.

The late afternoon sun beat in on her side of the vehicle, which smelled of beer and the previous driver's sweat. Dust kicked up by the tires sifted through the ill-fitting windows, exacerbating her physical woes. She ground her back teeth together, watching the blur of trees whizzing by, trying to figure out how long she could hang on until she could get some relief.

"If you need sex, say so," he said shortly, taking a corner on two wheels causing her to bang her shoulder against the door. "If not, then for God's sake stop squirming."

"There's more than one way to skin a cat, Dr. Compassionate." A few minutes behind a locked door by herself, and she'd be right as rain.

"I'm not going to be leaving you alone long enough to pick up some poor unsuspecting bastard in a bar," he said unyieldingly. "It's me or no one, sweetheart."

No one, she thought with grim determination. He shifted gears. He had long tapered fingers and lean, darkly tanned, masculine hands with short square nails. Big hands. Hands that she wanted to feel on various annoyingly throbbing body parts. Even the humid blast of the wind couldn't combat the sweat breaking out along her hairline and under her breasts.

A magnetic tide of arousal swept through her body. She pressed down uselessly on the cracked vinyl seat.

"Where are we going?" Anything, even trying to talk civilly to Kyle, was better than thinking about her demanding body parts.

"A small, clean hotel over on the other side of town. Be there in about forty-five minutes."

She could feel his eyes on her. A surge of heat flared on her skin. Even the sound of his baritone sent shivers of anticipation zinging through her. First the close confines of the helicopter, and now this tiny little jeep. It wasn't fair.

Pressing harder against her throbbing breasts with her crossed arms, she focused outside where road workers paused in their digging to watch them drive by at the speed of sound. The road was rough and uneven with patches of vegetation growing through the packed red dirt. Jungle pressed in on either side. Green danger.

Just like Kyle's eyes.

They reached the city just before dusk.

"Lock your door," he instructed as they drove into the center of town. She complied, staring at cars and pedestrians alike as they moved like frantic ants through narrow streets clogged with traffic. Everyone drove at a breakneck speed, often using the curb as part of the thoroughfare.

Kyle didn't even bother to tap the brakes. With nerves of steel and a total disregard for the red traffic light, they shot across a busy intersection. When Delanie opened her eyes again they were safely beyond the snarl and on a narrower side street.

"A red light here means 'go'?"

"It's dangerous to stop for lights." Kyle slowed to let a rowdy pack of children cross the street ahead. "More often than not drivers get robbed if they're not fast enough."

She let her gaze roam the streets of the city. Green wooden balconies bright with orchids and peonies jutted over narrow cobbled streets. Small bright spots in an otherwise dingy, depressing place. The poverty here was palpable.

Half-naked children by the dozen dashed between cars and pedestrians alike.

"Where on earth do all those children come from?" There must have been twenty or thirty of them. Delanie turned to look back, but the kids had disappeared into a narrow opening between the buildings.

"No birth control." Kyle turned onto a wider street. He indicated another yelling mass of skinny arms and legs on the sidewalk. "*Gamines*. Ratpacks of homeless kids. There're thousands of them here." He accelerated. "The parents can't afford to feed and clothe them so they're sent out to fend for themselves. They end up begging or selling whatever they can lay their hands on just to stay alive."

"That's appalling."

"The rich get rich and the poor get poorer. The only thing the drug trade has done for those kids is give them bad teeth from habitual cocaine use or put them to work in prostitution."

It was impossible to worry about her own list of complaints when presented with such bare, harsh facts. Delanie shivered despite the heat, sick to her stomach.

She'd pretty much raised Lauren on her own from when she was a kid herself. Their mother needed a caretaker, too. She was beautiful, and fun loving, and had the attention span of a hummingbird. But Delanie had always known her mother loved her. When she and Lauren were growing up they might've been dressed strangely, but they had never gone without shelter or food.

What she saw in the streets of San Cristóbal horrified and saddened her.

And nothing in her unconventional life compared to what was happening to her now. Suddenly she was surrounded with the pitiful dregs of a society. Where the buying and selling of drugs—or people—was a way of life. Here human frailties were used as weapons and Montero was lord of it all.

She'd been brutalized, threatened, and drugged.

And she was going back for more.

"Are you still determined to do business with Montero?" Delanie asked flatly.

"I know what I'm doing." A muscle twitched in Kyle's jaw. "You're just going to have to trust me."

"Oh, absolutely. You have such a sterling track record."

"Do you really want to dig up that corpse now?"

She swallowed roughly. Bracing herself for the next wheelie round a corner, she asked tightly, "What do you *want* from me, Kyle?"

"I want you to damn well trust me, even when your brain says you shouldn't."

An old man, wearing a blanketlike *ruana* despite the heat, was sweeping the sidewalk as Kyle cruised to a stop, not waiting for her answer. Which was a good thing. He'd have a long wait.

He parked with two wheels on the narrow curb as she scanned the face of the building. The "clean" part of "hotel" wasn't obvious to her. Perhaps dusk wasn't the optimum time to be viewing the neighborhood. She climbed out of the car and stretched cramped muscles.

"Is it okay for you to wear that out here in the street?" She tilted her head to indicate his shoulder holster.

"You think they have carry laws here in San Cristóbal?" His lips quirked. "I believe in advertising. Come on, let's get inside."

There were no streetlights to speak of. The shops were either abandoned or their owners just didn't give a damn. The Villa D'Este looked suspiciously like the dozens of other derelict hotels and businesses lining the city. *Gamines* of all ages and sizes ran wild here, too, dodging vehicles and fists alike. The common denominator was filth.

"Welcome to the Ritz," she muttered, keeping a tight hold on her bulging canvas bag. On spongy legs she followed Kyle into the dimly lit, grungy vestibule of the hotel.

The man behind the counter glanced up and broke into an enormous smile, showing several gold-capped teeth as he spared a moment to ogle her tight jeans. His stained T-shirt stretched over an impressive beer belly.

Delanie gave him a steely look in return.

He averted his gaze and hastily folded his newspaper to greet Kyle in effusive and rapid Spanish while she paced back and forth across the scarred linoleum.

Finally he handed Kyle a key from the wooden rack behind him.

"Let's go." Kyle took her arm and hustled her up a dark stairway. There wasn't much point protesting. She swallowed convulsively as her mouth filled with saliva. Icy sweat prickled her skin as the queasiness she'd felt in the car increased.

Their footsteps echoed loudly as they emerged onto a landing. Peeling brown paint and the smell of urine were the high spots in the decor. He unlocked a door halfway down the corridor and nudged her into the dark room.

"It's clean." Kyle found the light switch. "Gil can send someone over to the cantina for you later if you get hungry."

She had her room and a locking door; now all she needed was a little privacy. She tossed her bag onto the neatly made bed.

Kyle snagged her arm as she walked past him. "First things first. Now I want to—"

She shook him off. "—throw up," she finished, striding to the open door of the bathroom. Slamming the door, no lock, she sank to her knees before the bowl.

Throwing up with nothing in her stomach was painful. Retching, sweating, and shivering, she prayed for this to pass. It didn't help that Kyle was right on her heels. She tried to wave him out of the tiny bathroom, but instead he ran water in the sink.

She couldn't talk and didn't waste time trying. He held a cool, damp washcloth to her forehead, effectively holding her head up for her as she hugged the porcelain for dear life.

"Good girl, get the rest of the poison out." He braced her body as he supported the anvil weight of her head in his cool palm.

She wanted to curl up and die on the spot. Instead she accepted the brief reprieve from hostilities, letting him help her up when she was done. With shaking hands she fumbled through her bag until she came up with a travel-size bottle of Listerine.

"Hell, is there anything you don't carry in that thing?" He handed her a plastic glass filled with cold water.

She gulped most of it before swishing and spitting, feeling as though she'd been ridden hard and put away wet. Not a bad analogy, all things considered.

"Drink a couple more glasses of water," Kyle instructed.

Delanie was happy to oblige. Every cell in her body felt parched. She drank three glasses of tepid water, with Kyle watching every gulp, before she set the empty glass on the toilet tank.

Kyle waited silently as she dug around in her purse for a toothbrush and sample-size toothpaste, and brushed her teeth.

"Ready?" he asked politely when she threw everything back in the bag and slung the straps over her shoulder.

"Not really." But she stepped out of the small room anyway.

He followed her into the bedroom, then scanned her face. She must still look green around the gills; she certainly felt it. He had the appearance of a man about to restart the interrogation.

She held up a hand. "Give me a minute." Still shaky, she carefully sat on the bottom of the queen-size bed with its crisp white sheets and brightly colored cotton cover. There were a couple of bedside tables, a cane-backed chair, two mismatched lamps and a hideous hanging lamp near a table by the open bathroom door. Heavy drapes hung over a narrow window in the far wall. The wooden floor, while bare of rugs, was spotlessly clean and polished to a dull sheen.

"Gimme." He indicated her wrist. Delanie held it up like a paw and waited while he took her pulse and probably concluded she was half dead.

"You'll live."

"Where's your room?" she asked as he cupped her chin firmly in one hand and used a gentle finger to lift her right eyelid. She held her breath as he peered into her eye. His breath fanned her face, and his mouth tightened into a hard line as he lifted the other lid.

He swore, then released her to stroll over to twitch the heavy drapes more tightly across the window. "This is it."

"Oh no, it isn't!"

He glanced over his shoulder. "Still got the itch?"

"I believe you flushed the rest of it, thank you very much." What a humiliating experience. Just the fuzzy memories of what she'd demanded he do to her caused her cheeks to flame. The things *she'd* done to *him* made her inwardly cringe, and her skin ignite.

She rummaged in her bag for the small pack of saltines. They were in crumbled pieces. She picked out the largest chunks and let the salty crackers dissolve on her tongue.

Starting to feel considerably better, she glared up at him, said in her firmest voice, "I am not sharing this room with you."

"You didn't protest when we left Montero's."

"I didn't know what I was— Don't change the subject," she snapped. "I didn't want to leave there in the first place, damn it."

"That's right, you didn't." He sat down in the chair, watching her with those disconcerting pale-green eyes. "But here you are." He said it with enough satisfaction that she wanted to slap him.

"And now, my horny Miss Eastman, you are going to tell me exactly what the hell you're doing mixed up with Montero and his merry little band."

Perfectly at ease, he stretched out his long legs, leaned back, and rested his clasped hands on his flat stomach. Relaxed, but still dangerous.

"I want to know the what, the who, and the why. When you're done answering *those* questions you can take a nice cool shower and get a good night's rest before I put your sweet little ass on the first plane back to the States."

"Or else *what?*"

"Or else this, sweetheart."

She didn't even see him move. One moment he'd been sprawled in the chair across the room, the next he had his hand around her throat. He squeezed gently. She coughed on a crumb, glared at him, then swatted at his arm. His fingers tightened. She felt the pressure behind her eyeballs.

"You won't kill me," she managed with more bravado than belief.

He gave a small brutal smile, and said gently, "Don't bet

on it, sweetheart. There are far more important things at stake here than your interfering little neck."

"Don't be—" She had to lick her dry lips. He watched her with a total lack of compassion. This was *not* the face of a man who was kidding. "Let me go, damn it, I'll tell you."

His thumb traced the strumming pulse at the base of her throat as if he were contemplating the best spot to press. He was a doctor. He'd know exactly where to exert pressure—

The blood drained from her head. She kept her eyes steady on his face, praying he couldn't read the sheer panic in her features. He hesitated a beat too long before he withdrew his fingers. She gave him a dark look, then flopped back down on the edge of the bed to rub her neck.

"Now, what wild hair scheme made you hook up with someone like Montero?" He propped a shoulder against the bathroom jamb and folded his arms across his chest, trapping the long rope of his braid against his black T-shirt. He observed her through hooded eyes.

She got up and walked over to the window, shifting the drapes. The last rays from the setting sun filtered through a thin layer of fog over the squalor of the city, giving it a mellow, romantic aura it didn't have in the hard clear light of day. The hotel had been built on a hill; she had a hundred-and-eighty-degree view of San Cristóbal. Over the red-tiled roofs the last rays of the sun danced on the aquamarine waters of the crescent bay. Large white yachts were diminished to dots. She turned back to Kyle.

"He has my sister. Lauren worked for him at the Cobra in Vegas." She tried to slow down, to sound competent, but it was too late for subtlety, and she was so far out on a limb, rationality had long since passed her by. "He has my sister," she repeated brokenly.

Oh damn. She should have been more insistent that Lauren live at home with her. She should never have let her go off alone.

"Keep going."

"Lauren called me on a Thursday night, hysterical. She insisted I fly down to Vegas and help her. I couldn't understand half of what she said."

Delanie glanced up to find Kyle watching her intently. She swallowed roughly, staring at a spot on the far wall. "My mom is—flighty, for want of a better word, and Lauren takes after her. In spades. They're both beautiful and vivacious and attract men like honey draws flies. And Lauren is so trusting, so emotionally . . . needy. She's always in some sort of emotional crisis or another. Our little drama queen. Oh, God, it never occured to me before she disappeared that the time might come when I would be powerless to make things all right for her."

"She's an adult. She made her own choices."

"Usually bad ones." Delanie rubbed her nose with the palm of her hand. "I never know what's fact and what's fiction with Lauren. But suddenly she became totally paranoid. Every time she called, she was being watched or followed or chased by someone. I didn't know this time was any different. I thought I'd calmed her down. I waited ten days till school was out," Delanie said bitterly. "Ten days to get the lowest airfare I could.

"Lauren paid dearly for my being so conscientious and tightfisted." Her breath shuddered in her tight chest. "I should have said to hell with the last week of school and the cost, and left right away. I failed her when she needed me the most."

"Where were your parents while all this was going on?"

"My mother lives in L.A." *With the latest "love of her life," twenty-four-year-old Jason.* "My father's with his family. They live in D.C. I believe."

"You don't know where your father lives?"

"I've never met him. I guess *father* isn't the right word for him. 'Sperm donor'? He and my mother had a hot, tempestuous affair for ten years. And while my mother had Lauren and me in Sacramento, his *wife* was busy going to the PTA for his three sons and daughter in D.C. Not that we cared. We did just fine without him.

"Anyway, because Lauren is extremely headstrong, and

Mom is usually . . . distracted and can't handle her anyway, I'm the one who deals with her dramas."

Kyle mulled that over for several long seconds. What was there for him to say? The situation wasn't all that uncommon.

"What did you find when you got to Vegas?"

"I went straight to Lauren's apartment. She wasn't there. I asked her neighbors. They knew she had a rich boyfriend, and several of them had seen her leave with a man they described as Ramón—"

"*She's* headstrong?" Kyle shook his head. "So, *she* disappears and *you* decide to do exactly the same damn thing?" He rolled his eyes and rubbed a large hand over his mouth. "You should have gone to the cops."

"Do I look like a moron? Of course I went to the police. They put out an APB on her. But there was no sign of a struggle at her apartment; her passport was missing, as was a suitcase and half her wardrobe. They said wherever she'd gone it was obvious she'd gone willingly.

"All I had to go on was that phone call. And knowing my sister. While the LVPD did their thing, I went and applied at the Cobra to see what I could find out."

Kyle shook his head again, obviously in disgust. "What the hell did you hope to do? Hold Montero at gunpoint with that peashooter of yours and demand he produce your sister?"

"That son of a bitch took Lauren." There wasn't a doubt in her mind. "Call it gut instinct or whatever. He's got her up there. I don't know *why* he was her, but I'm going to find her and take her home. Do you understand me? Damn it, I'm going to take my b . . . baby sister home."

To her alarm and disgust, tears welled in her eyes. Impatiently she brushed them away. "I don't care if I have to hitchhike my way back up that mountain. I'm going to—" She stopped to give him a challenging look.

"The only thing that can stop me is if I'm stone cold dead. If you have any comments, save them till morning. I'm tired, hot, and cranky. I want a cold shower and peace and quiet."

He didn't move so much as a muscle as he observed her. "That's it?"

"No." Anger shot to the surface like foam on beer. "This is the last damn time you threaten to kill me, Wright. If you're going to do it," she said furiously, "get it over with."

"Why is it," he asked coolly, "Montero and company find my threats believable enough to keep a healthy distance, and you don't?"

"I don't believe you'd hurt a woman." Not with physical violence anyway.

"Is that so? Based on what assumption?"

"Based on the *fact* that I'm still alive."

"You have no idea who I am, jungle girl. No idea at all." He flexed his hands. "I'm not some tame boy from Sacramento that will do your bidding. Remember that."

She would.

Suddenly, what he'd just said dawned on her. "How do you know I live in Sacramento?" she asked suspiciously.

"I have ways of knowing things you're better off not knowing about."

"Bullshit, tell the truth."

"Sometimes the truth is a danger in itself, isn't it?"

"Only to people like you."

He rubbed a large hand over his jaw. "Jesus, woman, you sure as hell know how to ruin a party."

"Oh, excuse me for inconveniencing you."

"Yeah, well that can't be helped."

"I was being sarcastic."

"I wasn't." He pushed himself away from the door. "I'll find your sister. *Now* will you go back home?"

"No."

"No?" he parroted. "Do you trust *anyone,* Delanie?"

"There's only one person I'd trust with my sister's life." She stared him in the eye. "Myself."

"Are you basing your assumption that Lauren's on Izquierdo on anything concrete?"

"I told you. Her neighbors saw her leave in a black limo the same night she called me."

"Las Vegas is filled with black limos."

"Not ones that have COBRA1 as a license plate."

He stood staring at her. Did she imagine a flicker of admiration in his eyes? She couldn't be certain. It disappeared so fast, leaving his expression unreadable in the dim sixty-watt lighting.

"You're one tough cookie, aren't you, jungle girl?" He stepped right in front of her before she could evade him, and reached out, touching her gently on the cheek. "All right. We'll get her together."

And pigs will fly, Delanie thought, not believing him for a nanosecond.

She gave him a mild look, and after a moment he dropped his hand, tucking it into the front pocket of his jeans. "If we're going to find Lauren, you're going to have to believe I know what I'm doing and let me set the ground rules."

She knew all about men setting ground rules. And all about women foolish enough to trust them at their word. Delanie sized him up. Believing their BS was what got women hurt and left them spending the rest of their lives trying to fill the gaping holes in their hearts the men left behind.

But she wasn't stupid. If she was going to find her sister, she was going to have to go through the motions of accepting Kyle's help. *Pride* wasn't going to find Lauren.

But outright trusting him to take her back up the mountain with him would be downright stupid. She'd have to stick to him like glue not to be left behind.

Not that she was going to let on that she knew what he intended. "All right," she said quietly, and thought she saw his shoulders relax. It must have been a trick of the light. "I admit, I might need you."

"To find your sister."

"Of course, what else?" For the first time she noticed he looked as exhausted as she felt. Relieved to have a pause, however brief, in the hostilities, she flopped onto her back. Limp as a rag doll she covered her eyes with a bent arm, leaving her feet to dangle to the floor. At least she wasn't randy as a she-goat anymore, which was an enormous relief.

"Describe her to me."

"She's twenty-four. Five foot seven, angelically beautiful, shoulder-length strawberry-blonde hair, and blue eyes."

"She looks like you."

"Our coloring is nothing alike, and she's gorgeous. And a lot less determined. And more inclined to forgive." Delanie opened an eye. "She's *nicer* than I am." She blocked him out behind her eyelids again. "Under normal circumstances I wouldn't want you anywhere *near* her, Wright."

"These are hardly normal circumstances, are they?" Kyle said shortly.

"She's smart. Really bright." Another long pause before she said determinedly, "Smart enough to *do* something with her life. I was disappointed she didn't want to go to college." She gave a choking laugh. "Now I'd just be grateful if she's alive."

She realized how bitter she sounded and didn't care. She should have put her foot down and forbidden Lauren to—

"So you're a kindergarten teacher, huh?"

"They probably fired me when I disappeared for two months. But, yes, I am."

"And what," Kyle asked dangerously, "was a *kindergarten* teacher doing picking up a strange man in a San Francisco hotel bar?"

"I was lonely," Delanie said offhandedly.

"Bullshit. Where was Anthony-baby that night?"

Horrified, Delanie sat up. "Who told—? How did you—?"

"What happened, jungle girl? Anthony said you weren't woman enough for him, and when you arrived at his hotel to disprove it, he was busy with someone else?"

She swallowed roughly. "Something like that. Yes."

"So you decided to toss away your virginity on a total stranger. I'm flattered and honored."

"There were eleven men in the bar that night. You were closest to the door."

Kyle smiled. "No, I wasn't."

She shrugged. "I wanted to know what all the hoopla was about."

"And I was the lucky guy." Kyle moved to the bed and sat beside her. His weight tilted her body against his. Lord, but he was strong and solid. She shifted away from him slightly.

His eyes crinkled at the corners. "We connected in those seventy-two hours, though, didn't we?" He touched her cheek with his thumb. "We connected on a level you never experienced with anyone. Including good old Anthony-baby-the-jerking-son-of-a-bitch."

"The sex was great," she admitted. Overwhelming. Terrifying. She'd been consumed by him. Totally and irrevocably. She was, after all, *not* that different than her mom and Lauren. The thought had terrified her.

"You're a lousy liar, Delanie Eastman. There's a hell of a lot more we need to discuss, but this is neither the time, nor the place." With a last brush to her cheek he rose from the bed. "I have to go out. Want Gil to send up something to eat?"

"No thanks." She just wanted to be left alone. "Are you coming back?" she asked suddenly, opening her eyes.

There was a momentary silence. "Yeah."

She gave that a moment's thought. If he were lying she'd deal with the problem in the morning. She was so drained and exhausted he could go out and do the macarena all night for all she cared. She waited for him to open the door.

"Tell me something," Kyle said. "If Montero'd been straight, would you have slept with him to find your sister?"

"In a heartbeat," she said flatly. "I'd've done *whatever* it took to find Lauren."

Chapter Nine

Dim and smoky, the cantina, filled with lowlifes and twelve-year-old whores of both sexes, proved anything could be had for a price in San Cristóbal. Kyle felt the brooding malevolence of Montero's influence.

Delanie's words rang in his ears.

Whatever it takes.

Or *who*ever? he thought darkly as he nursed his beer.

Damn.

He'd cherished the memory of their brief time together for four years. Years when even a drift of familiar perfume could cause his heart to ache. The memory of her sweetness, her generosity of spirit, as well as her sensuality, had sustained him in some pretty bleak days between then and now.

He'd been in San Francisco for the weekend before hooking up with Montero on a journey into the dark side. Kyle had suddenly yearned for normalcy before the murky depths swallowed him whole.

He'd flown into San Francisco from Europe for some much needed R and R, with plans to meet his father for dinner his first night in town. And while he couldn't tell his dad exactly what was going down, Geoffrey Wright was a smart man and had three other sons with secrets. He'd read between the lines.

If his father had known what his youngest son was about to embark on, he wouldn't have been *mildly* worried when he wished him Godspeed and hugged him good-bye that night.

They'd lingered over coffee after dinner in Kyle's downtown hotel. But his father'd had to get back to San Jose to fly

out on a business trip the next day. Kyle had finally walked
him outside to his car, then, not wanting to go back to the
impersonal hotel room, stopped into the sports bar for a
leisurely nightcap.

He took a swig of warm beer and grimaced, remembering
the chilled brew he'd been drinking when Delanie walked
into the hotel sports bar that night.

The first thing he'd noticed was her air of vulnerability.
This was not a woman accustomed to sashaying into a bar
unescorted. He remembered glancing behind her to see who
the lucky guy was.

She'd been alone.

All the men in the bar had turned to give her the once-
over. She'd been quite a sight to see in that dimness. A ray of
midnight sunshine in a halter-neck dress of some yellow,
silky-looking fabric. A deliciously short skirt exposed long,
gorgeous dancer's legs and a goodly amount of slender thigh.

It took a while for Kyle's eyes to travel up that awesome
body to her face. Even her light brown hair had been
streaked with sunshine. Pretty without being outrageously
beautiful, she smoothed her hands self-consciously down her
short skirt and looked around uncertainly.

Fascinated, Kyle had leaned back, beer forgotten as he observed her. Joining a date? Hoping to spot a friend? Waiting
for her eyes to adjust? She'd been innocent entertainment
and a welcome diversion from his thoughts and misgivings
about this venture with Montero.

Their eyes met. Suddenly her slender shoulders straightened and her chin tilted—then she'd made a beeline straight
for him.

He'd never done anything like it in his life. He'd had several casual relationships over the years. Hell, he *liked*
women. He'd had a couple of long-term relationships that
had eventually fizzled—one after eight months, the other after a couple of years. The breakups had been mutual, and un-
surprisingly amicable.

He'd never picked up a strange woman and had a one-
night stand in his life. Yet he'd sat in that dim San Francisco

bar and known within minutes that if Delanie offered, he'd accept. Part of that, he knew, was the very real fear of what he was about to embark on.

God only knew there were a million things that could've gone wrong, no matter how extensive his expertise. He was by no means a pessimist, but Kyle had said his good-byes to his father that night as if they were his last. He'd written to each of his siblings, leaving the letters with his attorney in the event of his death. A chilling, and very real, possibility. Even now.

And while Delanie's precipitous departure had puzzled and hurt him, he was still grateful to her for giving him that glorious weekend to remember, always.

Perhaps in the intervening years he'd built on that shining memory because he'd needed something to sustain him. Perhaps he'd read more into what they'd shared that weekend than she had . . . Perhaps.

Even if she *hadn't* left, he'd known he had absolutely nothing to offer her. Not then. Possibly not ever. He'd've left himself the next morning.

All she'd done was gyp them of a few more hours.

All.

Yet he'd felt a painful wrench of betrayal when he discovered she'd left that night. The sex had been mind-blowing, wonderful, amazing. But Kyle had always felt that they'd connected on another level. A level he'd never found with another woman, before or since.

With a scowl Kyle twisted the bottom of the glass in a puddle of moisture on the scarred wood tabletop. Hell, just because they'd talked for all of an hour before he was upstairs with her in her room didn't mean she always behaved that way.

He'd been her first.

A *kindergarten* teacher, for godsake!

And even though she'd up and disappeared like a puff of smoke afterward, he didn't believe for one damn second that she'd have slept with Montero. She might believe it. But he sure as hell didn't. Acting like a bimbo and being one were two different things. She was even lousy at pretending she was such a hard-ass.

He'd get her to safety, then somehow he'd ensure someone found her sister for her. *Then* he'd go to Sacramento and demand that they start over.

Third time lucky.

He might not know her as well as he'd thought, but drugs or no drugs, Delanie would never have let another man touch her like he had this afternoon. *Never.*

She *belonged* to him, goddamn it!

He gave a strangled, half laugh. Jerk. He was feeling *used.* Christ, what a joke.

Having that brief conversation with Delanie earlier had made her behavior suddenly exceedingly clear. He felt a cold fist clinch his gut.

Unlike himself, who had always had a supportive and loving family, Delanie was it in *her* family. A flaky mother, a flakier sister, and an absentee father. A helluva lot easier to concentrate on fixing everybody else's woes than to look inward to her own needs. It was obvious that she needed her family to need her and took her responsibility as caretaker very seriously.

She was unbendingly stubborn, intractable, and single-minded. She was also annoyingly self-reliant. But he admired her grit, her sheer determination, and her unswerving loyalty that refused to be shaken, even when the deck was stacked against her.

Even when it pissed him off.

"Yo, Doc. Gonna cut that hair when we've nailed our man?" Darius, a T-FLAC team member stood beside the table. Kyle cursed. He hadn't seen the guy approach. This kind of ineptness could get him killed.

"I'd better. It's starting to grow on me," he said dryly, pushing the long braid over his shoulder and kicking out a chair from the table for the younger man. "Symbolism be damned," he drawled. "The stuff's a nuisance."

"We all do whatever's necessary to keep focused when we've gone deep." Dare sat. "What's got you so PO'd?" His dark hair hung loose to his linebacker shoulders. A puckered scar bisected one cheek, pulling the right side of his mouth into a perpetual snarl. Dare suited his name. He had a sense of restrained menace about him, as if civilization was a garment seldom worn.

"Preoccupied," Kyle corrected absently. He held up a hand. "Yeah, yeah. Just as dangerous as being PO'd."

Kyle drained his beer and signaled the waitress for two more. "Let me put it this way. A voice from my past, who *shouldn't* be on Izquierdo has somehow managed, in a few short days, to short-circuit my usually functional brain cells."

The waitress, wearing the shortest, most obscene, shorts he'd ever seen, slid two beers on the table in front of them. His glower encouraged her not to linger. When she'd huffed off, he quickly filled Dare in on Delanie's suspicion about her sister's kidnapping.

"You heading straight back tomorrow after customs?"

"Yeah, everything's set." Kyle drank some of his warm beer without tasting it. "I'll take care of Palacios as well, then get back up there for the grand finale."

"Can't wait for it to be over?" Dare asked with a trace of sympathy.

"It shows?" Kyle grimaced.

Dare shrugged, his fingers wrapped about his glass. "Hey man, you've got family, a real life. I'm in this for the long haul. There's a never ending supply of terrorists. Once Montero's gone it won't be five seconds before I'm needed someplace else."

"There's nothing like a nice quiet, predictable lab," Kyle admitted dryly. "I only took this on because I was the closest person they had to Montero. We went to school together. He trusts me. God only knows after four years of this crap I'm ready to cut bait. Doesn't it get to you?"

Dare shrugged, his scar taut across his face. "Nah. After

all these years it's what I know." He paused. "I just wished to Christ we didn't have to dick around with the real thing. Scares the crap outta me, man."

"I'm not too thrilled about it myself. But the poxvirus is safely contained, and no one can open the case other than myself. After I pick it up at customs tomorrow morning, believe me, I'll handle that suitcase and its contents like the lethal poison it is."

Kyle glanced around the misery-filled cantina. God only knew he didn't want an accident that would increase the wretchedness of these people's existence.

He met Dare's patient gaze. "Montero's paranoid, he'll have the vials checked as soon as I get back. For authenticity. Once that's done, those viruses are history. We're not taking the risk of this much manpower coming into contact, I assure you."

"And we're all behind you one hundred percent. The only thing you have to worry about is that little suitcase of yours. We'll do garbage detail so you can get back to your family."

The two men grinned, in perfect accord.

"Saw Michael last night," Dare told him. "There aren't any other SEALs involved. What'd he do? Quit? Or is big bro here to cover *your* puny ass?"

"Are you kidding? Michael is career Navy. He'd never quit while he has a breath in his body." Kyle smiled. "He took a leave of absence. Wants to make sure I do this right."

"Pal, if everybody wasn't *positive* you'd do this right, you wouldn't *be* here, trust me."

Kyle had never felt the weight of responsibility more keenly. He was grateful his older brother would be at his back in a couple of days. T-FLAC had eagerly included him in one of their elite teams for the duration.

With his brother and people like Darius behind him, Kyle felt confident he could do what had to be done.

Unfortunately not all the agencies involved were crazy about working closely with other agencies. Particularly with this many involved. But every country had a stake in the outcome of this particular mission. The chances of something going sour were too damn high. His men were used to being outnumbered, and they liked the challenge. But in this instance they didn't have anywhere near the manpower to field an operation of this magnitude.

To do this right they needed every pair of hands they could get.

After a few more minutes of business, Dare rose, leaving his untouched drink on the table, but slapping down a large tip. "I'll keep an eye on your woman at the café, then get her to the airport when you're on your way."

"I'd appreciate you keeping an eagle eye on her at the café. But negative on the transportation." It was flat, unequivocal. Kyle rose, too, and walked out with him. "Seeing her board that plane with my own eyes is the only way I'll believe she's safely outta here."

They stopped outside in the deep shadows of a nearby alley before parting. It smelled of rotting vegetables and things long dead.

"Sounds to me as if you're in grave danger of losing your objectivity here, Doc," Darius pointed out. "And I hope to God this woman hasn't caused you to drop your cover."

"I haven't forgotten what I'm doing here. And I don't need a reminder." Kyle gave his associate a direct look.

Dare held his own. "Get rid of her. You have two choices. Send her home or kill her."

Kyle dismissed the guard he'd ordered Gil to post outside Delanie's door at the safe house, and let himself into the room. The lights were still on. She lay in exactly the same uncomfortable position he'd left her in an hour ago. Feet on the floor, sprawled on her back, one arm over her eyes. There were dirty tear tracks on her temples, something he knew she wouldn't appreciate him seeing.

Damn it.

With a put-upon sigh, he removed his piece from the small of his back, checked the safety, and set it on the table by the bed. He didn't want to touch her. He'd erroneously thought his desire for her had been satiated this afternoon. Not so. The rolling boil had merely been turned down to a simmer.

Blinding. Dangerous. Unacceptable.

He saw her soft mouth, the delicate arch of her brows and one small pink ear poking through the strands of her honey-eyed hair. He remembered frantic hands clutching his back, hot wet thrusts, pleading eyes and avaricious mouth. He groaned.

If he wanted a semidecent night's sleep, she'd have to be moved. Which necessitated touching her. While he refused to undress her, she wouldn't sleep comfortably trussed up in her clothes. Reluctantly he lifted the front of her T-shirt and popped the top button on her jeans. The back of his fingers brushed her flat, golden-brown stomach, lingering for just a second on baby-soft skin.

He carefully pulled down the zipper, catching a glimpse of the skimpy, fire engine–red panties he'd had to force her into this afternoon—the ones she'd kept trying to get out of. Blocking his mind, he moved her farther up the bed and covered her with the sheet.

After turning off the lights in the bedroom, he took a quick, cold shower before crawling carefully onto the bed beside her. He'd redressed in his jeans. Body armor for his libido.

His medical residency had prepped him for sleep deprivation. He could practically sleep standing up. Fifteen-minute naps could, and had, sustained him for days. Residual adrenaline subsided the moment he closed his eyes. If it hadn't been for Delanie's presence, he'd have felt nothing more than the pleasant buzz of a job almost completed.

He rolled over, only to find his nose buried in her hair. He stayed where he was, enjoying the scent of strawberry and chlorine, trying to block out the arousing scent of sex still perfuming her skin from their manic bout at the compound.

They'd never made love languidly, never had time to linger. How was it possible to miss something he'd never had? Their affair had been like a firestorm, their need for each other too frantic, too all-consuming to think of slowing down. There had been too little time, too much they wanted to discover about each other's bodies. They'd thought they'd have all the time in the world, later, to languidly enjoy each other.

Without realizing it, his fingers tangled lightly in the silk of her hair, crushing the filaments with a yearning bordering on physical pain. She mumbled in her sleep, rolled over, and burrowed against him.

Kyle carefully slid his arm under her shoulders, pulling her head to rest on his chest. He breathed a sigh of contentment, tucked her head under his chin, and closed his eyes.

Sleep came down like a guillotine.

The cantina looked like a stage set. Cracked adobe walls, red geraniums in clay pots around the fountain in the tiny courtyard, and a plump proprietor with a stained white apron around his ample middle.

Delanie and Kyle were the only patrons. The rest of the wobbly, black wrought-iron tables were empty.

They slowly drank demitasse cups of *café tinto,* strong black coffee essence that did indeed look like ink. It was an acquired taste, but Delanie needed the jolt of caffeine.

"Doing okay?" Kyle appeared taller, leaner somehow, very sexy, she thought ruefully, in his well-cut, taupe-colored Italian pants, thin snakeskin belt, and crisp taupe-and-white-striped, long-sleeved dress shirt open at the throat. He'd come back from inside where he'd gone to use the phone. Bandbox fresh, and smelling of soap, he took the chair against the wall.

Wearing yesterday's jeans and a wrinkled red T-shirt, Delanie felt scruffy next to his sartorial splendor. She hadn't bothered with makeup, although surprisingly he'd packed a few items for her.

She shrugged. "Okay. All things considered." She sounded as contrary and uncomfortable as she felt. Her face felt warm.

She'd remembered more while she'd slept. Mostly jumbled images, all erotic. All annoyingly, tantalizingly out of reach, as though viewing a movie through a dense filter, a movie with long gaps of dark screen where her imagination filled in the blanks. And made it worse.

The proprietor arrived with huge platters of huevos rancheros, tortillas, and salsa, which he set before them on the rickety table. After a brief conversation in Spanish with the man, Kyle concentrated on his breakfast.

Other than those few words in the room, he hadn't spoken since they'd walked the two blocks to the restaurant. It was rather like waiting for the other shoe to drop. She ran her fingers through her still-damp hair and let it fall back on her neck.

"I'll drop you off in town to do some shopping." Kyle looked over at her, then drained his cup. "There's a café in the center of town where we can meet."

He glanced at his Rolex. "I'll be finished with my business by noon, I'll pick you up then. If you're hungry again, order lunch there."

The eggs, mixed with the thick, black coffee, had already turned to cement in her stomach. "I won't be hungry after this huge breakfast." She gave him a cool look. "Feel free to come and get me at any time. I have no intention of shopping or sightseeing while my sister's life is in danger."

"Good. Stay in the room."

"I'd prefer to stick with you."

"Sorry, babe, I don't have time to play. I have a business meeting."

"Actually, *babe,*" she said through her teeth, "I don't want to *play* either. I just want to make sure of my ride back up the mountain."

Kyle motioned for the waiter, paid him, then sat back while the man cleared the table. As soon as he was gone, he said briskly, "Get out your passport, and stick it under your clothes." He scanned her plain T-shirt and skintight jeans. "Somewhere."

He opened his wallet and handed her a couple of hundred-dollar bills. U.S. "Put these inside. The police or the soldiers can stop you at any time. They'll threaten you with jail, but they'll take a bribe to let you go. Give them *all* the money. And Delanie? For God's sake, *don't* give them any grief." He gave her that hard look she was coming to hate. "In San Cristóbal, if you're in jail, they throw away the key."

"I'll be sure to be my sweet little ol' self," she Marilyn Monroe'd, taking the bills and stuffing them between the pages of her passport.

He drained his cup, then set it down on the table. "You'll be safe as long as you don't go off the main thoroughfares." Kyle took a gold pen from his pocket, bent down to scrawl a number on a napkin, then tore off the corner and handed it to her. "Stick this in there, too, just in case your purse is lifted."

"What is it?" She glanced at the scraggly bit of paper, memorizing the number automatically. "Your Swiss bank account?"

"An emergency phone number if you get into trouble." He gave her the evil eye. "Don't get into trouble, jungle girl. I have a full plate today."

"I won't be with you," she said sweetly. "So I'll be on my *very* best behavior."

He stuck the pen back in his breast pocket, and said curtly, "Finish your coffee. I have another call to make, then we'll go back for the jeep."

Lined with flowering, brilliant yellow mimosa trees and picturesque sidewalk cafés, Avenida del Sol throbbed with a Latin beat. People crowded on the sidewalks of the main street seemed to have a rhythm in their step as they walked.

Delanie glanced at the clock on the City Hall tower across the street. It was barely nine A.M. Kyle had dropped her right outside the little café where they were to meet at noon.

The first thing she'd done was use the pay phone inside.

She hadn't expected an answer from Lauren's apartment in Vegas, but she tried the number anyway. No answer.

Next she called her mom in L.A.—it was the middle of the night there, but she got no answer there either.

She woke her Aunt Pearl from a dead sleep and listened to her litany of problems and complaints for several minutes.

"Tell Grandpa," Delanie said firmly, "that if he doesn't take his medicine, I said you can take him to the senior center and leave him there until I get home. He'll take them. And are *you* taking your blood pressure meds, Auntie P?"

Delanie listened patiently, heard all about cousin Sandy's latest drama and William's current girlfriend, a bimbo who had shifty eyes. There wasn't a damn thing she could do about any of it until she got home.

"I have to go. The tour bus is waiting." She cut her aunt off in the middle of a lengthy discourse on the perils of teenagers driving. Delanie presumed she was referring to one of her numerous cousins.

"Give everyone my love. Lauren and I will see you soon. Yes, the weather's lovely, and no we won't get too much sun on the beach. Yes, I'll bring you back an exotic souvenir."

She returned the phone to its hook and went to find a table. Nobody back home was in the hospital or in jail. For now.

She'd ordered a bottled water and nursed it while sitting under a red-and-white-striped awning outside the café. She cautiously slung her bag across her chest bandoleer-style and settled it on her lap as a prop for her book. But watching the lightning-fast pickpockets at work proved far more entertaining.

There were half a dozen people seated at the tables in the outdoor café. Three women, baskets filled with produce from the market, sat to her left. Delanie would've loved knowing what they were so animated about, and how on earth they could hear each other since they were all gesturing and talking very loudly all at the same time.

A wrinkled old man played chess by himself at a far table.

And two men were seated just out of polite line of sight. One, dressed in jeans and a black T-shirt, looked like a scared football player. The other, in a summer-weight suit, looked like a businessman. Delanie wondered absently what the two men had in common.

And thinking about a businessman— What *kind* of business was Kyle doing? When they'd gone back to the hotel after breakfast, he'd returned from the room wearing a jacket, a tie, and an expression impossible to read.

She reminded herself that she'd acknowledged the danger weeks ago. Kyle was just part and parcel of the same hazardous route to her sister.

She *hated* this. Hated feeling as though she weren't in control of herself or the circumstances. She'd never believed in knights and white steeds. She'd learned the hard way that people made and broke promises all the time. She accepted that. Which was why *she* never made a promise she couldn't keep. Her family needed someone they could count on.

She wished to God that thinking about Kyle didn't make her heart speed up and her palms sweat. Because tenderness slipped, like fragile beams of sunlight, between his moments of darkness. And a gentle touch from Kyle had a more frightening impact on her than his threats.

"Señora?" A child sidled up to her table. Black hair matted, wearing a too-small dress, the little girl looked about three or four.

Suddenly, and without warning, all the air in Delanie's lungs dissipated in a rush that bled the oxygen from her brain.

Oh God, not now, please, not now.

Unexpected pain, so sharp it took her breath, held her immobilized as she stared down at the pinched little face looking up at her.

Struggling to stuff a mountain of emotion back into a tiny corner of her heart, Delanie managed to refocus on the child before her. The moment the child had her attention, the little girl made a money gesture, rubbing thumb and fingers together, her eyes huge in her dirty elfin face.

"Do you speak English, sweetheart?" Delanie leaned forward, not surprised when her voice sounded choked. Brown eyes looked up at her with hungry, pleading despair. The waiter came out of the café and tried to shoo the child away, flapping his apron and yelling. Delanie glared at him and cleared the pain from her vocal cords.

"Please bring out a glass of milk and something for her to eat."

He didn't like it but he went back inside, muttering to himself. The child took a few steps back, but she didn't run. Her eyes never left Delanie's face.

In a few moments the man was back. He slammed a loaded plate on the table and spilled milk from the glass he set beside it. After handing him several bills, she beckoned the child, indicating the food was for her.

The little girl didn't hesitate. She rolled egg and sausage into a tortilla then stuffed it, oozing, into her pocket. Little brown fingers rapidly constructed another, which she gulped down hurriedly, her eyes focused on Delanie without blinking as she ate.

Delanie watched helplessly as the child mopped the plate with the last tortilla. All she could do was give her a handful of money when she was done. The child was off and running, dashing between the traffic and pedestrians alike as she forged across the busy road.

The child was defenseless, vulnerable, and all alone, and there wasn't a damn thing she could do about it. Delanie's heart ached for the little girl. Worse was the self-pity that swamped her, leaving her shaken and sad.

She had to snap out of this. *Now.*

Her fingers tightened on her purse as two soldiers, dressed in San Cristóbal military uniforms, came toward her table. She let out the breath she'd been holding when they strolled past her to talk to three pretty young girls at the newspaper kiosk beside the café.

Despite the climbing heat, Delanie shivered.

She was a woman alone in a deadly situation, unprotected and vulnerable, but hardly helpless. Kyle didn't give a damn about Lauren. He had nothing to lose by leaving her sitting right here waiting for him until doomsday. He knew she'd never find anyone to take her back up Izquierdo.

He wasn't coming back for her.

The bastard was *banking* on her chickening out and giving up.

"You aren't in Kansas anymore, Dorothy," she told herself grimly. Standing, she slung her bag securely in front of her hip, then hailed a cab.

Chapter Ten

Delanie sat in the passenger seat of the helicopter with the door open. The stagnant air, steamy-hot and oppressive, made her heavy jeans cling to her legs like a damp shroud. It was going to rain. She stared out at the empty dirt road snaking through the jungle and wondered when Kyle would decide to show up at the airfield.

Oh, he'd show all right. He had no intention of going back to the café to pick her up, she just knew it.

Damn, damn, and double damn. She popped a couple of Maalox, then decided it wouldn't hurt to take another. Holding the plastic bottle in her lap, she flipped the lid, snapping it up and down impatiently.

She wished to God the little girl hadn't jarred her memories to the forefront. Not here. Not now. She felt as raw inside today as she had in the hospital more than three years ago.

She squeezed her eyes shut, seeing the blur of the green curtains in the emergency room race by her gurney, hearing her own agonized, pitiful cries. Smelling again the instantly recognizable odor of a hospital. Antiseptic. Pain. Despair. Death. It was as though she was there again.

Alone.

Struggling uselessly to stay in control of what was happening. She'd had mixed emotions when she'd found out she was pregnant with Kyle's child. Her first thought had been delight. Unmitigated joy.

Then reality had reared its ugly head. Her family had been horrified that she'd even consider having the child. The baby would be yet another responsibility. Another mouth to feed. Another person to depend on her.

And hearing their outcry, Delanie had suddenly resented them. They'd all depended on her for years, and God only knew there was little enough time to wrangle what she had on her plate as it was. But she'd wanted the baby. Kyle's baby, damn it.

Delanie had felt small and selfish. But she'd been bone-deep tired of being the only one to fix everything in the family. She'd been only twenty-four, and had already felt as old as Methuselah. Alone. Always alone. But for the first time, she was going to do something only for herself. She was going to have Kyle's baby and love it. No matter how it might inconvenience the family.

In the five months following the magical and almost dreamlike time with Kyle, she transferred all her love and hope to his unborn child.

Only to lose her.

And afterward, when she had been taken up to a ward, when she lay cold and empty, her arms aching with her loss, did Delanie realize just how badly she'd *needed* his baby.

She pressed her fingertips against her dry eye sockets, and wished she could cry. It might relieve some of the pressure in her chest and behind her eyes. But weeping was a useless waste of time.

She wanted action.

She shot another glare at the empty road. "Where the hell are you, you sneaky son of a bitch?"

The cab driver had let her off half an hour ago. Too bad she didn't speak Spanish. The radio had been on in the car, and the earsplitting Spanish rock music had been blessedly interrupted by what sounded like a news flash. All she'd understood was *"El Presidente."* The driver swerved every time he crossed himself, but didn't speak enough English to explain.

Delanie shifted her sweaty back off the leather seat to lean forward as a familiar battle-scarred jeep hurtled down the road, trailed by a cloud of red dust. It swerved to a stop just feet from the pilot's side.

Kyle threw her a startled and furious glance as he pulled himself into his seat.

"Shut your door," he snarled, slamming his own door, and buckling himself in, almost in one motion. He flicked the generator switch, grabbed the throttle, and rolled it to the start position just as his entourage emerged through the trees.

"Damn." They were right on his ass.

"Hi, Kyle. In a bit of a hurry?" Delanie's voice came over the sound of the turbine engine shrieking to life. She stared out at the police cars, lights and sirens blaring, followed by three canvas-covered military vehicles. "Now what did you do?"

He watched the gauge showing the RPMs slowly rise. "Keep your head down," he said tersely. He was starting a cold engine. It was slow, excruciatingly slow. And damn risky.

And she was not supposed to be here, damn it.

He swore silently.

The five police cars came to a halt yards in front of the chopper, the trucks behind them disgorging Palacios's army. The uniforms sprang from their cars, taking cover as bits of dirt and vegetation, kicked up by the blades, pinged off their vehicles. The soldiers started unloading weapons from the trucks, yelling orders as they scrambled.

Kyle flashed Delanie a quick glance to be sure she was buckled in and had her head down. One out of two wasn't good enough. With one hand, he grabbed her skull and pushed. She swore. He didn't give a damn, just pressed harder so her head touched her knees. "Stay there."

A bullet ricocheted off the Plexiglas on her side. She flinched but stayed down. The cracks spiderwebbed across the window, but it didn't break.

He increased torque on the throttle, turned the inverter switch and went full power, then pulled in the collective, keeping the cold engine there as another bullet pinged against the body of Montero's brand new Tiger.

Kyle kicked the pedals.

With a shudder the chopper lifted. The bullets came fast and furious. The soldiers weren't very good shots; nevertheless, one out of three bullets made contact. He knew they couldn't penetrate the blast-shields or the boron carbide Kevlar, but there was a real danger of someone hitting the fuel tank or one of the MISTRAL missiles.

The men on the ground started running as the chopper made a slow assent. Kyle managed a tight turn away from the vehicles and personnel. The chopper hovered thirty feet off the ground. He pulled back on the cyclic, slowing their forward motion, gaining altitude as quickly as possible. Some smart soldier hauled out a handheld rocket launcher. Kyle didn't want to use the Tiger's firepower. He wouldn't need to, if he could get their butts outta here. *Fifth*with.

The skids skimmed the treetops by feet as they headed north, leaving twenty or so angry, frustrated uniforms shooting into the air. His options were rapidly dwindling as the storm front closed in. With the mountainous terrain and thick vegetation, there were only a few places they could go. Back into San Cristóbal wasn't one of them.

"You son of a bitch. You killed him, didn't you?" Delanie strained against her harness, her voice tight with anger as she jerked upright from her enforced crouch and put on the headset in front of her the better to yell at him. Her white-knuckled fingers clenched the seat on either side of her hips.

Kyle checked the clouds a hundred feet above. There was no way they'd make it up Izquierdo before the rain hit. Mentally he reconstructed the surveillance maps he'd studied before this mission.

"Oh God," she declared rawly. "Was *that* what your business was about this morning, Kyle? Did you come to town to assassinate the president?" Shaking out a couple of tablets from the bottle clutched in her hand, she shoved them into her mouth and crunched down.

"Of course it was," she answered herself furiously. "You told me yourself you were going to do it, the other night on the patio. Except at the time I had other, more immediate concerns."

"I told you something else a lot more recently." He eyed the oppressive cloud cover, knowing he'd have to land, and soon. Wind buffeted the chopper.

"What?"

The temptation to shut her mouth, one way or the other, was powerful. Unfortunately if he let go of the controls for even a second, the Tiger would immediately attempt to invert. "I told you I'd pick you up at the *café* at noon."

"A, I don't take orders very well. And B—" she sent him a fulminating look "—If you'd gone to pick me up at noon you could *not* have screamed onto the airfield at eleven, now could you?" She paused as the chopper dipped in the turbulence. He corrected it while she vented. "I knew damn well you weren't coming back for me, Kyle."

He'd watched her from across the street, through a window on the top floor of the City Hall building. Two of his operatives had been seated at the table behind her. She couldn't have moved a centimeter without his knowing about it.

Unfortunately, he hadn't known *where* in hell she'd gone, because she chose exactly the wrong moment to get into the cab. The two men seated at the café had another job to perform. If she'd stayed put they would have been able to complete running interference when the police and soldiers started chase *and* keep a visual on her. Instead, one agent had tried to tail her, and Darius had been hard pressed to distract the forces on his own. The damn job had almost turned sour because she'd refused to obey a simple order.

"You might as well tell me what—"

The words were bitten off as the chopper jerked violently. He made a quick recovery, pulling up on the collective as they lost altitude.

The Tiger rose briefly. Dipped. Rose and lurched.

He angled toward a clearing he remembered. The sudden

thunder of the tropical deluge was deafening as it hit. It was as though a faucet opened overhead. The chopper bucked like a demented bronco. It took all his concentration to touch down.

It was a lousy landing, but they were upright and on the ground.

For several minutes they just sat there, listening to the timpani of water hitting metal and plastic, to the whine of the blades as they slowed, to the escalating heat of each other's anger. Rain sheeted the Plexiglas. Visibility reduced to a green blur.

He looked over at her, water shadows danced on her ghostly pale face as she stared out of the front window.

"Well, hasn't *this* been a lovely day," she said with unnatural calm.

"A good day," he said through his teeth, "is a day when nobody dies. This has *not* been a good day." He ripped off his headset, the look he gave her scorching. "Listen up, jungle girl, I was trying to protect you from getting your ass blown to hell-and-gone. The least you could do is—"

Out of nowhere, rage consumed her, so intense her vision blackened. Before Delanie realized it, she'd flung off her headset and was out of her seat harness, blindly lunging at him, teeth and nails bared.

"You sick bastard." She slapped him so hard her hand went numb. "You murdering son of a bitch." She tried to rake his face with her nails, then struggled futilely as he trapped both her wrists in one large hand.

"Hey! Settle down, damn it!" Kyle held her bucking body away with one shackling hand.

She heard his seat harness snap open. She snarled, trying to kick his thigh in the confined space of the cockpit. She managed to get a hand free, beating at his upper arm with her fist.

"You killed that man for money, didn't you?" She was almost incoherent. Practically in his lap, she rained blows wherever she could, putting the full weight of her body into it. Adrenaline shot through her veins in a thundering, vital life force all its own.

"I-hate-you-I-hate-you-I—"

"Delanie—"

"You're a liar and a . . . a *murderer*." Her voice rose, words coming faster. "And a no-good bastard!"

On some level she knew she was out of control, her hysteria was rising. She'd never heard herself sound like this in her life.

She didn't care.

Tears of rage stung her eyes, exacerbating her anger. She swung again, this time connecting with his jaw.

"Ouch, damn it. That hurt."

"Good," she shouted with relish. "I wish those men had captured you and tortured you to a slow, agonizing death." Each huffing breath was punctuated by another punch. "I wish—" wham "—they'd—" wham "—shot—you—" wham "—I wish . . ."

"I get the picture." He'd stopped trying to hold her off. Her fist connected with a satisfying thump to his breastbone and he didn't even flinch.

Frightened of herself, Delanie flexed the fingers of her right hand before gathering up another head of steam. She could hear her own breathing as it escaped in harsh, uneven pants, rasping painfully from her throat. Emotions threatened to choke her.

"Done?" Kyle asked gently, cupping her shoulder firmly with one large, steadying hand as she paused to drag in a shuddering gasp of air.

God. She was a worse judge of character than either Mom or Lauren had ever been! Despite everything, she'd *cared* about him, wanted to have his baby . . .

Hurt, and absolutely furious with herself for her own stupidity, she shook her head vehemently, too out of breath to verbalize.

"Yes, you are, sweetheart." He used his other hand to brush a strand of hair off her lower lip. "Yes, you are. Shhh now." He pulled her into his arms. She fell against his chest, all the fight draining from her body in a dizzying rush.

The sudden absence of violence left her exhausted. Resting her damp face against his shirt, she breathed in the scent of danger and pure Kyle that continued to confuse her.

"That's a good girl." He rested his chin lightly on top of her head. "Take a deep breath and calm down." She felt his hand making comforting circles on her back through her T-shirt, subtly urging her closer. Her fingers clutched at his shirt in denial. She didn't want his comfort, but couldn't seem to move. His arms were strong, his heartbeat steady, his voice a low soothing rumble she felt rather than heard.

He settled her more comfortably across his lap, and her eyes closed as he ran his hand up and down her spine.

This was absolutely crazy, she thought, limp as a noodle, her hitching breath harsh and uneven, her emotions in chaos. *What am I doing?* She made a halfhearted attempt to push away from him.

"Stay where you are for a second, okay?" Kyle's voice was a husky rasp. "There's nowhere to go until this rain stops."

It took far too long for her to pull herself together and regain a semblance of calm. "God, I can't believe I just did that."

"What? Beat the stuffing outta me?"

"No, you deserved that," Delanie said with residual acrimony. "I've never been hysterical in my life."

His chuckle rumbled beneath her cheek. "I'd say after what you've been through in the last few weeks, you've had ample justification." It was impossible to read his expression in the dimness of the cockpit. "You'd have to be made of tungsten steel *not* to fall apart."

"I did *not* fall apart." She went rigid against him. "I was perfectly in control . . . For a while anyway."

He arched a meaningful brow. Before she could comment, he slid his hand around the back of her head bringing her up hard against him.

Then he kissed her.

His lips tasted compelling, tantalizing, provocative.

Deceiving, unreliable, and faithless.

She refused to open her mouth.

After a few moments Kyle lifted his head, his pale eyes enigmatic, his expression bland. She wondered what kind of experiment he was performing now.

"You are nothing if not predictable." Delanie used both hands to push against his chest, then slid off his lap. He let her go, and she wriggled back into her own seat.

"That's it for you, isn't it?" he asked quietly, leaning against the corner between seat and door, observing her through those eerie all-knowing, all-seeing eyes. "You allow yourself twenty seconds of comfort before you have to prove you're Superwoman again. No wonder you guzzle antacids like candy." His gaze was painfully direct. "It must be exhausting. Have you *ever* needed anyone in your life, Delanie, or do you always have to be the one in control?"

"Excuse me all to hell. But it's a woman's prerogative to say no." She gritted her teeth when her breath caught. "And for your information, I didn't *need* comfort. And it ticks me off that just because I'm handy, you assume I'm available for a little recreational sex to fill in the time until it stops raining!" She folded her arms and stared out the cracked side window.

Everything appeared distorted.

"And let me point out," she informed the blurry view of soggy trees and hateful green outside, "you've already *had* more than your allotted quota with me."

A low laugh escaped him. "I had a quota?"

Her blood pressure started climbing again. "Damn it, Kyle—"

"Jesus," he said, almost to himself. "I can't go on like this." He reached over and took her chin in a gentle, but inexorable hold.

She had no difficulty at all interpreting what was stamped into the hard map of his face. Exasperation and a good dose of pure male frustration. Poor baby.

"I hope you don't need your right hand for anything important," she said sweetly, " 'cause it's about to be bitten."

"Lord, woman, you are bloodthirsty, aren't you?" He tucked a strand of hair behind her ear before removing his hand. He looked at her a moment longer. "I can't believe I'm blowing my—" He paused, dragging air through his nose. "Palacios *isn't* dead, Delanie."

She raised both eyebrows. "Did you tell that to all those guys shooting at you?"

He stared up at the ceiling, as if asking for divine intervention. "I'm not what you think I am." He seemed to choose his words with care.

"What's that?" she asked bitingly. "A lowlife, drug-dealing assassin?"

"Delanie, I don't work for Montero, it's a cover. I work for an international antiterrorist organization called T-FLAC. And have been for the last ten years."

"Oh, really? Then why did you tell me you were a doctor?"

"I *am* a doctor. Look, I told you I was considerably younger than my peers, right? Well, I finished my medical residency when I was barely twenty. Nobody wanted a kid for a doctor, no matter how damn bright he was. So to take up some time while I waited for my face to get old enough to practice medicine, I went into research and specialized in epidemiology."

Delanie frowned her confusion.

"I research infectious diseases," he explained briefly. "I was working freelance, on the cult Aum Shinrikyo's sarin gas contamination in Japan for the CDC in Atlanta, when T-FLAC approached and recruited me. Terrorists are leaning toward biochemical weapons more and more, but the labs are damned hard to track down and conclusively identify simply because most could be legitimate medical labs. With my background I was perfect for the job.

"Put it this way. I've been busy ever since."

"You're a good guy." She stared at him narrow-eyed. "And it never occurred to you to tell me this rather important piece of information?" she demanded.

Kyle snorted. She wasn't sure if he was holding back manic laughter or holding onto the last thread of his temper. "You'd prefer I was a—what was that? Oh yeah, a lowlife, drug-dealing assassin?"

She searched his face in the water-wavering light. "*Is* this the truth?"

"Four years ago, if you remember, we didn't waste time *talking*. And on Izquierdo I had no idea just what role you were playing with Montero. If you were what you were pretending to be, four years of deep cover could have been blown."

"What's this got to do with Montero? I thought he was a drug dealer."

"The biggest. But his real pleasure comes from the thought of controlling the world by using biochemical weapons." His eyes hardened. "In this case, the virus for smallpox. And that's just a start."

She covered her throat with her hand. "God . . ."

"No weapon on earth is more capable of wiping out millions of people instantly. Montero is determined to have that power in his hands. He approached me, just before you and I met in San Francisco, to go into full-scale production of the virus. He plans to sell it on the world market. Bidding for the first batch opens on Thursday. A nice hefty infusion of cash. After that it's whoever has the bucks. Trust me, the phone will ring off the hook."

"Who . . . ?"

"Warring nations will pay big to get their hands on a missile filled with viruses. They could detonate it above a city, spreading the virus quickly and efficiently. An entire unvaccinated population could be wiped out. No fuss, no muss."

"He's insane," Delanie whispered, absolutely horrified. "Surely it would be easier just to use bombs to the same effect?"

"Not only are viral weapons considerably less expensive to produce, but a virus doesn't destroy buildings and vegetation. Besides, it would take hundreds of scientist-years and billions of dollars to develop working nuclear technology. Montero already had top-of-the-line equipment in his pharmaceuticals labs. So it only took *me*, and a *fraction* of that amount of money, and a matter of *months*."

"Why would you even pretend to help a man like that?"

"Because if I didn't, he'd've gone to someone else. And since, and I say this with utmost modesty, I'm the best in my field, we knew he'd want *me*. We banked on it."

Delanie rubbed her hand absently on her midriff. "That's why you didn't want me up there."

"You're damn right I don't want you there."

She bit her lip. "Damn it, Kyle, I'm sorry I didn't cooperate. I had no idea. I'm sort of used to being in charge—"

"*Sort* of?" Kyle smiled slightly.

Delanie leaned forward, her heart in her throat. "Do you have any idea where Lauren is, Kyle? Is she—is she being used for some godawful experiment or something up there?"

He reached over and covered her hands, which were clenched in her lap. "I haven't seen or heard of her. And I'm *damn* sure Montero would have bragged about her if she was up there. I swear, I'll put some of my people on it when they arrive. I won't let anything happen to Lauren if she is there. And if she isn't, we'll find her together when this is over."

"When is it going to be over?"

"Saturday."

"Four days from now. God. So much could happen to Lauren in the meantime."

"Yeah," Kyle said without prevarication. "It could. But unless I can find her before the raid, there's nothing I can do about it."

Oh, God. Lauren.

"As soon as the rain lets up I'll get you back to town and have one of my people escort you to the airport. I'll contact you at home when this is over."

"Home?"

"Sacramento."

"Could I at least wait for her in San Cristóbal? *Please,* Kyle?"

He hesitated a beat too long. "Sure," he rubbed a hand across his face.

"She's my top priority."

"Tell me, where does your own safety come in? Or is your whole life one of blithe self-sacrifice and denial?"

"My reason for being here is to find my sister."

"And how can you possibly help her if you're dead?"

"I'm not going to die."

"How comforting it must be to be so utterly self-confident."

"I'm holding you to your word that you'll help me find her." Delanie didn't for a moment believe he'd put her sister's safety before the job he was here to do. A job, if what he was saying was true, that was gigantically more important than the fate of one young woman he didn't even know. She had no intention of putting all her faith in a man who found lying as easy as brushing his teeth.

"I'll leave because insisting I go with you would not only be useless, it would also be stupid. But I'll only go as far as San Cristóbal. I'd be safe there, right?"

"Reasonably," Kyle admitted, not sounding particularly happy about it. "Okay. I'll get you to the Villa D'Este. You can wait at our safe house. If the shit hits the fan, an agent will get you out."

"Thank you." God only knew, she'd prefer being in the thick of things looking for Lauren herself. But she was *way* out of her depth, and knew it. She had no choice.

The rain didn't look as if it was going to stop anytime soon. "What was the deal with pretending to assassinate the president?"

Kyle leaned back, obviously trying to stretch his long legs as best he could in the close confines of the cockpit. "Caesar's the one who red-flagged us in the first place about Montero's latest interest in biological warfare."

"So you 'killed' him to protect him?"

"Yeah. Since Caesar's been in office he's kept relative peace in his country with the covert help of the U.S. military. But Palacios's position here is precarious. It won't matter

that the people want Palacios as president. Montero wants
someone else. If Caesar were to die, the country would be in
an uproar."

"Well Caesar is, for all intents and purposes, dead, and the
country is in an uproar. So what was the point, besides sav-
ing his butt?"

"Because this way we control what's happening, and when
it happens. Ramón Montero has someone more suitable in
mind for the presidency. Someone who embraces the same
ideology he does. Unfortunately, U.S. funding for aid has already been given to Palacios. On Monday Caesar Palacios
was to run against Montero's man for reelection."

"So I guess that means if Montero's man were to get in,
Montero would have an open money faucet straight from the
States."

"You got it. Hence the 'assassination,' " Kyle finished
grimly. "We had to keep Palacios under wraps until Montero
and all his lieutenants are taken care of."

"Obviously the president's army doesn't know the truth."

"Yeah. That was a bit hairy," Kyle said dryly. "The media
has been fed misinformation. There'll be confirmation that
the president is in critical condition in the hospital and isn't
expected to live. Tomorrow it'll be announced that he's
dead."

"Montero's a megalomaniac." Delanie shivered and curled
her legs under her to get more comfortable.

"We won't permit this to go any farther. If Montero had
his way he'd own the airspace and the sea lanes," Kyle continued, "and since there's no extradition from San Cristóbal,
he'd do whatever the hell he wants, then scurry back into this
convenient little hole on the other side of the world with impunity."

She wished she could see Kyle's eyes, but the rain blurred
all his features. "I don't know how you managed to keep up
the act for so long." She heard the tinge of acceptance in her
own voice. God, *was* he telling the truth this time?

"There was no acting required, jungle girl. I have an unbreakable cover. All I had to do was *be* my job."

The information he'd given her had set a clock ticking in her head. A reminder of how little time she had left.

Three days to find Lauren. She bit her lip.

Kyle touched her shoulder, and she almost jumped out of her skin. She turned to look at him. "What?"

"Let me do that for you," he said huskily and leaned over and kissed her.

She wanted to resist him again, damn it, she really did. But his hand moved from her shoulder to cup the back of her head, his fingers tangling in her hair. There was nothing aggressive about the kiss, only a tenderness that caused her throat to ache.

"Damn you," he said as though they were love words. "Damn you for being so stubborn."

"Hey! I—"

"Shut—" his teeth scraped her lower lip "—up."

Chapter Eleven

His tongue slid, moist, hot, seductively determined, between her teeth. His fingers tightened against her scalp. Delanie met his invasion with a challenge of her own and was rewarded with the hoarse sound of his groan as her tongue touched his. A shaft of pure fire shot through her.

She twisted to wrap her arms awkwardly around his neck. His eagerness sent her pulse racing as she met him halfway between the bucket seats. It was impossible to get their bodies aligned the way they were sitting, but she couldn't bear for him to stop kissing her.

She whimpered when he jerked his warm, wonderful mouth away. His face flushed, his chest beneath the crisp shirt heaving as he dragged in oxygen.

"Christ," he said roughly, "I want you so much."

Her breath caught at the heat in his brilliant green eyes.

"I have to touch your skin." He tugged her T-shirt free of her waistband. His large hands skimmed her sides, tantalizingly close to her breasts. She tried to twist her torso into his palm, and he jerked the thin cotton over her head in an impatient move that disengaged her arms from about his neck.

"What are you doing?" she asked huskily when his eyes moved slowly over her, his hands motionless on her upper arms.

"I want to memorize you like this. Your skin's like pearl in this light." His eyes were intent on her body, a visual caress moving like a charge of electricity across her flesh. Her skin prickled deliciously in reaction as anticipation unfurled its petals.

"Kyle—"

"Soft, translucent." Ignoring her moaning entreaty he continued, "Look at your nipples, jungle girl. Look at how they peak, just waiting for my touch."

She felt her face and chest heat with his words. Her nipples strained against the thin lace of her bra. There was no need to look to see how hard they were.

He ran his thumb gently across one peak, watching her reaction. "Does that feel as good to you as it does to me?"

Her skin burned. "Ye—" She had to clear her throat. "More."

"I want to taste them. Would you like that, little Amazon? Would you like it if I used my tongue on these sweet little buds?" She felt the heavy thrum of her pulse in the very tips of her aroused nipples as she nodded, her mouth too dry to speak.

He bent his dark head. She felt the wet heat of his open mouth through the thin fabric, and closed her eyes tightly as he sucked and lightly bit her through the gossamer-thin material.

She reached for his belt buckle at the same time he popped the top button on her jeans. She shifted her hips so he could pull down her zipper. Her fingers blindly fumbled his belt buckle free.

"God," he said rawly as he slid his cupped hand beneath the thin barrier of her panties and open jeans, "you're so pretty here." At his intimate touch, she shuddered.

"Hot, wet—" He wrapped an arm about her neck and dragged her closer, his kiss cutting off the inciting words.

As his tongue thrust deep into her mouth, she felt his fingers duplicate the motion deep inside her. She shifted restlessly as internal muscles tightened in exquisite anticipation. Beneath her outstretched hand, she felt his arousal, hard and insistent behind the prison of his zipper. She was powerless to do anything about it.

Shifting her hips, a movement hampered by her jeans and the bucket seats, she heard her own frustrated whimper followed by a rough chuckle from Kyle.

"No," she cried as he withdrew his fingers. She stiffened in shock, in protest, her own hand clutching at his blatant erection. "Damn you—"

"Get in back." He kept his eyes on her face as he stripped off his shirt, kicked off his shoes. "Now." He lifted his hips to strip off pants, briefs, socks.

He was naked, savage, the long dark rope of his braid snaking down across his chest to pool at his groin. Her eyes rose to meet his. She didn't trust herself to speak. God, he was the most magnificent male she'd ever seen.

"Now, damn it!"

Clumsy, impatient, and suddenly shy, she slipped between the front seats to the open area in back.

Don't do this, her mind shouted one last caution. She ignored the warning, fumbling with her clothes, not knowing which she wanted off first. She tore at her bra, fingers too impatient for the small hook-and-eye in back.

Firmly he pushed her hands aside, his eyes like living green flame caressing her skin as his hand reached behind her. The loosened bra brushed against her skin, making her shiver.

They knelt, facing each other, mere inches apart. She could smell his skin, feel his heat. He looked as fierce as a pagan warrior. She put her hand on his chest, and his muscles jumped beneath her fingers. "You feel so good," she said so softly she could barely hear herself.

He removed her bra, dropping it on the floor behind him. "Where?" he asked, sliding her jeans and bikini panties off. "Show me."

Using both hands she slid them slowly down the hard contour of his broad chest, until his flat, brown nipples peaked. "Here—" she leaned forward. "Like this—" Her tongue stroked him and his body tensed. His fingers gripped her hair. "And like this—" Her hands skimmed further down, along his ribs, to the shadowy indentation of his navel.

"I like to taste you," she said, in a voice barely audible, "here—" at the indentation of his narrow waist. "Here—" at the jutting bone of his hip. "Here. God, I love this spot." The silky smooth, vulnerable skin between hipbone and groin. "I think this is my favorite . . ."

"You're killing me, jungle girl." He tipped her over on top of him, bracing her descent with his arms. She nuzzled her face against his musky roughness, feeling his fingers plunging into her hair, stinging her scalp as her breath whispered across his chest. She licked a path toward his navel. He tasted exciting, dark, delicious. She raked her teeth from smooth, taut skin to the crisp hair at his groin.

"But this—" Her fingers curled around the pulsing hardness of satin flesh. She touched her tongue to the damp tip of his penis. "*This* is the best—"

"Jesus." He bucked as her mouth closed around him. She experimented, sliding her tongue along the length of him. Savoring the musky taste of him as she took him deep into the heat of her mouth, sucking gently, licking, lapping, nuzzling until he cried out, dragging her up his body practically by her hair.

"Do you want me to come without you?" he demanded hoarsely, kissing her eyelids, then her mouth, as she sprawled on top of him, every nerve ending in her body snapping and pulsing.

She spread her knees around his hips, centering herself, so hot she was ready to explode.

Kyle gave a jagged laugh. "God, you still want to be boss, don't you?" He watched her with heavily hooded eyes, his hard mouth curved in a small smile as he settled his hands on her hips. "You want control, sweetheart? You're in the right position."

She thought he was going to plunge into her, braced herself, anticipated the hard thrust, but instead he brought both hands gliding up her back, then around to cup her face.

"Have at it, sweetheart."

The rigid, throbbing length of him pressed against the wet heat of her. She wanted him *inside*. She wanted to tell him what she felt when he touched her so tenderly. But she didn't have the words.

She wanted him to know that being in control wasn't all it was cracked up to be. But she didn't have the courage.

Her heart filled with feelings she couldn't verbalize and a kindling, pulsing need. Reaching between them she took the rigid length of him in her hand.

Her fingers, cool and insistent, guided him home.

God. The sensation of hot, wet woman made him leap and pulse inside her. His eyes squeezed shut in pure ecstasy. It took every bit of discipline for him to allow her to slide, centimeter by centimeter, all the way down at her own speed.

She murmured low in her throat, head thrown back, eyes closed. He curled his hands more firmly around her hips. Holding her, savoring the texture of her silky skin. He slid his thumbs neatly into the creases between body and thigh, waiting for her to move. *Delirious* with the need.

Bringing his thumbs in, he touched her portal. She shivered.

And started to move. Unknowingly assisted by his large hands guiding her rhythm, she whimpered low in her throat as she rose and fell. He felt her small hands braced against his chest, her fingers digging in as her hips moved faster. Faster. Faster.

Slamming.

Sliding.

Grinding.

Riding him with wild abandon, clawing his chest. He groaned, arched beneath her, the sensations shooting through him in shimmering, violent waves.

He was close. So goddamned close. He wanted her with him. Sliding one thumb to the joining of their bodies, he found the slick heart of her.

Touched.

Stroked.

Incited.

She came in a shuddering rush, helpless to move. Her back arched, head thrown back as her internal muscles milked him to the point of insanity. His hands shifted to her sweet ass, fingers curled to touch. She spasmed against him, nails digging into his stomach as he made her move again.

Deliberately.

Slowly.

Exquisitely.

He felt the heat rising in her again. That quickly. God she was responsive. She tried to quicken the pace. His hands on her ass checked her. She growled like an animal in heat, pressing down on him, her nails embedded in his flesh.

"No more," she begged weakly, her breathing harsh, her skin wet and slick against his. He'd never felt anything more sensuous in his life. "Mercy. White . . . f-flag. Uncle."

"Yeah?" he could barely speak himself. The discipline it took to hold back, to let Delanie have it all, was costing him. His heart threatened to explode in his chest.

"Hmmm." Her lashes, spiky wet, drifted to her flushed cheeks.

He clenched his teeth with the pleasure of prolonging it, tormenting himself as he dragged her from one plateau to the next. Until the oxygen was so thin they both gasped for breath.

The instant he felt her body gathering, he slowed. She turned dazed eyes to his face. He had her off balance now, her body slowly being fine-tuned to his; receptive, malleable, responsive to the tiniest touch. He led her into a slow dance. And where she'd begged for mercy before, now she pleaded for speed. For another release.

Before she could protest, he kissed the pulse in her temple, the peak of her brow, the tender skin behind her ear. He felt her internal muscles quiver around him, but refused to relent. His control of his own body was complete as he allowed her to simmer, her knees pressed insistently to his sides, her hands clutching his belly.

Even when she bowed, he held still until the moment tamed. Delanie rested her breasts against his chest, her skin fevered.

"Don't rush it. We have time." He pressed a kiss to the pounding pulse in her throat. "Lots of time."

"You're torturing me," she groaned, sitting up again so she

could press down, shifting restlessly, spiking his temperature.

He touched her breasts, stroking hot, silky skin. He examined her hard nipples with exquisite care for detail, bending her so he could suckle one sweet hard peak. She made a pleading little sound in the back of her throat. He sucked harder and she groaned.

He could feel the fiery heat of her around him, the hard heavy drum of her heart beating in rapid counterpoint to his own. And still he kept his hips steady. Until almost every vestige of her impending climax was gone.

Only then did he guide her hips into a plunge and thrust rhythm, again and again. Rebuilding speed until he imagined the chopper vibrated around them and he could feel her hands on his shoulders, his chest, his stomach. Her nails became tiny darts of ecstatic sensation.

The sweet scent of her skin drove him mad. This was like so many of his dreams. "Are you real?" he asked, as her legs tightened exquisitely. The memory of her had kept him alive for so long, but nothing compared to this reality.

Her silky legs tightened as she threw her head back and her muscles gathered— "Damn you! Why do you keep stopping?" she cried in frustration. "It's like turning down the flame just as I start boiling."

"I don't want you boiling again. Yet." He smiled at the metaphor. "Just keep at this nice, steady simmer."

"You make me crazy. What do you call this darn technique of yours?"

"Torture. Torment. Teasing."

Delanie had been glaring down at him; now a slow grin appeared as she said impishly, "Technical difficulties?" She pressed her hips down and did a slow deliberate grind. Her smile widened at his instant response.

He laughed. God, what the hell was he going to do with this woman? "Technical difficulties? I'll give you technical difficulties."

Giving her no more time to think, he turned with her in his arms, brought her flat on her back against the carpet and plunged inside her to the hilt. She gave a gasp of surprise; her eyes flew to his face as he kept up a hard, steady rhythm, giving her no quarter.

Her body bowed beneath his, her eyes squeezed tight, her nails imbedded in his ass.

He showed her the power he'd been holding back.

She screamed as she came.

The rain had stopped, the sky now bright with the beginning of a spectacular rain forest sunset. Brilliant red, orange, magenta, and deep plum, the colors were almost garish in their intensity.

Kyle cradled her with a tender strength that magnified how different they were. *This is nice,* Delanie thought, drowsy, satiated, and strangely at peace, *lying here, safe in his arms.* Even her stomach felt happy. In a little while they would have to go back to San Cristóbal, but for now—

"Rise and shine," Kyle said, his voice rumbling beneath her ear. She thought he was asleep, and his low baritone startled her. She sighed, shifting slightly. The humidity had climbed while she'd dozed causing their bodies to stick together.

"One more hour," she begged, wanting to postpone the inevitable a little while longer.

"Montero's waiting for his report," Kyle said, sounding as reluctant as she felt. "I'm late as it is. And we still have to get you back to town."

"Right." She sat up, dragging her crumpled red T off the back of the front seat and pulling it over her head. "What's the bet Palacios's men will be swarming the place, watching every airport for you?" She took a second to flip her hair out of the neckline, looking at Kyle as he stretched his long length on the floor, his arms behind his head. The sunset bathed his lean body, highlighting the hard planes and angles. He looked sexy as hell. She concentrated on getting dressed.

The corner of Kyle's mobile mouth kicked up in a smile as he watched her squiggle into her underwear.

"What?"

He snagged her hand as she reached for her jeans, and yanked, effectively toppling her onto his chest.

He held her face between the splayed fingers of both hands, their gazes locked. It was as though he were trying to see inside her brain with X-ray eyes. Or worse, do a Spock mind-meld.

"What do you see?" she asked, trying to keep her voice light. He looked very intense, and her heart knocked against her rib cage.

"A woman who's devoted, loyal to a fault . . ."

"Great," she said lightly, "I sound like a faithful hound."

"An incredible lover." His eyes raked her features one by one before meeting her gaze again. "And a woman who doesn't trust easily."

No kidding! "I trust you."

He kissed her. Slow and deep.

It felt like good-bye.

"Let's talk about what needs doing when the shit hits the fan."

"When?"

"Trust me on this, jungle girl. There's no *if* about it. We need contingency plans," he said dryly. "Okay, here's what we have to do . . ."

He didn't like being cornered, didn't like being hemmed in with zero options. He was not a happy man.

Soon after liftoff, Delanie had taken a wide roll of electrical tape out of her bottomless purse and taped up the window beside her. Her head rested against the silver X, and she'd fallen asleep, having fought off exhaustion for hours. She rested in a sort of alert doze. A technique he'd often used when there was danger about. As a civilian Delanie shouldn't have acquired that knack. Nor should she ever have had the need for it.

He glanced over at her pale face in the gathering dusk and the muted lights of the instrument panel. Her eyelids were slightly swollen. It was as though she allowed herself only so much emotion before burying it.

He might have known, despite their wild lovemaking, her defenses would be firmly back in place the moment it was over. As for her telling him she trusted him, hell, he'd never heard a lie emphasized with such veracity.

He wanted to tell her what a fool's mission she was on. If Montero did indeed hold her sister, there wasn't a snowball's hope in hell the girl would be salvageable. That was providing she was alive. The odds were stacked against Lauren. And if Delanie allowed herself to acknowledge what she already knew about Montero, she'd pray her sister had died quickly. Damn quickly.

Something about Delanie reminded Kyle of his grandmother. Not in looks, but in temperament. Grammy had had the same stick-to-it-ness as Delanie did. Martha Washburn had *also* been stubborn, opinionated, and pigheaded. She'd also loved her family above all else. Hell, Kyle bet Grammy would have killed to keep her loved ones safe. And if anyone had dared to kidnap a member of her family, his grandmother would've been here on Izquierdo just as Delanie was now. Without question.

Kyle rubbed his jaw, and heaved a sigh. Yeah, two peas in a pod. God, he missed the old broad.

He took a turn over San Cristóbal's two airports in the hope the dogs had been called off. They hadn't. An assassination attempt was grounds for instant death in this neck of the woods. No questions asked. Both small airports were crawling with soldiers and police, spotlights and dogs.

Out of options and out of time, with just enough fuel left, he woke Delanie, and reluctantly headed back toward Izquierdo.

He had a bad feeling. A *very* bad feeling.

They got back to the compound well after dinner and saw no one on the way to their room. Delanie, drugged with fatigue, stumbled into the shower while he summoned a servant and ordered a light meal for her.

By the time she emerged, silk robe clinging to damp skin, the meal had arrived. A vaporous cloud of steam followed her into the bedroom. Tendrils of wet hair, loosened from a haphazard topknot, were plastered to her neck. She smelled enticingly of his soap and her own strawberry shampoo. She eyed the wheeled table and its white linen and silverware with disinterest before pulling the bedcovers down.

"My stomach's hungry, but my mouth hasn't got the energy to chew." She yawned, got into bed, and curled her arms around her bent knees. Her eyes appeared exceptionally dark surrounded by smudges of exhaustion. She yawned again. Heat shot unexpectedly to his loins. She made even the act of yawning sensual, and looked so damned seductively sweet and sexy sitting there watching him with that slightly unfocused gaze.

"Have something before you keel over. You haven't eaten since this morning." He gave her a considering look when she scowled and shook her head. "You have to fuel your body, Delanie. Doctor's orders. Come on." He nudged the cart closer, removing the domed silver covers. The savory smell of the spicy soup made him realize just how hungry he was himself.

"Want me to feed you?" He unbuttoned his shirt, then picked up a roll and bit into it.

Swinging her legs free of the covers, she used both hands to draw the cart closer and picked up a spoon. Nudging the note he'd received, she asked, "A summons from our host?"

"Yeah." Kyle tugged off his shirt, holding the half-eaten roll between his teeth as he did so. He finished eating it before he continued. "Wants that report." Her eyes followed his hands to his belt buckle. He'd dropped his pants and shorts before she apparently remembered the dry spoon in her hand and averted her attention. He bit back a smile.

"Eat. I'm going to take a shower."

She snapped him a rather limp salute. "Aye-aye, mein Capitan."

Walking naked into the steamy bathroom, he chuckled. "I think you have your metaphors mixed, but I like the sentiment."

After a leisurely shower and a change of clothes he'd

come out of the bathroom to find her in the same position he'd left her in. Supporting her heavy head with a braced hand, she pretended to nibble at the salad, he suspected just to have something to do until he left the room.

"Okay, let's skip dinner." He shifted the cart out of the way, and she glanced at him, her eyes glassy. "As exhausted as you are right now, I'm afraid you'd drown in the soup."

"I'm fine." She sounded as indignant and petulant as a five-year-old.

"You'd say that if you were a suttee and the flames were dancing around your feet." He stripped off the damp robe, swinging her silky legs back under the covers. Her acquiescence was a mark of her exhaustion. "Close your eyes because you want to."

"I can take care of mys—"

She was asleep midsentence. Stubborn little witch.

She'd had one hell of a day. It was impossible to miss the dark shadows under her eyes and the soft droop of her slightly swollen mouth. She appeared as fragile and vulnerable as he'd ever seen her. He hardened his heart and went to report the success of his trip to his host.

Chapter Twelve

The air-conditioning chilled the room to an unnatural fifty degrees, presumably so Montero could enjoy the snap of the roaring fire in the white Carrara marble fireplace in his pseudo-English library. Kyle strolled to the bar where Montero stood smoking a cigar, elbow propped on the rich, mahogany surface, Brioni-shod foot braced on the brass foot rail. Montero spoke softly to Bruno, who played bartender for the evening.

The sharp fragrance of Isabella's distinctive perfume mingled with that of cigar and applewood smoke. Kyle figured she'd departed moments before his arrival.

Montero held up a crystal glass. "Whiskey?"

"Yeah." Kyle took the drink, waved away the offer of a Montecristo, and sank into the closest leather armchair.

"The newscasts were predictable. Caesar apparently had a mild heart attack." Montero's teeth gleamed in the firelight. "You were absolutely right, *amigo,* when you predicted they would withhold the assassination from the public. How soon do you think they will announce his death?"

"Hard to say. Feelings are running high as it is. He was a popular man, my friend." Kyle shrugged. "I guestimate by late tomorrow."

"As long as it's done by Monday." Montero leaned back, puffing his cigar. "On the news, they claim twenty thousand troops were called to full alert."

He smiled when Kyle snorted. "Indeed. The general public does not need to know that the number is closer to two thousand."

Kyle turned the glass in his hand. "I've paid off our insiders. The riots and looting will begin tomorrow just before noon. They'll order a curfew and a ban on alcohol immediately. Velasquez will be ready to step in the moment Palacios's death is announced. The hospital personnel can't be kept quiet for long. Someone will reveal that the president isn't there," he reminded Montero blandly.

"So," Montero said with relaxed satisfaction, "everything goes according to plan. It went well?"

Kyle arched a brow. "Of course." He took a swallow of his drink, the smoky flavor smooth on his palate. "Exactly as predicted."

Montero closed his eyes against the smoke of his cigar, then observed Kyle through the thin haze. "You are the only man I could have trusted with such a delicate job. Thank you, *amigo*."

"De nada," Kyle said dryly.

Son of a bitch was as cold and deadly as ice. Kyle kept his expression inscrutable and his anger hidden. There was no room now for either a false step or inattention.

"And the viruses? Everything is as it should be?"

"Of course. I took the live cultures to the lab before coming up to the house.. I'm ready to start production when we know the size of our first order."

He wondered what Delanie would have done had she known the deadly viruses were on the chopper with them. "What time are the final bids expected Thursday?"

"Lunch, our time. The first round will go to the highest bidder. That will set the watermark for future purchases."

"Excellent. I'll start production first thing Monday morning," Kyle said easily. Monday morning Montero would be awaiting arraignment.

"In fact," he said with a thin smile, "your gift arrived in the second shipment, too. I have it in my room. I'll give it to you tomorrow."

"You bought me a gift?" Montero asked, obviously pleased. Like a child at Christmas he demanded, "What is it?"

"You'll have to wait," Kyle told him coolly. "It's packed with some last minute additions I needed for the lab—I'll give it to you at breakfast."

"You are a tease, *amigo.* Very well, I will await my gift patiently." Montero sighed elaborately. He changed the subject with a roll of the smooth cigar between his fingers. "And the girl? She was with you when you iced Caesar?"

Kyle crossed his ankle over his knee, leaning back against the supple leather of his chair. "Naturally I didn't take her with me. Why? Did you want her to watch?"

Montero was edgy; it was plain to see in his soulless black eyes. He sure as hell hadn't suddenly developed a conscience about offing the president. This was about Delanie.

Kyle caught the glance Ramón gave Bruno over his shoulder. "I sent her shopping. She had no idea."

There was something he needed to resolve. "Just out of curiosity, what the hell were you thinking, drugging her? She's a goddamn loose cannon as it is. I was put in the position of having to haul her horny ass into San Cristóbal earlier than planned. I don't like being manipulated, Ramón. Even if my partner is extraordinarily inventive," he added.

"It is our new product. She received just a *muestra.* A little sample. Effective, no?"

"Effective, yes," Kyle agreed, letting a little of his savagery leak into his tone. "It's effective as hell. Would've been nice to have had some kind of warning though. I don't appreciate being used as a guinea pig, *amigo.*" He gave Montero a lazy glance. "We will, however, make a fortune from the stuff. Has it been street tested?"

"No, not as yet. The cook has only just perfected it."

Kyle knew of Dr. Montgomery, a professor of chemistry and biology lured away from Stanford to work for Montero in the "kitchen" on Izquierdo. His first job was turning the raw cocaine into white powder. He was as crooked as a donkey's hind leg. By next week he'd be manufacturing license plates.

Montero rolled the stem of the snifter between his long elegant fingers. "Unlike Rohypnol, the user is perfectly aware, and can enjoy the effects. There is the possibility of some memory loss, but we aren't sure how extensive that will be. The cook felt there might be some other minor adverse side effects." The drug lord smiled.

"The good news is that it is, of course, highly addictive after perhaps three or four uses. Unfortunately at the moment all of our test subjects have had a disagreeable tendency to become dribbling idiots after prolonged use." He waved away the inconvenience with his cigar.

"There's no limit to our customer's appetite for new and creative drugs. Dr. Montgomery is working on the minor side effects of our new product. We can't have our customers incapable of accessing their own money, can we?"

Fury pounded behind Kyle's eyeballs, although he knew he appeared perfectly relaxed and only slightly interested. Every instinct in him demanded he crush this scumbag beneath his heel.

Long before Saturday.

"Who was used for testing?" he asked.

"Locals. *Putas,* many *gamines,* no one of consequence."

Rather than obliterate the bastard's face, Kyle rose slowly and sauntered over to the bar. "Should make us a dime."

Montero laughed. "Oh yes. We shall call it Impulse, I think." He laughed again, delighted. "It can be taken in either pill form, a bubble pack our marketing people are suggesting, or a powder in a time-release—"

"This is all fascinating data," Kyle interrupted, resuming his seat and appearing bored. "But I'm not particularly interested in the marketing angle. Not until the product starts making money. Where are we manufacturing?"

He was going to take great pleasure in taking out the drug lab when he disposed of the biochemical lab.

"Here on Izquierdo. I planned on taking everyone to inspect the lab tomorrow."

"How close are we to distribution?"

Montero beamed. "I am assured, no more than a month."

"Perfect," Kyle said, genuinely pleased. Not a damn thing was on the streets yet. In four days the factories would be rubble. "It appears, my friend, that you are achieving everything on your wish list." He toasted his partner with a raised glass.

"Our wish list surely?"

"My list gets shorter by the moment," Kyle assured him in a soft feral voice. Time to do a little shaking. "You do trust Kensington and the others then?"

"Naturally, I—"

Kyle inserted a disbelieving snort. "Surely you realize the tong has more than a healthy interest in Sugano's presence here? Are we really so sure of the people we've used to infiltrate the organization? After all, neither of us speaks the language. How the hell can we be sure . . ." he allowed his voice to drift off.

"What are you saying? We can't trust our associates?"

Kyle shrugged, "Distrust has kept me alive. I'll watch your back, *amigo.* You watch mine."

"What about the girl? You took her with you into a situation that could have become volatile if she'd talked to the wrong people."

"I took her because you'd pumped her full of your new aphrodisiac, and it was in my best interests to do so. I believe," Kyle said coldly, "we've been over how I feel about being interrogated. It was your mistake bringing a woman here at the most critical time in our plans. And the only reason I got stuck bringing her back was because she was waiting for me when I got to the chopper with the National Guard riding my ass."

Kyle set his glass down on the side table with a click and fixed Montero in place with his stare. "Since I'm stuck with her, I'll avail myself of her not inconsiderable charms for a couple more days."

Kyle's eyes narrowed as Montero averted his gaze. Crap'nshit, here it comes. "Why? Is there something about her I should know?"

The other man squirmed uncomfortably in his seat. "Kensington thinks she might be DEA."

Kyle couldn't help it, he laughed. "Wouldn't she have to

have a brain for that?" he asked dryly, glad the lady in question wasn't in the room to hear him. She had a mean right hook.

Montero swallowed his drink. "She's asking too many questions, talking to my men, to the servants. She's been poking around the compound while she's supposed to be out jogging . . ." He shrugged.

"You shouldn't have brought her here." Like the tip of an iceberg, Kyle allowed a portion of his fury to show. "Your damned vanity might blow this whole thing apart. What the hell were you thinking? There's not a goddamned soul here who gives a shit who you screw. Christ, Ramón. Luckily for you she's too stupid to have caught onto anything."

"You're sure?"

"Look, she's creative as hell in the sack, but she's real light in the brain department. The only things she's interested in are money and whatever the hell else she can get her avaricious little hands on."

"I'm concerned that our partners are suspicious of a mere *puta*."

Kyle fixed him with a hard look. "I'll take care of her, don't worry."

"I admit, bringing the woman to Izquierdo at this time was not a good idea." Montero got up to refill his glass. "Yes. Take care of her *amigo, de una vez*." Once and for all. "Then none of us need worry."

Kyle gave Montero his present the next morning over breakfast. The prototype of the new Z-769 handgun could fire forty-five rounds in almost as many seconds. It had so many features for its size, they supplied it with a manual.

A guard had hand-carried the ultrasecret weapon all the way from the States to San Cristóbal. Kyle had had to do one helluva lot of talking to get the Government boys to release it at all. They'd only acquiesced after making several minor but strategic adjustments to the weapon before he could give it to Montero. Right now Kyle could've kissed the collective booted feet of Uncle Sam.

All the players were present. Sugano, Kensington, Danzigger, and Dr. Montgomery, who'd arrived early that morning. They'd gone to the lab before breakfast. The pox-virus vials had been inspected by the doctor and deemed acceptable. Kyle had stated he'd be back later that morning to infect the chicken eggs. In point of fact he was going to dispose of the virus before the shit hit in a couple of days.

Montero's merry little band, happy as pigs in shit at the prospect of all the money they were about to make, trooped into the dining room with ravenous appetites.

Everyone was in a damn fine mood.

Montero recouped the weapon from Sugano's scrutiny and stroked the bronzed nose like a lover, all beaming smiles and oily goodwill.

"Perfectly balanced." Montero seesawed it across two fingertips. Not once had he checked to see if his new toy was loaded. "After breakfast you must share more of my present's capabilities with us, Kyle."

Kyle casually plucked the Z out of his host's fingers on the downswing as he heard footsteps approaching along the slate corridor outside the dining room. There was an imperceptible pause before Delanie appeared in the doorway.

Like a good actress, she was right on cue. All smiles, she sauntered into the long formal dining room. Conversation stopped. Even wearing black slacks and an oversized plain white shirt, she looked good. She had her canvas bag slung like a bandoleer across her body.

Kyle felt his cotton shirt stick to the small of his back as the already harsh sunlight poured through the open shutters behind him. His pulse pounded a little faster than usual as he fixed his attention on the woman drifting beneath the arched doorway to the room.

"Good morning, gentlemen. Isabella." Her voice was a little thick. Sleepy-eyed, and sexy as hell, her hair brushed back and tamed in some kind of braid, gold gleaming at her throat. She glanced around the table with a smile. Taking in the already filled breakfast plates and chafing dishes on the sideboard, she moved to pull out an empty chair.

Her knees dipped imperceptibly, and she steadied herself on the chair back. She hadn't even glanced at him, but he saw her pupils, large and dark, eyelids heavy, skin pale under heavy-handed makeup.

He had to work fast.

Steady as a rock, Kyle rose slowly from his place at the table, the Z-769 steady in his hand. In his peripheral vision, he saw Montero and the others turn as if in slow motion. The weapon had no safety.

Someone gasped.

Delanie's head jerked up. She blanched, eyes wide.

Kyle fired.

A hair off, the bullet missed her by a fraction of an inch, shattering the priceless Ming vase on the credenza, then splintering the wall-size mirror behind it to smithereens. A shower of glass tinkled to the Tabriz carpet. Flowers and water cascaded over the sideboard.

For a moment she stood, transfixed, eyes unbelieving. Dark with shock. Before she could even scream, Kyle took aim again. The second shot hit her in the center of her chest between her breasts. A flower of blood bloomed. She staggered. Blood welled obscenely against the white fabric of her shirt. Beside her, the chair fell over with a soft thud.

She gasped, skin gray.

She was still standing. Beside him Kyle heard Kensington's murmur. Montero inhaled sharply.

He calmly readjusted the sight on the Z and pulled the trigger a third time.

The impact made her stagger back, then teeter forward. Utter stupefaction crossed her face. The force of the hit had knocked the air out of her lungs. Her eyes rolled as she fell hard against the table before crumbling to the floor in a cacophony of silverware, china, and glass.

Pandemonium reigned as everyone suddenly found themselves with a lapful of breakfast. Scrambled eggs and grilled tomatoes followed the roses in a liquid mess to the floor.

Dr. Montgomery, the closest to her by Kyle's design, pushed away from the table to kneel at Delanie's side, two fingers at her throat. Impressed, he turned, and said quietly to Montero, "She is quite dead."

Danzigger knelt beside the doctor and slid a hand into the front pocket of Delanie's pants. Kyle grabbed the back of his shirt. He swore and reeled back, shocked, as he was hauled to his feet.

"Her body isn't even fucking cold yet." Kyle shook him loose to go down on one knee beside Delanie's sprawled body.

Danzigger readjusted the collar of his shirt. "Search her." He gave Kyle a defiant look, but stepped out of his way. "She's sure to have had some kind of communication device." He sounded both pissed and afraid. "She would have been making cont—"

"She wasn't a DEA agent. She wasn't *any* kind of agent, just a foolish, not-very-bright woman in the wrong place at the wrong time." Kyle glanced down dispassionately.

Delanie looked very small lying there.

And extremely dead.

Chapter Thirteen

"That was really too bad of you, Dr. Wright," Isabella said, annoyed. She held the front of her egg-splattered green silk dress away from her body with two fingers. "I do wish you had waited to see if other plans had been made for Miss Eastman."

"I don't hang around waiting for someone else to make a decision. She was damn inconvenient. None of us trusted her. If you don't like the way we conduct ourselves here, Isabella, I suggest you take the next sky cab home. This is men's business."

"How dare—"

"Mamá, *no importa,* it is done." Ramón calmly rang for a servant. "José will take care of the mess." He looked sadly at the shattered Ming and shook his head at the loss. His eyes didn't stray to the body on the floor for even a second. "Come gentlemen, we can continue our discussion in the library."

Kyle handed the Z back to his host. "I'll take care of my own garbage. Go ahead. I'll join you shortly."

He knelt beside Delanie's body, feeling for a pulse. Not a flutter. Things had progressed much faster than he'd anticipated. Surreptitiously picking up the shell casings beside her, he stuffed them in his pocket, then swiftly deactivated the necklace before wrapping her body in the blood-soaked carpet. Ignoring the onlookers, Kyle slung it over his shoulder, almost putting out Sugano's eye as he passed. He strode through the French doors and out into the blazing tropical heat.

Delanie and the damn carpet weighed a ton. By the time Kyle crossed the compound, he was drenched in sweat. He came to the deep shade of the jungle and checked behind him. No movement. Montero was so damn sure of him now, he wasn't being followed.

The thick, dripping foliage camouflaged him almost immediately, and he moved faster, shifting the rolled carpet as his eyes adjusted to the dimness. Insects clung to the sweat on his face as he pushed his way deeper, in a hurry now. The wet, enervating heat threatened to suck out his very breath, and he wasn't the one mummified in a thick wool carpet. He shifted to an easy jog.

As soon as the jungle closed in behind him, he paused, every sense tuned and alert for humans. A parrot screeched. The bass tone of the insect population counterpointed the high notes of monkeys and birds. There wasn't a breath of a breeze.

The path, cleared the other day for the nature walk, was relatively easy to follow, and eventually he came to the small pool. Forcing himself to ignore the godawful smell coming from a tree to the right of the shimmering water, he carefully lifted Delanie off his shoulder and laid her on the thick ground cover beside the water.

Rapidly he uncovered her. Her clothing was drenched, as if she'd taken a shower in them. The blood spread obscenely across her shirt. Her face was crimson and shiny; rivulets of moisture ran down her temples into the stringy wetness of her hair. She still had her canvas bag slung over her body. Obstinate little witch. He'd told her to bring nothing. She'd insisted on a change of clothes and her peashooter.

Kyle felt her pulse. Barely there, but at last detectable. He checked his watch. Probably another half hour at least before she regained consciousness.

By the time she'd walked into the room, she'd already had the capsule under her tongue. The pill had been formulated for a man his size. Two milligrams, less than a quarter dose had worked faster than he'd estimated. God only knew what risk they'd taken to pull this off. No doubt her body still re-

tained some of the crap Montero had given her two days ago.
He had no idea how the hell the two drugs interacted, and
would never have taken the chance if there'd been any other
way.

He'd figured out the secret catch to Delanie's necklace last
night while she'd slept, totally unaware of what he'd been doing. He slid it off her neck now, dropping it into his pocket.

Holding his breath, he dragged the decimated carcass of
the boar from behind the tree where he'd hidden it. He'd
managed to kill the thing late last night, on the way back
from the lab, when it had come to the pond to drink. In the
past few hours various life-forms had consumed chunks of
the rapidly decomposing pig as a smorgasbord. The visual
wasn't much better than the stench. Ignoring the gore, he
hauled the pungent carrion to the edge of the pond. Digging
in his breast pocket, he took out the twenty-four–carat gold
necklace, complete with clever little tracking device, and attached it to a half-chewed hind leg.

He tossed the carcass into the center of the pool.

In seconds the calm water became a pink froth as the piranha dined on boar du jour. Butterflies rose like coral smoke
as the water came alive. Kneeling at the water's edge, he
quickly rinsed his hands before dipping his handkerchief
into the tepid water and going back to Delanie.

She hadn't moved, but her color was slowly returning. He
stroked the back of a finger across her smooth, hot cheek,
then ran the damp cloth over her skin before applying the insect repellent he'd taken from her purse to her face and
hands. That done, he picked up the carpet and tossed it high,
to land to one side of the pond. It settled half in the water
and half on the thick vegetation growing on the far bank.

Scene set, Kyle strode back and picked Delanie up in a
fireman's lift. She felt light and far too still as he shouldered
a looping vine out of his way. He had to push the concern he
felt for her out of his mind with the same dispatch. He didn't
have time to stay with her while she came out of it. He sped
up, stepped on something that hissed underfoot, and forged
ahead without looking back.

Thick and putrid, the stifling blanket of muggy air made him remember how much he hated jungles. Hated the cloying heat, hated the brightly colored insects whose bites could be agony, hated the red ants that swarmed over everything. And the damn snakes. Small as a hair, or fat as his leg, he hated the damn snakes the most.

Streams of golden-dappled sunlight came through the tree canopy high above him. He detoured around the edge of the compound to get to the far side of the clearing. Beyond the perimeter of the main hacienda was an innocuous little hut, no bigger than six by four, and almost covered by vines and thick undergrowth.

Kyle pushed through the vegetation until he found the door. He'd discovered the structure with infrared surveillance months ago. At the time he hadn't known how handy Montero's one-man bomb shelter would be. Last night he'd parted the vines and other vegetation, clearing the doorway.

With the key he'd swiped off Montero's key ring last night, he unlocked the door. The titanium, bulletproof door creaked open. Two dozen cement steps led sharply down to a small dark room. Kyle pulled the door closed behind him, then flicked on a small penlight.

Although the confined space smelled stuffy, it was surprisingly cool. And clean. A narrow bed, covered by a red satin spread, stood across from a small propane stove on a museum-quality antique table. He lay Delanie down on the comforter, propping her head on a satin-covered pillow with a ruffled sham, and crouched down beside her.

"Hey, gorgeous . . ." His thumb stroked the soft paleness of her lips. She didn't stir. Glancing at his watch, he saw he'd been gone almost half an hour. Enough time to dispose of a body.

He let his gaze run over her face. Unconscious, she looked very young and far too vulnerable. Trailing his fingertips across her cheek, he felt the unnatural chill on her skin. He closed his eyes. When she'd stumbled over that chair, her eyes wide with feigned surprise and horror, it had been too damn realistic. He glanced down to find her eyes open and staring up at him groggily.

" 'm I dead?"

"Alive and well." Kyle casually held her wrist. "How do you feel?" Her pulse throbbed, weak and thready.

"Like I was shot." She sounded as if she'd been on a four-day bender. He gingerly unbuttoned the shirt and tugged off the Kevlar vest underneath. The small glassine bags, filled with boar blood, came off with it.

"Jesus."

Delanie struggled to glance down at her chest, then let her head flop back on the pillow, obviously not completely with it yet. "Jus' a bruise." She licked dry lips. "Doesn't hurt too badly."

Yeah, right.

He poured a cup of bottled water, holding her head up so she could drink. It dribbled from her numb lips.

"You said 'hangover.' " The words lost resolution. Her eyes were still unfocused. "I never had one—" she had to lick her lips "—before. Don' like it."

"That bad, huh?" Amused, he would've bet the ranch on the fact she'd never lost control enough to get plastered. Too bad; she made a cute drunk. She seemed softer, less prickly with her defenses down like this. He wasn't surprised she didn't like the feeling.

He'd had to resort to using the stuff once. The sensation of "coming alive" was similar to the day after a three-week bender. His finger dipped and rose over the swell of her breasts, tracing the livid marks the blanks had left. "Think of it like an anesthetic, you've had an anesthetic, right? It wears off in a couple of—"

Without warning tears filled her eyes. He saw a lifetime of pain there before she squeezed her eyes shut and limply turned her head to the wall.

"Damn," he said softly, and carefully gathered her in his arms. "Don't cry, sweetheart, it's just the drug. It's like being hung over. It'll dissipate soon, and you'll be back to your normal feisty self. I promise. Shh now, you'll feel better soon."

He felt her soundless, hot wet tears soaking his neck and the collar of his shirt. He rubbed her back, trying to reassure her. "I scared the shit out of myself shooting you like that. Must have scared you even more. Shh, now. You're okay." He lay down on the bed beside her, holding her in his arms, wishing he could hang around until the effect of the drug had time to wear off. "Don't fight it."

"I'm sorry," she said thickly, her face pressed against his throat, "I'm so sorry."

"Sorry about what?"

"Forgive me . . . didn't mean it." The rest of her words blurred together. Her arms tightened around his waist, and a lump formed in his throat.

He had no idea what the hell she was talking about. Half the words were so slurred as to be unrecognizable. From somewhere deep inside her, a hurt she'd buried had come to the surface.

She cried without a sound, which made her pain more profound, more intolerable. Tears ran in an unrelenting stream down her temples into her hair. He'd take the tears she'd shed when she was uncontrollably furious over this silent outpouring of grief.

He held her until she'd tumbled into exhausted unconsciousness.

Her defenses were down, inhibitions temporarily gone. He considered waking her just enough to find out what the hell tormented her.

Smoothing her damp hair away from her face, Kyle watched her in the half dark. He couldn't delay his return without causing speculation.

He rose, careful not to jar her, and stripped her pants and shirt off her lax body. In this heat they'd be dry by tomorrow. Placing two fingers beneath her ear, he checked her pulse again.

She'd be fine. Feel like crap, but fine.

His eyes raked her face; he had no choice but to leave her
here.

Alone.

With tears on her face.

Groggy and disorientated, Delanie opened her eyes to candlelight. Not romantic by any stretch of the imagination, although the white vanilla-scented candle was in an ornate
silver candelabra. Bless you, Kyle!

She closed her eyes again, trying to ignore the massive
ache in her chest. Everything about the day was a blur. She'd
slipped the pill he'd given her under her tongue just before
she'd walked into the dining room. He hadn't been sure how
long it would take to act. She could tell him. A minute or
less. She'd actually felt the capsule dissolve at the same time
it leeched the strength from her muscles and bones and made
the rhythm of her heart falter in her chest.

She remembered almost falling to her knees. Too soon.
Holding onto a chair back. Kyle. And his eyes.

One thing she would never forget as long as she lived was
the look in his ice-floe-green eyes when he'd pulled that trigger.

There had been no hesitation. No emotion. No remorse.

And she'd thought, in the split second before he'd fired,
that he *could* kill her after all. *After* she'd mindlessly, and
conveniently, accepted and taken a drug he'd given her.

Lord but this heat was making her stupid, she thought,
swinging her legs cautiously over the side of the bed. It hurt
to draw in a deep breath because of her bruised ribs.

She snagged her purse off the bedside table and removed
the change of clothes she'd brought with her. Dizzy, she held
onto the wall as she dragged on khaki-colored cotton slacks
and a fresh, long-sleeved dark green T-shirt. The blood-
soaked white one she stuffed to the bottom of her bag.

She felt like hell. Sore and stiff. But grateful.

And thirsty.

She dug in the purse for the orange she'd tossed in at the

last minute. Finding a paring knife on the table—she hated pith under her nails, especially when she couldn't wash her hands afterward—she used the knife to peel the fruit and dropped the peel into her bag. Tossing the knife back on the table, she glanced around as she savored the sweet, tart fruit.

Pretty ritzy bomb shelter. Red satin and antiques. Trust Montero. Delanie sat on the side of the bed. What was going on up at the house? Had Kyle made her death look convincing?

Lord, she'd been awake for all of ten minutes and she was already stir-crazy. How on earth would she make it down here in the bowels of the earth for three whole days?

She emptied her purse on the bed beside her and rummaged through the odd contents. Ate two M & Ms she found at the bottom. Sipped some of the water Kyle had left for her. Poked at the candy bar—she'd eat that later—and inspected the bookmark in her book. Halfway done. That should last her a while.

She took as long as she could to finish the orange. When she was done, she used the last of the wet wipes in her purse to freshen her face and clean her hands.

Boy, she was going to be a basket case at this ra— "Oh, geez, this is all I need right now!"

A fist-size iridescent beetle scurried across the floor from beneath the bed. She lifted her feet out of the way automatically as it disappeared beneath the bedside table.

Nothing like a challenge, Delanie thought wryly.

Very careful where she put her feet, she rose, and started looking for something to catch the beetle in. There was no way on God's green earth she was staying in the tiny room with that thing. "One of us has gotta go, bug. I choose you."

She found a crystal candy dish, empty of course, with a lid, and took it back to the bed with her. Sitting cross-legged, she replaced everything, except the paperback, in her purse. The thing weighed three tons.

She waited out the bug, but it was happy under the table. At least for now.

She decided she'd read two chapters, try again to catch her roommate, then take a little nap. Stretching it out that way she could probably manage to make the book last at least until sometime tomorrow. Maybe.

Without thinking she dropped the purse on the floor beside the bed so she could stretch out.

The smell was immediate and overpowering, causing her eyes to water profusely. "Shit!" She'd smashed the damn beetle with her gargantuan purse!

Hand over her nose, she leapt off the bed and cautiously lifted the bag. Yep. Dead bug.

"Oh, man. This is not a good thing." She coughed as tears ran down her face.

Think. Think. The bug carcass had to go and the bomb shelter had to be aired out.

Grabbing the satin pillow sham, Delanie went up the steep and narrow stairs. She'd clean the bug guts off the canvas, wash it as best she could with a little of her water, and leave the door open for as long as she dared to air the place out. How long could that take? An hour?

It would have to do. She couldn't stay out there indefinitely, and she couldn't stay inside with the pungent and overpowering smell.

A small penlight retrieved from her stinky purse helped her climb the stairs. The heavy door opened with surprising ease, letting in murky predawn light, and the welcome fragrance of loamy earth and wet soil. Racing outside, she dropped her hand from her face and took several deep, cleansing breaths.

The door slammed shut behind her with a dull thunk.

She took her time cleaning off her bag, using the red satin pillow sham dipped in a bit of the water and dirt as an abrasive, and a bit of mouthwash to dilute the smell. It still stunk to high heaven, but it was the best she could do.

It didn't take Delanie long to figure out that she couldn't get the door open again. Not without a key.

Kyle would be back to check on her. When he could. *If* he could.

In the meantime she was outside and unprotected. She looked around. Now what the hell was she going to do?

Find Lauren, a little voice urged. She was for all intents and purposes dead. Invisible, if she kept her wits about her.

Not a good idea. She had no idea how far away the compound might be. Or how close. For all she knew she was in spitting distance from where the action would take place on Saturday.

Three days, though . . .

. . . but what if Kyle returned to find her gone?

It was unlikely, Delanie decided. Kyle had enough on his plate in the next few days. He knew she was resourceful and could take care of herself.

If she kept her wits about her, and the fence of the compound in visual range, she could check the buildings she hadn't checked before, without getting lost. She'd come back here in the early evenings before it got dark and use the wall of the small structure as protection against the elements and the critters.

It didn't sound particularly smart to leave, she admitted. But she wasn't going to stand here all day with nothing to do, and nowhere to be. At least she could do *something* constructive.

And when she found Lauren they could both return here to wait for Kyle.

Making sure the foliage around the entrance appeared undisturbed, she slipped into a wall of green, going a little deeper into the jungle before veering off when she saw a glimpse of the fence glinting in the thin stream of yellow from her flashlight.

Now all she had to do was keep parallel to the fence, and she wouldn't get lost. Senses alert, her eyes adjusted to the dimness. Even this early, the jungle was alive with the raucous sounds of life. But it didn't appear as if anyone in the compound had stirred. Yet.

The fecund smell of rotting undergrowth blended with the sharp scent of climbing orchids and rich black topsoil. The oppressive wet heat seemed alive as her clothing immediately clung to her skin. Pushing aside a fern frond, she paused a second to get her bearings. The enervating heat sapped her energy as she wiped dripping perspiration off her neck and throat. She hadn't even been out an hour, was only a quarter way round the compound, and was already wilting.

She pushed farther. Walked faster. Prayed harder.

And decided she'd make only one circuit before heading back to the dubious protection of Montero's little bomb shelter. Daylight came slowly. The texture of the light changed, easing from olive-black to blue-green, then emerald and citrine. Delanie'd had enough of green, hot, and wet to last a lifetime.

Pushing aside a sawtooth leaf twice as tall as she was, she forged ahead. It wouldn't be hard at all to get turned around and end up miles from civilization with no way out. And although she had never been afraid of dying, she would prefer it to be *quick*.

She had to make sure her death didn't become a reality. Yesterday had been a near thing. She had no intention of getting caught now. There were several more unexplored buildings yet to go. The sky was lightening, giving her more chance of detection. She passed around the back of three small buildings she'd checked the other day. The fourth, fifth, and sixth were no more than tiny metal storage sheds. There were no windows in the corrugated iron walls, and the heat would be asphyxiating. If anyone were hidden in any of them, they'd be dead by now. A quick reconnoiter revealed none of the sheds were locked. She checked inside just to be sure.

Dark and odoriferous, the first held fertilizer and insecticides. The second, tools. She flashed her penlight into the third only to see shelves of paints and folded drop cloths. Nobody and nothing hiding inside. She turned off the flashlight as she exited, peeling herself away from the incinerating heat of the prefab. The sky between the trees was now a pale milky blue.

What was Kyle doing right now? Probably sipping an icy cold drink in the shade by the pool, or he might still be asleep.

She slipped behind the low building she'd just checked.

And backed right into someone's arms.

Not missing a beat, she used a quick backward jab with her elbow and was gratified by her assailant's sharp, surprised hiss. His arms tightened. One around her waist, the other hard around her throat. A knife gleamed. She felt the muscles in his arms bunch as he dragged her, kicking and struggling, back into the jungle. She dared not make a sound.

Between their bodies she could feel her useless gun. Her nails dug into his forearm trying to loosen it from around her neck.

"Stay still, you little hellcat." Delanie's foot, ready to deliver a kick, dropped to the ground. She swiveled her head in the hammerlock and glared up.

Kyle.

He'd tied a rolled-up white handkerchief around his forehead to keep the sweat out of his eyes, and his braid hung over one muscular shoulder. His only concession to the jungle was combat boots, which he wore with navy slacks and a pink golf shirt. Half civilized gentleman, half predator.

And totally pissed off.

He let her go abruptly and she staggered. "All you had to do was say hi." She regained her balance on the spongy ground and rubbed her throat.

"Hi? Shit, you might say I'm just a little irritated you didn't stay put." His voice was dangerously soft. He was furious. She noticed the scratches she'd made on his arm. "Damn it, Delanie. What the hell are you doing out here alone? I told you to—"

Stupid is as stupid does, Delanie thought, not blaming him a bit. And because she was guilty of doing just what he accused, no matter *how* good the reason, she snapped back. "Nobody tells me what to do, Wright. I'm a big girl. For your information, the do—" *Locked behind me.*

"You're a *stupid* girl if you think—"

That did it. "I'm not a *girl*. I'm a *woman*. A woman who doesn't need a man to tell her what the hell to do. Got it?" She spun on her boot heel and marched deeper between the trees. Not going anywhere but away.

He grabbed her elbow. It didn't hurt, but it effectively stopped her. "You're hurting me," she said coldly.

"No, I'm not. But I *could*. You seem to forget little details like that."

She shook off his hand and stepped out of his way. "I don't forget *anything,* Tarzan. Not anything." Her temper shot from cranky to downright furious. Hot and tired, sweaty and dying of thirst, she was just spoiling for a fight. And her Maalox had been left at the house. Her stomach and her temper were both flaming.

Grinding her teeth, she glared at him.

He glared back.

"The plan, since you've had a brain fart, was for you to stay put while I search for your sister." He returned the knife he was carrying to the ankle sheath. "Wasn't that what you agreed to last night when we discussed this?"

"As I recall, you *told* me what was going to happen. I *listened.* And I *was* doing the sensible thing, except I smashed—are you even listening to me?"

Obviously not.

"I'm here to do a job, and I plan on doing it alone. If your sister's here, I'll find her. No help. No assistance, no questions. *Capisce?*"

"Fine. Do you have the k—"

"You could get hurt, damn it! Now go back to the shelter. I have to get back to the house before anyone misses me."

Delanie rubbed an itchy welt on the side of her neck. "Let me know when you're done ranting so I can get a word in edgew—"

"You don't even want to know what these animals will do to you if they find you alive." He was on a roll. "You saw what Montero did to the pool kid. What do you think he'd do to you, for God's sake?" His eyes narrowed; he was almost gnashing his teeth. "Why the hell do you think I saved your ass in the first place, Delanie?"

"So I could show you just how ungrateful I am and shoot you?" Her hand balled at her side so she wouldn't take a swing at him. "I'm not exactly running naked into the compound waving my arms to attract attention," she pointed out. "I'm trying to tell you—"

To hell with it. He wasn't listening. Delanie grabbed the front of his shirt, stood on tiptoe, and kissed him.

It was supposed to be a shut-up-and-listen kiss. Quick. Dry. Over in two seconds.

But then, this was Kyle. The kiss wasn't quick, nor dry, nor was it over in two seconds.

When he finally lifted his head, Delanie's hand was still fisted tightly on his pink shirtfront.

His eyes glinted. "You know what we're going to have to do, don't you."

"What?"

"Duke it out or make love." His teeth shone white in his darkly tanned face. "Either way, jungle girl, it had better be hard and fast. And now."

Delanie glanced at the ground, literally moving with vegetation and insects, and then back at his face. "I don't like it hard and fast," she lied coolly.

"Yeah you do." His hand on her belt loop tugged her closer. The placket on his trousers brushed against her, sending an electrical shock shimmering over her skin. He smelled of clean sweat and chlorine from the pool. His mouth looked grim, his eyes hot. She looked up at him, just daring him to push his luck.

His hand shot out to cup her through two thin layers of cotton. He rubbed erotically against her mound. She backed away. He followed.

"You know doing this here. Now. Is insane, don't you?"

"Yeah." She grabbed his wrist. "Don't start something you won't be able to finish." She walked backward to elude him.

"I'll never be finished with you." His voice was a seductive purr as he stalked her.

"Yeah, right."

"What the hell is it with you?" he demanded as he caught her hips and pulled her against the hard length of his body, looking down into her face with eyes blazing. The muscles in his chest felt like rock against her breasts. Her body burned. "Well?"

"Go to hell."

His mouth crushed down on hers, effectively shutting her up. For the moment. His tongue swept inside her mouth and she reciprocated, spearing him fiercely, not letting him win. He tasted of breakfast coffee. Hot, dark, and rich. Son of a bitch.

Without letting her up for air, he dragged her T-shirt off her, breaking the lip-lock for only a second. His shirt felt rough on her naked skin as he pulled her against him.

Wedging a hand between their bodies, she snapped open the top button of his slacks, revealing an arrow of dark silky hair. "This is insane . . . someone will come . . ."

"Both of us, I hope." He dragged her pants down to sag around her knees. Delanie heard the thunk as her gun dropped to the mossy ground beside her shirt. She staggered, and he hauled her against him again to kiss her senseless.

She came up for air, breath ragged, her struggle with his zipper made impossible by the hard bar of his arousal behind it. His damp breath scorched her swollen mouth.

She bit his lip, then said fiercely against his mouth, "You are *not* taking me on the ground."

"Okay."

He swung her against a tree trunk instead.

Chapter Fourteen

Kyle had almost knocked the breath out of her. Frustration made her impatient, but Delanie finally managed to tug his zipper down, sliding her hand into the wedge to find his shaft silken smooth, hard, and pulsing. Her fingers tightened. He kissed her savagely, his teeth raking across her lower lip before he plunged his tongue into her mouth.

He inserted his knee between her bare thighs. His skin was hot and erotic, sliding against her softness as he wedged his foot into the sling of fabric, hobbling her, and stepped on her pants. She had to let go as he lifted her up and out of them, leaving her wearing nothing but her boots and a scowl.

She managed to drag his trousers to his knees, then held a cheek in each hand, digging her short nails into his lean, bare flanks. He took a deep, shuddering breath and she knew he was inhaling the scent of her arousal, which excited her even more.

He lifted her higher and pressed her spine against the hard bark of the tree. Leaves showered down on their heads. Her empty hands now found purchase on his shoulders. Delanie felt the flex and play of his muscles beneath his shirt, smelled the sharp aromatic odor of vegetation and sweat on his skin.

She wrapped her legs around his waist, her fingers stroking across the front of his shirt before she ripped it open. Buttons popped. Cloth ripped. She found the rough mat of hair on his chest and leaned forward to bite him just above his nipple. With a feeling of triumph she felt his growl vibrate through his chest. She bit again.

He grabbed her by her hair, pulling her head back, and like a vampire sucked at her neck until she squirmed against him. Her blood turned to molten lava.

His teeth climbed her throat, taking stinging little nips on the way to her mouth.

Delanie ran her fingers down the dark silk of his braid, then wound it around her hand, holding his head still in a fisted grip. His green eyes, mere inches away, blazed into hers.

She slowly licked a drop of perspiration from his upper lip.

His fingers tightened in her hair.

She arched her spine, away from the unyielding tree, hard against an unyielding Kyle Wright. Between a tree and a deliciously hard place.

The heat they generated made a hazy mirage over them, sweat glistened on Kyle's tanned skin, his hair curled around her fingers like liquid embroidery silk. He bit her bottom lip, hard enough for her to gasp, and then laved it with succulent swipes of his tongue until she felt a throbbing pulse deep inside her.

She wrapped her arms around his neck, seeking his mouth with lips and tongue, delirious for the taste and touch of him. Beneath her fingers the muscles in his back rippled as he settled her higher against their bumpy, vertical bed.

He kissed her with a voracious hunger, tasting and insisting she reciprocate. He was heavy against her. She whimpered with impatience as his erection rubbed erotically against the open heart of her.

"Ever done it against a tree?"

"No." She could hardly get the word out. "And if anything bites me anywhere private I expect you to kiss it better."

"If anything bites you anywhere private it's going to be me." He crowded her against the broad tree trunk, his chest pressing against her sensitized breasts. Using both thumbs he outlined her mouth, staring into her eyes, before crushing her lips with his. His tongue swept inside, ravishing her mouth, sending a darting, intense pleasure to the juncture of her thighs.

"Damn you," she cursed when he let her up for air, then she pulled his mouth back down to hers. Bark scraped her soft skin. She didn't even feel it. The foliage around her became a blur of vibrant spinning greens as Kyle braced her with the weight of his body.

She drank the moisture from his lips, drunk with wanting him, her blood fevered and surging as she felt his large hand cover her breast. Delanie squirmed, her nipple too sensitive, too engorged for such gentle contact. She arched her back and he plucked the hard nub between his fingers with just the right amount of force to make her shudder.

She climbed his body, her bare legs wrapped around him as he pinioned her to the tree. Her boot heels dug into his butt. She felt one large hand slide beneath her for support. His finger delved deeply, finding her hot and wet, as his mouth came down on her nipple, sucking hard. She heard the soft, feral moan deep in his throat and her pulse spiked, her breath fast and shallow.

"You said . . ." She tried to talk without panting and found she couldn't. He had big hands. But not big enough. "You . . . said . . . hard. Fast . . . and now!"

He entered her with one quick thrust, filling her completely. Her climax came instantly, before he could even begin a rhythm. Her body rigid, clenching around him, Delanie went deaf and blind. She had the sensation of being shot like a rocket into space.

"Jesus. Not *that* fast," he managed to complain dryly, his chest heaving before he drove into her with a pounding intensity that stole her breath. She bucked and held on, whimpering as he drove into her.

She wasn't done with one climax when she was suddenly catapulted into the next. The orgasm seemed to last forever as Kyle moved against her, bringing with him smaller aftershocks until Delanie couldn't tell one from the other.

She responded in a delirium of need. The powerful weight of his large body hammered against hers as if he would drive her through the tree and out the other side. She couldn't think, she couldn't reason, only feel. She responded like a wild thing.

Bathed in sweat, bodies glued together in a primal mating in this primal place, they shut out everything but their own unquenchable desire.

An affirmation of life.

Kyle came hard, his breath ragged against her ear. Hers was nothing more than thready moans against the dampness of his neck.

Delanie wanted to consume him. Her breath sawed as she labored to drag great gulps of wet air into her tortured lungs.

A parrot screeched high in the treetops.

She jerked out of her sensual trance and became aware of tree bark scoring her backside and something unpleasant crawling across her shoulder. Sweat stung her eyes.

Kyle kept her pinned to the tree with his hips, flicked the bug off her shoulder with his finger, then reached up over her head to a fork in the tree.

"What . . . She blinked her eyes back into focus. "Your gun? In the heat of the moment you remembered to put your damn weapon within easy reach?"

"We're not in a zoo, for Christsake. We're in a rain forest. There are all sorts of—"

"Thanks for reminding me." She could still feel him inside her. "Will you please let me go?" Delanie disengaged her legs as he carefully lowered her to the ground.

Naked except for her boots, she became painfully aware of the subliminal buzz of the insect population in counterpoint to the painful thudding of her heart. Swatting a big black winged thing that landed on her hip, she picked up her shirt, and shook it briskly before putting it on. Only then did she bend down to grab her pants from the mossy ground.

"Now that's a pretty picture." Kyle drawled, cupping her baby-bare behind. He handed her the scrap of black cotton he'd snagged from a spray of fire-red orchids several yards away.

"I can imagine." Delanie dusted off her behind, shook out

anything unwelcome from her underwear, then pulled them on.

"Trust me. I've never seen anything sexier in my life." Kyle cupped her hot, sweaty cheek and dropped a quick, fierce kiss on her swollen mouth. With a fingertip he wiped away the sweat from the corner of her eye. "Are you okay now?"

"Now?" Delanie did up the top button on her pants before sticking the Colt into her waistband. She glared up at him and repeated. "Now? What does that mean?"

"You were hyper and stressed out." He shrugged. "Are you—"

Delanie took a menacing step toward him. "You had sex with me for my . . . nerves?"

"Isn't that like asking the man if he's stopped beating his wife? Hey! Wait a sec, where're you going?"

Delanie turned and looked at him over her shoulder. "Is your hearing aid turned up?"

"Huh?"

"I was trying to tell you something important but you kept rudely interrupting. I was outside, and the door to the shelter locked behind me. I can't get back in."

"Shit. I'm sorry. Here." He dug in his back pocket. "Take the key. Can you find your way back? I'm meeting the stooges at the lab five minutes ago."

"I'll be fine. It's not far." Delanie stood on tiptoe to brush a kiss on his mouth. "Watch your back, okay?"

Kyle grabbed her about the waist before she could step away. "I have plans for this bod. Keep it nice and neat and all in one piece for me, jungle girl. Don't loiter. I'll try and come tonight after everyone's gone to bed."

"If you come I guarantee you'll come." She smiled to cover her concern. "Be careful, Tarzan."

He dropped a quick kiss on her mouth. "Go."

Walking until she couldn't hear him or see him, Delanie paused briefly to readjust her clothing and do a quick check of her gun for debris before heading back to the shelter.

When she took a sip from her canteen it was only to find

he'd exchanged her almost empty one with his, which was full.

Like the sound track from a jungle B movie, the rain forest's musical score kept her company as she pushed her way through the undergrowth.

It took several moments for her to sort the distinctly human sound from those of the jungle. She was dumber than a stump. Hadn't she learned her lesson yet? She fumbled for her gun, stepping behind a tree just as a man in camouflage moved within yards of her. He stopped, rested his Uzi against a tree, and lit a pungent cigarette.

The element of surprise might be on her side, but she had no intention of alerting him to her presence. When he was done with his cigarette he'd move off, and she'd be on her way. She inhaled a stray whiff of secondhand smoke and relaxed her muscles to wait him out.

A sharp sting on her ankle caused her glance down.

Oh damn. The ants must have heard a dinner bell.

They marched in a slow column up her left boot. Carefully, centimeter by excruciating centimeter, Delanie removed her foot from their mound. With a fatalistic sensation she felt the canteen slip from its hook at her waist and fall with a soft thud to the mossy ground. She held her breath as it rolled several feet, paused as if in indecision, then rolled again, hitting the soldier's Uzi with a small, metallic click.

The man's head jerked up at the out-of-place sound. He moved for his weapon. Before he could snag it, she stepped in front of him, balancing on the balls of her feet, keeping eye contact, as she'd been taught to do in the self-defense class she'd dragged Lauren to.

Given Lauren's lifestyle, Delanie had decided her sister would likely need the knowledge. She'd never imagined *she'd* need it, too.

The guy had been one of the soldiers assigned to guard her at the swimming pool, and he was sure surprised to see her.

"Madre de Diós!" His eyes bugged as he crossed himself. "But you are dead!"

"Reports of my death were greatly exaggerated." She used the Colt to wave him away from his weapon, keeping herself loose as they circled each other.

In some vague distant part of her brain she saw herself standing, legs braced, a gun in her hand in the middle of a South American jungle. She didn't recognize this person she'd become.

His surprise changed to challenge. "*¿Qué quieres?* Shoot me, *puta gringa.*" He dared her, his feet kicking up leaves as he moved slowly around her. "In minutes *mis compañeros* will come. They will take you to *El Patrón,* and he will kill you himself this time."

"You'll be dead, and I'll be long gone, pal." Brave words from a woman who was about to wet her pants with sheer fright. She didn't dare risk the sound of a shot, and that was if she could manage to figure out how the hell the gun worked in the first place!

She was still between the soldier and his weapon. Keeping an eagle eye on him, she leaned down and picked up the Uzi by the barrel. With an underhanded throw, she tossed it into the brush.

He swore virulently and pulled a knife, the blade about ten inches long and wickedly sharp. Heart firmly in her throat, legs braced, Delanie pointed the business end of the little gun at him. "Don't even blink!"

He rushed her, easily knocking the weapon from her hand. Her fingers stung. She jerked her knee up into his groin and he screamed and buckled over clutching his balls.

This would be a great time to run like hell, Delanie decided. She frantically did a visual search for her gun, then gave up. She wasn't hanging around for this guy to quit groaning.

She started to race into the trees, then stopped short. Holy Hannah. If the soldier went back to the hacienda, which he would, he'd tell everyone she was alive. And when he did, Kyle's cover would be broken.

Think. Think.
Go back?
Run like hell . . . ?

The soldier made the decision for her.

He came up behind her, grabbing her by the back of her shirt, dragging her to where the undergrowth had been flattened earlier by their feet.

Delanie flailed around in his hold, not getting her feet under her enough to steady herself.

Trying not to think about the knife in his hand, Delanie twisted violently out of his hold and backed up.

Hands loosely at her sides, she allowed the circle to tighten. He came closer and closer until she could smell sweat and cigarette breath. Calling out Spanish insults, he jabbed the knife in the air, close to her face, playing with her.

Her persona as the ditzy blond was standing her in good stead. He felt confident enough to come up close and personal.

An adrenaline rush, so powerful it pounded through her veins, made all her neurons jump to life.

"Come on, you ugly bastard," she taunted, dancing just out of his reach. She was the dog barking at a car. She had no idea what the hell she'd do if he *did* rush her.

He moved like lightning, coming at her like a bull at a red cape. Without thinking, Delanie used his momentum and applied her left fist to the man's jaw.

Ow. Ow. *OW!* Her hand stung.

He staggered backward, then came at her again, the knife flashing.

She did a *grand battement,* a ballet step she'd done a zillion times, only this time, instead of controlling the kick, she threw her leg high and hard. She kicked with power, the full weight of her body behind it. Her foot caught him square in the stomach. He grabbed her ankle as he fell, bringing the two of them to the loamy earth, jarring her shoulder.

She continued kicking and punching.

He swore in guttural Spanish as he forced her onto her back. His fist against her already bruised solar plexus vibrated through her body, driving all the air out of her lungs. He dug a knee into her already bruised diaphragm. Black swirls blurred her vision as she felt her arm being wrenched out of the socket. He dragged her roughly to her feet. Her head hung to her chest while she forced back the panic of not being capable of drawing in air.

After a few seconds of agony, air leaked slowly into her billowing lungs. His grip loosened slightly as she wheezed, her head down, hands on her knees. He grabbed a handful of her hair.

She executed a *tour jeté,* leaping in the air, scissoring her legs as she spun, both legs parallel to the ground. Her boot hit the man squarely on the jaw. His eyes widened, rolled, and he fell to the ground.

She kept a careful eye on his inert body as she dragged thick, wet air into her laboring lungs. Sweat poured off her in rivulets, stinging her eyes and attracting every damn flying insect in South America. Her breath sawed, the muscles in her calves and thighs ached, her hand throbbed.

But she was standing.

She'd won.

This round.

Sort of.

Now she had to do something with him to keep him quiet. She lacked the stomach to kill him, which would have been the safest, most efficient way to silence him.

She tucked the soldier's knife in the top of her boot, then dragged his dead weight deeper into a thicket of dense underbrush. It was heavy going, the guy weighed a ton. As soon as she figured he was far enough off the beaten path, Delanie let go of him and went back to where she'd dropped her tote and pulled her roll of silver electrical tape from the depth of her purse. Some women couldn't live without their glue guns. She carried the tape with her everywhere. Quicker, and more easily accessible than rope, it had been used for everything from auto repair to getting lint off a sweater. But she'd never used it to tie up a man she'd knocked unconscious with a ballet kick!

With shaking hands she clumsily strapped his feet, then his wrists, together. A couple of inches across his mouth should keep him quiet for a while.

The adrenaline was subsiding in a dizzying rush. Sick to her stomach, she couldn't believe what she'd just done.

Tree trunks, foliage, and shafts of sunlight oscillated in a dizzying blur as she ran back to the shelter, moving as quickly as she could, pushing aside foliage and jumping over downed branches and low vegetation.

The sudden, blinding pain on the back of her head was intense and absolutely unexpected.

Her last thought was annoyance. Then everything went black.

Chapter Fifteen

•

Because of the flood of calls expected at one o'clock, lunch was served early. Kyle opted for a swim instead of food. He needed to expend some of the taut anticipatory energy filling him before he sat for long hours.

The culmination of four years' hard work was about to come to fruition. Every sense needed to be sharp, clear. Defined. No more thinking about a certain brown-eyed nymph. She was safely tucked into Montero's bomb shelter and smart enough to stay there until he came for her.

The hundred laps had taken the edge off, and he arrived at the appointed time, alert and ready for anything.

A long room at the back of the house had been set up as formally as a board room. Montero, white linen Armani suit immaculate, sat at the head of the koa wood conference table, his manicured hands folded. An ashtray, a pad, and several pencils neatly lined up in front of five red telephones with the lights of their multiple lines blinking like Christmas trees.

Behind Montero stood the ever-present Bruno, arms akimbo, expression blank. He was a nice touch.

The other members of the elite cartel were seated, the silence palpable. No one liked or trusted anyone at the table enough for small talk. Nevertheless, excitement and anticipation manifested themselves as tangibly as another presence. The room was already filled with cigar smoke. Sunlight streamed across the table, bouncing rather significantly, Kyle thought, off the diamonds in their pinkie rings.

"Come, *amigo,* we wait only for you." Montero waved Kyle over to the empty chair on his right.

The seat allowed Kyle the French doors at his back. Not that he needed a hasty escape route today. But it was good to have the option, he thought dryly, pulling out the cowhide chair and slouching in his seat. Everyone else came to attention as Montero brought the meeting to order.

"We have twenty-five calls on hold." Montero smiled and glanced back at Bruno. "Take them in the order in which they were received. We will call them back within the hour."

Bruno moved off, surprisingly light on his feet, and settled at a desk across the room. He picked up the first phone and spoke into it quietly.

The buttons on Sugano's Hawaiian shirt strained over his corpulent chest and belly as he leaned forward. Next to him, Kensington seesawed a pencil between his fingers in an unconsciously nervous gesture. Out of the corner of his eye, Kyle saw Danzigger's pale chalky hands, clasped together on the tabletop.

Kyle leaned back, seemingly relaxed. He'd felt a nagging buzz since breakfast. Nothing he could put a finger on, yet here, in this room, the buzz had gotten louder. He never ignored his instincts. He examined Ramón from under half-closed lids. The man's attitude was natural and calm. Whatever was going to happen, Montero didn't know about it.

Yet.

Kyle was prepared for anything, and as usual had worn his gun in a shoulder holster over his T-shirt in full view.

"Gentlemen." Montero smiled. "Our hard work and diligence is about to pay off." He picked up a pile of file folders and passed them down the table. "As you will see, each and every one of our deadlines has been met. Thanks to Kyle, Palacios's death will be announced later today. Velasquez is ready to take over the presidency. We now await the acceptance of our first offer for our poxvirus. Kyle goes into production on Monday morning." He shot his cuff, then glanced at Bruno. As soon as he dealt with each call, a new light started blinking. Biological warfare was big business these days.

Kyle knew all the calls were being traced and monitored by international intelligence operatives temporarily based in San Cristóbal.

Montero and those present were the last pieces of the puzzle to be gathered before The End could be written.

Paper rustled as each man opened files and scanned the contents. Surreptitious glances at Bruno betrayed the players' interest in the almost silent bidding war going on across the room.

Montero closed the open file folder in front of him. Folding his hands he surveyed the others. "We have done well, gentlemen. And we shall do even better when we own worldwide distribution of both the virus and vaccine."

"What about that little problem we had in Canada?" Sugano asked.

"You will find the resolution documented on page nineteen." Montero made a chopping gesture with his hand, his smile white and all encompassing. "Now then gentlemen, we await only the last-minute reports, and the final outcome of—" The only black phone in front of him rang, cutting him off.

Montero picked up the receiver at the same time as the fax machine behind him spat out a message. He snagged it out of the machine, reading it as he listened to the voice on the phone, plucking at his eyebrow.

Kyle shifted slightly in his chair. He couldn't identify the caller, nor could he hear what was being said. Montero's expression was unreadable. All Kyle knew was that it was *not* one of the lieutenants they'd been expecting to hear from this afternoon.

Montero snapped the receiver back onto the cradle, the sound sharp and precise in the now dead silence of the room. Every eye focused on the man whose smile had slipped from his face like shit off glass.

"Troubling news, gentlemen." He rose from his chair, balancing his weight on palms flattened on the tabletop. He scanned the men seated on either side of him briefly, before black eyes rested on his right-hand man.

Kyle kept his relaxed posture, meeting Montero's glance with a measured look of his own.

And he knew, right then, four fucking years had just gone up in smoke.

Delanie stifled a moan of pain and opened her eyes. It took a moment to focus. Ropes tied with cruel disregard for tender skin secured her wrists behind the chair in which she sat. The strain on the muscles and tendons of her shoulders and her numb hands indicated she'd been this way for some time.

How odd. Her hair was wet and dripped coldly down the back of her neck. And she wasn't wearing her own clothes, just a thin cotton muumuu. She felt a clutch of panic. Oh God, she should've been more damn careful. Should've run faster, should've—

Had she blown Kyle's cover? Did they have him here, too—wherever *here* was—or was he already dead? Heart like lead, she choked on guilt and sorrow.

Then she thought: Captured? Dead? Kyle? Never. He was too tough, too mean, too smart to be caught.

Without moving her head, Delanie glanced through slitted eyes, trying to orient herself. Dim and cool, luxuriously furnished with crystal lamps, jewel-toned velvet sofas, and plush area rugs, the large windowless room was unfamiliar. Out of the corner of her eye she could just see an elaborate stereo system and a high, sheet-draped massage table at the far end of the room in front of a wall-size mirror. The sybaritic room exuded malevolence.

Every hair follicle prickled at the *tap-tap-tap* of heels on the marble floor as someone paced impatiently back and forth behind her. Wherever she was, whatever was about to happen, Delanie knew she wasn't going to like it. Goose bumps rose on her skin and her tongue stuck to the roof of her dry mouth. The location might be unfamiliar, but the perfume in the air was unmistakable.

Wearing skintight leather pants and a matching sleeveless vest Isabella came into her line of sight. She turned on the state-of-the-art CD unit against the far wall, but the soft swell of Brahms did nothing to calm the flight signals humming along Delanie's nerve endings.

Isabella turned and contemplated her prisoner speculatively as she strolled closer and drew up a small, gilt chair and sat down. She lit a cigarette. "I am very disappointed in you, *chica*." Blowing out a thin stream of acrid smoke, she snapped the flat, platinum cigarette case closed and slid it onto a nearby table.

"I can't tell you how that breaks my heart," Delanie answered dryly. "Mind telling me whose dress I'm wearing?" The blue cotton was thin and voluminous, leaving her arms and legs bare. "And while you're at it, why's my hair wet?"

"We were required to bathe you, *mija*." Isabella tilted her head, hair blue-black under the lights. "You smelled of sweat and sex when you were brought to me. And although I am not usually offended by such aromas, in this instance I prefer cleanliness."

Delanie's goose bumps got goose bumps. "Who's *we*?"

"Two guards and myself. You have nothing to be ashamed of, *bonita,* you have a lovely body."

All five-foot-seven inches of Delanie's "lovely body" quivered in outrage. "How dare—" Delanie's brief spurt of indignation morphed into trepidation as water drizzled down the back of her neck. She wasn't sure just what this woman had in mind, but she was damned sure she loathed the idea of Isabella and two guards bathing her.

"I was *quite* annoyed when the doctor shot you."

"Can't say I was crazy about it mys—"

"Tell me," Isabella swept on. "Which are you? An ignorant *puta?* Or a wily agent?

"Oh, *definitely* the wily agent." Delanie tried to wriggle her fingers without wincing. God, that hurt. "An agent the United States government isn't going to let disappear off the face of the earth. They'll want to know where I am when I don't check in." *I wish.*

"Which agency?"

"All I'm required to give you is name, rank, and serial number."

Isabella shrugged. "It makes no difference. If this is true, your superiors will be led to believe you became a victim of the jungle. They will shake their heads and express concern about ever using a woman agent again."

"You're all heart."

Isabella crossed her legs, leaning forward in a cloud of Chanel and cigarette smoke, showing too much cleavage. Chocolate-brown leather creaked as she moved. "Exactly how much of my son's operation have you divulged to your superiors?"

"Everything," Delanie lied flatly, wishing like hell it were true. "Everything I know, they know."

"You lie, *mija.*" The slap came out of nowhere, quick, sharp, and impatient. Delanie's head jerked back. "You know nothing." Isabella watched her through a veil of smoke. "You are no agent. *Dr. Wright* is the agent. *Qué no?*"

Cheek stinging like fire, left eye watering, Delanie clenched her teeth. "Don't be ridiculous. He and Ramón are partners."

Isabella stubbed the cigarette out on the marble floor beneath a high-heeled boot. "Don't play games with me, *chica.* Your being alive is proof enough of his perfidy."

A chill of foreboding raced up Delanie's spine. *Kyle.* Don't think about it now, she warned herself fiercely. She had to stay focused in the here and now.

"Where is the doctor?" Isabella snapped.

"I have absolutely no id—" Delanie flinched, a knee-jerk reaction as Isabella's hand shot up. She tried to disguise the shrinking of her body as the other woman backhanded her. This blow was considerably more forceful than the slap. Tears of pain lined her lower lids; lifting her face she blinked them back.

I'm not scared, she told herself, mouth dry, heart in her

throat. The ropes binding her to the chair bit into her chest and hips. She was afraid her fear had a smell to it that would provoke another attack.

I am not scared. I am not scared—

—Oh God. Of course, *I am. I'm terrified!* "That's the last time you hit me. Don't do it again."

"Oh, I do like the show of spirit, my dear." Isabella's black-cherry eyes glowed. "Such zest is always welcome. This will manifest itself so creatively later." She reached out to stroke her prisoner's cheek. Cold fingers lingered against the heat of the slap marks.

Delanie twisted her head away, flesh crawling, spine pressed hard against the slatted back of the chair.

Isabella's thin, red-painted lips lifted in a mocking smile. The heavy chain around her neck glinted, outlining the deep V of the leather vest. Delanie's attention was suddenly captured by the lights flickering on the strangely barbaric gold necklace Isabella always wore.

A necklace that wasn't an arum lily at all.

The necklace depicted the head of a cobra, fangs bared.

The same cobra Montero and his partners wore as rings.

"You're part of your son's operation, aren't you?"

Isabella gave a dry, sophisticated laugh. "While the family business of terrorism and the drug trade are lucrative, that is man's work. I have my own vocation to amuse me, *bonita.*"

"Look, I really don't care, okay? Tell me what you want from me and let's get this over with."

Isabella sighed and stroked Delanie's cheek with cool dry fingers. She flinched and Isabella gave her a silky smile. "You are a very pretty girl, *chica.* I'm going to enjoy breaking you."

Delanie wanted to puke. Literally.

Isabella smoothed her hand up Delanie's arm. Slowly. "You will come to be grateful for my many years of experience. I'm in the prime of my life, *bonita.*"

"*Geographically* speaking," Delanie said with barbed irony, as she tried tucking her arm against her side, impossible the way she'd been tied. She felt the solidity of her back against the chair, the coarse rope around her wrists; and pressed her bare feet against the cool floor to focus on anger, instead of morbid fear.

A wash of color rose under Isabella's perfect makeup. "You would be well advised to keep that clever tongue of yours hidden until I request otherwise." Isabella leaned forward. "I only need the bindings until you are malleable. There are only two choices for you here in my house."

She gave Delanie a malevolent look. "Compliance or pain. I could show you what resistance looks like, *mija*. I recently had a girl returned to me because she proved to be unsatisfactory. It isn't pretty. Too much Impulse and you will become an addict, good for nothing except future drug testing."

Delanie's heart pounded in painful thumps. "What the hell *do* you want from me, Isabella?"

"I will train you," Isabella said huskily, eyes glowing with an unholy light. "Soon you will understand."

Delanie was already afraid she understood, but her brain needed confirmation. "Trained to do *what?*"

"Oh, didn't I mention the nature of my business? I train and sell sex slaves. A lucrative and enjoyable little hobby." Black eyes glittered. "Eventually you will be sold. A wealthy European, not squeamish, but very particular in his or her tastes, will be your new owner." She paused. "Unless your performance is so exceptional I decide to keep you for my own enjoyment. This happens on occasion. Some of my personal pets have become excellent trainers themselves. Would you like that, *bonita?*"

Bile and fear rose in Delanie's throat. She swallowed hard, and managed to keep her cool by a mere thread. "Here's a news flash, Izzie. Slavery went out with the Civil War." Her voice sounded hoarse, her heart raced, and her palms felt damp. "And in case you haven't noticed, I'm not exactly the docile type."

"By the time you have an intimate acquaintance with Impulse, you will do *anything,* with *anyone,* for the next fix. You *do* remember the delightful effects of our new product, do you not?" Isabella asked with a sly smile.

Only too well. A rush of heat swamped Delanie. "*You* gave me the drug that day by the pool."

"A little in the wine you drank." Black eyes glittered. "Unfortunately, now and then new girls refuse to cooperate. They have no idea what a life of ease and pleasure I offer them." Isabella exhaled a put-upon sigh. "Stupid little fools. Of course, our new product will now make my work so much easier and more pleasurable than other products I've used."

Lauren. Oh God. Lauren.

Isabella smiled dreamily. "My clients are particularly fond of blondes. I have an unparalleled reputation for training my girls well, and business is thriving." She ran a sharp nail up Delanie's arm, leaving a long cruel red scratch on her smooth skin. "Nobody has ever managed to elude me. No one has ever escaped."

She'd be the first, Delanie vowed. Somehow. Some way. "At least untie me, I can't feel my hands."

Ignoring the complaint, Isabella rose, crossed the room, and returned with a glass of water. "You must be thirsty."

Mouth desert dry, eyes averted from the clear refreshing liquid in the glass, Delanie found she could barely breathe. "I don't want anything from you."

Isabella smiled. "You will want *everything* from me, my dear. I will become the water you drink. The food you eat. The very air that you breathe. Come, drink."

Water trickled down her chin as Isabella forced the glass painfully against her lips. Alarm zapped through Delanie like tiny droplets of ice as she looked up into eyes that promised the depths of hell.

"*Basta!* We are wasting time." Isabella set the glass sharply onto a nearby table and yanked open a drawer. She removed what looked like a remote control, swung her chair around and sat down beside Delanie. "We will begin."

The lights went out, plunging them into pitch darkness. Brahms cut off mid beat.

The room filled with the overpowering scent of Isabella's perfume. Delanie believed she could even smell her own primordial fear mingled with the excitement of the woman sitting so close beside her. Unnerved, she stared into the impenetrable blackness.

Waiting.

Darkness and absolute silence.

"Pay attention, *chica*." Isabella's lightly accented voice broke through the thick oppression. Instantly a light flickered on the far wall to capture Delanie's attention, and an enormous concealed TV emerged from the floor. For a moment Delanie stared at the wide screen without comprehending what she was seeing— Bodies.

Naked bodies. Skin against skin.

Repelled, Delanie squeezed her eyes tightly shut. Panic slammed into her like a freight train. Oh, God.

She wanted out.

Now.

She could hardly breathe.

"Open your eyes, *querida*." Isabella laughed, and gave her arm a savage pinch. "You must watch."

"Go to hell." Isabella couldn't *force* her t—

Electricity shot in an agonizing ring about the base of Delanie's throat. Her fingers clawed the rope binding her wrists, trying to get free; the rope about her chest tightened as her body arched. It was over as suddenly as it had happened, leaving her shaken and chilled to the core.

She shot her chin up and hissed at Isabella between trembling, bloodless lips. "B-bitch."

"I told you to watch. That was just something for behavior modification." Isabella's eyes glittered in the flickering light. "Silly girl, I'm not going to hurt you. The shock lasts only a few seconds. I am quite annoyed that I had to replace your pretty necklace." A chilling pause. "Do what I tell you, or—" She repeated the demonstration.

The current zinged through the delicate membrane of Delanie's throat. It felt as if every tendon and bone in her body bowed. Bile rose in her mouth. Tears sprang to her eyes. She wanted out.

O. U. T.

Now.

Isabella took her thumb off the control.

Immediate, blessed absence of pain.

Delanie drew in a ragged breath and held it. *Don't lose it. Do not lose it,* she warned herself, knowing instinctively Isabella got off on her terror. She tilted her chin and held the woman's reptilian gaze.

"I will continue until you obey me. The discipline is for your own good, my dear," Isabella said tenderly. "Don't make me have to hurt you unnecessarily."

Delanie froze as the woman ran the back of her knuckles down her throat in a caress. "Pain can become pleasure, *chica.* Later we will explore how choking heightens the moment of sexual release."

Delanie swallowed convulsively as nausea surged, sinking into herself as Isabella resumed the tape. She went still, refusing to assimilate anything Isabella said. The only thing she could do was keep her mind blank and change her depth perception to make the screen blur.

It was impossible.

Her heartbeat threatened to choke her.

And God help her, Delanie knew this was only the beginning of the horrors Isabella had in store for her.

Chapter Sixteen

Kyle bounced a couple of times on the marble floor. The solid door closed with a final thump, and he rested his cheek against the cool tile. He listened to the triple click of the tumblers as Montero's goons locked him in, then departed.

They needed some work on their treatment of prisoners.

Montero had come unglued after the fax and phone call. Within seconds, Kyle had been out of his chair and sprinting across the brick patio, soldiers right on his ass.

His bound hands went to his throat. They'd put a necklace on him when he'd been unconscious, and the metal felt uncomfortably warm against his skin.

Brain sluggish, Kyle frowned into the pitch darkness. The rope binding his hands in front of him was neither tight nor hard to remove.

Too easy. He untied the bindings, tossed the rough hemp away, and quickly fingered the intricate lacing in his boots. They were exactly as he'd tied them this morning. Which meant he wasn't without resources.

Odds were the room was bugged. The damn necklace, almost identical to the one he'd removed from Delanie, was impossible to remove himself. So even if he managed to make it out of here he'd be fried if he crossed the sensor. And he didn't know where the sensor was. Hell.

A faint, barely there, sweet odor permeated the air.

Easing himself back, he rested his head against the slick, cold wall, his hands hanging over his bent knees, every sense alert to his environment, to any sounds outside the room. He flexed his tingling fingers.

Why hadn't Montero tortured him or killed him outright?

Hell. There *was* something worse than death. It all boiled down to one word.

Delanie.

He shifted, bracing himself on his flattened hands against the cool floor, wincing as something sharp punctured his palm. He picked up the small metal object, an earring by the feel of it, idly twisting it between his fingers before absently sticking it in the breast pocket of his shirt. One never knew what might come in handy.

Shapes materialized out of the darkness as his eyes adjusted, assisted by the trace of light from under the door. Thickheaded and lethargic, due no doubt to the blows he'd taken to the head, he rose to his feet to survey his cell.

An enormous four-poster bed took up most of the room. This was like no prison he'd ever been in. What was wrong with this picture? He swung around as someone approached him slowly from the side. He braced for combat—only to find himself confronting *himself* in a wall-size mirror.

Curiouser and curiouser.

He stood very still, alert for any sound. What he heard made him scowl, and accounted for his lethargy.

Gas.

No wonder his bindings had been so ineffectual. Carefully walking on the balls of his feet he followed the barely perceptible hiss. Using his hands and sense of smell, he searched the room. And found the tiny nozzle cleverly tucked beside the frame of a painting on the far wall.

Anesthetic?

Poison?

Nope. By his symptoms, the tingling fingertips, depressed vision, and increased hearing, Kyle deduced it was nitrous oxide. He sure as shit didn't feel like laughing. The N_2O wasn't going to kill him, just keep him sufficiently loopy to be ineffectual. Or so they obviously hoped.

With the sensitivity of a safecracker, his fingertips traced around the edge of the painting. The nozzle came directly out of the wall. No way to remove it without asphyxiating himself in the process. A turn to the right and the hiss became louder; a turn to the left reduced the sound. He'd have to be satisfied. There was no way to turn the damn thing off completely. He adjusted his breathing to accommodate his environment.

Damned if he'd turn on the bedside lamp—someone was probably on the other side of that mirror observing him. Kyle moved around the dark, well-appointed room like a caged animal. He couldn't make out color, but the textures were rich, luxurious.

A narrow table held a plastic jug. He picked it up. Water. Nothing in it as far as he could tell after he'd swigged down enough to moisten his throat. His frown intensified.

Further down the table he fingered . . . medical supplies? A small plastic bottle, cotton, bandages. Hmmm.

He paced to the door. Twenty-three steps.

First things first. He unbuckled his belt and turned the buckle into position to finesse the lock on the door, but the insidious need to sit down and relax made him want to jog to get his energy level up. Which would require more oxygen.

He stared at the belt in his hand blankly.

Door. Lock. Yeah, right.

He had to get to Delanie and make sure she was safe. Had to contact his people and—get this damn lock picked.

He forced himself to concentrate. What did Montero expect?

He expected him to make a break for it.

Kyle dropped his belt onto the table by the door. Hell. He didn't feel like running around the jungle dodging Montero's goons for hours. Especially not with this dog collar on. He might as well bide his time. If he could stay where he was until tomorrow noon, he'd be able to get out of here and head straight into the fray at the hacienda.

Yeah. He was here for the duration. Hell. Face it, he could use the rest. Delanie was safe and sound in the bomb shelter. She'd be good until tomorrow when he went to pick her up.

He started back toward the door for another lap, lungs aching with the desire for a deep cleansing breath.

When they'd caught him, the soldiers had stripped him of his more obvious weapons, but they hadn't taken everything. He had more than enough equipment on his person to be ready for almost . . .

He scowled, losing his train of thought for a moment.

—anything.

Christ. The stuff was effective.

Feeling the ache of a new bruise on his upper arm, he gripped it between his fingers and gave himself a good pinch. Hurt like hell, and lessened the fuzz around his brain.

Delanie. Tomorrow night this would be over and they could sit down and discuss—

Kyle's musings were sliced off by a high, piercing scream that froze his blood and sent his pulse into overdrive like nothing else could.

Chapter Seventeen

Delanie's shrill, agonized shriek cut off as swiftly as a hot knife through butter, then silence. Thick. Oppressive. Gut-wrenching, fill-in-the-blanks-yourself silence.

Palms sweating, mouth dry, Kyle tried not to imagine what they'd done to make her scream like that. Unfortunately, he couldn't control the images racing through his mind.

Fueled by fear and rage, feeling helpless, he started to pray. Quick disjointed promises. It'd been a while.

She was still alive. He knew it in his gut.

He also knew Ramón Montero was a sick son of a bitch, so the quality of her life was the thing.

Every sensory system on red alert, Kyle grabbed at the door handle, rattling it uselessly before slamming his shoulder against the solid wood.

Then again. *Bam.*

Please, God . . .

Again. *Bam. Bam. Bam.*

God. Please—

He pressed his forehead against the solid door beside his clenched fist.

The scream had come from close by. Possibly the room next door.

He grabbed the belt from the table and fumbled for the lock-picking device, his fingers made clumsy by the N_2O and urgency. He slid the thin metal between the door and jamb.

The tumblers clicked. *Snick. Snick. Snick.*

Resisting the urge to bust through the door, he eased the heavy wood open just a crack to see what he could see.

Satisfied, he stepped into a wide, empty corridor, inhaling deeply of the fresh air as he paused to listen.

Footsteps sounded. Two men headed this way, carrying something heavy, judging by the cadence of their gait.

Kyle slipped back into the room and shut the door, positioning himself against the wall. Timing was everything.

He relaxed into a state of ready alertness as the footfalls stopped outside.

A key scraped. Scraped again. The door flew open. A stream of light from the hallway fell across the bare floor, illuminating the room.

Kyle had eyes only for Delanie as two soldiers tossed her unceremoniously at his feet like a sack of garbage.

Before the door had closed, Kyle lifted her rag-doll limp body onto the mattress, leaning over to click on the light beside the bed. Something alien and terrifying shimmied down his spine as he looked at her stark white face.

Delanie's eyes were open.

And fixed.

Exhausted shadows highlighted the gauntness of her skin and the bruise on her left cheek. Her sightless eyes appeared black in the subdued lighting, empty.

Around her neck was a familiar gold necklace.

A primordial groan rose in his throat. "Christ, what the hell did he do to you, jungle girl?"

No response.

The knowledge that Montero had laid his filthy hands on her . . . had hurt her in some way, would torment him into his next life.

He picked up her flaccid wrist, feeling the weak pulse, his own heartbeat all but choking him. Her chest, under thin blue cotton, barely moved. A hand waved close to her eyes elicited zero reaction. Kyle framed her face in both hands. Her bone-white skin felt cold, clammy.

"Come on, sweetheart, snap out of it."

He removed his hands reluctantly. There wasn't time for

guilt or remorse. He had to find out what the hell was wrong with her. The first thought that came to mind was drugs. He checked her pupils. Almost normal.

Frantically he scanned the room. For brandy, whiskey, hell, anything to bring her out of it. He settled for the water and got up to pour some, then came back to the bed, setting the plastic glass on the table beside the lamp.

"Come back to me, damn it!" He barely recognized his own voice as he grabbed her shoulders and shook her. "You're scaring the crap out of me, sweetheart. Come on now, wake up."

He shook her again, harder this time.

Her lashes fluttered. He held his breath.

"That's it, come on now, jungle girl, you can do this." She blinked again, obviously disoriented. His smile felt ragged as she focused vaguely on his face.

"Ky—?" she asked on a dry, rasping breath, groping for him blindly as her eyes closed. Her fingers encountered his hand and she clasped it in a death grip against her face.

He held the glass to her lips with his other hand and after a moment she greedily gulped down the tepid water.

He felt every neuron in his body firing up again. "Tell me what he did to you." Her gaze went from vague to aware between one heartbeat and the next. Her eyelids slammed down like automatic garage doors.

"No way, lady. You can sleep later. Open your eyes. Now."

Delanie dragged her eyes open to look up at Kyle's face. The skin across his cheekbones appeared brutally stretched; his pale green eyes grimly hollow. She felt thick and stupid, and frowned because she couldn't figure out what was—

She gasped, then moaned, biting her lower lip as the pain bit into her with a vengeance. Burning. Brutal. Unrelenting. It radiated up her leg in a sharp undulating rhythm in time with her furious heartbeat. Her vocal cords ached with the need to scream.

And scream and scream.

Silently he took her in his arms, pulling her around to lie against his chest as he sat propped against the headboard.

Strong arms tightened around her, her breath hitched. The hot ball in her chest burst open, and she wept, out of control, like a child increasingly frightened by its own sobs. There was no beginning to the excruciating pain, no end.

"Shhh." Kyle folded her against his chest, tucking her head into his shoulder, stroking her hair, rocking her in the safe harbor of his arms. "Shhh, sweetheart, shhh—"

Delanie squeezed her eyes even tighter . . . seeing Isabella.

Nausea rose in her throat.

She convulsively swallowed, struggling in Kyle's hold. He refused to let go, keeping her pressed against the steady pounding of his heart. Arms wrapped around his ribs, nails digging into solid flesh, she tried to make her breathing shallow. The terrified sobs came harder. He rubbed her back, whispering words of comfort. Terror poured from inside her in a tidal wave of such magnitude she knew she'd never be the same.

"Christ, sweetheart, tell me what I can do to help you?" Kyle's voice sounded raw; she felt his fingers against her scalp. Firm, trying to soothe.

Her grief and terror seemed endless, coming from a bottomless well, but the paroxysm of tears eventually eased to hiccupping tears and a runny nose.

She felt him stretch, then he held a piece of cloth under her nose. "Blow."

Delanie took the fabric from him. Her hands shook as she blew her nose several times on what appeared to be a lace table runner. Sitting up carefully, she balled the material in her fist.

Kyle raised his hand to touch her. Involuntarily she flinched. His hand dropped, clenching on his own thigh before he reached for the glass on the table beside him. He handed it to her, and then wrapped her fingers firmly around it before he let go.

"What the hell did Montero do to you?" he demanded, soft and feral.

She drew in a shuddery, watery breath. *God*— Gulping

the water, she handed the glass back. "It wasn't Ramón. It was . . ." Gall rose in the back of her throat threatening to choke her. She could feel the length of his legs, stretched out against her thigh as she half sat, half sprawled beside him on the wide bed.

"It was?" He pulled back the curtain of her hair, eyes scanning her red, swollen features.

"Isabella." She raised her face to look at him. "It was Isabella." Pale eyes gazed back at her steadily as his hand dropped from where he'd been touching her hair. His knuckles turned white, fisted against the bedspread.

A muscle jerked in his jaw. "Tell me."

"T-the soldiers brought me to I-Isabella. She made me watch h-home movies." Delanie shuddered. Kyle rested his head against the ornate headboard, his gaze never leaving her face. The pain in her leg made her grit her teeth as she switched to a slightly more comfortable position. Perspiration collected on her upper lip and she licked it off.

"Lauren was here. Here, in Isabella's house. I saw her on one of the videos—"

"Get to your *sister* later, Delanie. What the hell did that bitch do to *you?*"

"They t-tied me down. S-strapped me to a t-table and— Oh, God—she gave me a physical—to make sure I was c-clean and healthy f-for her customers—"

"Jesus."

"Then s—" Delanie swallowed convulsively. "Then she b-branded me."

The acrid smell of her own burning flesh seemed to fill her head. Horrified, terrified out of her mind, she'd lain there on that damn table, tied down like a broken butterfly pinned to a board, while Isabella had stirred a metal rod into a small brazier beside her.

The anticipation of worse to come had almost obliterated the painful indignity of the physical examination Isabella had subjected her to only moments before.

The long metal branding iron in Isabella's hand had seemed so slow, almost torpid. The devil-red tip had warmed her skin a split second before it bit. For several horrific seconds there hadn't been any pain. Just numbing anticipation. The sudden agony had exploded, wrenching a high-pitched scream from between her bloodless lips.

Ohgodohgodohgod.

Overwhelmed by helplessness, powerless to stop the torture, Delanie remembered praying she *wouldn't* pass out, leaving herself open and completely vulnerable to Isabella.

"She *branded* you?" Kyle's lips went white. "Where?" His hands on her shoulder, while excruciatingly gentle, were implacable. "Show me *where*."

The pain encompassed her entire leg. She wasn't sure where. Was too scared to find out. "Somewhere on my right leg— No!" Delanie cried in alarm, as Kyle shot off the bed and started peeling the cotton dress up her legs. His hands felt cool on her knees.

She couldn't.

She just could not.

He gave her a steady look.

Delanie hesitated, then slowly, reluctantly, parted her knees, yanking the material down to cover what she could. She lay back against the warm spot he'd left on the pillow, her eyes squeezed shut. Every internal female organ contracted, as muscle and nerve resisted a second invasion.

His damp breath fanned her stomach. "Where? Where did she—"

The pain wasn't localized, and Delanie was afraid to ask Kyle if she'd been branded where she thought she had. "Is it—?"

He shook his head.

Her breath came out in a rush, tears filled her eyes again, and she bit her lip as, hands gentle, Kyle checked all the way down her leg until he came to her right ankle. He cradled her foot in a large warm hand as he inspected the burn.

"The head of a cobra. Right on the medial malleo—ankle joint," he told her, voice grim. "Right on the bone where the skin is thinnest. God *damn* that fucking bitch."

He looked to the far end of the room, his jaw working as if

he could feel the sharp searing of muscle and nerve. "Give me a minute."

"We don't have any time to waste," she said urgently, sitting up, not without a considerable amount of agony. "I *have* to find Lauren now, don't you see? She might still be he— What are you doing?" She yelped in alarm as he gripped her shoulders with steely fingers.

Something wild and dangerous flared in his eyes. "I don't want to hear about your damn sister. Do you hear me, jungle girl? I-don't-want-to-hear-one-more-goddamned-word-about-your-*sister*, right now!"

Delanie looked up at him blankly. She had never in her life seen anyone so angry. For several taut seconds they stared at each other.

Kyle cursed. Dropping on the edge of the bed, he hauled her against him, pressing her tear-swollen face against his chest. His heart beat with an unsteady, heavy thud beneath her cheek. After a brief hesitation, she put her arms around his waist. It felt good to be held.

In a voice so soft she had to strain to hear him, he whispered roughly against her hair, "I'm sorry, sweetheart. I'm so damn sorry."

She must have dozed, fading away with the feel of his arms securely around her. She roused to find Kyle beside her.

"What're you doing?" she asked, feeling drugged and sluggish. Her leg throbbed from toes to hip, but it seemed more distant now.

"They left some first-aid supplies. We can't leave this open, not in this environment. I'm sorry. This is going to hurt."

The room was dim. In the mirror across from the bed, she could see Kyle's back as he bent over her. His body blocked hers from view.

"How bad?"

"The burn looks as bad as I'm sure it feels. Nothing a good plastic surgeon won't be able to eradicate when you get home." He paused. "Brace yourself, jungle girl, this is gonna hurt like hell."

"Worse . . . worse than hell." She bit the back of her hand as he carefully applied salve to the wound. The pain was so intensely agonizing that it wasn't localized. Yet.

She felt sick. "It feels *huge*. But it's only about the size of a dime, right?"

"Yeah. *Only* the size of a goddamned dime." A muscle in his jaw jerked, and he finished dressing the wound with his teeth clenched. "Okay?"

She nodded. He gave her an approving smile, which didn't reach his eyes. He barely had himself in check. "Good girl. Here." He took something out of his pocket and handed it to her. "See what you make of this."

"It's Lauren's earring." Her voice broke. "I gave it to her when she graduated high school. Kyle, where did you find it?"

"Over there on the floor."

"Isabella told me Lauren had been sold months ago."

Kyle cocked a brow. "I wouldn't believe anything that bitch says." He carefully bandaged her wound. "Okay, that should do it."

"Do you think she's here? Oh Lord, Kyle, do you?"

"I'll check it out." He snapped off the light, plunging them into darkness.

"Leave the light on."

He leaned forward, his chest brushing her breasts, and said very, very quietly against her face, "I turned it off so they can't watch us anymore."

Her gaze swept the room for a camera, a shiver running across her skin.

"The mirror, one-way glass." His voice was low, matter of fact. "Do *not* go to sleep. You understand, jungle girl? *Don't* fall asleep. There's nitrous oxide being fed into the room. Not enough to knock us out, but enough to keep us docile. I turned it down as much as I could."

Delanie tensed and felt his knuckle brush her cheek. "It's a more efficient way to keep us here than tying us up." She felt his fingers lightly touch the base of her throat. "Same goes for these damned dog collars."

Actually she hadn't given it any thought at all. In fact, she decided, lying there in the darkness beside him, thinking had already gotten her into enough trouble. His face felt scratchy with five o'clock shadow. He smelled sweaty. She liked it and inhaled deeply, immediately feeling the fuzzying effects of the gas on her brain. She struggled against it for a moment and then wondered, why bother?

The opulent room could have been the ritzy guest room on a French estate, she decided. The bed was comfortable, the darkness hid a multitude of fears and dangers, and thinking could wait. Her brain had overloaded hours ago. The darkness pressed in on her.

"Tell me the rest." He said, his voice grim.

She told him quickly, wanting to get it over with. She skimmed briefly over the "training" movies Isabella had forced her to watch. Where she'd seen Lauren. Where she'd seen herself and Kyle. She told him about Isabella's rich clients and how many girls Isabella had bragged about selling.

And she wished with all her heart that he'd left on the light, or that he'd wrap his arms around her. The darkness felt weighty, oppressive. She reached out, found his braid and ran her fingers carefully up and down the bumpy rope.

She imagined Isabella on the other side of that wall-sized mirror, avidly watching them. Delanie shivered, then realized that, at every point, Kyle had covered her body from view. She gave his braid a subtle tug.

He maneuvered her to the center of the bed, enfolding her in his arms as she finished.

"So Mamá trains and sells sex slaves."

"Said it was very lucrative."

"I don't doubt that for a second."

"She put the drug in the wine she gave me and filmed us in your bedroom."

"I swept the room a dozen times a day. How the hell did I miss the cam— Never mind."

"And I thought she had the hots for *you.*"

He exhaled sharply. "I would have traded places with you in a heartbeat."

They lay in the silence for several minutes. "You have to stay awake," he reminded her, but it didn't seem to be that important anymore. He was very relaxed—damn. What the hell was he doing? "Delanie!"

"Hmm?"

"I want you to count for me, okay?" He let go of her, and she felt him get off the other side of the bed.

"Backwards?"

"Forwards," he said grimly.

"Hmmm. One. Two. Three . . ."

"Keep going."

"Four. Five. Six."

"Seven. Eight . . ." he prompted, removing a small tool from his belt and applying it with a surgeon's precision to the door lock.

Snick. Snick. Snick.

"Seven. Eight. Nine. Thirteen. Five . . ."

"Why don't you try singing instead?" he suggested dryly.

" 'K."

Kyle paused, gripping the doorknob as Delanie started singing an old Beatles song.

Hell, he didn't want to leave her. Acid ate at his gut for what she'd endured. He bent to remove the small Beretta from its hiding place in the double seam on the back of his boot, and slipped through the opening, closing the bedroom door quietly behind him. If he didn't get them out of here fast, there'd be no payback. And he wanted that retribution so badly it was a heady flavor on the back of his tongue.

Fresh air and the adrenaline rush pushed the last bit of tranq gas out of his system. Keeping to the wall, he followed the wide corridor to the left. The sound of men's voices came from the back of the small house.

There were no surveillance cameras out here. There was no need. Isabella kept her visitors drugged. If the women she held somehow managed to revive and get past a locked door, they'd be fried the moment they stepped across the invisible boundary outside while wearing the damned necklace. He fingered the herringbone, now fully understanding Delanie's phobia about the damn necklace around her neck. He didn't like it either.

But first things first.

Elbow crooked and tight against his side, muzzle of his weapon close to his face and pointed to the ceiling, he paused outside the door of what appeared to be the kitchen. He could smell strong coffee and the distinctive smoke of Piel Rojas, the fat stubby Colombian cigarettes the people inside were smoking.

Three men were playing cards by the sound of it. From their conversation, he gleaned the next shift wouldn't relieve them for several hours. Kyle listened, standing dead still. Like most of the men at the compound, these were trained for simple guard duty, not heavy combat. They were loquacious, bored, and pissed because Isabella had not allowed them to play with the *virgen*.

He hoped to God the virgin was Delanie's sister. The girl appeared to be her reason for living. He desperately wanted to give her something to hold onto until he could get her to safety.

He stepped into the brightly lit kitchen. "*Buenas noches,* gentlemen.*" Three pairs of eyes shot up, startled. All three sprang from their seats at the same time, fumbling for weapons they should have been wearing, but had left hanging on pegs by the door. Cards and coffee mugs went flying. A full ashtray skidded over the edge of the table, spraying butts all over the floor. A chair clattered as it fell.

One man crossed himself, while coffee dripped on his boots. His friends, never taking their eyes off Kyle, started a slow circle around the table. The pincer movement might have worked, but Kyle was much too fast and wily for these three goons despite the gas.

He had the soldier closest to him in a headlock before the other two had moved three steps.

With a snap he broke the man's neck.

He was taking no prisoners. The situation had always been life and death.

But now it was personal.

Deeply personal.

He let the man's body drop. "Next?" he asked coldly, tucking the Beretta into his belt. He figured, no weapons and only two to one, the odds were about right.

They rushed him.

His booted foot shot up and out, striking the one on the left in the esophagus. The man went down without a peep, a look of surprise on his face as he crumpled on top of the body already on the floor.

Two down, one to go.

Kyle fixed his eyes on the last soldier. There was something in the eyes looking back at him that made him relish a bit more of a challenge.

"Alto!" the soldier warned. *"Nunca pasara! Le mato primero!"*

Kyle snorted. "I've been threatened with death by better men than you, asshole. Come on, I've got things to do and places to go." Keeping his eye on the last soldier, Kyle unhooked the three Uzis from the wall beside him. The man bent low, covering his throat protectively, circling around the bodies on the floor, almost missing a step because of the debris under his feet. His expression didn't change when he saw Kyle holding their weapons.

Kyle tossed the Uzis out into the corridor and stepped over the two bodies. The soldier moved quickly to put the table between them.

Kyle watched him toss his small Toledo steel knife from hand to hand, and recognized the type—vicious, lightning-fast reflexes, and no conscience. Probably no room for one in his small brain.

The kitchen was compact. Rudimentary appliances, a stove, small refrigerator, a coffeepot. A table and chairs in the center. No window. One door.

The floor was linoleum. Old, worn from dozens of booted feet, and dirty. Perfect traction. Without warning Kyle propelled himself across one corner of the table, surprising the hell out of the guy as he slammed into him.

They crashed to the floor. The force of Kyle's bulk and

momentum put him on top. Just in time, he saw the flash of the knife and broke its descent to his face with a steely grip. The tendons in the man's wrist snapped under the pressure. The knife clattered to the floor.

"Donde está la virgen?"

"Yo no sé, Yanqui."

"Wrong answer, *asqueroso.*" Kyle grabbed his hair, slamming the guy's head sharply on the floor. "Where is the virgin?" he asked again, his fingers on the man's windpipe. The soldier's eyes rolled. Kyle eased up. Infinitesimally.

He choked; his eyes glazed. "Señora Isabella took her, Señor."

"When?" Kyle pressed gently, and the man gagged.

"When she go to *El Jefe*'s house. An hour ago, Señor. No more."

With clinical detachment, Kyle used gentle pressure to cut off the man's air.

Rising, he glanced at his watch. It was practically the middle of the night. No doubt Isabella and her bag of tricks would be here first thing in the morning.

Wasn't *she* going to be pissed.

He dragged the men one at a time, dumping them in a small utility alcove off the kitchen. He took the time to inventory the contents for weapons, ammunition, and supplies. Clean uniforms were stacked on shelves above the washer and dryer. Kyle snagged a bundle before he turned off the lights and exited down the corridor, picking up the Uzis on the way out.

He paused outside the bedroom where he could hear Delanie's off-key rendition of "Eensy-Weensy Spider." Kyle knew time was of the essence.

But first things first.

Depositing the clothing, weapons, and supplies on the floor beside the door, he strode to the next room.

Chapter Eighteen

Kyle opened the door and found a light switch.

He stood in the doorway for a moment, eyes raking the dimly lit room. It stunk of cigarette smoke, Isabella Montero's perfume, and Delanie's terror.

The table was at the far end of the room.

Booted feet traversed marble and carpet in ground-eating strides. He fingered a three-inch-wide leather wrist strap that had restrained Delanie as she lay there open and vulnerable, pinned, like a fragile butterfly.

Terrified.

Calmly he released the buckled strap. It flopped back on the crumpled white sheet as he circumvented the table with even steps.

A large, smoked mirror covered the wall. Even with the light out in the bedroom next door, he could discern Delanie sprawled on the bed. Depressing the button on what was obviously a speaker, he heard Delanie's watery, off-key humming as she struggled to stay awake. He felt a muscle tick in his jaw and clenched a fist, dragging his eyes off her and back into the ambient lighting of Isabella's chamber of horrors.

Next to the table stood the small brazier. Almost tenderly, Kyle plucked the slender metal rod out of the faintly glowing coals. Twisting it between his fingers, he inspected the cobra head at its tip, then hefted the weight of it in his hand.

Light. Tensile.

With a roar of pure animal rage he gripped the edge of the table, flinging it to the floor. Sheet and mattress skidded across marble, and the legs snapped off with one blow of the metal pike. Leather restraints screamed in protest as he ripped them out of each corner with his bare hand.

The brazier came under attack next, crashing to the floor in a shower of ash and live coals. Dust swirled in violent air currents. A crystal lamp shattered into a million diamond pieces with a strike of the lethal weapon applied with virulent force. A mirror came next. Fragmented to smithereens. Razor-sharp shards shattered at his feet.

The still-warm branding iron ripped through silk and satin, velvet and crystal, leaving a path of complete destruction as he systematically demolished the room. He disected the sofa and chairs, and the floor became littered with kapok, foam, glass shards, and wood fragments. Shattered vases bled water into the worthless remnants of priceless Persian rugs. The giant TV imploded. The stereo system became plastic rubble. Speakers became mangled boxes of splintered component parts.

He cleaved the giant coffee table in two with three well-placed blows of an antique chair.

He hacked. Slashed. Severed and smashed. Coldly. Ruthlessly. Until nothing in the room was recognizable.

Twisting off his ring, he tossed it into the destruction. Without a backward glance he walked out, closing the door softly on the Armageddon he'd left behind him.

Pausing outside the bedroom, he dragged air into his billowing lungs, sweating as if he'd just completed a decathlon. Kyle focused on regulating the cadence of his breathing and heartbeat before he opened the door.

He strode over and flicked on the lamp beside the bed. Delanie blinked up at him with a dopey, and incredibly adorable, grin on her face.

He had to touch her.

Touch something *soft*. Innocent. *Clean*.

Lightly, he brushed strands of silky hair off her forehead, allowing his fingers to linger on warm, smooth skin for a moment.

"Hi." Her voice sounded raspy; she'd cried again in his absence.

"Hi, yourself, jungle girl. What say you get up and at 'em and we blow this joint?" He helped her sit up and gently swing her legs over the edge of the bed. She swayed between his hands. Kyle kept a close watch on her eyes for the first sign of pain.

The tranq gas had served a purpose; she was too looped to care. Efficiently, he reapplied the antibiotic salve he'd used earlier, then stuck the tube into his back pocket before bandaging the wound.

Delanie wasn't much help, but eventually he got her into a pair of camouflage pants and a long-sleeved shirt over a cotton T-shirt. It was pretty much like dressing a doll. She didn't fight him. A couple of times he gently removed her fumbling fingers. With her assistance they'd get out of here a week from Sunday.

"Hope these boots I found fit." He didn't offer where, and she didn't ask. He could depress the toe of each boot by a good three inches, but it beat her walking barefoot. After stuffing the toes with the leftover cotton bandages, he tied the laces.

"Stand." He held her upper arms. The pain, when the blood rushed down to her ankle, was going to be—

"Aggggg!"

Excruciating.

He held her forehead against his chest as she panted through it. Eventually she pulled away, her face shiny with perspiration. Her eyes were much clearer, but the pain was all there.

Nothing he could do about it. "Let's go."

Despite being a trifle wobbly on her feet Delanie gamely followed him down the corridor. "Where do we start looking?" she asked, her eyes becoming clearer as she glanced about.

There was no time now to coddle her. "Lauren isn't here." He opened the door to a small closet and found exactly what he was looking for. Beneath the communications control panel, gas tanks for the backup generator squatted on the floor.

A quick detour to the kitchen and he was back with a half-filled five-pound bag of sugar. Just enough of the sweet stuff to contaminate the gasoline and foul up the generator. Next he gutted the communications panel.

"Did you look?"

He scrutinized her over his shoulder. She was leaning against the far wall. "Yeah, I did." Her face paled even more, but he hardened his heart. It didn't matter that he wanted to cradle her in his arms and take care of her. The fact was, she was at her strongest when she was pissed. And right now she'd need all the strength she could muster.

"If your sister's anywhere on or around this compound we'll find her."

He didn't bother mentioning that he'd disabled all of Montero's choppers before he'd gone into that meeting in anticipation of the next day. If Lauren had been on this mountaintop at some time in the last twenty-four hours, she was still here.

Somewhere.

He wanted to be deep in the jungle before reinforcements arrived. If he remembered correctly from the infrared photos taken, he had erroneously thought this building part of the drug lab—therefore they were perhaps thirty, forty minutes from the hacienda through the jungle.

By the time the relief guards got here, found their friends, discovered the phones didn't work, and returned to the main house, hours would have elapsed.

Delanie muttered a curse as she rammed four fingers into the space between her neck and the chokehold of the gold necklace, making a fist. "Get this off before we go." If she kept yanking at the damn thing, she'd eventually decapitate herself.

He moved behind her and touched the back of her neck. Delanie quickly bunched her hair out of his way.

"Can't find the lock?" she asked, her voice husky. His breath whispered warm on the back of her neck, and she felt the callused rasp of his fingers brushing her nape. It felt like forever until the warm links slid free over her skin.

"My turn." He came around her, turning his back, then

crouched at her feet. "Run your fingers underneath until you feel several uneven links."

He was close enough so she didn't have to do anything but move his braid over his broad shoulder to bare his nape. His shirt felt slightly damp, his neck hot. She ran her fingertip carefully inside the necklace, trying to feel the small ridge indicating the lock.

"Your hands are cold."

Dizzy with nerves, worried sick about Lauren, she didn't answer. She tried to find the clasp, again and again. The muscles in his neck and shoulders bunched as her index finger moved slowly beneath the flat links. She touched his skin, smelling the faint compelling scent of him. Her breath moved the fine dark hair at his nape.

Kyle had to explain more than once how the mechanism worked. It was intricate, and impossible to see. Eventually she found it. They both felt relief as the gold slithered from around his neck into his waiting hand. Kyle rose, stuffing both necklaces into his back pocket.

The ghostly brush of his fingers at the nape of her neck lingered as they walked down the hallway.

"Will you promise me something?" she asked calmly, feeling perspiration clammy on her skin as they walked past the room where Isabella—

"Yeah?"

"If for some reason I don't make it out of here, will you promise to find my sister and get her to safety?" He gave her an odd look. "I have a life insurance policy. You can have it. It's small, but— Will you see she's taken care of?"

Something dangerous flared in his eyes. "No."

Blood drained from her head. "No? My God, Kyle—"

"This is a war, jungle girl." He sounded harsh, grim. His eyes froze the marrow in her bones. "You aren't supposed to be here. As it is, you've already jeopardized this mission. I'm not a frigging baby-sitter or nursemaid. The people up at the hacienda want to kill me just as badly as I want to exterminate them. Hundreds of other people are involved in this mission. In twenty-four hours the real fun will start." His pale eyes glittered. "If you want to make sure your precious sister gets your insurance, you'll have to hand it to her yourself."

Chin up, shoulders back, Delanie glared at him. "Fine. I'll do that."

"Delanie Eastman. Always her sister's keeper. What are you going to do when you find her? Carry her yourself?"

Her throat ached. "If that's what it takes."

"You can barely walk yourself."

"I can walk," she said with unnatural calm. "Not very well maybe. But I *can* walk."

"Leap buildings in a single bound, too?" he asked ferociously, stepping away from her. "Has it ever occurred to you that maybe, just maybe, you can't always handle everything by yourself? That perhaps you might need someone else once in a while?" His voice was ragged, angry, almost bitter.

"I just asked you for your help, and you turned me down flat, remember? No problem. I did just fine taking care of myself long before you came along, and I'll continue to do so long after you've disappeared into the sunset. I'm strong enough to take care of myself."

"No one's that strong."

She fought off a feeling of helpless despair. Kyle had promised his help, then suddenly withdrawn it.

He gave her a savage look. "You'd goddamn rather break than bend, wouldn't you?" He searched her face for who knew what. "Okay, let's get the hell out of here." He didn't sound ecstatic. "Do everything I tell you, *when* I tell you, or we'll both be dead."

"Trust me," Delanie assured him with utmost sincerity. "I will. What do you want me to carry?"

He handed her a nasty-looking gun on a webbed strap, and a burlap bag.

Imitating Kyle, she slung the weapon over her shoulder and marched outside like a good little soldier.

Dawn hovered. The air, thick with the smell of vegetation, felt cool against Kyle's face. He hadn't realized just how long he'd been in that room. Damn. No matter how mild the tranquilizing gas had been, it had still robbed them of hours of travel time.

They headed north, deep into the jungle. Away from Isabella's house of horrors, and away from the compound. Roughly calculating the time it would take to reach the rendezvous point, Kyle figured three-plus hours travel time.

Everything around them was in shades of gray, the path away from Isabella's house relatively free of undergrowth. Later he'd have to use the machete tucked in his belt. He checked their position on the GPS compass built into his watch, which the stupid bastards hadn't taken off him, thank God. The global positioning satellite would lead him to the meeting point where he'd stashed emergency supplies, and where his team would be gathering in just under nine hours.

He'd really like to contact them, give them the heads up. But somebody had swiped the communications device from his room days ago, and the sudden change of plan in San Cristóbal had prevented him from replacing it. Hell, nothing he could do about it now.

He made out shapes and movement in the dense undergrowth as the narrow beam of his stolen flashlight strafed the trees. Behind him, Delanie crashed and stumbled without complaint, her breathing harsh, and her gait uneven.

Tenacious. Stubborn. Unyielding. And loyal to a fault.

He'd instructed her to hold firmly to his belt until visibility improved. Her slender fingers had leather and fabric bunched in a sweaty death grip at the small of his back.

The Uzi felt comfortable against his chest, thirty-two rounds in the ammo magazine times three. He'd stuffed a couple of spare clips in his pockets and carried the machete in one hand, the flashlight in the other. The Beretta was tucked in his belt.

Delanie carried the bag with the supplies and an Uzi. The bag also contained the rest of the magazines, which weighed a ton. He'd have carried everything, but naturally she'd made a federal case out of shouldering her share of the load. She could barely carry herself, let alone an Uzi and the sack, but she'd insisted vehemently.

The smell of vegetation was suddenly obliterated for a moment by the pungent stink of bug.

"Hang on a sec." Delanie released his belt and limped off before he could stop her.

Now what?

She returned seconds later with a familiar black canvas bag, held at arm's length, and a smile on her face. "Look what I found!"

"Yeah, one more thing to carry." The damn thing stunk to high heaven.

Delanie ignored him, slung the straps over her shoulder, and grabbed hold of his belt again. "Let's go."

For a brief moment he questioned whether she could make the three-hour trek to his stashed supplies, then laughed grimly to himself. Hell, yeah. If anybody could do it, it was the woman keeping pace behind him.

After an hour he knew she needed a break. Her breath caught on every step. He'd pushed her past her endurance. Even so, she probably would have continued until she dropped at his feet rather than utter one word of complaint.

"Sit down and take a load off. I'll be right back." The flashlight beam arced as he tossed it to her.

"Where—?"

"Drink some of the water." Not looking back he melted into the trees.

Using the machete to clear a path deeper into the jungle, Kyle checked his bearings on the illuminated dial of his watch.

Whack. A lopped off, wrist-thick vine dropped at his feet. It felt good to vent some of the excess energy he'd been stockpiling. *Whack. Whack. Whack.* A nice steady rhythm built.

There were at least twelve hours left before the party started.

Whack. Whack. Whack.

The charcoal light changed gradually to slate. He'd given her a thirty-minute break. More than he could afford. He headed back.

Delanie was where he'd left her, leaning awkwardly against a nearby tree. She hadn't sat down. He suspected because it was too painful for her to get back up again.

"How are you holding up, jungle girl?"

"Fine." She straightened, drawing in a breath as she took a step. She picked the Uzi up by the webbed strap and slung it over her shoulder. It was almost full light, and he clearly saw the gray cast to her face. Sweat shone on her skin, and her damp hair curled about her face. She looked like hell. And he wanted to kiss her so badly, his lips throbbed. "Ready?"

She nodded, and they worked their way down the path he'd cleared. Given the topography, most of the ground they had to cover was on a downward slope, giving them momentum. Anything in their favor at this point was a plus.

Delanie hadn't asked once where the hell they were going. For all she knew they were walking back down the mountain to San Cristóbal.

"I stashed a tent and some supplies about an hour from here. Think you can manage another sixty minutes?" More like another two hours, but even twenty minutes must seem like an eternity to her.

"Yes." Her bumpy knuckles prodded him in the back where she once again held onto his belt in a death grip. It was plenty light enough for her to see quite clearly now. He didn't comment.

Delanie's breath hitched with every step she took. Kyle clamped his jaw, wishing to hell he didn't feel every painful step with her. He couldn't afford to feel anything at the moment, not when their lives depended on his undivided attention.

They reached the end of the cleared section in minutes. Using the machete, he hacked back at the tangle of vines and thickly veined leaves. He felt her hand slip from his belt.

During the last mile, her limp had become more pronounced. He was going as slowly as he dared. They were now well out of audio range of the compound, but there was still a lot of ground to be covered. "Need to stop?" he asked grimly.

"No," she said, not unexpectedly.

His admiration for her grew. How the hell was she managing to walk? To talk? To stay upright?

He wanted to pick her up and carry her, protected in his arms. Get her away as far and fast as humanly possible. He fought back a wave of tenderness. He didn't want this agony of worrying about her. Couldn't afford to screw up this assignment even more by being distracted.

Wasn't going to happen.

Her tenacity was going to keep her alive, and he was going to stay focused. Kyle could practically hear her mind whirring. She'd be going over and over what had happened to her at Isabella's hands. She'd probably have nightmares about this for a long, long time.

Hell. So would he.

Shafts of sunlight streamed through the upper branches. The heat and humidity intensified in direct proportion to the increasing level of light. Her breathing was harsh enough to cause him real concern. He hacked away another couple of feet of vegetation. "Stop and take a break."

"If you were alone would you be taking a break?"

"I'm not alone."

"I didn't think so. I'm fine, keep walking."

She was hanging in there. He kept walking and sought something else for both of them to focus on. The fact that she had a short fuse would help, he thought wryly. Her anger seemed to produce adrenaline. It wasn't hard for Kyle to think of something to piss her off, and he said mildly, "You're very good at dissociating yourself, aren't you?"

"What?"

"Dissociating yourself. Separating yourself from what's going on around you."

"Boy, I wish *that* were true."

"Oh, it's true all right. Isabella tortured you, and you allowed twenty seconds to think about yourself before you started worrying about Lauren. Is it easier to worry about other people than it is yourself, Delanie?"

"That's ridiculous. This conversation is ridiculous."

"Is it?" He paused. "Tell me why you took me to your hotel room that weekend."

"What does one thing have to do with the other?"

"Depends on your answer, doesn't it?"

"You don't want to know."

"Oh, believe me, jungle girl, I do want to know. Why the hell did you go into the bar and pick me up that night?"

A long pause. Her steps altered as she shrugged. "I told you. I was engaged to Anthony Russell. We'd been engaged for seven months, and I hadn't been able to bring myself to sleep with him. Don't ask why. I don't know. I just hadn't wanted to. He was getting irritated and started mocking me and giving me a hard time about it. He was going to a conference in San Francisco, and he told me before he left that if I wanted to keep him around I'd better be prepared to sleep with him when he got back."

"You should have told the asshole to take a long walk off a short pier," Kyle told her, attacking a man-size fern with the machete. "Then what?"

"I decided to go to San Francisco and surprise him. I borrowed some of Lauren's sexy clothes, packed the bare minimum, and arrived unannounced at the hotel."

"He was there with someone else."

"Yeah. How'd you know?"

"Figures. A jerk wouldn't change his spots."

"Hmmm."

"So you decided not to waste the weekend and got rid of your virginity with a total stranger."

"Something like that." The trail had widened and she came alongside him. "We had great sex, what are you complaining about?"

"Great sex?" He lopped off another branch with considerably more force than necessary. "Great sex, huh? I thought we had more than that."

"Okay. We had *three days* of great sex." Sweat caused the

shirt she wore to cling to her delectable curves. She wiped her arm across her flushed face, then took the shirt off, tying the sleeves around her waist. The dark green T-shirt she wore underneath clung to her skin like a latex glove.

He took the bag she carried, withdrew a plastic bottle and handed it to her. "Drink as much as you can." Her hands shook, and he had to help her remove the cap. He kept his worry to himself. "I'm astonished you'd do something so rash and irresponsible."

"So was I." Delanie measured the liquid content of the bottle visually. "You have no idea how out of character that was for me." She chugged exactly half the water before handing him back the bottle.

Kyle sighed inwardly. He had a *very* good idea how out of character that weekend had been for her. Putting together bits and pieces, he was learning a great deal about this woman. He chugged. The damn water tasted of the purification tablets.

"Don't tell me that's all I was to you, either."

Her eyebrows rose. "Luckily, I never built up any expectations, so I wasn't disappointed when you left."

He felt the blood pound behind his eyeballs. "I came back, damn it. And *you* were gone!" *She* was supposed to be the one getting pissed off, not him. Christ, she was tying him up in knots all over again.

She scowled. "What do you mean you came back? When?"

"Twenty minutes after I went down to get my clothes from my room." He'd left her snuggled under the covers, and not wanting to waste one second when Delanie was awake, he'd zipped down to his room to pack. He'd returned to find the door of her room ajar and no sign of her.

"I had a plane to catch."

"At two in the morning? Without leaving so much as a frigging note?" His jaw tightened on a fresh serge of disbelief. "I was halfway in love with you, goddamn it."

"Were you? After three days? How sweet."

How sweet? How *sweet?* "There was a hell of a lot more

involved than just *sex*. We connected on a primal level that I'd never experienced before or since. And neither, I'd be willing to bet, have you."

She shrugged.

He didn't realize he'd moved. Suddenly he was so close to her he could see the darker ring around her irises. There was a sheen of sweat on her upper lip. "And *sweet* had nothing to do with it." He gripped her nape and he brought his mouth down on hers, to punish himself because her words had ripped his heart out, to punish her for being the one woman in the world he'd rip out his own heart for.

Her obstinate mouth resisted. He used a gentle implacable pressure, nibbling at the fullness of her bottom lip. His tongue traced the stubborn line denying him entry. Her bunched hands pushed ineffectively against his chest. He tightened his hold. Her lips parted slightly. More than likely to deliver some sort of diatribe he didn't want to hear. He took advantage, spearing his tongue into the heat of her mouth. She tasted sweet. God, she tasted sweet. He was dying of thirst for her.

Her tongue darted away from his. He followed it, tangling with it until he felt her fists loosen between them. He cradled the back of her head in his hand, twisting his fingers into her hair, slanting his mouth on hers until he felt her hands move up his chest and eventually twine around his neck.

God, he thought on a prayer. Thank you, God.

The T-shirt she wore was damp, and clung to her skin. It was as though she were naked against him. He felt the erotic rub of her nipples through two layers of fabric. It made him want to tear their clothes off and take her there. Against a tree again. Naked and panting in the tropical heat. He felt delirious for her. Filled with the taste and scent of her. His brain short-circuited by want, and need to reaffirm life.

Her hand gripped his braid in a fist. Urging him closer. His fingers tightened on her scalp. His body burned, throbbed. It took every last vestige of his control not to shove his knee against her groin where he knew the pressure alone would make her come.

As hot as he was, he hadn't forgotten what she'd just been through and that they were still two hours from camp.

They broke apart, both sucking in great drafts of thick humid air. She opened heavy-lidded eyes, her gaze meeting his. He slid his hands down her back until he held an ass cheek in each palm.

She stood on her toes, arching her back. "Kiss me some more," she demanded, closing her eyes again, lifting her face.

His hands tightened on the firm flesh of her behind, fingers spread as he pulled her harder against him, letting her feel how hard he was. Rubbing her against him until he was almost mindless with wanting her.

"You're mine, jungle girl. And it's a hell of a lot bigger than 'just sex.' " Her mouth scorched his, shutting him up. Her clever tongue dueled with his, not giving quarter. Taking prisoners and fighting dirty. He eased her backward, so her spine was supported by the tree trunk and leaned into her, just enough so he could feel the soft mounds of her breasts flatten against his chest.

The heat they generated made the air around them seem downright balmy. God, they were nitro and glycerin together. "I love your mouth," he said roughly, "and this sweet little ass. I love your verve for life. I love your stubborn loyalty." His mouth crushed hers, drawing life from her kiss. They were equal in every way. He'd never had that with a woman before or since. He felt her low moan, taking it into his own mouth.

Unbearably aroused, knowing they wouldn't be able to do any more right now than kiss, he shifted his upper body to look down at her, bringing one hand up to cup her face. He drew in a ragged breath. "I love you, Delanie."

She snatched her arms from about his neck. A shiver traveled up his spine as she looked up at him, eyes shuttered. A narrow shaft of sunlight filtered down, illuminating her hair and the golden tips of her lashes. A golden Madonna, with a kiss-swollen mouth. Tenderness welled inside him.

"Did I hurt you?" The question took on a double meaning

when her shoulders didn't relax. She couldn't move away physically, he had her pinned to a tree, but emotionally she was gone. His heart plodded to a stop at her closed expression.

"No," she gritted out.

He wondered which question she'd just answered. The past or the present?

Somehow she squeezed herself free. Moving a few feet away she stood with her arms wrapped around her waist, her expression closed as she looked him right in the eye.

"I'm sorry, Kyle," she said flatly, "but I just don't love you back."

Chapter Nineteen

Delanie's heart ached as though she were the one to have taken the blow. Kyle seemed to have taken her declaration in his stride. And she was the one hurt by her own words.

What really fried her cookies was that he hadn't said a word. Not one damn word. She stepped over the fly-infested carcass of a small, dead animal in her path. Okay, she hadn't expected him to keel over in mortal anguish because his black octagonal heart had been broken, but it would have been nice if he'd shown some sort of emotion at her words. Even indicating a little blasted disappointment would have appeased some of her pent-up acrimony. But oh, no.

He'd come back.

For four years she'd believed he'd left her like a thief in the night. But he'd come back. Not that it mattered, really. He would have left sooner or later anyway. And sooner had been better.

How dare he say he loved her? Damn it, how *could* he? He didn't *know* her. Not the real her, anyway. He'd only seen her when she was a poor replica of Lauren. Take away the sexy clothes and too-blonde hair, and she was just an ordinary, forgettable woman. Face it, he probably wouldn't even *like* the real her if he'd met her first.

Love schmuv.

Delanie bit back a sigh. Thank God at least one of them had 20/20. Their physical attraction was undeniable; he didn't have to tell her he loved her to justify it.

As far as she was concerned, romantic love was a highly overrated emotion. It always came with strings attached, strings that bound one tighter than a noose. Strings that when severed, brought one pain instead of relief. Delanie considered herself a quick study. Years of observing her mother and sister, both in and out of love, had proven her theory.

Bottom line. Love hurt.

Luckily she was immune.

Sort of.

It took all her energy just to walk doggedly behind him, eyes on the sway of his braid down the center of his broad back. The burn on her ankle, still agonizingly, fiery hot, hurt like blazes.

A snake dropped in front of her face. She paused, lacking the energy to scream, then stepped over it as it slithered beneath the carpet of leaves on the ground. A month ago, her heart would've done a flip-flop at the sight of a thick-as-her-wrist, five-foot-long black snake. Now it was simply same old, same old.

She glared at Kyle's back. For all he knew, she'd fallen into a nest of the darn things a mile back.

A man must measure time in the same way he measured inches, she thought irritably, trudging along almost blindly. The hour he'd promised had turned into two before they came to a clearing of about nine by nine feet. One "wall" consisted of three gigantic trees, their trunks grown together; another, an enormous boulder.

"This is it," Kyle said, stopping in the center. "Home sweet home. Lay out the—"

She dumped the contents of the burlap bag at his feet and had the canvas ground cover laying on the uneven terrain of the jungle floor before he finished asking.

He gave her a searching glance, which she met with a steady one of her own. She kicked a corner of the mat flat, then lowered the Uzi she carried, feeling inexplicably frustrated and somehow achingly alone. God, she was exhausted.

She leaned wearily against a tree trunk, too tired to care if something unpleasant crawled on her. The jungle closed in.

The darkly tanned muscles of Kyle's forearms bunched as he erected the wire-framed tent: a small, dark green dome, floor and walls all in one. It was awfully small to house two people who weren't talking to each other.

Her heart still thumped with an uncomfortable erratic beat as she watched his swift and economical movements. The air, thick enough to eat with a spoon, was hard to draw into her aching lungs. A living, breathing, *green* presence. And it started to rain.

She was tired to the marrow of her bones; tired of being stoic about the pain in her leg; tired of being brave and tough and resilient and resourceful. Tired of being strong.

She wanted to fling herself down on a nice soft bed in a cool room, and sleep for ten years. Then she wanted to wake up and cry for another ten hours in a cold shower.

Then she'd be a brave little toaster again.

Her clothes clung to her sweaty skin, her eyes felt gritty, exhaustion dragged at her. And her heart felt painfully shriveled, like one of those apple-head dolls she'd once bought her sister at a fair.

She *didn't* love him. She didn't, she told herself, watching a beetle carrying a leaf five times bigger than itself scurry across the tarp. She brushed a fat drop of rain off the bridge of her nose. And then another and another.

"Leave that bag of yours out here, and get in while I get the rest of the stuff. Here." She caught the heavy duffel bag he tossed her. "There should be medical supplies. Check it out. As soon as we're situated, I'll make coffee and something to eat. Then we need to get some shut-eye."

Delanie grabbed her own bag and tipped it upside-down, so the contents spilled on the floor of the tent. Then she tossed the smelly thing as far as she could into the trees.

"Wait a minute— Let me see that."

"This?" Delanie picked up the little portable radio and handed it to him. "It doesn't work."

"Yes, it does. Thanks to your sticky fingers, now I can alert my team."

"Glad I could be of service." Delanie crawled into the tiny tent—the tiny, *dark* tent—and flopped down on her back, covering her eyes with a bent arm. Stretching out her legs, she listened to Kyle mumbling on the radio and stewed about their unfinished conversation.

Rain pounded the sides of the canvas in a steady, somehow comforting beat.

She sat up as soon as Kyle crowded in, shifting her legs out of his way. The atmosphere inside the small space was thick and uncomfortable, and despite it being somewhere around midmorning, dusk dark. "Did you reach them?"

"Yeah."

Delanie bent over her upraised knees and rested her head on her folded arms. As long as she could make both of them believe she didn't care, she'd be safe. Love had caused her mother to carry on an affair with a married man for years, and bear him two children. She'd never spent a holiday, birthday, or even a weekend with her lover. And yet she still searched for him in every *new* lover she took—more than ten years after he'd found someone younger and prettier.

"Here."

She glanced up. Kyle handed her an antimalarial pill and a canteen of water.

"Thanks." She swallowed the pill and handed back the bottle.

"Let's take care of that leg before we get some sleep."

"It's fine."

Naturally he ignored her. He concentrated on unlacing her too-big boots, then eased them off and tossed them aside. Then he pushed up the leg of her fatigue pants, removed the bandage he'd applied earlier, and dragged the first-aid box to his side.

"What's that?"

He tore into a small package with his teeth. "Pain patch."

"I don't ne—"

"Want a shot instead?"

"No," Delanie said reluctantly. God. She wished she'd shaved her legs.

"Now why are you scowling?"

Because despite everything she wanted to be smooth and

clean and smelling wonderful when she was with him. Even if he was the most annoying man on the planet. "Do you have predator blood in you, or what?" she demanded. "How can you see in the dark?"

"It's not that dark. I see you clearly, jungle girl. Very clearly indeed. Does this hurt?"

Ow! "No."

He laughed, then efficiently cleaned and dressed the wound. Which of course felt considerably better after the application of the patch. "Okay." He drew down her pant leg and twisted to close the lid of the first-aid box. "That should do it for now. Lie back and take a nap."

She missed the contact already. *Idiot*. "And what are you going to be doing?"

"Prepping for tomorrow. Sweet dreams."

Oh, sure. Delanie flopped on her back and turned over to face the dark canvas wall inches from her nose. Well, to hell with him. If he didn't want to talk about it, then neither would she. She'd said her piece.

Fine. Damn it. *Just fine.*

Eyes closed, she rolled over, scrunching her butt against the canvas to give him more room to do whatever it was he was doing.

Kyle was aware of every blink, every breath she took as he fieldstripped the weapons. Too damn frustrated to complete the conversation they hadn't concluded to his satisfaction earlier.

But they *would* get back to it, he promised himself, dismantling the last Uzi. The finish on the guns resisted rust, but he still wiped everything down with an oily rag, then ran a toothbrush along all operational parts, checking to see that springs were taut and magazines were clean to prevent misfire.

He glanced over to see Delanie watching him, her face pale. There were things that needed to be said. Promises that needed to be made. And as much as he knew she was waiting for a response from him, his acrimonious little love was damn well going to have to learn a little patience.

Right now he had to focus on what had to be done in the next several hours. Extracting the knife he'd commandeered, he tested its sharpness before pulling his braid over his shoulder. He'd grown the damn thing for four years. Every inch had brought him closer to this moment. He cut through the braid with one swipe of the small, sharp knife. The loss of a yard of hair felt amazingly liberating.

A promise made and kept.

Delanie gasped. "I can't believe you just did that."

"I only grew it for the role." He finished whacking it off to shoulder length, then tossed the thick rope aside before finding the knife sheath in the bag beside him. He strapped the leather onto his forearm, then slipped the knife into the sheath like a homecoming.

Delanie sat up and retrieved the discarded length of his hair, twining it between her fingers. Kyle felt a ridiculous surge of lust, as if she were running those slender capable fingers over his body.

"I didn't thank you for hauling me out of Isabella's house." She glanced up to catch his eye. "I wasn't quick enough getting back to the bomb shelter. It was my own fault I got caught." She half shrugged. "I should have stayed there in the first place to wait for you." She absently caressed his braid, her hand sliding up and down the length. Slowly.

"Whether I could get back inside or not was immaterial. You were absolutely right to be angry with me. I'm sorry, Kyle. I regret that my actions put you and your job in jeopardy. I probably didn't move as fast as I should have. I was pissed off. I'm not used to anyone telling me what I should or shouldn't do."

She gave a small self-deprecating smile that damn near broke his heart. "Actually, I'm not used to anyone worrying about me, one way or the other."

Oh Christ. Not now. They needed to have this conversation. Soon. But not now. This was neither the time, nor the place. Kyle wanted comfortable surroundings in neutral territory to say what he had to say.

"Then you'd better practice getting used to it," he said simply.

"It wasn't the best of scenarios," he added. "But it's done."

Delanie stared off into the distance for several moments. Rain pounded the canvas in the steady heartbeat of the jungle.

"After I find my sister, I'm going to do . . . *something* to Isabella." Her voice was fierce. "Something," she promised grimly, "of apocalyptic proportions."

"Revenge would be sweet," he agreed tersely, expecting and ignoring the suddenly mutinous expression on her face when she realized that wasn't going to happen. "However, the second my team gets here, you're going to be far away from Isabella Montero. Don't worry, I'll take care of her for you."

Her eyes were dark in her pale face and he saw her lips tighten for the inevitable rebuttal. "I can take care of her myself."

"I understand your need for revenge, and if it's possible I'll make sure she's gift wrapped and handed to you. A hell of a lot more than *your* damn wants and desires ride on the outcome tomorrow. I'm sorry as hell for what she did to you, but I can't allow you to get in the way."

"But—"

"Conversation closed." In a lightning-quick switch he asked, "Tell me where to find you when this is over."

She rattled off her address in Sacramento so fast, he knew damn well she didn't expect him to remember it.

She kept her eyes fixed on him. "Don't tell me you plan on seeing me again."

"Why not? I love you. No, don't give me that bull about not loving me back. I don't believe it. You love me, all right. You're just too stubborn to admit it."

He wanted to jump to his feet and pace, but he was damned if he'd go outside; the rain was now coming down in torrents. Frustrated all to hell, he settled for listening to his back teeth gnash and feeling the sweat stick his shirt to his skin.

"Know what, jungle girl? I think I have this figured out now. Every time you refuse my help, and insist on doing it for yourself, you're putting out a challenge. You want me to *prove* to you that you can depend on me."

"That's ridiculous—"

"You want me to *show* you that no matter what, I won't walk away. Convince you how much I want you." He gave her a hard look. "Isn't that what this is all about, Delanie?" He made a move to toss the tail end of his braid over his shoulder, remembered it wasn't there, and snarled. "Every time we have a conversation, or make love, or look at each other, it's another way for you to test me. To see just how damn quickly I'll fail you."

"You don't know what you're talking about," she said tightly.

"Hell yes I do. Everyone has failed you, so you keep people at a distance. You're their judge, jury, and executioner. And everyone is set up to fail. That way there are never any nasty surprises because you always know the outcome, don't you?"

"Are you trying to analyze why I don't love you?" Once again she was listening without hearing.

"Damn it, Delanie, can't you see? I'm trying to make you understand that you've been hurting yourself. Look at what you've done with your family. You've made them your whole existence. You enable them, not giving them the opportunity to stand on their own two feet. You're selfless in your devotion to them, and in doing so, you never give any of them the room to make their own mistakes."

"They need me." She tried to shift as far away as she could in the claustrophobically small tent.

"You enabled your mother, you overprotected your sister, and they ran like hell to get away from you. Tell me how that helped either of them?"

"I love my family. I take care of them the only way I know how."

"And I bet there are more people who you take care of than your mother and sister. Why don't you give me the list so I can fully form the picture?"

"Why don't you go to hell?" she suggested sweetly. "Unless you have a psychiatry major somewhere in your long list of degrees?" She gripped his shorn braid in her fist.

"Who needs a degree? You're a textbook case. So? Who else do you have?"

Delanie shifted on the lumpy canvas floor. "My grandfather and aunt live with me. He has early Alzheimer's—it's not as though it's his fault!"

"And your aunt? What's her problem? One eye and a wooden leg?"

"She had a shattering divorce."

"And when was that?"

"Nine years ago."

"Nine years? You were nineteen when she came to live with you?"

Delanie shrugged.

"So you're the one everyone in the family runs to when they need their problems fixed."

"Not everyone is self-reliant or strong."

"And who do you go to, Delanie? Who do you depend on to comfort you when life is crappy and things don't go right?"

"I make sure my life stays on an even keel, and I take care of myself."

"Must be nice to be so autonomous. Not to need another living soul. No woman is an island, you know."

"Philosophy, too? Boy, you're multitalented. What would you suggest?" she asked, voice calm. "Throw myself in your comforting arms because I have no one else? I don't need anyone, haven't you got that? Holy Hannah! What do you want from me, Kyle?"

"Jesus Christ." He ran his hand roughly over his eyes. "What I want should be so goddamned simple. I want you to know instinctively that I would never do anything to cause you harm. I need you to trust me unconditionally. As automatically as breathing. You have to learn that loving someone doesn't make you weak."

"I don't *have* to do anything. And I trust you just fine."

"Bullshit. Part of this is because you've been smarting that I didn't contact you after the weekend in San Francisco, isn't it? I understand where you're coming from, but surely you can see now *why*. When I left you, it was to start this mission. It got more complicated than any of us expected."

"You should have told me what you were, what you were doing. Given me something to hang on to."

"And said what? I think I might be falling in love with you, but I'll be gone for four or five years, so please hang around and wait for me? We can talk about it when, or *if*, I get back?"

Kyle scrubbed his jaw and tried to unclench his teeth. "I was darkness to your sunshine, and frankly I wasn't sure what I'd have to offer you when this was all over. Or if I'd be in a position to offer you anything at all."

There was a long pause filled by the sound of saturated foliage dripping water into the puddles already formed on the ground.

"I had my own problems, Kyle," she said tiredly.

"I realize that now. Christ." He ran his hand over his face again. If only they'd taken the time to talk four years ago. How different their lives might have turned out.

How the hell was he going to get through to her?

She was so damn close he could feel the heat of her body and smell the elusive fragrance of her skin mixed with a healthy dose of clean sweat.

She needed loving, lots of it.

She needed to know she didn't always have to be the strong one. For once in his life Kyle struggled to find just the right words, words to penetrate her emotional blindness. Anything worth having was worth fighting for. He'd learned that truth a long time ago. His lips quirked in a rueful half smile.

Delanie was worth World War Three.

"Could you quit trying so hard to be a hard-ass for the next few hours?" he asked softly. "For now—at least until we have to leave here—could you just be who you really are?"

"Sure. Whatever."

The gates were going up. Kyle touched her cheek. Warm. Soft. "This isn't the time or place for this conversation. I've got something more constructive to do with our next couple of hours."

"Oh, you do, do you?" It obviously took an effort to achieve that tone. But she did it.

"Lie back and let me show you something," he said quietly.

She raised her eyebrows, and her pretty mouth turned up at the corners. "I've already seen it, thank you."

"Smart-ass. Close your eyes and let me show you how I feel."

Delanie ran her hand up his arm to his shoulder. "You feel terrific." She lowered herself to the tent floor, eyes dark as she watched his face.

"Close your eyes, woman. And don't move," he added.

Delanie dutifully closed her eyes. "At all?"

"For as long as you can stand it."

Delanie smiled slightly. "Wake me up when you're done, Tarzan."

"Ten bucks says I can make you move in the next five minutes."

She opened one eye. "Is that a dare?"

"Yeah."

Delanie stretched out her arms in fake supplication and shut her eyes. "Have at it, Valentino."

Kyle smoothed her bangs off her face. "Good girl."

Delanie snorted.

"Let's see . . . where are we?"

"Sweating in a teeny-weeny tent in the middle of the jungle?"

"Whose fantasy is this?

"Yours, apparently."

"Hotel room," Kyle decided, his breath warm beneath her ear. She hadn't realized he'd moved closer. "Doesn't matter where. It's cool. The shutters are open. Can you feel the soft ocean breeze on your skin?"

Kyle's breath fanned her neck. He licked, then blew softly down the damp skin of her throat.

"Uh-huh."

"I want this to be slow. Can you understand that? I don't want to wait for a real bed . . . *can't* wait for a real bed. So use every bit of your imagination, jungle girl, and think of a king-size, with crisp cotton sheets. We're going for a slow, slow ride." He kissed the corner of her mouth, and she felt the jackhammer of his heart where his chest rested against her side.

Delanie turned her head a fraction and laid her closed mouth against his. He nuzzled her lips with his own, making no attempt to deepen the kiss. Nevertheless a buzz of arousal hummed across her skin as he moved his head slowly from side to side just grazing her mouth. The tip of his tongue painted a feather-light trace of moisture across her lower lip. Delanie's breath sighed as he blew softly to cool down the heat he was generating.

She could have told him the ploy wouldn't work. She was already experiencing internal combustion. Supersensitive now to the lightness of his touch, and the soft puffs of cool air, Delanie opened her mouth just wide enough to take his upper lip between her own. She sucked gently and felt a rush of heat as his answering groan caused her lips to buzz.

Stroking her cheek with his fingertips, Kyle reversed the action, alternately nuzzling softly, and tenderly sucking at her lower lip. Delanie almost came up off the ground.

Kyle kissed her eyelids, her temples, her nose, chin, below her eyes. Her eyebrows. Varying from smooth and dry, to cool and damp. He nipped and soothed, until it was impossible to tell one insanity-inducing action from the other. Finally he lifted his head, eyes glittering, and whispered, "Feeling cool yet?"

She was hot enough to explode. But God, this was amazing. Slow, thorough . . . incredible. "Oh, sure." There was nothing cool about what he was doing to her. Even her brain felt hot. And she wasn't going to move until she absolutely *had* to.

His chuckle brushed her throat. Her lips missed his. He took small tender bites from her neck, alternating with soft cool breaths that made her shiver and moan and long to squiggle about.

Her chest felt cool, and she realized he'd lifted her T-shirt at some point. Sneaky man. She waited vainly for him to touch her breast.

"Ah—?"

Kyle brushed a maddeningly lazy kiss on the curve between her neck and shoulder. "Got a bus to catch?"

"I'm five minutes past *ready*," Delanie grumbled brokenly.

"The room's paid through tomorrow." Kyle rubbed a slow finger across her mouth and continued feasting on her neck. Delanie dampened his finger with her tongue, then sucked the digit into her mouth and sucked on it to pay him back. He groaned and lifted his head long enough to peel the thin, cotton T-shirt over her head.

When he came back it was to her mouth. God she was ready. *More* than ready. He French-kissed her deeply. Maddeningly, frustratingly slowly. The tip of his tongue ran lightly against the roof of her mouth, then traced a line across her teeth.

Delanie slid her tongue against his. Leisurely. Take that. *Stroke*. And that. *Stroke*.

She was excited far out of proportion to the actual physical contact. Just the anticipation of where he would touch her next was driving her crazy. It seemed they kissed for years, a century, before she felt the brush of Kyle's hand on her breast. She wanted him to hurry. She wanted him to slow down. She felt boiling hot, and freezing cold. Her nipples were so hard they hurt. Kyle's fingers gently soothed, then made the small erections feel a hundred times more sensitive when he licked and blew across them just as he'd done an eon ago across her mouth.

"I'll . . . pay . . . you back for . . . this."

He bit down gently. "I'm banking on it, sweetheart. I'm banking on it." The low, soft register of his voice made her shiver and ache. He stroked and kissed and petted her breasts, and with each new torment his hair brushed across her bare midriff.

Delanie reached out unerringly to curl her fingers around the ridged length of his penis through his pants. He removed her hand. "Na-ah. No touching, I'll go too fast. This one is strictly for you."

"No fair. I want to play, too."

"You will. Later. Much later."

She tangled her fingers in the rich black silk of his hair and pressed his mouth to her right nipple. "Here," she told him firmly, then took his hand, and slid his fingers down the front of the thin, cotton fatigue pants she wore, so that he finally, *finally* touched her. "And here."

Kyle curled unhurried fingers to cup her while he paid attention to her nipple.

Nerve endings on fire, unable to keep her body still, Delanie tried to get a grip on her spinning senses. She could barely draw enough breath to lodge a complaint. "Kyle! Damn it. The world has ended. Dinosaurs are back on the planet. The stars have aligned. The polar caps have melted—"

Kyle's laughter was strained. But he *finally* shifted his body over hers and effectively shut her up with a languid, succulent kiss. *Then* he slid inside her like a benediction, inch by agonizingly, *dillydallying* inch.

And holy Hannah, did he know how to make a good thing last. And last and last. Delanie was a limp noodle when Kyle was done with her.

"I'll mail you a check," Delanie managed, more than twenty minutes after they'd made love. She lay cradled, okay *glued,* to his side, his arm beneath her head, her cheek on his chest.

He was playing with her hair as he said a weak "Huh?"

"I don't have any cash on me."

"Ah, the ten bucks."

"I moved."

"You did?" Kyle sounded surprised. "I thought it was the earth."

Delanie smiled. "That, too." The hair on his chest was crisp and springy. She ran her fingers through the mat and followed it down to his groin. They both still wore not only their pants, which were at half-mast, but their combat boots as well.

Too exhausted to do anything other than touch, Delanie trailed her hand back to safer ground. She rested her hand over his heart. Kyle draped his arm over her hip and trailed his fingers back and forth over the dip of her belly button.

Tell him, she thought. *Tell him now while we're physically close.* When she didn't have to look him in the eye. *Coward.*

"I can practically hear your agile little mind ticking away. What are you thinking about?" Kyle asked against her forehead. God, the man's intuition was terrifying.

The rain stopped as suddenly as it had started, leaving a pulsing silence inside the confines of the tent.

"I was pregnant," Delanie said so low and strained he almost missed it.

He rose on his elbow to stare down at her. "What?" A strange sensation unfurled inside him, almost of sweet anticipation. "You were pregnant?" His heart started beating again in a triumphant rhythm. "We have a child?"

Delanie sat up and pulled on her T-shirt, covering her rosy breasts. "No." She drew the fatigue pants up to her waist and curled her legs under her like a mermaid.

Kyle closed his eyes, inhaling sharply. He didn't give a flying continental fuck that his family jewels were exposed. He opened his eyes to pin her in place. "You had an abortion?"

Her chin jerked as if he'd administered a blow. "What the hell difference would it have made to you? You weren't there."

"I would have moved heaven and earth to be with you."

He listened to the water drip off the canvas, the silence inside the tent absolute, before she said roughly, "The doctors called it a spontaneous abortion."

He held her prisoner with his gaze. There was a look in her eyes he'd never seen before and found hard to interpret. Anger?

No. Guilt. And bottomless pain.

He wanted to hold her so badly his throat ached. But before they could comfort each other, she had to purge that pain and bone-deep sorrow. She held her eyes steady. Her chin tilted belligerently, daring him to . . . what?

"And you didn't care because you hated me that much?" he asked softly. Not believing it for a moment. *Oh, jungle girl, what in God's name am I going to do with you?*

"Do you blame me?" Her breath shuddered, but Kyle held himself still. For both their sakes it was better not to touch her right now. He pulled up his pants and moved a few feet away, his fist clenched on his knees.

"I thought about having an . . . having an abortion. I was so angry. Angry at you. Angry at myself. Angry that my *family* was angry. My head knew it was the most practical solution, the most logical— But my h-heart— In the end I couldn't do it." Her throat moved convulsively and she blinked rapidly, obviously struggling to hold back tears. She whispered brokenly, "I loved her too much, and God took her away."

Her eyes filled.

Hell with it.

He reached out and pulled her into his arms. "How much you loved her had nothing to do with it," Kyle told her gruffly. Her face felt hot and damp against his neck. His own throat felt tightly restricted as she cautiously slid her arms around his waist, as if doubting her welcome, then held on tightly.

He buried his face in her hair, his damp eyes squeezed tightly for their shared loss. "You had a right to do whatever was necessary for your family's survival," he said, his hand gentle on her back as she rested her head against his chest.

"You were gone. And all I could think about was that I would have another mouth to feed, another person dependent on me. Another eighteen years before . . ." She laughed brokenly. "What an irony that my guilt at the *thought* of it has been a bigger burden than the baby could ever have been."

His fingers spanned her back. God, she felt frail under his hands, her bones delicate, her skin soft. He was so used to her roaring like a lion, it was always a shock when he touched her and rediscovered she wasn't made of steel.

"My arms still ache to h-hold her."

Kyle held her safely in his arms and let her cry for both of them.

Delanie felt raw inside and out, relieved she'd finally told him about the baby. Sharing the burden with Kyle had made it easier to bear. She rested her swollen face against the steady beat of his heart. It felt so good, so achingly wonderful to have his large hand stroking her back through her shirt. Her eyes stung and she squeezed them shut, trying to memorize his scent and touch. Something to recall later. She shifted and he immediately released her.

She felt cold without his arms around her. Not that he could move too far away. The tent was crowded to capacity and she could feel the heat of his body as he sat beside her.

She surprised herself with a yawn. "Talk to me."

"Want a bedtime story?"

"Hmm. With a happy ending. Tell me about your family."

"Okay, but lie back and close your eyes. It's been a hell of a day, and you need to get some rest."

Delanie curled on her side and shut her eyes. "Talk."

"I've been damned lucky. My family's terrific. We've always been close."

Delanie heard the smile in his voice seconds before she felt his fingers sifting absently through her hair. She wanted to purr.

"Your dad's a widower?"

"Yeah, Mom was killed the day after my seventh birthday. Drunk driver. God. I just remembered . . . We still had chocolate birthday cake in the fridge on the day of her funeral."

"I'm sorry," Delanie said softly into the silence. "Forget it. Talking about family isn't always the most cheerful of subjects, is it?"

"Actually, I have lots of terrific memories of my mother. Not enough, but great memories nevertheless. She'd frosted my seventh birthday cake with white sailboats on a navy blue ocean, and we all had blue tongues at my party." Kyle grinned. "She was something else. Loved sewing our Halloween costumes, no matter how crazy we wanted them to be. She always claimed she'd popped out all us kids one after the other so she and Dad could get all our teenage years over with as quickly as possible and enjoy their old age in peace."

Kyle lay back and slid his arms under her neck, bringing Delanie's head to rest on his chest. She heard the steady beat of his heart beneath her ear, and rested her hand on his hard, flat stomach.

"She loved all of you."

"God, yes. There was never any question of that. But it was the love she had for my father that I'll always remember. Of course as a little kid I thought all that kissing was gross."

"And your father never remarried?"

"No. But he dates now and then."

"No woman's touch?"

"Oh, sure. My grandmother moved in with us after our mom died. She was awesome—tough as an old boot, with a mushy heart. She ruled us with the proverbial velvet glove." Kyle stroked Delanie's cheek. "I loved that old girl. She died last year."

"And your brothers and sister?"

"You'll meet Michael later. He's the oldest. Navy all the way. I've never seen anything that ruffles him. He's rock solid. Then there are the twins, Derek and Kane. Derek's a rancher. I'm damn grateful I met you first. Derek is charm personified, not to mention he's okay looking."

Okay looking? Delanie smiled. "And Kane?"

"They're twins. So same looks, but completely opposite dispositions. Claims he's a photographer."

"What is he?"

Kyle shrugged. "Let me put it this way, he takes pictures in some very strange places."

"And what about your sister?"

"Marnie," his voice softened. "She'll love you, and you two will get along famously. My little sis is one of the nicest women I know. She had a bad heart as a kid, and we tended to spoil the hell out of her, but she's come through with shining colors . . . God. She must've had the baby by now . . ."

Delanie forced herself not to stiffen. Women had babies all the time—

"Sorry," Kyle murmured. "I didn't think—"

"That's okay. Tell me more."

"Later. Your turn. Tell me about this vast family of yours."

Delanie shrugged. "Not a whole lot to tell. My mom has three sisters. So, three aunts and their assorted families. Lots of cousins. It's like wrangling greased eels." She chuckled. "Trust me, there's never a dull moment."

"And they all live near you in Sacramento?"

"Most of them, thank goodness. They're easier to corral that way. My mom's lived in Los Angeles for the last ten or so years. She's an actress. I'm really proud of her. She's had several bit parts in made-for-TV movies, some commercials. Lauren gets her looks from Mom, who doesn't look old enough to have adult daughters."

"And who do you take after?"

She felt the brush of his hand on her hair. "I'm a hybrid, I guess."

"No contact with your father?"

"Nope. He has other interests."

"What could possibly be more interesting than two beautiful daughters?"

"He already had a wife and family when he and my mother had their affair. Lauren and I didn't have any impact on his life one way or the other."

"That must hurt," Kyle said softly. "I can't imagine what it would be like not having my dad around."

"I didn't miss what I never had."

There was a pause before he said quietly, "Such a tough cookie."

Delanie smiled sleepily. "They call me the Rock." Of Gibraltar. Always there. Always on duty. Twenty-four/seven/three hundred sixty-five.

His shirt smelled of rain, damp under her cheek; she could feel the heat of his skin through it. "What will you do when you get back to Sacramento?"

"Find another job. I never went back after spring break. They've probably replaced me by now. Take care of Lauren."

"Realistically you must know that's not going to happen," he said against the top of her head. He sounded as weary as she felt.

"Why not?"

"Look, this conversation can wait until we find—"

"Why not?"

He hesitated, "If she's alive, and if she's still up here—two big *ifs*—chances are she's already addicted to whatever Isabella forced on her. You're not the right person to help an addict. No matter how much you want to."

He pulled her farther up his chest, his arm tightening around her back. The night closed in around them. Rain started again, thudding intermittently on the canvas overhead.

Delanie tried to relax.

"*Wherever* she is, we'll find her. My people have an incredibly good clinic where she'll be well taken care of, whatever her needs are when we find her."

"She's not dead."

"If she's got half your tenacity, I'd bet the ranch she isn't."

His mouth brushed across her hair, but his hold on her felt

impersonal for all that they were practically on top of each other.

To her disgust she realized she was crying. It wasn't even a satisfying cry, she was just too tired to hold back the waves of emotion that had been building since she discovered Lauren's disappearance. The tears leaked from beneath her lashes, saturating his shirt and chest in a steady flow.

"It kills you that you can't fix this, doesn't it?"

"Of course I—"

"You need her that much?"

"Lauren will need me, and I'll be there. Just like I've always been there for her."

She felt his hand against her hair. "And I'll be there for you, jungle girl."

"I told you. I don't need anyone."

"Don't you?" His thumb brushed her mouth in a caress. "How many guys have you slept with in the past four years?"

"None of your business."

"That's where you're wrong," he said softly. "How many?"

"None," she admitted. "So what? I have a low sex drive."

Kyle threw his head back and roared with laughter.

Her cheeks flamed and she would have socked him if she'd had the energy. "It's not necessary to talk about this."

"Yeah it is. I think the reason you jumped into bed with me so quickly when we first met was because you *did* need someone. Desperately."

His finger pressed gently over her mouth when she started to protest. "Get some sleep, it'll be time to get up before you know it. I'll wake you when the others arrive."

She closed her eyes, too tired to protest. Just as she toppled over the edge of sleep she thought she heard him whisper, "What the hell am I going to do with you, jungle girl?"

Chapter Twenty

The call of nature could be a real pain, Delanie decided, pulling up her pants quickly. Kyle had tried insisting he go with her. Lord, he'd seen everything there was of her to see, but she drew the line at him standing guard while she peed. His presence wouldn't have prevented the something that had bitten her bottom.

She scratched the welt as she walked, being careful where she stepped. The ground was squishy, the foliage leaked water overhead, and her pants were already wet up to her knees from the undergrowth. She'd never realized how homesick she'd be for her own utilitarian white-tile bathroom and a light switch.

It was darker than pitch. The flashlight only illuminated about four feet in front of her, and she could feel things watching her as she passed. "Seven, eight," she mumbled under her breath, counting off the bits of white bandage she'd industriously tied to branches to find her way back.

"Nine. Ten." The beam strafed a plate-size acid yellow orchid, which she pushed out of her way without admiring its beauty. She wasn't going to miss the rain forest one bit. The flowers were pretty, but the next time she saw an orchid she wanted it to be in a vase.

Darn. She could have sworn she hadn't gone that far—What was that? Pausing, she clicked off the flashlight. A twig snapping? A branch broken? She knew the birds were silent because she'd passed beneath their perches, but was there someone else out here? One of Montero's men? She froze in place, tilting her head to get a better look through the leaves. It was too dark to see *anything*. A residue puddle of rainwater tilted the leaf it was on, splashing her arm as she stood dead still, straining to see.

A frond moved off to the left. Suddenly an arm came around her throat, pulling her off balance and scaring the crap out of her. Her body was drawn against a hard male form. Not Kyle, she knew immediately. Whoever he was, he was bulkier.

"Let go, you son of a bitch!"

Delanie elbowed him in the stomach. He grunted, but held fast.

She let her body go limp for a second. His arm dropped. Springing away from him, she found her balance on the loamy earth and swung her leg in a high arc, aiming for his chin. She drew in a sharp hiss at the agony the movement caused her ankle.

With incredible speed the man grabbed her ankle as her foot came within inches of his temple. He barely glanced at her as he held her leg above her head for a moment and then tipped her slightly so that she fell on her bottom with an ignominious yelp.

God, he was quick. Before she knew it, he hauled her to her feet and imprisoned her against his chest, his forearm around her throat, an unforgiving arm around her waist. Her nails dug into his muscular forearm as he carried her wriggling into camp.

Kyle, standing in a dim circle of light made by a small kerosene lamp, greeted them with the business end of an Uzi.

The arm across her windpipe loosened somewhat. Delanie took the opportunity to kick back, eliciting a grunt and a muffled laugh. "Yours?" The amused tone behind her was gruff.

"Hiya, bro. Yeah." Kyle's eyes held an answering glint of humor as he dropped the weapon to his side. "Mine." He reached out to snag her arm, drawing her to stand beside him.

Instead of moving away from his proprietary hold on her,

Delanie shifted closer, keeping her eyes on the other man. She subtly wiped the perspiration off her face against her shoulder. The burn throbbed painfully. She gritted her teeth and ignored it, focusing on the two men instead.

Good Lord, a Kyle clone. Not quite. This one was more muscular, and he looked a little more civilized than Kyle, not that that was saying much. His dark hair was cut military short; he wore fatigues, heavy boots, and a big grin.

"Shoot him," she told Kyle pithily, rubbing a hand over the seat of her pants, which were now soaking wet from her fall.

"Nah." Kyle grinned. "He's a good guy."

"Isn't that an oxymoron?" She reluctantly moved away, then bent to pour herself a cup of coffee.

Freshly shaven, and with that buzz cut and spotless fatigues, Kyle's brother made Delanie feel like a bag lady who'd just emerged from her home in a Dumpster.

"Ah, hell." Michael groaned catching the look that passed between them. "You're sleeping with her."

Delanie almost choked on a sip of coffee. "I *beg* your pardon!"

"She's San Francisco," Kyle said flatly.

"Is she now?" his brother asked, glancing from one to the other with deceptively lazy eyes. "Serious?"

"Death and taxes."

"Rules?"

"Bangkok," Kyle said dryly, and both men laughed.

Michael glanced back at camp. "Where's the other one?"

"Haven't found her yet. Delanie, my brother Michael. Delanie Eastman."

"You two must have attended the same charm school," she said sweetly, coming up beside Kyle with a steaming mug of coffee in her hand.

Kyle took the cup from her, drank, then passed it back. "Others close behind?" he asked his brother as he laid a possessive hand on her nape under her hair.

"Right behind." Michael withdrew a mug from the small pack he carried and moved over to the burner and the coffeepot. "Want a cup, Tin Man?" he asked without turning as another man emerged through the gloom.

Lord, Delanie thought as the man stepped into the light, *another big one.*

"Thanks," the new guy said quietly, looking strangely relieved to see Kyle.

"Hey, man. What're *you* doing here? I thought you were involved in training up in the Sierras these days." Clearly surprised to see him, Kyle clasped the second guy on his broad shoulder and squeezed.

"Are you kidding?" Tin Man—*Tin Man?*—grinned. "Marnie insisted I be here for the curtain call. She was getting worried. Besides, you have a fairy princess waiting back home to meet you. Your new niece has to be seen to be believed. We wanted to be sure you got back in one piece."

"Nice to know everyone has so much confidence in my abilities," Kyle said dryly. "Delanie," he drew her into the group to introduce her, keeping his arm around her shoulders. "Jake Dolan. Friend, brother-in-law. Delanie Eastman." No qualification this time.

"Hey." His brother-in-law acknowledged the introduction without looking at her. "Doc, our confidence in you is rock solid. It's the other teams we're not so sure about."

Several men entered the clearing, drifting in like shadows to stand just out of the feeble glow of the lantern. In camouflage and with their faces painted, they were almost invisible, their movements stealthy and sure as they moved about with purpose.

Delanie moved to the tarp on the far side of the clearing and sat down, watching the men as they gathered and silently separated into groups, checked equipment and weapons, and conversed in the kind of shorthand Kyle and Michael had used earlier, only this time, in deadly earnest.

Over the next hour a dozen more men slipped into camp. They moved about silently, using hand gestures as a form of shorthand.

Eyes burning with fatigue, Delanie dozed. It was only

when the men started stripping off that she focused on what was happening around her. Holy Hannah. She'd never see so many naked, buffed men in her entire life.

Kyle came over and hunkered down beside her. His mouth twitched with amusement. "Close your mouth, jungle girl. They're off limits."

They also didn't care that there was a woman in their midst as they quickly drew strange, skintight black bodysuits over their naked bodies and started strapping on an arsenal of weapons. A shudder traveled up Delanie's spine.

"It's show time. I have to go ahead," Kyle told her. "These two will lead you back to the bomb shelter and stay with you." A couple of guys, a Mutt and Jeff team of tall and short, floated out of the darkness. "Lynx, Savage, take good care of her."

They both wore black paint on their faces, which obscured their features, and formfitting headgear as part of the rubber suits. Only their eyes reflected what little light the lantern cast. Lynx was the big silent one who mock-saluted Kyle.

The little Savage gave Delanie a rude up-and-down glance. "If she hadn't screwed up in San Cristóbal, we wouldn't have to play bloody baby-sitter."

Delanie's eyebrows shot up at the sound of a husky, feminine voice. "You're a woman!"

Narrow shoulders stiffened under the tight black suit. "And your point is?"

"If you can't handle the assignment, Savage," Kyle said coolly, "say so."

"I can handle it just fine," the woman said coldly, keeping narrowed eyes on Delanie. "But it would be easier to get rid of her here. I'll do it."

"You and Lynx will take her to the appointed drop-off and hand her safely off to the men stationed there. Then you can take your designated places," Kyle told her flatly. "Is that clear?"

"As a bell. Come on, Lynx." She gave Delanie a you-are-such-a-pain-in-the-ass look. "We'll be over there, ready to change your nappy before we go." She stomped off across the camp, her partner in tow.

"She's charming," Delanie said, watching the woman's narrow back disappear into the darkness.

"I've seen Savage kill a man with her bare hands. She'll get you to the shelter safely," Kyle told her, wrapping her in his arms. "Stay put until either Michael or myself come for you."

His breath smelled of coffee, dark and rich. Delanie closed her eyes and felt the brush of his hair against her face and the warmth of his fingers curve against her cheek. "And don't try anything heroic, okay?"

"You don't have to warn me. I'm already scared."

"Scared is good." He didn't smile. "The men know to look for Lauren. If she's anywhere on Izquierdo, she'll be found and brought to you."

His thumb caressed her lower lip and she tilted her face. He kissed her softly on the mouth, his lips lingering before he rose, pulling her up to stand beside him. "We've got plenty more talking to do, jungle girl. Keep yourself safe until I come for you."

"I won't do anything stupid. I promise." Delanie paused. "What exactly are *Bangkok* rules?"

Kyle grinned. "There aren't any."

Three thirty-three A.M., pitch dark and dead quiet. No lights on, inside or outside the house. Kyle observed the quiet compound from behind the chain-link fence and the cover of the trees just outside the clearing. In the green glow of his night-vision goggles, he scanned each building and the wide gravel areas between them for signs of life. Something wasn't right. There wasn't a guard in sight. His sixth sense kicked in big time.

Standing motionless, every sense alert, he heard the imperceptible—more a feeling than a sound—*whop-whop-whop* of the choppers as they came in from east and south. The sound faded in and out, too far away for someone not on the alert to hear. Right on time, he thought with satisfaction. Through the lenses of the NVG he saw more of his men melt into place along the perimeter.

Jungle noise, a few chirps and clicks from birds and insects, the rustle of something moving through the low vegetation deeper in the jungle. He walked carefully, narrowly missing an olingo only because he'd seen the red glow of the furry creature's eyes glaring at him just before he stepped on it. It ran like hell, its soft tail trailing it like mist. The air was dead still and hot, the humidity its usual ninety percent.

They all wore voice-activated radio headsets with lip mikes. Through his earpiece Kyle heard the Mossad check in, then the DEA, Interpol, the Europeans, and finally the two T-FLAC teams on the far side of the compound. That done, they'd maintain radio silence unless absolutely necessary.

Everyone was in place. Party time.

He restrained himself from checking on Delanie one last time before he went in. She was as safe as she was going to be, and well away from the action.

Behind him two T-FLAC men set up a squad automatic weapon on its bipod, canvas ammo pouch unzipped on the ground beside them. The SAW's two hundred rounds were ready, and several other pouches lay next to the first.

Kyle switched his headset to T-FLAC's frequency. "Alpha team, close in. Doc, over."

Click-click. The signal heard and executed by the others.

Michael took point, moving like smoke toward the fence. Kyle only knew his brother was there because it was where he was supposed to be. Michael had the uncanny ability to blend in with his surroundings like a chameleon.

Three meters away, Kyle spotted a sentry standing on the other side of the fence, his back to the jungle. He was smoking a cigarette, and the pale smoke drifted straight over his head like a specter. Out of the corner of his eye, with the help of his NVG, Kyle spotted the identifying firefly attached to the shirt of one of his men. He motioned him forward, indicated he could take the soldier, then left him to it, creeping behind the two men quietly in the dark. He heard a sharp but faint grunt and then a thud as the body hit the dirt behind him.

As ephemeral as vapor, the rest of his team materialized beside him. He gave the signal to scale the fence.

The house was over five hundred yards away, all of it in the open the moment they cleared the fence. Other than the half pergola roof over one end of the pool and the rock waterfall, they would be as bare as a baby's butt for a good two and a half minutes as they crossed the brick patio to the hacienda.

Heaven, Kyle thought with a grin as he joined the others on the compound side. Enjoying the hell out of the adrenaline rush, he pivoted his head and saw the same intense concentrated expectation on his men's faces.

They were on the north side of the house, almost directly opposite the boardroom. Every room in the house opened up to the patio with French doors. It hadn't occurred to Montero just how vulnerable his impenetrable hideaway was. In sign language Kyle indicated for the others to fan out as pre-arranged.

There were too few operatives in this phase of the operation to provide backup. Until individual assignments had been achieved each man was on his own. According to the T-FLAC sentries posted, no one had left the compound all day. Everybody was snugly in bed inside the main house.

Kyle stepped from the gravel onto the brick patio, his booted feet silent as he crouched low, stealthily and rapidly crossing the open area. He heard the sibilant whisper of voices. Three soldiers were shooting the breeze, taking a smoke break in the deep shadow close to the house. The glow of their cigarettes made them prime targets in the dark.

Pushing up his goggles because they tended to blur anything close up, Kyle removed the knife from the leather sheath on his wrist. Holding it loosely in his right hand, he crept up behind the least vocal of the men. He applied the knife with deadly intent high up, into the kidneys so the guy dropped without a sound. The second the body dropped, he had the attention of the other two. The soldiers looked at him in dumbfounded surprise as he vaulted over their friend, arms outstretched. His momentum carried him between the two soldiers, still fumbling for their weapons.

"Hey, *amigos,* remember me?" he asked, colliding with them at the same time he hooked an arm around each thick neck. Holding them cradled in the crook of his elbows, he exerted pressure with his biceps and shoulder muscles to bring their heads together with an audible thump. They dropped like stones to the ground. He dragged the bodies deeper into the shadows and opened the French door into the dark, quiet conference room.

A protracted burst of automatic weapon fire broke the silence, slicing the night with noise and light. Half inside the room, Kyle froze in his tracks.

Someone swore ripely in his ear through the bone-conducting headphone. He dittoed the sentiment. What the hell were they firing *at*?

"Hell," Kyle snarled under his breath as gunfire erupted, closer this time, lighting up the room. He spun to check outside and saw one of the good guys hanging limply over the chain-link fence, yards from where he and his men had gone over. Another burst of fire caused the body to jerk and fall back on the jungle side.

Like a frigging sunrise, the floodlights sprang on around the perimeter, blinding anyone wearing NVGs. The element of surprise was gone. The cameras would track every movement now. He quickly stepped inside, closing the door behind him.

Those men who hadn't already entered the compound were now neatly trapped beyond the fence.

"Alpha leader. What the hell happened? Doc, over," he demanded, holding his finger over the earpiece as he stepped to the side of the French door, observing the reigning pandemonium through a twelve-inch square of glass. The headset attached to the satellite radio, and the signal went twenty-two thousand miles to a geosynchronous communications satellite in less time than it took to make a telephone call. The satellite radio was encoded. The algorithm, based on the timed transmissions from NAVSTAR satellites, was on computer disc so that no one could break the security or duplicate it. Which was all moot at this point. The shit had hit the fan, and they might as well goddamn *yell* instructions to one another.

The radio crackled in his ear. He repeated himself, watching as half-dressed men tumbled out of the barracks several hundred yards away from the main buildings. The gravel crunched under their boots as, blinded by the floodlights, they fumbled for their weapons. They might have been alerted, but they still moved around like frantic half-awake ants. Kyle shifted his M4 into position. After several seconds of static, he heard Dare reply through the earpiece as something exploded behind the house, sending up a shower of sparks and rocking the ground. Christ, the Interpol team was covering that quadrant, and there weren't supposed to be any big explosions until the house had been secured and cleared of people and all the evidence as well as Montero's extensive collection of stolen artwork had been removed.

The hacienda was now lit up like a Christmas tree. He could see some of his men outside although most blended with the vegetation.

"The assholes from Interpol decided to go in early. Tin Man, out." Jake. Where the hell were Dare and Michael? He didn't have time to find out. While the early attention wouldn't degrade what was to come, it was damn irritating that the other team hadn't followed the directives from their last briefing.

"God damn it!" There was another short burst of gunfire. More lights went on. Doors slammed. Footsteps pounded on the slate floor of hallway. Shouts.

The gunfire outside was erratic, Montero's soldiers shooting more to hear themselves than at any target. In his headset he could hear the soft commands of the team leaders urging their people in.

The Mossad team called in their confirmed capture of
Kensington, Sugano, Danzigger, and the cook, Dr. Montgomery.

Now, where the hell were the Monteros?

Another steady burst of fire, this time directed at the
house as more soldiers poured from the barracks, fanning
out across the compound. They were too skillfully deployed
to be the goons Kyle had seen playing at training all week.

It was two hours till dawn. The throb of the choppers got
louder. Activity escalated as the soldiers started randomly
shooting at the lights in the sky.

Trusting his people to take control of the situation, Kyle
made his way around the koa table, smelling the thick scent
of old cigar smoke and greed. Montero was going away for a
long, long time, and his pretty face was going to be a real li-
ability where he was going. Sanctimonious bastard should
be sweating about now, Kyle thought, weapon ready. Ramón
and Isabella must know there was no way they were going to
escape.

Overhead he heard the first call for surrender. Choppers
flew low over the compound. Floodlights strafed the buildings. A megaphoned voice repeated in Spanish and English
for everyone to come outside with their hands up.

Every light blazed inside the house; the corridor crawled
with uniforms. Ducking back into the doorway, Kyle ditched
his headset and NVG, then tucked the knife back into his
wrist sheath before stepping casually from the boardroom
and sauntering down the wide hallway. Two soldiers outside
the library straightened, almost saluting as he strolled by.
Neither stopped him as he gave them a half smile and
opened the door.

Taking in the room at a glance, Kyle's eyes found Delanie
across the room where she stood in the shadows, Montero
directly behind her.

Shit.

The man who stepped into Montero's library was different
from the one she'd parted from in the jungle a few hours ago.

With his face painted, hair loose about his shoulders, he looked a hell of a lot scarier in the light than he had in the dark. But it was neither his clothing nor his face paint that sent a primitive shiver up Delanie's spine.

Not a scrap of softness touched him, no latent tenderness in his eyes, no compassion, no spark of humor. This was Kyle Wright, soldier of fortune. Hard, silent, and lethal. She didn't realize how relieved she was to see him, until she felt her shoulders drop with the taut expulsion of air from her lungs.

Kyle shot her a quick molten look before closing the door behind him. "Jesus, woman, you sure as hell know how to get into trouble." He stepped away from the door, an extremely nasty-looking gun in his hand.

"Some of his soldiers grabbed us on the way to—"

Montero goose-stepped her farther out into the room, his arm hooked around her throat, his mother's branding iron in his other hand. The tip had cooled enough to go from bright to dark red. One wrong move, he'd promised her, and he'd burn her until she begged to have her neck broken. She believed him.

Kyle's eyes narrowed as they flickered to her face for a second. "All right?" he asked, the words belying the brutal indifference in his voice.

"Not really." She could barely hear with the blood pounding so hard in her ears. She wasn't quite sure if she wanted to throw up, wet her pants, or just faint. She swallowed and had to lock her knees as she felt the fiery heat against her right cheek. The wound on her ankle pulsed painfully in tandem with her frantic heartbeats. She stared dry-eyed at Kyle.

"Put the gun down, *amigo,*" Montero said silkily. "I have a much more effective and immediate weapon right here."

Her nostrils flared as the sweet smell of heated iron moved closer; then she flinched as she heard, then smelled, the sizzle of her hair. Sweat prickled her scalp and underarms, and she clenched her teeth on a scream.

"Just shoot him," she said through dry lips. The hole in the end of Kyle's gun rose so she could practically see down the barrel.

"Let her go. Now."

Fascinated, Delanie couldn't take her eyes off Kyle's finger on the trigger. She knew he'd go for Montero the second he had a clear shot. And as the man was the same height as she was, she'd better not flinch. *Do it,* she thought urgently. *Oh God, please just* do *it.*

She braced herself.

"Whatever the hell you think you can negotiate for, forget it."

Behind her she felt Ramón tense. His arm tightened around her throat. She could smell his nervousness through the overpowering sweet smell of his cologne. Her dry eyes burned. All she could think about was the branding iron an inch from her face. A drop of sweat trickled down her temple. She didn't know which was worse, Montero with a steady, sure hand, or Montero with a nervous twitch.

"Your resurrected playmate wishes to know where her sister is, *amigo.*" Montero's arm almost cut off her air and the heat didn't waver. "If I am dead, she will never know. Drop your weapon, or I will take out her eye." She could see the image of the cobra on the tip of the metal rod.

Stalemate.

Delanie stared straight ahead. Kyle knew what he was doing. When he wanted her to do something he'd let her know; in the meantime she'd do her best not to pass out, scream, or choke while he thought about it.

"I don't give a rat's ass what she wants." Kyle's voice carried over the sound of gunfire and helicopters overhead. "I've come for *you, amigo,* and I've waited a long, long time."

Montero laughed. "You believe I will go with you? A lamb to the slaughter?"

"Hear that?" Kyle pointed the barrel of his gun directly at her chest, indicating the sounds outside with a tilt of his head. "That's *adios* to the rest of your new cartel and goodbye to selling off the smallpox. I destroyed the virus before the meeting yesterday. Let her go, Montero."

"You think I won't burn her?"

"I know if you do, you'll be dead half a second later."

"Will my death matter, when your woman has no eye? I want a helicopter with a pilot and safe passage to San Cristóbal."

She didn't believe Kyle would actually do what Ramón wanted, so she was horrified when he tossed his gun aside.

"Don't—"

But Kyle's eyes were fixed on the man behind her. "He won't shoot me yet," he said blandly, not in the least perturbed. "He needs both of us to get out of here. Isn't that right, you little chicken turd?"

Montero dragged her closer to the doors, glancing at the men swarming all over the patio. Heat lay like a blazing strip across her cheek. Another fraction of an inch, and that iron would fry her skin. God. She *hated* this.

"You'd better warn your men it's you," Kyle said grimly as Montero opened the door. Not that he gave a shit if one of the soldiers hit Montero, but he sure as hell would object to either himself or Delanie catching a bullet.

Christ. How the hell had the bastard found her? Not that it mattered. He'd been purposefully trying not to look at her terrified face. He could feel the scream hovering behind her lips, a scream he recalled chillingly from Isabella's house. Eyes enormous in her pale face, she looked at him just before Montero motioned him to walk outside first.

A strafe of gunfire lit up the still water of the swimming pool, shooting up pellets of water. An enormous explosion rocked the walls. Thick plumes of black smoke billowed into the bleached blue of the dawn sky.

"There goes your new drug lab," Kyle taunted. Smoke hung thick in the air as he stepped outside. His eyes scanned the area for his own men. They were well concealed, but everywhere. By full light he knew there would be nothing left of the factory but rubble. He saw it in his mind's eye. Destruction of apocalyptic proportions.

"I will build another," Montero said with all confidence,

and then shouted out in Spanish for the men to stand clear. He dragged Delanie beside him, presumably so both factions held their fire.

Kyle observed the branding iron, still hot enough to do Delanie serious damage as Montero rested his arm on her shoulder. Without warning, Delanie dropped like a rock, slipping out of Montero's hold and coming down hard on the brick in a tumbling roll. She immediately scrabbled like a crab out of his reach.

Montero swore.

"Atta girl!" Kyle shouted, as a sudden blast of light indicated a shot from beyond the chain-link fence. Montero howled with pain as a bullet ripped through his upper arm. He dropped the branding iron with a clatter, then hunkered down, doubled over, whimpering like a child.

Out of his peripheral vision Kyle saw Delanie glance over her shoulder at him. Her eyes widened. Kyle shifted a fraction of a second too late. The blow to the back of his head dropped him to his knees.

Chapter Twenty-one

"Don't you dare pass out," Delanie ordered.

Kyle opened his eyes to see her crouched beside him, looking worried. He hadn't seen her move. He frowned. She wrapped her arms around his waist, and he felt a rush of relief that she was all right.

He helped her stand, felt her heart pound against his chest. The smell of cordite filled the air. Over the sound of the choppers he heard the repeated stutter of machine-gun fire.

As if reading his thoughts she said swiftly, "Bruno boinked you on the head then took off with Ramón." She grinned, eyes sparkling. "I used those Bangkok rules of yours. Good move, huh?"

"Very." He rubbed the back of his head where a hefty lump had already formed. His arm hurt like hell. Stifling a hiss of pain he glanced down to see shiny black on his sleeve. Yeah, just as he'd thought, the bullet marked for Montero had nicked him, too.

"You've been shot!"

"Law of averages. Did he burn you?" He searched her chalky face in the shifting light.

She shuddered. "No. Can we go now?"

"Hell, yeah." He raised a hand, cautioning her to silence as he paused to listen.

A metallic click. A scrape. The sound of a jammed, then cleared, breech.

He was ready when a soldier appeared around the end of the building, almost stumbling over them. Kyle flung himself sideways, drawing the man away from Delanie. He slammed into the soldier, bringing up the Beretta and squeezing off a round. The guy flew backward, firing as he fell; bullets sprayed a line into the stucco of the house.

An explosion rent the air, rocking the ground where they stood. Smoke billowed black across the faint apricot glow of the early morning sky.

The viral chem lab. *Yes!*

Flickers of light came from the deep shadows behind them. They were going to get shot if one of the goons got lucky.

"We've got a target-rich environment out there." Kyle thrust his gun into her hands. "My people know who you are. If anyone gets in your way, *anyone,* point and shoot."

He raced back into the library and picked up his SIG from where he'd thrown it earlier.

He checked his ammunition clip. It was ready for use. Hell, *he* was ready for use. He strode outside again. "We're going to have to run like hell to reach the fence. Forget trying the gate. It'll be locked. Go diagonally across the patio, behind the pergola. We'll be in shadow there. Ready?

"Hey!" He grabbed her chin, forcing her to look at him. Her eyes were wide. "Don't look back, just run flat out until we hit the fence."

He jerked her into motion. Their long legs syncopated as they flew, feet barely touching the ground. Their boots slammed down on the brick of the patio, picking up speed. Breath sawing, hearts pumping . . . out into the middle of the patio, beyond the pool. The open stretch seemed like miles instead of yards.

The flare of light from the explosion illuminated her face. They were closing in on the fence. Movement in the darkness straight ahead warned him they were being tracked. He jerked her aside, his hand on the back of her shirt, putting himself in front of her. "Down. Get *down.*"

She immediately crouched low, but they kept moving. His eyes scanned the dark shapes several hundred yards ahead before he hauled her upright, running flat out. Two, no three, of his people, on the other side of the fence.

"Go-go-go!" Kyle shouted.

He appreciated the sudden burst of covering fire as he and Delanie hit the chain-link fence at a dead run. He put his hands on her butt, propelling her up and over, then hied his own ass after her.

He came down beside her in a crouch. She was flat on her back, face flushed with exertion. Leaves and debris clung to her hair as she lay there, her breathing rasping in and out as she looked up at the early morning sky.

Kyle knelt beside her, having waved off the guys who'd covered their butts. Hands on his thighs he sucked in air as he waited for her to regroup.

"God." Her voice was definitely shaky, but she sat up smiling. "That was awesome."

He bent down and nuzzled his face against her sweat-dampened neck as he chuckled. "You are certifiably nuts, you know that?"

"Where'd he go, do you think?" she asked, wrapping her arms around his neck. He could have taken her right there. With bullets practically whizzing overhead, percussion grenades exploding, and choppers filling the sky. *I love you,* he thought, stunned by the sheer intensity of the emotion all over again as he looked at her shining face.

He pressed her back to the spongy earth, cutting off whatever she'd been about to say next, and kissed her hard. Her mouth was pliant, hot and welcoming, and just as urgent. She shuddered, and he tasted her moan into his mouth.

Automatic fire erupted and he let go of her, lifting his head. For a moment they stared at each other, breathing hard. Her eyes were dilated, her lips still glistening from the moisture of their kiss.

"Bet he's gone to the bomb shelter," she said shakily, finishing what she'd been about to say before he kissed her.

"You're probably right." He stood and pulled her to her feet. "Guess it's no use asking you to stay out of the way while I look for him?"

"Hey, if you can't beat 'em—" She lifted one eyebrow and he grinned, reluctantly amused. Christ. She was having the time of her life. He shook his head. Damn if she didn't do the unexpected every time.

"Stay alert, and keep that thing ready to use."

Her heart pounded in excitement, half fascinated terror, half the sensation of an exhilarating roller coaster ride. Her fingers curled around the Uzi he'd given her as they slipped deeper into the jungle. The hail of gunfire, followed by a series of loud booms followed them into the dense jungle.

"Come on, Wright. Move it," Delanie said over her shoulder, her long legs moving swiftly. Foliage whipped back as she forged ahead. Slashes of lime-green sunlight arrowed through leaves and foliage as the sun rose over the jungle canopy. The vegetation had been flattened by dozens of running footsteps coming and going; consequently, travel time was cut considerably because they had no need to hack a path through the undergrowth. The air reeked of gunpowder, smoke, and fear.

Out of sight, the loud *whop-whop* of the evac choppers grew louder as they lifted into the sky, carrying the first batch of prisoners bound for San Cristóbal.

They'd have to pass through the pond clearing to get to the shelter. Delanie saw the break in the trees ahead, then heard a grunt behind her.

"Delanie," Kyle shouted, "Run!"

Before she could turn, someone jumped out of the thick undergrowth, knocking her flat on her face. Her gun flew one way, she another. Hell.

Just out of sight, she heard Kyle wrestling with his own set of problems. A short volley of shots from that direction had the monkeys shrieking from the treetops. She didn't have the opportunity to find out who'd been shot.

A booted foot connected with her ribs as she spat out vegetation.

Holy Hannah. That *hurt*. Before she could flip over, the man was on her, twisting her arm up high. He pressed her face to the jungle floor with his boot, laughing as he forced her arm even higher. Delanie bent her knee, bringing her heel up sharply behind her. Right between his legs. Bull's-eye.

Montero screeched like a wounded animal.

She jumped to her feet.

The macho drug lord was grabbing his balls with both hands, tears in his eyes, lips drawn back in a rictus of agony.

He recovered too fast and came at her again. Eyes manic, swearing vilely in Spanish. His head battering into her stomach. She staggered, grabbed him by the hair, and slammed her knee into his chin.

Montero dropped to his knees, grabbed her around the waist, and pulled her down. They tumbled down a small incline, legs and arms tangled. The sharp, sweet fragrance of the orchids around the piranha pond filled her senses with a pungent warning as they crushed the flowers beneath their thrashing bodies.

He had her by the hair, his fingers gouging her scalp as he pulled. She reciprocated, pulling his hair with all her might. Both refused to let go. Her breath came in fast uneven gasps as she struggled to draw in the thick wet air.

She fought him like a wild thing, using every weapon at her disposal. She bit what she could reach, pummeled his head and shoulders with her fists, and kicked whatever came her way. He reciprocated, and they rolled on the damp ground twined together like vines.

She managed to gouge his cheek with her nails.

He thudded his elbow into her stomach.

Air whooshed out of her lungs.

He smiled.

She kneed him. Missed by a mile, but had the satisfaction of hearing a growl of pain. "Not . . . so . . . damn . . . brave now, huh? No . . . branding irons, no guns. Just nice tidy hand-to-hand. The way I like it." If BS could kill, he'd be stone dead.

Montero hit back.

She sank her teeth into his dirty white shirt and bit his shoulder. Hard.

He yelped, his hands going for her throat, his lips drawn back in a snarl. "I should have let my mother have you sooner." His fingers tightened. Black spots flickered in her vision.

She twisted her head to bite his wrist, and tasted blood. That earned a backhanded slap.

Go for the nose. Delanie shot out her hand, palm up. Montero's head snapped back from the blow. He let go of her throat to clutch his face. Blood spurted between his fingers.

Bracing her feet apart, Delanie kept her focus. She kicked Montero's leg out from under him as he tried to stand. He fell, screaming invectives, his face scarlet, blood streaming from his broken, swelling nose.

She straddled him, bringing her knee up to pin his chest to the ground. He screamed obscenities.

Delanie sat there for a moment, panting, wondering what the hell she was doing. She had no idea what came next.

He slammed his fist into her jaw. She bit her tongue, tasting her own blood, as he rolled over and jumped to his feet. Sweat stung Delanie's eyes, as she staggered upright to swing blindly at his head. *Focus, damn it. Focus.*

"I am going to kill you, *puta*. Make no mistake." Blood smeared his handsome face and stained his shirt as he advanced on her. This time he had a knife in his hand. A large, lethal, shiny knife. Where the hell had he found *that*?

"Funny," she taunted, "that's not what *I* was thinking." She kept her eyes on his, ready for a move. "I want *you* to live a long, long time, Ramón." She backed up slowly as he advanced. "In a small, filthy, crowded jail cell. We'll see who's the *puta* then, won't we?"

A brief succession of shots sounded in the trees. A yell, a curse, and then silence.

Montero charged.

She took a step to the side, miscalculated, and felt the water close over the top of her boot. She used both hands to wrest his hand away from her throat, pushing hard, using her full body weight until he was forced back. The wet leather of her boot caused her to slip. The water came almost to her knee. Her other foot started losing traction on the crushed vegetation. Her heart slammed up into her throat.

Montero grabbed her, spinning her around to face the water, one arm wrapped around her throat, holding the knife close to her eyes.

"Take a last look around before you are blinded, *puta*." The hand holding the knife shook as he brought it to the bridge of her nose. Delanie's heart pumped faster. Her elbow slammed back into his hard stomach. The knife dropped from her face, splashing into the water. She turned, using both hands clasped together as a club to swing at him, hitting him hard on the temple.

Stumbling, his foot came down hard on the edge; soil and ground cover crumbled into the water. Off balance, he screamed as his foot sank. He tottered precariously, his arms windmilling for balance. One foot sank ankle-deep in the water as he tried to regain his equilibrium on shifting sand. His other foot failed to find purchase on slick, wet vegetation.

"*Madre de Dios!* Help me, help me." He staggered. His hand brushed the water, and he shrieked hysterically.

God. Had she come to this? Delanie grabbed his flailing arm.

"*Ándale! Ándale!*" He threw himself toward her, grabbing her forearm with both hands. "Delanie! *Ayúdame!*"

She *was* trying to help him, damn it. Bracing her feet as best she could, she struggled with his dead weight, trying to pull him upright.

He was now thigh deep.

Her foot slipped a few inches, water splashed her legs. She dug her boot heels firmly into the tightly woven ground cover.

Suddenly she felt strong hands on her other arm and she was jerked backward a few inches.

"Ever heard the expression 'No good deed goes unpunished?' " Kyle asked laconically, keeping a death grip on her upper arm and almost ripping it from its socket.

Montero held fast to her other arm. Blood dripped from

his nose and arm, creating delicate pink ripples in the clear water. Small bubbles formed on the surface. There was a flash of silver. Then another. Then another.

"Ah, Kyle? Could we speed this up a little?"

Montero's hands slid down her arm, causing heat friction. Her foot slid a fraction closer to the water.

Kyle gave her a sudden sharp jerk, sending her sprawling in the dirt behind him. Montero shrieked as he toppled over with an enormous splash and went under. He shot back to the surface, propelled by hysteria, screaming. And screaming. And screaming. He went under again. A cloud of pink water floated around him. Bubbles shot rapidly to the surface.

Delanie staggered to her feet, coming to stand beside Kyle. Silvery shapes materialized around Montero under the water. "Oh God, we can't—"

"You feel compassion, after what he's done to you?"

"No. Yes. I don't know. But we can't just stand here while he's eaten alive!" Montero's terror sent chills down her sweaty spine.

"Sure we can," Kyle said coldly, watching the other man's head go glug-glug beneath the water again.

Now there were a hundred silvery ribbons flashing, weaving around Montero. He beat the water with his arms, incoherent with terror.

"I'm going to throw up," Delanie yelled above the gurgles, loathing Montero, yet unable to watch him die literally by inches. "Please, get him out."

"Those damned fish aren't going to eat a human being," Kyle assured her. "Not a *whole* one, at any rate."

She stared at him, appalled. "That's worse!"

Kyle looked down at her. "Your call. Really want him out?"

She shuddered. "Yes."

"Doc to Dare," Kyle said quietly. He held her gaze.

"Yo."

"Can you do a garbage pickup at the pond?"

"On my way."

"Walk *slowly*," Kyle instructed grimly. "Out." He dropped his arm around her shoulders. "Let's go." Delanie glanced back and gagged. "Don't puke, jungle girl. Time's a-wasting."

Montero's screams followed them as they took the route to the hidden bomb shelter.

"Block it out," Kyle advised, his arm still around her shoulders. He detoured to pick up various weapons from the path. She noticed several man-size dark lumps in the foliage and averted her eyes without comment.

Now that the adrenaline rush had ebbed, nerve endings all over her body screamed. Her jaw ached from clenching her teeth so she wouldn't cry out. The pain in her leg returned with a vengeance, and made her want to double over and whimper. She was bruised from head to toe. Yet she'd never felt more alive in her life. After handing her a handgun and an Uzi, Kyle wrapped his arm around her again and they walked two abreast.

"All he has to do is keep his head and *walk* out," he told her. "Hell, the dickhead could be out of there before Dare arriv—" His words cut off at the sound of an avalanche of gunfire. Close. Too close.

"Oh, no. Not again!" she wailed as Kyle pushed her down flat in the rotten vegetation. She obeyed without a whimper, sweat stinging her eyes, heart pounding. More than happy to lie still for a moment.

He dropped onto his stomach beside her, eyes constantly moving, gun pointed at the path they'd just left.

Sighing, Delanie lifted her Uzi and aimed it in the same general direction. "I'm getting pretty sick of all this action, you know," she groused, feeling his length beside her. She leaned her chin on his shoulder, watching for more bad guys. He smelled strongly of jungle.

Her head shot up as they heard more shots. Closer now. A few yells. English. American. "The cavalry." Kyle grinned at her, his teeth very white in his dirty face.

He was as sweaty and exhausted as she was. Delanie leaned over and kissed him. Hard. "How're you doing, Tarzan?"

"Good. You?"

She shuddered. "Peachy. What happened to good old Bruno?"

"He died of acute lead poisoning." He touched her cheek. "Ready to find your sister now?"

Chapter Twenty-two

They hadn't seen anyone as they'd headed toward the bomb shelter. Delanie walked beside him on autopilot. Kyle put his arm out to stop her. She glanced at him. He jerked his head, indicating someone hidden behind the structure.

"Show yourself," he said softly, holding the SIG ready. A man stepped around the corner, his weapon extended. Kyle relaxed, recognizing one of his own men. He lowered his gun. "Anything?"

"One in, no one out, sir. As instructed, I haven't been inside, if you'd like—?" He was young and eager, but Kyle shook his head.

"We'll do the—" He spun on his heel as another man melted through the trees. "Hell, it's a party. Couldn't find any more action, Dare?"

Beside him, Delanie's eyes went wide at the size of the man. He topped Kyle by two inches. His size alone was intimidating; the scar bisecting his cheek, grotesque.

Delanie didn't even blink. "You're the guy from the café."

"And you're a shitload of trouble, lady." He gave Delanie what was supposed to be an amused glance. Unfortunately it looked more like a grimace. Dare shrugged. "I left the cleanup to the others. You two seem to be having all the fun; I thought I'd follow you and see what else came up."

"Give us a few moments for a private party. I'll yell if we need you." Kyle turned to her. "I don't suppose I could prevail upon you to stay up here with Dare?"

She looked at him as though he'd lost his mind.

"Yeah, that's what I thought. Okay, jungle girl. The second

that door opens, whoever is down there will be ready for us. Keep to the wall. Get down to the bottom fast. Step sharply to your left, and be ready for anything." He gave her a searching look. She held the gun he'd given her close to her face, pointing to the sky, just as he'd shown her.

"Let's do it," she said, and he could practically see the adrenaline race through her.

Kyle nodded to the young soldier, who opened the door with no difficulty. That wasn't a good sign. If Isabella was hiding down there, she'd have the damn door barricaded against intruders. Instead the door had been left slightly ajar. The only thing missing was the damn welcome mat.

They raced down the cement steps together. There was no need to be silent; the glare from the sunlight was their calling card.

The second Delanie's feet touched the last step she saw her.

Lauren.

Eyes closed, face slack, her sister lay on the red satin cover like Sleeping Beauty. She wore the familiar blue muumuu, and Delanie's heart beat like a trip-hammer at the sight of it on her sister. It took a moment for her to notice the IV stand on the far side of the bed. It held a plastic bag, dripping clear liquid into Lauren's left arm.

Delanie took a hasty step forward and was brought up short by Kyle's hand on her arm. Her head shot up, and she saw why he'd stopped her.

"Dr. Wright," Isabella said dulcetly, stepping out of the shadows. "And my own dear Delanie." She positioned herself between the two sisters. Her ecru linen pants and matching shirt were soiled with moisture and dirt, her usually immaculate hair hung wildly around her shoulders. She pointed a small pistol at Lauren.

"Both labs are gone and your son and the others are on their way to Florida to await trial." Kyle didn't lower his own weapon. "There's nothing left here for you, Isabella. Come quietly and avoid getting hurt."

Isabella laughed. "What I want, my dear Dr. Wright, is a

helicopter to fly me to San Cristóbal and a guarantee of safe passage to my home in Switzerland."

"Sorry, just turned down the same dumb-ass request from your son. Not going to happen." His smile was cold and savage.

The air in the small room felt close and still smelled of dead stinkbug. But it was the scent of Isabella's perfume that made Delanie break out in a cold sweat. She swallowed the dryness in her mouth. Isabella couldn't harm her. She had a gun and Kyle was standing right here with her. That Darius guy and the other man were waiting above ground . . .

But God, just hearing the woman's voice made her sick inside. Fear kept her immobile. *Get a grip,* she warned herself. It took several agonizing moments for her brain to focus on the present.

Kyle and Isabella had a standoff. Why didn't he . . . *do* something? Then she saw why he wasn't going to rush the bitch. It wasn't Isabella's gun holding him back, it was what the woman held in her other hand.

A small, familiar black control panel.

Blood drained from Delanie's head. Oh, sweet Jesus.

Mesmerized, her eyes remained glued to the small horror.

"You recognize this, do you not?" Isabella purred, glittering black eyes focused on her.

Delanie resisted the urge to put her hands up to her throat. "You sadistic bitch. I hope you rot in hell for what you've done."

"I could have made a fortune with you, my dear. You were quite responsive. No," she warned, stepping nearer the bed. "Do not come any closer." She used the plastic box in her hand to indicate Lauren. "Your sister, I believe?

"I didn't think it possible for two girls to be equally uncooperative. This one was returned to me," Isabella informed her, her voice cold and venomous. "Returned! Never has this happened to me. Never! *Madre Dios,* I was shamed. No matter how much of the drug was administered, this little bitch refused to cooperate."

God, Lauren's face was gray, and there was no sign of life. "Is she dead?" Delanie was surprised her voice didn't break.

"Hmmm." Isabella shrugged. "Let's see . . ." Before either of them could move, Isabella pressed down on the control panel in her hand. Lauren's body bowed in a hideous arc before she fell bonelessly back on the bed.

Rage, black, violent, and immediate, mobilized Delanie. Without premeditation her leg shot out in a *jeté*. The thick rubber sole of her heavy combat boot hit Isabella square on the chin. She dropped like a rag doll across Lauren's legs.

"Damn!" Kyle said admiringly. "Nicely done, jungle girl." He grabbed Isabella's unconscious form and tossed her aside. Delanie fell to her knees beside the bed.

"Oh God, baby, what have they done to you?" Her voice broke. The necklace had to come off, she thought hysterically. The damn necklace. Had. To. Come. Off. Her sweaty hands shook as she fumbled to find the magic links to free her sister. Her fingers were too slow, too shaky, to do any good.

Kyle gently pushed her hands out of the way and removed Lauren's necklace for her.

"Thanks." Her voice cracked. She picked up her sister's limp hand, holding it against her cheek as he checked Lauren's eyes, then felt for a pulse at her throat. She gave him a beseeching look.

"We have to get her to a hospital. Now." He moved to detach the IV from the vein in her wrist.

Delanie stroked Lauren's gaunt cheek. The bastards had struggled to find one more place to insert the needle. Her entire arm was a mass of purple, yellow, and green bruises. She shot a loathing, venomous glare at the unconscious woman on the floor.

Tears burned the back of her eyes as Kyle wrapped her sister in the bedspread.

"Yo, Dare?" Kyle shouted over his shoulder.

The man loped down the stairs, taking in the scene at a glance. He studied Lauren. "She alive?" he asked no one in particular, crouching down beside Lauren, and touching a gentle finger to her face.

Delanie instinctively took a step forward.

"Unconscious." Kyle stepped over Isabella to come around the bed to stand beside them. "Predictably, drug-induced. You can see the bruising on her wrists where they bound her some time ago. Apparently she wouldn't cooperate, so the bitch drugged her to the gills."

Dare ran the back of a finger down her sister's cheek. "Poor little bit, had a hard time of it, haven't you?"

Delanie scowled at him.

Dare had insisted on carrying Lauren. Kyle bit back a grin. While his pal was Rhett Butler carrying Scarlett, he had Isabella slung over his shoulder like a sack of manure. Delanie walked beside him, a fierce glower on her face.

Midmorning, and hotter than a sauna. A haze hung over the treetops like mist; a combination of smoke from the fires on the compound and steam evaporating off the wet ground and foliage. Mosquitoes swarmed in clouds, attacking any exposed skin they found.

Kyle brushed a tiny red bug off Delanie's cheek, just for the sheer pleasure of touching her. She gave him a small, distracted smile before turning back to keep an eagle eye on Lauren.

She'd taken great pleasure snapping Lauren's discarded necklace around the older woman's throat before they'd left the shelter, and now walked with the control box gripped in her hand. God help Isabella if she so much as blinked.

"Where to now?" Delanie asked, voice raised over the noise of an ascending chopper as it cleared the trees.

"San Cristóbal International, Miami. Then wherever you want to go."

She touched her sister's hair draped over Dare's arm. "Home, Sacramento, I guess. I have to find somewhere right away for—" She obviously caught the look he and Dare exchanged over her head. Her eyes narrowed. "What did I miss?"

"I'm taking your sister to T-FLAC's clinic in Montana," Dare said, making Delanie's head whip around in his direction. Kyle sighed. He'd tried to warn Darius.

"Like hell you are," Delanie snapped. "I don't know who you think you are to be making *any* decisions about her welfare. Lauren and I live in Sacramento. That's *California.* Not Montana. I'm taking her home."

Dare glanced over her head at Kyle, then back to her. "We have a facility in Montana. I've arranged for one of our people to meet us in Florida before transporting her there." The scar on his face whitened. "She'll have the best of care. You have my word on it." The most words Kyle had ever heard his friend utter in one string.

"It's not only the drug addiction we have to worry about, jungle girl. Lauren must've been through hell and back psychologically. God only knows, Isabella gave *you* a taste of it. She drugged and sold Lauren. And your sister was *returned.* She must have fought them tooth and nail, despite them pumping her full of drugs. She's going to need a hell of a lot more than a regular detox center. She'll need heavy-duty counseling—"

"PTSD," Dare inserted.

"Yeah, for posttraumatic stress, which dollars to donuts will be a major concern. The T-FLAC clinic is one the best of its kind in the world. They know what they're doing."

Several hummingbirds swooped overhead. The jungle closed in around them. They weren't far from the compound. Ten, fifteen more minutes tops.

Kyle relaxed somewhat when he saw a portion of the chain-link fence about two hundred feet ahead.

"And when that's done," Dare snarled, "I guarantee you, home will be the last place she'll want to be."

"Kyle, tell your friend to *shut up.* He doesn't even *know* my sister."

"Cease fire, you two." *Been there, done that.* Kyle knew what Dare's chances would be of getting Lauren anywhere more than two feet away from her sister.

Zero to none.

Were his chances stacking up to the same odds? Delanie's thoughts were exclusively on her sister. With no room for anything else. Would it always be that way?

The going was considerably easier here. Shorter vegetation had been flattened, matted by dozens of booted feet. Delanie immediately moved up parallel with her sister and Dare.

One moment Kyle was about to draw abreast of them to play referee, Isabella's head bouncing down his back, the next he had no load.

In a move so slick he had to admire it, Isabella levered herself off his shoulder and did a neat tuck and roll.

Before anyone knew what she was about, she had an arm wrapped around Delanie's neck in a stranglehold. She had to stand on her toes to do it, bending a startled Delanie back at an awkward angle. The small knife in Isabella's hand reflected the greenery around them as she held it to Delanie's throat.

Kyle sighed and cocked the SIG. "Damn it, I'm too tired for this crap. How about you, Dare?"

He heard the action click on Darius's weapon.

"Back off, Dr. Wright. I dipped the edge of this knife in poison. I would love to cut her for all the trouble she has caused." The paring knife stroked slowly up Delanie's throat, then lingered directly over her pulse point.

"Do it, and I'll shoot you." Frost chilled Kyle's voice, but this was one time in his life he was terrified to call someone's bluff. "Hell, I'm itching to do it."

Brown eyes held his. "Kyle, *please*." Delanie slid her hand into her pocket and stood perfectly still in Isabella's hold. "I can do this."

"Yeah. I know you *can*." His tone was grim. "But why should you? I know you're rabid about paying your own debts, sweetheart. But let me do this for you this once. I'd really enjoy it."

"My charge, my credit card."

Ah, shit, he should have anticipated this. "Sure?" There was no one in the world besides the two of them.

"Oh yes." Delanie's eyes glittered. "I want to do this."

Isabella laughed. And nicked her with the sharp paring knife. Kyle saw the frantic flutter of her heart there, like a trapped bird. Blood drained from his head. He could take the woman with one clean shot. He stepped forward aggressively.

"Kyle, no!" Delanie stopped him. "Shooting her is too quick. She's lying, there's no poison on the knife."

He tried to see her pupils to ascertain how fast the poison would work. Knowing Isabella, he didn't consider her words a bluff. Delanie looked just fine. Pissed, but controlled. He stayed where he was and refocused on Isabella.

The older woman smiled. "Now you will have to wait and see if I am lying, or if the poison is slow-acting." She paused meaningfully. "How do you feel, *querida*?"

"Like I've got nothing to lose," Delanie snarled, slamming the butt of the Uzi she carried back, hard into Isabella's belly.

"Yes!" Kyle shouted, seeing her bright, determined eyes. "Play dirty," he instructed her, his chest tight, his fist clenched. Rage ate through his stomach like battery acid. It took every ounce of control he possessed to stay where he was.

"Jesus, Doc," Dare said incredulously, coming up beside him. "Surely to God you aren't going to let her *do* this?"

"It's a damn big debt." He captured Isabella's eyes. "If Delanie doesn't kill you, take it to the bank, I *will*."

Delanie swung her body around and came at Isabella like a raging bull. Her Uzi went flying. Kyle swore.

And then they were down. Yelling and screaming, kicking and biting, scratching and gouging. The knife flashed in Isabella's hand. Isabella drew blood. Kyle swore vilely, jaw tight.

"Ditto," Dare agreed, protectively holding Lauren higher against his chest as he moved out of the way. "Aren't you going to do something?"

"She needs to do this on her own." The hardest words he'd said in his life. His damn heart was in his throat as Delanie did a high graceful kick, hitting Isabella a solid whack in the middle of her chest, knocking her onto her back. Isabella rolled, but Delanie, a feral expression on her face, jumped on her and pinned her down, one knee on the woman's chest, the other on her knife arm. Grabbing two handfuls of black hair she smacked Isabella's head in the dirt.

"Hell when the boot's on the other foot, isn't it," Delanie told Isabella calmly. She wasn't even panting.

"I *like* you on top, *querida*."

Again, Delanie pounded the woman's head sharply against the ground. *Harder,* Kyle silently encouraged, teeth clenched. *Much harder.*

"Man, she's incredible," Darius said admiringly. "But I've gotta tell you, pal, this one's going to give you gray hairs before your time."

"That's the pla—keep that hold, jungle girl!—damn." He scowled as Isabella bucked Delanie off. Delanie swung a punch. He winced with her as it connected. "Did you see that? Go, sweetheart, go!"

Women fought so damn differently than men, he thought impatiently. "Damn it," Kyle yelled as she tried again. "Stop hitting like a *girl*. Hit *harder!*"

The two women circled, feinted, and parried. His fingers twitched on the butt of his weapon. *Come on, come on, come on,* he urged silently, mentally coaching Delanie from the sidelines.

Isabella lunged to her feet, knife flashing.

Delanie circled her like a wary cat. Whipping out the little black box she had stuffed in her pocket, Delanie looked calm and composed. "Let's see how you like some of your own medicine." She extended her arm and pressed her thumb down.

Isabella clutched her throat. "I like it, *mija*," she said, but with a small grimace. "Do it again."

Sick bitch.

"Okay," Delanie said obligingly, extending the box and pressing again. For considerably longer this time. There was no way Isabella could pretend that didn't hurt. "Oh, hell, this is *too* easy!" She tossed the plastic control off into the shrubs, dancing from foot to foot like a prizefighter.

Delanie felt amazingly revitalized, so energetic she could leap buildings in a single bound. In the periphery of her vision she could just see the two men standing at the tree line. Kyle looked as though he was chewing glass—

Isabella threw herself forward. Delanie executed a grand jeté, one leg shooting out to strike Isabella's right hand. The knife flew through the air in a high arc. Isabella shrieked, stumbling backward into a tree trunk, staggering to maintain her balance. Eyes wild, she pushed herself upright and came at Delanie at a dead run.

As soon as Isabella was close, Delanie stepped aside. Isabella kept going, screaming like a banshee.

Dragging in gulping drafts of sticky air, Delanie ran after her; she wasn't done with Isabella yet. Not by a long shot. Eight feet away, Isabella stopped as abruptly as if she'd slammed into an invisible wall. Her shriek cut off midoctave. Her body arched. Jerking, as if caught in a monsoon, she whipped around, held in an invisible grip. Her body convulsed, an expression of utter stupefaction on her face. Black eyes wild, she opened her mouth in a silent scream, grotesquely chilling to watch.

"Get the hell away from her!" Kyle yelled, running toward Delanie.

Delanie stopped on a dime, her unbelieving eyes going from Isabella's blanched face to the coarse filaments of the woman's black hair, standing straight up, and out, from her head. Sylvester the cat with his tail in a light socket. Steam rose from Isabella's skin and clothing. Her eyes bulged hideously.

Delanie slapped her hand over her mouth, gagging at the smell of superheated flesh. Transfixed, she couldn't take her eyes off Isabella, who'd finally been thrown to the ground. Her body contorted, bowed in an arc. Twitched, then lay still. *Dead* still.

Stunned, Delanie started running toward the fallen

woman. Kyle grabbed her tightly, picking her up off her feet, his arm like a vise.

"Wh—"

"Electrocuted," Kyle managed hoarsely. He spun her around and gathered her to his chest, holding her so tightly she could barely breathe. He buried his face in her hair. Delanie wasn't sure which of them was shaking more. But she wasn't planning on letting go. Her knees were jelly.

"What the hell was *that*?" Dare came to stand beside them.

Kyle held her in a steely grip, her face pressed to his sweaty shirtfront. His heart drummed unevenly beneath her ear. "Underground electronic fence." He sounded shaken, his voice hollow.

He pressed Delanie's face against his shoulder. "By the look of her, I'd guess about a thousand volts. Buried just beneath the soil. The very *wet* soil. Activated by the control in the necklace Isabella's wearing."

Delanie's body was plastered against his. Not even a sheet of paper could have passed between them. She mashed her nose against his shirtfront, her arms tight around his waist. Shivering as though she were in the Arctic instead of the tropics, she was grateful for the strength and support of his arms as he held her close.

"Where the hell did you learn to fight like that, jungle girl?"

"B . . . ballet school." Damn, she couldn't seem to stop shaking. Kyle rubbed her back and she closed her eyes, leaning against him, drawing strength from the vast well of his.

After a few moments she forced herself to pull away from him to check on her sister. "We'd better get going," she said quietly.

Chapter Twenty-three

Several helicopters sat at the small landing strip behind the hacienda. All had the cobra logo painted on the side. Kyle selected one and opened the cargo door.

"Get Lauren settled," he told Dare, not looking at Delanie. "I'll go get the parts I yanked out the other day. Be right back." He strode across the packed dirt to the hanger.

Pushing her hair out of her eyes, Delanie watched him go, then turned back to help Dare lift her sister into the back of the chopper.

"He's crazy about you," Dare told her as he jumped in beside Lauren. Delanie gripped the door frame, levering herself inside. Having baked in the sun all morning, the inside was as hot as an oven. Though it wasn't anything like the one Kyle had used to fly her into San Cristóbal, she had a flash of a memory that threatened to rip out her heart. Pushing it aside, she found a blanket, folding it to put under her sister's head.

"I came to Izquierdo to find my sister," she said doggedly, smoothing Lauren's hair off her face. "She's found. We're going home."

"What about Kyle?"

"Lauren needs me."

Dare jerked his chin at his friend striding back from the hanger. "Think he *doesn't*?"

"Look," Delanie said tiredly, "I don't want to be rude when you're getting us out of here, but what I think about Kyle is none of your business."

"So you're coming to Montana?"

"I'm going wherever is best for my sister."

"She's going to Montana."

"Then so am I." Delanie glared at this scarred stranger who thought he could do whatever the hell he liked with her baby sister.

From the open doorway she watched as Kyle came closer, his arms full of boxes. He must have ditched his shirt in the hangar. The beige tank top he wore showed off his broad tanned chest and shoulders. She couldn't drag her eyes away from him as he walked up to the door. Sitting on the floor as she was, they were at eye level.

Muscles shifted under tanned skin as he tossed the boxes behind the second row of seats. "Purified water, fruit juice, and whatever I could scrape together to eat." He talked exclusively to Dare. "I'll just get these parts back in—"

"I'll do it," Darius insisted, jumping down. He took the greasy parts from Kyle and disappeared from view.

"Better buckle up, jungle girl."

"Yeah, I guess so." She started squeezing between the two rows of seats, then changed her mind. "I'd rather stretch my legs for as long as I can before we fly out." She turned back, sat on the floor in the doorway, where Kyle stood, and dangled her legs, ready to jump down. He put his large hands around her waist and swung her to stand in front of him.

"Thanks for letting me take Isabella on my own." She grimaced. "It was a little more dramatic than I'd anticipated, but I guess it was poetic justice after all."

"Yeah, it was. Feel all right?"

"She was bluffing."

"How would you know that?"

"Because the last time that knife was used, I peeled an orange with it. I could smell it when she stuck it in my face."

"I wish to hell I'd known." He looked off into the middle distance, then turned back to her. "Jesus, that scared about twenty years off my life."

The shadow directly overhead from one of the rotors covered Kyle's eyes. She wished she could see his expression. There was a long silence. Emotions swirled inside her.

His pale eyes searched her face. "Going to Montana, jungle girl?"

"Yes." A painful ache settled around her heart. She had no idea how to tell him things she'd only begun to understand herself. She heard Dare clanking away at something in the engine. A transport helicopter took off nearby. People shouted orders in the distance. The sun shone.

Frustrated, Delanie glanced back to check on her sister, who still hadn't regained consciousness.

"Lauren will be fine," Kyle assured quietly.

"From your mouth to God's ears."

"While you're there, have the surgeon take care of your ankle."

"Okay."

"Here." Kyle removed something from his back pocket, and took her hand. "Sell these when you get back, should give you a comfortable little nest egg." He opened his fist and poured three gold herringbone chains into her palm.

Instinctively she flinched, her eyes narrowed with distaste. "The last thing I'm going to do is take these things home with me."

Kyle closed her hand around the warmed gold. "More poetic justice. Do some good with the money."

Reluctantly she stuck them into her front pocket. The necklaces, and what to do with them, were least of her problems. She stared at him suspiciously. "Why are you giv—" Oh, God, what— "Aren't you going with us?"

"No, I'll bug out tomorrow. There're still some ends I need to tie up here."

"But I thought—" He shook his head and she swallowed, her mouth dry.

"Stay with me." He didn't touch her. "I trust Dare with my life; let him take Lauren to our clinic where she'll be helped. I doubt they'll let you see her until she's stable. Could be weeks—"

"But I'll be close by— Oh, God, Kyle." Somehow she prevented a catch in her voice. "Don't make me have to choose."

"I'd never make you do anything, Delanie." He raked his hair back, sounding exhausted.

"I'm all she has."

He sighed. It sounded sad and soul deep. "I know."

He reached out and almost touched her cheek, and she wanted to press his hand there. Keep it there. Against her face. Close enough to smell him, to see the pale green of his eyes looking back at her.

He stuck his hands in his front pockets.

"Then I guess this is good-bye," she whispered.

"Yeah." His eyes narrowed. Whatever he'd been looking for obviously wasn't there. "Bye, jungle girl."

Delanie struggled for air, feeling tears swim in her eyes. "Kiss me good-bye," she begged achingly.

He shook his head no. He wouldn't even allow her that.

"Kyle—" She didn't know what to say. And even if she did, she'd never be able to speak over this aching lump in her throat. Her chest felt tight.

It should be raining.

But the sun shone and the brilliant birds flittered around chirping happily. The darn trees grew five feet a second, and the mosquitoes flourished. All was right in this green hell except that her heart was being ripped out. She started digging in her pocket for a Maalox, remembered she didn't have any, and dropped her hand. Great. Just great.

"Ready to roll?" Dare shouted impatiently. Delanie hadn't even noticed he was inside the helicopter. The rotors started turning, slowly.

Delanie looked back at Kyle, heart in her eyes. Regrets tasted bitter on her tongue. Needing to touch him, she reached up to brush a strand of hair off his cheek. He flinched as if she'd slapped him.

"Kyle. I—" The words fell tonelessly from her mouth as, without a word, he turned and walked away.

"Lady," Dare said above her, hand on the door ready to slam it shut. "Fish or cut bait. Lauren and I are leaving."

Chapter Twenty-four

Perfectly aware everyone in the bar was staring at her, Delanie nursed her fifth cup of bad coffee. Back to the corner, seated at a small, sticky-topped Formica table, she willed Kyle to walk through the front door. Now.

Four months and three days. Who knew she'd miss the man so much it would become a physical ache?

It was early afternoon, and the bar was already half full. The clientele consisted of dock workers and a group of scantily clad women she presumed were hookers. A stunning redhead sat alone at a table, silently drinking a soda, obviously waiting for someone. A couple of guys dressed in jeans and T-shirts, tourists by the look of them, pored over maps and guidebooks spread out on the bar. And two stevedore-types who hadn't taken their eyes off her since she'd come in hours ago. Delanie removed the small can of Mace from her purse and held it firmly in her left hand under the table.

The smell of rotting wood, tar, and brine mixed with cigarette smoke, cheap liquor, and even cheaper perfume. She was out of her mind for being here. In this bar, and in Rio de Janeiro. She'd had third, sixth, and ninety-ninth thoughts all the way from Montana to Brazil.

The kamikaze cabdriver had taken her through the shantytowns and barrios of Rio at breakneck speed, darting down narrow lanes and dank streets to end up at the Last Chance Bar and Grill near the docks in a screech of bad brakes.

Her desire to see Kyle outweighed the danger.

Last Chance.

How appropriate. She wondered, not for the first time, if Darius had lied and sent her halfway around the world to find a man who wasn't there, just to get rid of her.

The bartender came over and picked up the empty mug she'd nursed for the past hour. "You pay rent, senhorita?"

Delanie opened her purse, extracted one of the twenty-dollar bills from the "bribe" compartments of her purse, and handed over the money. "I'll have a bottle of . . . whatever's local."

He gave her a salacious smile, gold-capped teeth flashing beneath a bushy black mustache, before he shuffled back to the bar to fetch her order.

One of the sailors got up from his table, said something to his companion, then sauntered over to her. He reached out drunkenly and grabbed her bare arm.

"Hey!" Her purse slipped off her lap as he hauled her to her feet.

"How much?" he demanded, his breath beery in her face.

"Let go of me!" Delanie depressed the sprayer for the Mace. The spray hit the guy squarely in the neck. Damn it. *Higher.* "I'm not—"

Suddenly the redhead stood at her elbow. Looking as furious as Delanie was indignant, she grabbed the man's beefy bicep and burst into a spate of rapid Portuguese. Slowly he grinned as the woman stroked his arm, then proceeded to pull him toward the front door, still talking.

Delanie fell back into the chair and watched them disappear into the sunshine outside. She gave mental thanks to her unlikely guardian angel. She hadn't taken the woman for one of the hookers, but she was relieved the redhead had been so territorial.

The bartender returned with a fingerprint-smudged glass and a smoky bottle, both of which he slammed on the table before going back to his other customers without leaving her change.

Ignoring the pale worm curled at the bottom of the bottle,

Delanie filled the glass, then wrapped both hands around her "rent" and held on as though her life depended on it.

Darius had informed her that Kyle came into the bar every afternoon at three. She'd been here since two, just in case he showed up early. It was now after four. Where the hell was he?

Her body, her mind, her very soul ached to see Kyle.

When she'd chosen to get on that helicopter with Lauren instead of staying with him on Izquierdo, she'd known she'd hurt him. God only knew, by leaving as she'd done, she'd hurt herself. Every day apart had deepened the self-inflicted wound on her heart.

She'd come halfway around the world to make it right.

Lauren would make a full recovery; Dare wouldn't have it any other way. He'd reluctantly arranged for Delanie to stay in a small cabin on the ranch where T-FLAC had a training camp, within walking distance of the clinic. In the past four months she'd met all the doctors, the nurses, the orderlies, and the psychiatrists there. She was more than satisfied with Lauren's care.

She'd half expected Kyle to show up in Montana. But he hadn't. The first few weeks there had been hell. Her sister hadn't been a good, or willing, patient. When she'd finally acknowledged that she couldn't do anything useful in Lauren's recovery, she'd felt painful, desolate despair that Kyle hadn't contacted her. Although, God only knew, she shouldn't blame him.

Weeks followed, with still no word, and her grief turned to mild annoyance. Where *was* the man? So much for loving her, damn it. If he cared as much as he'd said he did, he'd have at least contacted her.

Then after three months with no word, Delanie had gone to the gym on the grounds and worked off her anger on the dummy. It felt good punching it. It would have been better if the hard body had been Kyle's—

And think of the devil . . .

The door opened and here he was. Kyle Wright in the flesh. Delanie's heart leapt. Oh God, he looked good.

Wonderful. Familiar. Dear. His hair hung to his wide shoulders, and he wore his ubiquitous black silk T-shirt, black jeans . . . And a clinging redhead on his arm.

Delanie stuffed the Mace in the pocket of her ankle-length floral skirt, slung her purse over her shoulder, and pushed her chair back. Then she strode toward Kyle and the hooker with purpose in her step and blood in her eye.

"Excuse me," she said coolly, peeling the woman's hands off Kyle's bicep. "I appreciated your help earlier. But this one's taken."

Kyle gave her a mild look. "Hello, Delanie."

"She's going to lead you a merry dance, love," the redhead told Kyle in a husky, vaguely familiar voice. She raised her hands in surrender when Delanie glared at her, then grinned and went to join the two men at the bar.

Narrow-eyed, Delanie briefly observed the people across the room, then turned back to Kyle. "She's that Savage woman, isn't she? I suppose those tourists over there are your people, too?"

"Did you really think I'd let Dare send you into danger?" Kyle headed straight for the table she'd vacated and sat down.

Delanie gave a broken laugh as she followed him and resumed her seat. "You knew I was coming."

"Of course."

Wasn't he pleasantly calm about it? "Then why couldn't we have got together at my hotel?"

"I wanted to see how far you'd go to find me."

"Obviously halfway around the world, and totally out of my element. Again." She met his eyes. The intensity in the pale green depths seemed to see right through to her soul. By walking away that day on Izquierdo, he'd accomplished what he'd set out to do all along. He'd turned her into a desperate, lovelorn female who not only hungered for his touch, but ached from wanting him any way she could get him. And now that he'd accomplished his goal, he seemed disinterested in the prize.

His smile made her throat constrict. "Is this the real you,

Delanie?" As if he couldn't sit this close without touching her, Kyle reached out and brushed a gentle hand to her back-to-normal brown hair.

"Not blonde. Mousy," she said defensively, the withdrawal of his touch, as meager as it'd been, a painful loss. "I did tell you."

"Pretty mouse." His gaze traveled to her feet. "Those the Birkenstocks?"

"My favs," she told him sweetly, lifting her foot off the floor to admire the heavy sandals and pale pink nail polish on her bare toes.

Kyle laughed and Delanie wanted to fling herself into his arms and bury her face in the warm curve of his throat.

The door opened and shut, letting in half a dozen men talking animatedly as they headed for the bar. Happy hour. They turned as one six-headed monster to stare at her.

Delanie ignored them. "I'd feel considerably more comfortable on my own territory."

"I know." He examined her glass. "Have you drunk any of this?"

Bewildered, Delanie shook her head. The longing she had to touch him was a physical ache. God. She needed him to kiss her. To hold her in his arms . . .

"Yo, Henry!" Kyle shouted across the bar, "Couple of sodas, heavy on the ice? Thanks." He turned back to her. "So, jungle girl, how's your sister?"

Her eyes widened. "My *sister*? Um, Lauren's doing much better. Still a long way to go, but much, much better. The doctors at the clinic are excellent. It's better for her if she concentrates on getting well without me hovering."

"Amazing. You figured this all out by yourself."

"I had some counseling while I was there," she admitted. "You were right about some of the things you said to me that night." He just sat there watching her, his expression unreadable. She refused to look away, but had to swallow before she could go on.

"But you were dead wrong about my wanting *you* to prove yourself. The challenge was to myself. Not you." A brittle laugh escaped the lump in her throat. "I didn't trust my own instincts."

God, what was he seeing when he looked at her like that? He was so damn inscrutable. "Would you please *say* something?"

"I don't see vulnerability as dependency. Loving, and being loved, gives us strength. We get that by trusting each other, by allowing each other the chance to take a turn being the hero. By growing together. Being strong when the other needs it. By loving each other. It's a full circle, Delanie. But you'll have to meet me halfway."

"I'm here, aren't I?" Her voice caught and her palms began to sweat as Kyle continued to sit there with his arms folded in front of him on the table, his eyes hooded. She briefly closed her eyes, squeezing her hands together before staring at him from burning eyes.

"Why?" he asked.

Because I dream of you whether my eyes are closed or open. Because I think of you twenty-four hours a day. Because I miss you. "This is where you are," she said simply.

"I've been plenty of places. You weren't in any of them before. You going to drink that?"

She shook her head. "You're going to make this hard for me, aren't you?"

He finished her cola and set the glass down on the table. His silence answered for him.

"Why?" she whispered.

"Because nothing worthwhile comes easy."

She closed her eyes for a second, then looked at him with her heart in her eyes. "I l— care about you, Kyle."

The look he gave her was indecipherable, almost sad. Which was ridiculous. She'd just told him what he wanted to hear.

"I don't need rescuing, Delanie. In two days I'm bugging out of here for home." At her puzzled look, he said mildly, "Since Lauren's taken care of, I presume you're between crises on the home front. I don't need you to bail me out of anything, jungle girl. You'll have to find another cause."

"Didn't you hear what I said?"

"Oh, yeah. Loud and clear." His eyes were cool.

Bewildered, and feeling the slow burn of irritation, she frowned. "Are you paying me back for lying to you?"

"Which lie was that?"

"When I told you— When I told you I didn't love you."

"Was it a lie?"

"I was wrong not to trust you," she said softly, a catch in her voice. "But when you said you l-loved me I was scared. Afraid to believe you. If I allowed myself to believe you, and it turned out not to be true, I couldn't've handled it. I had to protect myself. Look," Delanie said desperately when he didn't say anything. "Could we *please* go somewhere else and talk about this? Back to my hotel?"

"I don't want to be alone with you right now. Want a hamburger?"

"For God's sake why not?" Delanie demanded.

"Because," Kyle told her calmly, as he signaled for the bartender, "we'd be all over each other like white on rice. And we already know we're terrific in bed— I'll take the special, extra crisp on those fries, and another soda, better make that two. Delanie?"

She stared at Kyle incredulously as he gave the man his order. Both men looked at her expectantly. "Nothing for me, thank you." Her voice was arctic.

To hell with him. She'd come halfway round the world to find the damn man, spent months coming to terms with her feelings and fears, and he didn't have the decency to listen to her. Pain and hurt turned into a furious, soul-burning rage.

She waited until the bartender was out of earshot, until she could gather her defenses. Until she didn't feel as though someone had punched her in the stomach. "I was a game to you, wasn't I? The words you spoke weren't worth the air it took to say them." She shook her head in disgust. At herself. "God. What a stupid, naive little fool I was to think— Lord, I made it easy for you, didn't I? First *I* picked *you* up, then I was conveniently served to you on a silver platter."

"There was nothing *convenient* about it."

"Whatever." Delanie stood and glared down at him. "Have a nice life."

His hand shot out and grabbed her wrist. "Sit down. We're not done talking. Not by a long shot."

"Yes we damn well are. Let go of my hand. I have a plane to catch."

Kyle tugged and she tumbled back into her still-warm chair.

"Where would we live, Delanie?" Kyle asked genially, leaning back.

She glared at him, a strange, unfamiliar tightness in her chest. "Do you have a mouse in your pocket?"

"Sacramento? San Francisco? How far away from your family would you get before they tug you back into the spaghetti of their lives? Seattle?"

Delanie narrowed her eyes. He wasn't asking her to live with him. He was making a point. Damn. How could she have been so wrong? He obviously didn't give a rat's patoot about her. And despite knowing better, she'd fallen for his lines. Lock, stock, and barrel. She'd resisted this all her adult life. She'd *known* not to fall, and here she was. Twenty-seven, and in love for the first time.

Well, love sucked. It hurt. It was messy and unpleasant.

She hated being in love.

She didn't want to feel like this. She didn't want to need him like this. She didn't want to sit here three feet away from the warmth of his body. She didn't want to lust after a man who could so easily keep his own hands off *her*. Damn. Damn. Damn.

"Chickening out?"

"No. Cutting my losses," she told him curtly. It hurt to breathe. It felt as though a giant hand had reached inside her chest and was squeezing her heart in a tight, mean fist.

Kyle rubbed his hand over his face, then sighed. "I thought you claimed to be in—to *care* about me."

"Are you going to make me say it a million times?"

His lips twitched. "So far you haven't said it *once*."

God. He wanted complete surrender. No safety net. No

crying uncle. A total rout. Delanie looked toward the front
door. Torn between running like hell to get away from him,
and dragging him into a back room to remind him just how
compatible they were. Damn, she was pathetic. Her throat
closed up. She fished a piece of ice out of her empty glass
and popped it in her mouth. He wasn't finished breaking her
heart. He was obviously determined to humiliate her as well.

And she was going to let him. Because to be with Kyle, on
his terms, was better than being without him on her own.
"Tell me what you want from me, Kyle." Her voice was quiet
and sure, her gaze steady. "Whatever it is, it's yours."

He continued to watch her. "Why?" he asked softly.

The pounding of her heart was deafening in her ears.
"Because I love you with my heart and soul. I— Why are
you looking at me like that?"

His smile was brilliant, his eyes glittering. "You love me?"

"Of course. I just sai—"

"Say it again."

She scowled. "I love you."

"And again."

"I love you."

Kyle's hands were suddenly on either side of her face; his
fingers tunneled through her hair.

"And I want you, Kyle, so much that I thought I'd die
without you for all those months."

His thumbs brushed her cheeks. "You're damned pigheaded, you know that, jungle girl?"

"I can also be bossy. And judgmental, and—" Delanie
racked her brain for all her bad points. There were plenty.
She didn't want him to have any illusions.

"Trying to scare me off?"

"Can you be?"

"No. Because I know you too well. I know you'd carry me
if I needed it, and you'd bop me over the head if I needed
that, too. I know you love children, and animals, and are kind
to people less fortunate than yourself. I know your eyes haze
when I make love to you. I know where to touch you to make

you go wild in my arms, and I know where to touch you to make you melt."

Kyle combed his fingers through her hair and held her face in both strong hands, his mouth an inch from hers. "I know that when I'm with you I'm a better person than I am without you. I know that no matter what, you'll always have a wide stubborn streak in you. I know that without you, my nights would be bitterly lonely, and my days forever dull. And I know—" Kyle smiled. "—*that's* just the tip of the ice-berg."

God. He did know her.

"I also know, without a shadow of a doubt, that you love me," Kyle snuck in before she could speak again.

"I don't have a job, and I'm homeless. I sold my house to Auntie Pearl. She's going to take care of Grandpa. I thought I'd better have a healthier cash flow in case I had to follow you all over the world like a camp follower."

"Did you now?" His eyes were hooded as he watched her. "How would you take care of your family if you followed me all over God's creation?"

"They're going to have to learn to take care of them-selves." She smiled. "I want to spend the rest of my life with you at my side. Not in front of me, or behind me, but with your hand in mine no matter what."

"You're sure?"

"I've never been more sure of anything in my life."

"Well, then, I guess there's nothing left to do but get mar-ried, move to the suburbs, and start making our own baseball team." He stood up and dropped a twenty on the table.

The next thing she knew he'd swept her off the chair. There was a loud cheer from the bar patrons as Kyle lifted her in his arms.

"What are you doing?"

"Taking you to your hotel before I take you right here, woman."

Her heart soared. Laughter bubbled as she twined her arms around his neck and demanded, "Kiss me."

"Not until I have you naked." He strode to the door. "I have a research grant at Stanford. What do you think of living near San Francisco? Close enough to your family for *real* emergencies, and far enough away so they don't all drop in every Sunday for dinner?"

Her smile lingered as she touched his face. "I love you, Kyle Wright."

Kyle's grin broadened. "Damn right, you do, jungle girl. And about time you realized it. I don't think I could've delayed another moment not seeing you. I was going to give you another couple of weeks to realize what you were missing, before I went to Montana, or Sacramento, or wherever the hell you were, and kidnapped you. You don't think I'd let the woman I love hide from the future we're going to build, do you?"

"God, I hope not. What did you have in mind?"

"We're going to get married as soon as we get back home. I'm going to make love to you morning, noon, and night, and one of these days we're going to make beautiful babies together. We're going to love each other, jungle girl. We're also going to fight and make up. But we're going to know that no matter what, we'll love one another till our last breath, and beyond."

Delanie nuzzled her nose into the curve of his neck. Soon they'd be naked, and she'd be doing a lot more than kissing his strong throat. "You're a *very* smart man," she told him primly.

Kyle kicked open the front door, letting a breath of fresh, sunshine-bright air into the bar as he carried her out to a waiting taxi. "I've got *you,* don't I?"

"Yes," she whispered, brushing his mouth with hers. "You have me." And her mouth met his in a soul-searching kiss that left them both awed and shaken with the promise of all their tomorrows.

Together.

"A sexy, snappy roller coaster ride!"
—Susan Anderson

KISS AND TELL

by Cherry Adair

Marnie Wright has seen more than her fair share of testosterone. Growing up with four overly protective brothers was one thing. Now a mountain man named Jake Dolan has invaded a peaceful day of soul-searching at her grandmother's secluded cabin. Sure, she was trespassing on his private property, but did he have to pull a gun on her? There's more to this longhaired soldier of fortune who calls himself the Tin Man, but she's not sure she wants to stick around to find out what. Then he stashes her in his secret lair—an underground techno-fantasy complete with security monitors and an arsenal—and Marnie realizes the guy is military, top secret military. He's also got the most beautiful mouth she's ever seen.

Published by Ivy Books.
Available at your local bookstore.

I GOT YOU, BABE

by Jane Graves

On the run for a robbery she didn't commit, Renee Esterhaus is stuck in the middle of Texas with a broken car and a sadistic bounty hunter hot on her trail. Desperate for a way out, Renee decides to make a promise she never intends to keep—offer the first man she meets a night of unforgettable pleasure in return for a ride. A night to remember, all right, since the handsome guy turns out to be a cop with a pair of handcuffs and zero tolerance for sweet-talking criminals…

Published by Ivy Books.
Available at your local bookstore.